SMI   Smith, April,
             1949-

Be the one.

$24.00

DATE			

BAKER & TAYLOR

ALSO BY APRIL SMITH

North of Montana

BE THE ONE

APRIL SMITH

BE THE ONE

ALFRED A. KNOPF NEW YORK

2000

THIS IS A BORZOI BOOK
PUBLISHED BY ALFRED A. KNOPF

www.aaknopf.com

Knopf, Borzoi Books, and the colophon are registered
trademarks of Random House, Inc.

ISBN: 0-679-45096-3
LC: 00-104374

Manufactured in the United States of America
First Edition

For Ben and Emma

Endless love

PROLOGUE
NOVEMBER 1994

She was that close to busting the record for the most consecutive bull's-eyes made under the greatest influence of alcohol, when the bar phone rang.

It was three o'clock in the morning in a local dive in Laguna Beach called Papa's. By then she had been throwing darts almost four hours, ever since the challenge by the French kick-boxer. The guy had looked like a cokehead, like he'd been put through a pencil sharpener, stringy tendons and collapsed cheeks. She had seen him staring at her and known what he was thinking: Here's one of those tall, all-American babes with the blonde braid and great body who lives for beach volleyball. Not too friendly, not too cool, but for him—une piece of cake.

He hadn't counted on fire and desire.

Her first toss drilled straight through the center of a red cork circle the size of a quarter.

He took his beat-up aviator jacket and split, and she kept it going until the place emptied out—except for the other two icons of Papa's, Mary Jo Martin, a TV newswriter who came in around midnight to work on a screenplay about a TV newswriter, and Big Tyson behind the bar, in his all-season leather vest and wool beanie.

The sound system was tuned to a jazz station and Cassidy Sanderson was working with the same smooth despair as Miles Davis's Kind of Blue, hitting the sweet spot seventeen times in a row. She had come straight from the stadium; khakis limp, the armpits of the white cotton button-down shirt translucent with sweat, but she had no idea. She had reached that state of detachment it takes Zen masters a lifetime to achieve: The point seeks the innermost circle, it is inevitable.

She walked seven steps back to a worn yellow line on the splintered floor. Another dewy glass of lager was waiting on a stool, illuminated, it seemed, by a spotlight of gold. It was an obscure microbrew from her home state of Oregon that she claimed made her feel "evergreen." She fingered the grooved shaft of the dart; warm brass, like a bullet.

"Cassidy!"

"Don't talk to me."

"Phone call."

"It can't be for me. My life is pathetic."

She had been thinking about stopping by her trainer Marshall Dempsey's place, waking him up, and getting laid. It wouldn't be the first time.

Mary Jo looked up from a laptop. "Who is it?"

Big Tyson shrugged. "Some kind of weird connection."

Reluctantly Cassidy came to the bar. Her bangs were damp and the look in her eyes was smeared.

"Damn it, my streak."

"What can I say?"

Tyson held out the cordless. Cassidy hesitated, seeming to be fixated by a large turquoise rock in his ring. Mary Jo put a comforting arm around her buddy's shoulder, which was like embracing a piece of granite. The pressure on Cassidy at work these days was intense enough to liquefy stone.

But Cassidy said hello and broke into a puzzled smile.

"It's Uncle Pedro," she told them. "Calling from the Dominican."

Mary Jo and Big Tyson exchanged a relieved look. Who the fuck knew who Uncle Pedro was but at least Cassidy wasn't breaking furniture.

Obviously they didn't read the sports page. Pedro Pedrillo was the most successful bird-dog scout in the Dominican Republic, which meant he drove a hacking old Datsun seven days a week across cattle country and fields of sugarcane looking for boys to fill the farm teams in the United States, but hoping to find the phenom—talent so pure it would light up the game like a fireball that doesn't burn. Cassidy Sanderson, a baseball scout as well, the only female scout in the major leagues, put a hundred thousand miles a year on her Explorer, driving the freeways of Southern California looking for the same light in a different forest.

"Where are you?" Pedro was asking.

"At my pub."

"But I dialed your home number."

"We have call-forwarding. New technology. I can send my calls anywhere I want."

"To a bar? That doesn't sound good."

"It's fine."

Cassidy stared at the collection of weirdness behind the walnut bar. A kind of pressed aquarium in a mother-of-pearl frame with dried-up sea horses and guppies. An old straw hat. Shark jaws gripping a rubber human hand.

"I have found a ballplayer," Pedro was saying.

"What kind of ballplayer?"

"A pure hitter."

"Yeah?"

"Cassie . . . I like this kid."

"You like this kid."

"Yes, I do."

"Well, great. I'm very happy for you."

"I want you to see him. Fly down tomorrow."

For a moment she was lost, listening to the static.

"Are you there?"

"Yes, Uncle Pedro. Hold on."

She walked outside into the cold. Somebody's bare feet were sticking out the window of a Suzuki, We will, we will, rock you! blaring from the radio.

Cassidy pivoted in the opposite direction, past a sunglasses gallery and some beachy boutique, Candles 'n Crap, pacing with the phone to get a clear channel.

"You found a hitter. What's his name?"

"Alberto Cruz. You don't trust me?"

Pedro had played ball with her dad in the fifties. He was her godfather.

"How can I begin to answer that?" she said.

"You know how I look at a ballplayer."

"The intangibles."

"I got a list of fifteen things we can see with our eyes and another fifteen we cannot see with our eyes—"

Cassidy smiled, loving it—the list, the lecture, the oral history of baseball—hearing it evolve, full of pomp and fantasy, soothing as a bedtime story.

"I'm talking of the heart, the guts, the aptitude—" Pedro was going on, "and this kid's got it all. Exceptional talent. A center fielder with a quick bat, really drives the ball. Soft hands, good glove."

"The good face?"

"The good face," he echoed solemnly. "It's the dead season, the mills are closed, but they play in the sugar leagues maybe one time a week. Get here tomorrow and you can see Alberto Cruz in a game on Friday. They said on the news there's a big storm coming but you can beat it."

"Hello, Edith."

"What?"

"Talking to my dog."

A small white terrier had padded out of the bar looking for Cassidy, shaking her hide and yawning. Edith, rescued from the pound, still had abandonment issues.

Impatient: "Got a problem?"

"Not a biggie. It's just three thousand miles out of my territory. They'll annihilate me, Pedro, they're just looking for a reason."

"This kid won't last. The other organizations are gonna be all over him."

Cassidy knelt to touch the soft reassuring curls of fur and gazed across South Coast Highway at the Laguna Life Guard Station, a landmark built like a miniature lighthouse. There might be dolphins crossing the bay.

"You said this kid is playing—?"

"Day after tomorrow."

Cassidy looked at her watch. The numbers were meaningless.

"I'd have to call my supervisor. Travis. Raymond. Someone. I can't just get on a plane."

"Okay," he said, "forget it."

"But Alberto Cruz . . ."

"One thing I learned after thirty years: There's always another ballplayer."

In Pedro's silence she heard a resounding affirmation of the ability of this boy and a shot of adrenaline pierced the boozy high. A batter has a quarter of a second to commit to the swing.

"I'll be there."

Pedro's wife, Rhonda, came back into the room of their apartment in the Gazcue district of Santo Domingo. He had finished talking on the telephone and was seated on the edge of the bed smoking a cigarette, staring into nowhere with that heavy-lidded look. She knew it was not the time to be too strong, so she sat beside him and stroked his white hair. They had three sons living in the United States. When she thought of her new grandchildren her heart would break.

"Pedro," she said softly, "when are we going back to Miami? We can do it now. We can move."

He didn't answer.

"When are you going to give up this dream?"

"I just gave it up," he told her. "I just gave it away."

When Cassidy finally passed through customs in Las Américas International Airport, Pedro was not there to meet her, nor was he at the baggage claim. She took off a black silk Planet Hollywood jacket and tied it around her waist. The listless air smelled like lukewarm vegetable soup. As the crowd of passengers thinned, she alone continued to pace the terminal, scanning a sea of black faces.

American airports are dead at night, this one was like a block party — laughter, and boom boxes playing Latin music. Too much was being transacted for an outsider to begin to understand. The place was teeming with men and boys — hordes of boys under the age of twelve swarming the arrivals for spare change, and men lined up along the walls, watching.

Cassidy was used to being looked at, a big blonde girl with broad hands and hard wrists. She pretended to ignore them, but in sidelong looks at the lean bodies and sinewy long limbs there was an irrepressible thrill: the classic Dominican baseball physique, the template on which great players have been built. The men stared and chattered as she passed, Afro-European-Caribbean faces glazed with heat, and she realized her high school Spanish, sturdy enough in Los Angeles, would be as viable here as a child's red wagon on a freeway.

Her mouth was dry. She was coming down fast. The flight to Santo Domingo had been delayed in Miami, so she sat in the Admirals Club and drank with a guy she met, good-looking, older, a business type. He was buying, it was raining, she went way past her quota. Past four extra-strength Tylenol and a liter of Evian water. And now, reality. Her feet were walking, all by themselves, it seemed, on foreign soil. She had no Dominican money. She had not called her supervisor. The cost of the ticket had maxed out her credit card.

Suddenly a wiry little hustler slipped the duffel right off her shoulder. Not more than ten years old, with bony arms and no shoes, he said in authoritative English, "Come with me," and she went, following the boy outside to a line of ramshackle vehicles, some of which had the word *Taxi* decaled on or simply scratched into the paint.

"What is your hotel?" he asked.

"I'm waiting for someone."

Beyond the overhang of the terminal roof there were no electric lights. The parking lot did not have lights, neither did the road. God knew where the city was or even the next house. Behind the last taxi was nothing but darkness.

"No, gracias," she told the boy, and tried to take her bag from him.

But he would not let go.

"This is mine." Her heart kicked up hard.

"Lady, tell me your hotel. I want to help you. I want to make you happy in my country," he said and continued with a loopy laugh.

"I am very happy."

She searched his eyes, strangely dark and shining.

"I need my bag."

Okay, he was ten years old, but in her country ten-year-olds carry guns. And there could be others. Yes, two more coming toward them. Her boots were tipped with steel. Another instant and she would blow out his knee.

In one quick move she gripped the strap and yanked forcefully. There was no struggle. No attitude, no Saturday night special pulled from the waistband of the tattered shorts. The boy had no weapons other than a sullen disappointment.

She started up the ramp. Someone was calling her name but she kept walking at top speed until she looked over and glimpsed a familiar white head keeping pace.

"Uncle Pedro!"

She ducked beneath a railing and they embraced—his broad chest and scent of cigars, her strong sure arms—as the boys continued to wheedle and beg. Pedro made a subtle hand gesture, a slow-motion flick of the fingers, and they trotted away.

As they crossed the unlit parking lot, he hardly looked at Cassidy, delivering a lecture instead about what a sad indication these street children are of the way things have become.

"They buy glue from the shoe repair and use it to get high. A few pesos for a bottle. It's worse than cocaine."

Cassidy recalled the darkness in the boy's eyes; looking into them had been like watching through peepholes as his brain turned into tar.

"And the shoemaker sells it to them?"

"The shoemaker has to make a living." Pedro gave a wry shrug. "This is a poor country. We know what we got in the Dominican Republic, we are not proud to the poverty."

"But you've got ballplayers."

"No doubt about it, the Lord blessed these kids with the ability to play the game." He unlocked the door of the battered Datsun. "Some people say it is His only blessing."

Inside he pointed the key toward the ignition with a disturbing shakiness Cassidy hadn't noticed the last time they were together.

"Thanks for coming to get me," she said, vigorously upbeat. "The flight was canceled because of the storm. Looks like you missed it here."

"I don't think we gonna miss nothing. Another hurricane is now in Cuba. We get what they get."

The air-conditioning was an unexpected relief. Cassidy hadn't realized her face and neck were slick. The road from the airport was absolute black, the view through the windshield blurred by streaks of dried mud. As they rounded a bend the headlights flared over a group of soldiers in camouflage gathered in the bush, machine guns on their shoulders, tracking the Datsun with their eyes, young indifferent faces receding into darkness.

"What's the matter, Uncle Pedro?"

"I don't like your drinking."

"My drinking?"

"Your phone calls come to a bar!"

"It's my pub. My home away from home."

"Cassie—if you are in trouble, you have emotional problems, you talk to someone, talk to me. You're my kid."

His big meaty hand clamped down on her knee. He was paying her the highest compliment: treating her like one of his prospects, one of his sons.

"Just leave the drinking alone."

"You saved my life," Cassidy said finally. "Getting me back to the game."

"Well, your dad"—he jerked a thumb skyward—"he got an eye on me."

"Is that why you called? Because of my dad?"

Pedro gave the finger wave as if he wished the question would disappear like the boys. Finally he sighed.

"Your dad was not only a talented pitcher but one of the best human beings it was my honor to know. Your dad was a baseball man and your brother was a baseball man, and you are also a fine baseball man. I don't say 'baseball woman' because it don't make no sense—"

Cassidy let loose a wild laugh of relief.

"—You got the stuff. You're as sharp as any of the men scouts I got working for me. If the organizations in the United States couldn't see that without someone pointing it out to them, it is because they were only looking with their eyes."

Suddenly Cassidy never felt happier.

A faint line of palm trees became visible to the east. They passed beach stands lit by neon signs that looked as if they hadn't changed in forty years—Tropicale, Noche Azul—open-air cement bunkers painted funky screaming turquoise with walls of glistening bottles, a three-man band. Mostly they were empty but the bands played anyway and the neon crackled and sputtered in the dark.

They had reached the Ozama River. At a stoplight on the Puente Duarte a boy threw water at the mud-stained windshield, polishing quickly with a piece of newsprint. Pedro gave him a few centavos. Through the shining glass they could finally see the city of Santo Domingo with burnished clarity: a shoreline docked with mammoth barges, a cluster of high-rise hotels, an enormous billboard for Winston cigarettes, a sixteenth-century Spanish fortress.

On the other side of the bridge, cars and bicycles, públicos and pedestrians, swarmed around a traffic circle in the center of which stood a military monument, a floodlit obelisk of large gray stones.

As always, the beam of the lighthouse Faro a Colón, monolith to dictators, sliced above Santo Domingo like a white-hot saber.

A phrase came back to Cassidy, something they used to say about old-time baseball scouts. "Ivory hunters," they called them. Driving slowly through the congested streets of this exotic city observing the shadowy crowds under strings of weak colored lights along a shorefront drive called the Malecón, Cassidy felt what the hunter feels, crossing the border at midnight, ahead of the others, senses primed.

The hunter may have never been to this particular place but she has the gift, the locus, so that if she came down anywhere she would begin to hunt, and she would be right, and in the end there would be a death, even if it were only the death of a mother's dream about her son, the dream that he would never leave.

Her heartbeat quickened with a jolt of euphoria.

"Tell me about Alberto Cruz," she said.

JANUARY 1995

1

Cassidy Sanderson and Alberto Cruz have jogged nine miles, through a working-class Los Angeles neighborhood and twice around Elysian Park, and now the kid is starting to complain he's tired, they should quit, so she reaches past the ache in her thirty-five-year-old knees and sets an unforgiving pace, through a stand of pines up Stadium Way, panting, *"What do you want?"* a mantra she often uses to get young players focused on a goal.

"I want to fall in love with you," replies Alberto Cruz, and gives the wondrous smile.

"Not possible."

"I make a joke."

An unseasonable intrusion of hot desert winds has combusted the wet winter weather like a Christmas tree going up in your living room. The air is scathing. Her allergies are acting up. It feels as if someone's done her nasal passages with a bottle brush. "It's the dry air" is supposed to explain a lot: the flu that nailed the family over New Year's. A freak tornado that blew out the windows of a restaurant in Long Beach.

Things are stirring with a will of their own. Men in business suits have begun to appear at Dodger Stadium on their lunch breaks to buy tickets. The sky has a smooth shining quality, the air whisper-thin and clear, and sometimes the Santa Anas blow, knocking over power lines and café umbrellas, creating supernatural eddies of hot and cold in the most ordinary places, like the backyard.

It is hard to run up the mountain in this kind of heat, coming off in sheets from the hard-packed trail, scalding the calves and wicking moisture from the throat.

"What do you want? You want to be a Dodger?"

"Sí, I want to be a Dodger."

So she burns it. This impressive burst of speed will cost her, but it will send an important message. What *is* the message? Sometimes she wonders. Certainly she has nothing to teach Alberto Cruz about running—eighteen years old, he runs like a deer—while she has long since compromised the breath, nothing left in the legs, glucose-depleted, everything hurts, half a mile of straight-up switchback to go.

They pass an Asian mother and two daughters on their way to the playground. The girls are walking primly beneath Little Mermaid umbrellas while the mother shields her face from the sun with the *Los Angeles Times*. She may find it unusual to see a black man and white woman trot by—both in incredible shape, both wearing backpacks and carrying baseball bats like some sort of sports SWAT team—but her urban wariness reveals nothing.

For her part, Cassidy would never let the rookie see how much more it's hurting her than him, so her eyes stay fixed upon the horizon, singed this morning like a candle passing close behind a page. She keeps the features of her Nordic face relaxed, not strained, as if she's not preoccupied with a hundred other tangles, long blonde braid whipping sweat off her back. Loping easily beside her now, Alberto snorts with adolescent disdain as the trail yields in small rocky falls beneath the aggressive hammering of their high-tech neoprene soles.

The road rises at a steep angle along a brushy slope and Cassidy and Alberto break their third or fourth major sweat, tossing bright drops into the chinquapin and yucca. As they ascend, the view of the Los Angeles basin expands into an arc from Century City all the way around to Glendale. Coming at them directly ahead is the downtown cluster of high-rises and the shriek of jackhammers where they've finally begun to demolish buildings and excavate a huge pit, digging the bones of the old pueblo for a new sports and entertainment center.

Each day's heart-busting effort is Cassidy's deliberate reminder to Alberto of the work accomplished and the work ahead. When she scouted him in the shantytown of Río Blanco he had been laboring in a sugar mill. Seven weeks later, she has taken him an extraordinary distance—signed by the organization and brought to the United States to train. Now, as they reach the summit, the reward comes into view: beyond a picnic area and down a hill they can see Dodger Stadium itself, set in the center of the bowl of Chavez Ravine like a three-quarter crown with the crest turned away so you can look directly into the field.

Fifty yards to go and an old instinct kicks in and Cassidy pours it on, sprinting to the top, beating Alberto by a footfall and feeling a ridiculous amount of sneaky satisfaction in pulling it off, although now she has to bend over and concentrate on counting to twenty in order to keep from retching.

It is strange up here, high above the city. The lone woman with a big dog, the four Caltrans guys sitting motionless in a yellow truck, seem isolated and surreal, as if the constant desert winds have scoured the surface of ordinary things, turning them into symbols of ambiguous intent. They skirt a tumbleweed, then jog slowly past a Mustang with a vivid royal purple paint job, like the powdered candy that comes in envelopes and stains children's palms.

"Drug deal," Cassidy remarks.

Alberto keeps his eyes ahead.

A volley of shots resounds from the police academy below.

They head toward Bishop's Canyon Park, ditching the backpacks and squirting water down their throats.

"How did you sleep last night?" she asks.

"Good."

"What did you eat?"

"*Pollo.*"

"In English."

"Chicken."

"What did you do?"

"Watch TV."

"Did you help with the dishes?"

"She don't let."

"It's polite to call somebody by her name."

"Mrs. Dulce don't let me wash the dishes," Alberto repeats, and Cassidy sees she will have to have another talk with Dulce Rodríguez, administrative assistant in the scouting department and den mother to young Latin players, who puts them up in her house when they first arrive in the United States and spoils them silly, just like back home.

"How about the laundry?"

Alberto rolls his eyes.

Cassidy pulls a warm-up jacket out of the backpack and slips it over the black halter sports bra slashed with hot pink.

"Oh, I see. You think doing laundry has nothing to do with playing ball. Laundry is for women. Ball is for men."

Alberto shrugs with shoulders so loose they pop up to his ears.

"You tell me."

He perches on top of a picnic table, knees jutting out of huge baggy shorts, gastrocs flexing the long stringy calves; six foot three, he will need to gain at least thirty pounds to compete. He is wearing the same shirt with the Aztec zigzags as when she first saw him at the mill, and the same gold chain with the Virgin inside a plastic heart. Even with the pencil mustache and shaved step hair he does not look like every other skinny homeboy. He looks exotic, uncomfortable in woodsy North American light.

And yet the good face shines, the eyebrows flying off the forehead like butterfly wings, a wide and hopeful look; in his eyes, the intangibles that make a ballplayer—openness and balance, fire and desire—and the smile, still that of a boy who is eager to please.

"You may be a rookie who hasn't even been through his first spring training," Cassidy is saying, "who hasn't made it to the minors, who might be sent home tomorrow, but you are still a professional ballplayer. You have already beat out thousands of kids for the honor and responsibility of representing the Dodger organization, and in doing this you have also agreed to be a role model. Do you know what 'role model' means? To show other kids how to be a good person. We are privileged to play this game. We don't just take, we give back. You're a guest in someone's home? Find a way to help. What's the matter?"

Alberto's face squinches up. "You talk like my big sister."

In reply, she tosses him a 32-32 Adirondack bat.

"Ready to work on those hips?" recalling Alberto's swing in effortless detail from scouting him on the rock-strewn playing field in the DR. Pedro had been right about his arm strength and ability to run: she had seen right away he was locking his lower hips. There had been flies and merengue and scampering boys wearing nothing but bathing trunks, and sweat and dust and Alberto's hips not fluid, not rotating into the ball. He has to open his hips and keep his head down, learn to trust his hands.

He hasn't moved.

"What's the matter?"

Alberto shrugs again.

"Is there a problem?"

"*Yo no sé.*"

Enough of this crap.

Cassidy pulls out one of her coaching aids, a file folder labeled SLUGGERS. Before the talk of body balance and wrist action, before the soft toss and repetitive swings, they are going to take a look at the batting stances of the Old Timers in magazine photos she has laminated.

Before Alberto creates history, he's going to learn it.

"Who's my top player of all time?" Cassidy muses, although Alberto hasn't asked. "Roberto Clemente."

She flips the plastic sleeves, past Willie Mays and Mickey Mantle and for a moment they are blinded by a spot of sun sliding across the plastic.

"I'd even put him ahead of Griffey."

A hot wind sends curlicues of brown eucalyptus leaves floating down around their shoulders.

"Clemente could do anything. Run, hit for power. The whole picture."

And she shows it to him: the famous Puerto Rican right fielder on the follow-through of one of his sizzler line drives, enormous extension, shoulder in, chin pointing toward the ball. She's got a portrait of him, too, in which his deep brown face is cast in shadow and you can see, in the furrowed brow and eyes not looking at the camera, the tension in a hitter with a lifetime average of .317 who would always be an outsider.

Cassidy becomes so engrossed in looking at the picture she fails to notice Alberto has been holding something out to her, a scrap of paper worked between his fingers.

She takes it from him. In childlike printing on lined paper it reads in Spanish: *Dear Señor Cruz, I know what you did. Worry when you see me. Pay $10,000 by 1 February or you will die. Box 182, Nagua, DR.*

It is so preposterous Cassidy smiles. "Gee. What-all did you do?"

Alberto says, "I do nothing."

The paper has been folded and massaged so often it feels like cloth. Cassidy realizes he has been worrying it over and over, trying to rub the message away.

"Players get stuff like this all the time."

But his wide-hewn handsome face remains grim.

"Forget about it. Not your problem. I'll give it to security."

Then Alberto reaches into his pocket and comes up with three more identical notes.

Worry when you see me. Pay $10,000 by 1 February or you will die.

"Where did you get these?" Cassidy sifts through the damp soft papers, a lot less happy now.

"They coming to the stadium."

"No envelopes?"

"I don't know. I throw out."

More frustrated than she would like, "It would help if we had the post-marks. The dates." Then, "Are there more?"

Alberto shakes his head and sits back down, looking toward the San Fernando Valley. Now Cassidy knows why he has been lagging, why the good face has become a pout, carrying the weight of this, afraid to say any-thing, afraid to hold back.

"Where is Nagua?"

"In the north."

"Who do you know in Nagua?"

"I not go there."

"You didn't do something back in your country that might have made somebody mad—"

"No! Why you not believe me?"

"I didn't say I don't believe you."

But she knows very little about his past. On Friday she had seen him play, by Sunday she had made the deal and was out of there.

Alberto picks up a twig and breaks it.

"I do nothing."

Cassidy tries to ignore the pressure building in her chest. Threats against players on the Internet, pornographic letters, crazy fans acting out in the stands—there must be so many incidents of sports rage every day in professional ball you'd need a team of computer geniuses just to keep track. Still. You could dismiss one or two stupid notes, but four? Four is starting to sound like an obsession.

"We'll take care of it," she assures Alberto, hating what she has to do next, which is report to her scouting director, Raymond Woods, there is some trouble with this kid. The one kid, of course, she risked her job to go out and sign. It would be less agonizing to run up the mountain again, backwards, wearing ten-pound ankle weights.

Alberto says, "Okay," and picks up a piece of the twig and starts to tap it against the picnic table.

He had extinguished *a welding torch and come slowly through the ash-white smoke. He had taken his time, not intimidated by strangers waiting for him. Cassidy had liked that. Underweight, but tall. She had liked that, too, an elongated figure moving with an easy gait through a huge open threshold, out of the shadows of the sugar mill and into the searing humid sun.*

When it was explained the blonde American woman had come to the ingenio *in the middle of the afternoon to see him play baseball, Alberto did not betray surprise and did not look away.*

His fawn brown eyes held hers, as they do now, in a shaded grove at the top of Los Angeles, with curiosity and patience; as if he were used to waiting a long time for things that mostly don't turn out.

2

In baseball there is always somebody watching.

Even when there is no game and nothing to see, in the dead of winter, buried under snow, you will always find someone lurking around a ball field. A commuter home in time to walk the dog. A kid sister who has climbed to the top of the bleachers. *Just to make sure.*

At big old professional Dodger Stadium during the January off-season, the watching eyes belong to Chief of Security Oskar Kvorcziak, from a Balkan country not known for its collective sense of humor, who is paid to scan acres of deserted parking lots for vandals and lost media types—but who (Cassidy has always known) is secretly a member of the International Mind Police, *just making sure* nobody is even considering the notion that it would be the thrill of a lifetime to skateboard from the top of the steep bowl of Chavez Ravine all the way to the slaloming between the parking cones over super-smooth newly resurfaced asphalt.

Nope. Here he comes, tucked into his golf cart like a giant praying mantis, while Cassidy has no choice but to let the Explorer coast downhill across three empty feeder lanes to a space near the administrative entrance where a dozen cars are parked haphazardly.

"Hi, Oskar," she calls innocently.

He rolls by without a wave.

She slams the door and the sound reverberates in the still canyon air. Along with gym bag, bat bag, and the perennial nest of water bottles, scouting reports, Thomas Guides, and crusty towels, there is a splintered old skateboard in her backseat, waiting.

Not today.

Maybe tomorrow.

Let's face it. Never.

She shoulders her black leather backpack, checking to be sure the extortion notes are neatly stacked inside. Maybe she is making too much of a deal of it, putting each letter in a separate plastic sleeve, but she figures they are evidence and should be protected from contamination. Mostly she wants Raymond Woods to see she is actually capable of taking something seriously.

Not only is it becoming harder to get up in the morning after a workout like yesterday's, it is painful just walking across the parking lot. Cassidy's arthroscopically reconstructed knees are holding up okay, a few tweaks, but her neck aches from pounding up the mountain and her energy is sapped. At the age of thirty she would have been at the gym this morning, no problem, but now she can count on feeling depleted for another couple of days. Dang, she might even need to take a nap.

The glass doors open automatically to the club level and an off-season calm. No stampedes, animal odors, garbage, cries; everything harmonious and still. Orderly tiers of folded seats—yellow, orange, red, blue. Gray cement floors so clean they look waxed, the outfield steamy and dreamy, bright green grass like a well-kept public park, except it is not: it is a timeless amphitheater in which the vibration of everything that has been played and everything that is yet to be resonate together in the whispering air.

There have been times Cassidy has stood in this spot in the quiet of a non-game day and actually choked up. Here is a monument that holds no purpose other than to play the game of baseball, but she knows such monuments are doomed. Gilmore Field is gone, a neighborhood park that used to be on Fairfax Avenue. Cassidy's parents met at Gilmore Field: Smoke Sanderson a starting pitcher for the Hollywood Stars and Maggie a cheerleader, bobby sox and all. And now, just two miles from here, a three-hundred-million-dollar sports and entertainment center is hatching from the pit—multipurpose arena, shops, private suites, theme restaurants, arcades, and malls—that will render Dodger Stadium too plain, too downscale, to survive.

She turns into the lobby of the management offices, past the gold pantheon for the World Series Championship of 1988, through an inner door and down a bright blue corridor, cheered by the low-tech nature of this high-bucks biz. If it were the season, the game would be playing—not on big-screen TV monitors, but on cheap transistor radios on secretaries' desks—multiplied a dozen times, small and urgent. Phones would be

ringing and people would be going about their business, but everybody
would be staked to the outcome of the same event, like bookkeepers at
NASA listening to the launch of *Apollo* 13.

Dulce Rodríguez swivels away from her desk and heads for the copy
machine, papers in hand. She is always meticulously feminine—denim
dress, stockings and heels—always doing four tasks at once.

"To what do we owe the pleasure?"

Dulce's English is softened by the muffled consonants of a Spanish
speaker born in Guatemala. A pair of barrettes pull brown wavy hair off
her face, which, like her name, is soft and sweet, structured on the broad
cheekbones and flattened nose of the Maya.

"Hey, I bought something for Jasmine."

"Why?" asks Dulce. "You already gave her a Christmas present."

"You said she was having trouble in math, so I got her one of those
computer games. This is for Rosa," handing Dulce a stuffed kitten. "So
she doesn't get jealous."

Dulce takes the gifts, shaking her head.

"You are too good. Thank you."

"I don't have kids, might as well spoil yours."

Dulce's back is to her. Two moments pass. Two copies spit out of the
machine.

"Raymond around?"

"On the phone." The door to the scouting director's office is closed.
"Want to see Travis?"

"No, thanks."

As they walk back Dulce says, "I'm sure Travis wants to see *you*," and
smiles suggestively, still young and naive enough to believe Cassidy and
her supervisor could be a match.

On Dulce's desk, beside snapshots of her daughers in confirmation
dresses, is a collection can for victims of Hurricane Gordon, wrapped
with a photo of a little boy with the dazed stare of a survivor, standing near
a house that looks as if it had been bombed flat.

Cassidy slips a fiver into the slot. Every time she comes to the office
she feels compelled to make another contribution. She'd had a taste of
the hurricane when she was in the Dominican, caught in a downpour
that hit the windshield with the force of a fire hose. Two days after she left,
the thing ate the island alive—winds like a buzz saw, floods, mud slides,

whole villages swept out to sea. Across the Caribbean, they said, a thousand were dead.

The can is heavy with money.

"Has Alberto heard anything more from home?" Cassidy asks casually.

"He doesn't talk about it."

"How's he making the adjustment to your house?"

"Okay, except my son keeps asking why 'the Dodger' leaves poopy toilet paper in the bathroom wastebasket."

"What's up with that?"

"They have tiny pipes in the DR. You don't flush toilet paper there—"

Cassidy rubs beneath her bangs. Maybe everything is okay. If Alberto were receiving threatening calls, if hooligans were waiting outside in cars, Dulce would not be talking about plumbing.

"That's *it*?"

"We're working on the toilet paper."

The door to Raymond's office opens.

A pause as the winds shift around the boss.

"Cassidy Sanderson is here," Dulce announces although Cassidy is standing right there.

"Have a seat," Raymond says. "I'll be right back."

"Thanks," says Cassidy, and stiffly walks into the Cell.

Raymond Woods has been with the club twelve years and there is nothing on his desk. Nothing on the bookshelves nor on top of the credenza. He keeps it all in his head—stats, reports, rankings, strengths and weaknesses of all the top prospects. Sometimes you'll see him staring at a single sheet of yellow paper and it's scary. All he has in the office (maybe all you need in life) is a great view of the ball field through an ample window behind his desk. Swivel. Bam. And there you are, in ballpark space. Cassidy knows every angle on the game, but the first time she saw the field from the executive suite on the club level it took her breath away: the big picture. The way you look at baseball when you own it.

"Why are you hiding out in here?"

Startled, Cassidy jumps.

It is not Raymond in the doorway but her supervisor, Travis Conners.

"Hey!" she says brightly. "Why don't you give me a front office?"

"Take mine—" Travis quips. He barely has a cubbyhole. None of the area scouts has permanent digs, communication is from the road by e-mail, fax or phone. "—along with my body. Anytime."

Cassidy wishes she had been alert to the scuffle of his damn cowboy boots.

She smiles. "Still no takers?"

"Saving it for you."

Cassidy folds her arms. "You're having a good hair day."

Golden hair, long and layered. Flinty eyes in a hard, handsome face.

"Always."

Travis places his right butt-cheek on the edge of Raymond's desk and poses there, torquing his chest to display the broad shoulders and narrow waist of an ex-pro who has stayed in condition. The body of a ballplayer, thinks Cassidy, the mind of a yenta. He is wearing his usual garb—tight wrangler shirt, tight jeans, with a belt buckle the size of a dinner plate from one of his pals in the Hollywood stuntmen's union.

"Why do you want to see Raymond?"

"We've got some trouble with Alberto Cruz."

His eyes widen.

"Not Wonder Boy?"

"Probably nothing. Just being cautious."

"Since when is 'cautious' even on your screen?"

"Why don't you just let it go?"

Travis begins rolling up his sleeves, revealing forearm flexors square as two-by-fours.

"I'm your supervisor. I take the heat."

"And the glory."

Travis snorts. "Like Gordon and Cappalletti?"

Cassidy socks him on the shoulder.

"This is *not* Gordon and Cappalletti!"

"Some people feel pretty strongly that you get unfair special consideration around here," Travis continues smoothly as if the blow were moth-breath. "Smoke Sanderson's kid. Pedro Pedrillo's stamp of approval. Whatever."

Cassidy's cheeks are flaming.

"*Whatever*, I took the risk. I went down there and signed a hundred-thousand-dollar player for twenty. You should be on your knees."

"Is that an invitation?"

"Asshole."

Raymond enters briskly. "Bring me up to speed."

He sits behind the mile-wide empty desk.

Travis says, "Cassidy just called me an asshole."

Raymond leans back. His weight makes the chair creak. "All kidding aside."

For a non-athlete, Raymond keeps himself in pretty good shape. His height carries him, and the authority of a mustache. His skin is black with a delicate undertone of ultra blue. He recently got a fade haircut which makes no attempt to hide the gray, kind of hip with the Brooks Brothers windbreaker and navy slacks.

Cassidy pops it quickly: "Someone is threatening to blackmail Alberto Cruz. He's been receiving letters—"

"What letters?"

"Right here."

Cassidy hands over the plastic sleeves. Her fingers leave moist marks.

"Can you read the Spanish? It says, *I know what you did. Worry when you see me.* There are four notes, all the same. Alberto didn't keep the envelopes, so unfortunately we don't have the postmarks, but they come to the stadium. He's supposed to send ten thousand dollars to a postbox in Nagua by February first."

"Or what?"

"They'll kill him, I guess."

She gives a goofy shrug; it sure sounds lame.

"Who wants to kill him?"

"I have no idea."

Raymond blows air out the sides of his mouth.

Travis: "Where the hell is Nagua?"

"That's high school geography, you wouldn't know."

"Oh, I'm hurting."

Raymond is skimming the notes. "This dude didn't make it much past first grade."

He turns his big, steady face toward Cassidy.

"What does the boy say?"

"He doesn't know anything about it."

"You believe him?"

"Yes, I do."

The men exchange a look.

Raymond: "We could have Pedro check it out."

Travis: "We could."

Cassidy interrupts, "Cruz is my prospect, guys. Pedro passed him off to me."

"We know that," Raymond says evenly. "I'm thinking Pedro could check it out because Pedro's already down there."

"Right."

She tries to make it sound nonchalant, but they've already seen her unease. It is not that she worries Pedro would suddenly claim Alberto Cruz as his own. One of the few Latin American scouts with a National League contract, Pedro is on salary and does not receive a bonus for the boys he signs. For him, giving up Cruz would mainly mean denying himself the sugary, envy-laden fruit of recognition from his peers; over the years he's gorged on plenty of that.

Cassidy knows that Pedro gave up Cruz because of some unfinished business with her dad—an honor or a buried debt he did not want to discuss when she'd asked him about it in the Dominican—and that Pedro would not go back on that obligation now. She finds it hard to trust, however, that respect for a friendship in the past would stop anyone else (like Travis) from trying to snatch the prize right out of her hands.

They sit in silence as Raymond flips through the notes.

Finally, "It's in the boy's favor that he brought these to you."

"I thought so."

Travis, respectfully, "What's your gut, Ray?"

"I think it's horseshit. Jealous rival. Practical joke. You know how many of these we get a week?"

"Right."

"Let's keep an eye on it." Raymond tosses the notes so they slither across the desk. "I'll pass it along to security."

"Great."

Travis gets up and stands behind Cassidy, squeezing her shoulders as hard as he can, payback for the hit.

"Look at these shoulders! Relax!"

"Thank you. I'm relaxed."

He shakes her body, getting as much flexibility out of it as a piece of sheet metal.

"Don't worry. Be happy. Give the lady a cigar."

Raymond opens a drawer and pulls out a box of illegal Monte Cristos made in Cuba.

Travis cracks up laughing and Cassidy's stomach contracts to the size of a lime. The day she left Santo Domingo she had ducked into an indoor market to buy some merengue tapes and cigars. Suddenly the lights had gone out—not unusual in a city half without electricity—and when she had gotten back to LA (sneaking through customs with heart failure) and presented the booty as a gift to Raymond, the illicit, fragrant Cubanos had mysteriously turned into stale tubes of straw. During the blackout, the boxes had been switched.

"Okay, you guys."

Raymond chuckles, "Just a joke."

Like shaving cream in a uniform pocket, or shoeblack on the rim of a cap. Harmless locker-room stuff.

Raymond likes to be seen as playing it loose. On-the-surface loose. He is dealing with a double whammy—being African-American and having come up through management, an ex-marine and college coach with an advanced degree in sports management. He is not, as Cassidy is not, someone who played in the majors, a "baseball man."

You would think this would make them allies.

Dulce sticks her head in. "Travis? Skip O'Donnell's calling from the road."

Travis leaves.

Cassidy gets up to follow but Raymond prevents her by closing the door.

"I got another call from Jacinto Rincón."

Director of Latin American Operations, oh shit.

"How is Jacinto?"

"Pissed. His own scouts, the ones down there beating the bushes every day, want to know what happened with Cruz. Why didn't they get the tip?"

"It's a favor from Pedro. He's my godfather."

"Their perception is Los Angeles is horning in on their territory."

"Give me a break."

"They think it's because you're my girl."

"Your *girl*?"

"Those were Jacinto's words: 'What are you doing, sending your girl down here?'"

Raymond's eyes hold hers, then look away. Suddenly they are both embarrassed.

"What else can they think?" he says. "I've lost control of my staff?"

A small bulldozer is crossing the field. Guys are digging around third base.

Cassidy's voice drops to a mumble. "I'm sorry if I messed things up for you."

"You're the one whose percentages have been down."

"I know."

"You've still got to prove yourself to a lot of people. These threats don't help—"

"They'll go away."

"—especially after Gordon and Cappalletti."

Gordon and Cappalletti, Gordon and Cappalletti, twin anvils of failure hammered over and over every day since the June draft. Gordon and Cappalletti, Cassidy's top two high school prospects, both pitchers, both drafted in the first ten rounds—a *good* percentage that would have gone a long way toward bolstering her credibility as the only woman scout in the majors. Instead she lost both players and wound up skewered on the sports page.

Cappalletti didn't sign because at the last minute he opted for an athletic scholarship to Princeton. Fifteen hundred on the SATs, a handsome kid from a well-to-do family in Newport Beach, he was altogether too good to be true. Still, they had a handshake deal and the father unapologetically went back on his word. Why let your son play the game he loves when he could grow up to be an investment banker?

Not her fault, maybe. But Gordon.

Gordon's people (an earnest African-American family from Gardena) pleaded not to sign him before the California State All-Star Game because it would have made him ineligible to play in the last big event of his high school career. Cassidy, not wanting to take that away from the kid, let the signing hang. In the fifth inning of the All-Star Game her boy Gordon tried to be a hero and dove for the bunt in a crushing collision with the catcher that shattered his right wrist. The contract flew off the table like a petal in the wind.

Two early-round draft picks wasted.

Raymond Woods is not a screamer, doesn't have to be: "You never should have let Gordon play in that game."

Adding: "You're too nice."

Just a toss-away as he headed down the hall, but in thirty years as a competitive athlete nobody had ever accused Cassidy Sanderson of being nice. *Read my clips!* she should have shouted.

Then there was the article in the *Los Angeles Times* bemoaning the lost art of baseball scouts. "Ivory hunters," fierce individualists who carried the heart and history of the game across the American Serengeti in their Chevrolet sedans. They knew every nuance of the sport and would lie, cheat and steal to sign a prospect: promise 'em anything and carry cash. Romantic. Colorful. Loners, drinkers, misogynists—gone! Replaced by the national draft. In fact the job has become so downgraded, they've even given it to a girl.

Take a look at Cassidy Sanderson, the writer went on to suggest. Played softball for UCLA, superstar all-American shortstop once named "best defensive player in the world," goes on to play professional hardball for the all-female Colorado Silver Bullets, retires at age thirty-three and becomes a scout for the forward-thinking Dodgers. Gets two of her prospects drafted in the first ten rounds and what happens? Unaccountably, she allows them both—Gordon and Cappelletti—to drift away. Couldn't make the sign. Clearly not a "baseball man." Another sad example of the corruption of the game.

"The media loves to pull that horseshit," Raymond had said. But the heat was on. Being first, being visible, she would pay.

Gordon and Cappalletti, two bad-luck ghosts who stuck around long past Halloween. She had turned over rocks in schoolyards from hell, logged the miles in the Babe Ruth leagues, amateur ball and area code games, but nobody surfaced outstanding enough to break the spell.

Until Alberto Cruz.

"I took a flier going down there, but you approved the sign," she scolds Raymond. "I tried him out under the worst conditions, the most crapped-up field in history, then I called you, and what did you tell me? You knew I was in Jacinto Rincón's little kingdom. Did that stop you? What did you say?"

The playing field *had been nothing but a gap in the center of town, as if whatever had been there had atrophied and blown away, leaving dried clay and weeds bordered by scrub jungle of acacia and mesquite. Cassidy stood where the third base line would have been if they'd had a third base. The groundskeepers—two eight-year-olds in swim trunks—set out the bases, which were rags held down by rocks. Cassidy marked off ninety feet with her tape measure, but after second base they ran out of rags. No chance of running out of rocks.*

But this, she knew, was Alberto Cruz's field of dreams, and felt with him that excruciating pregame rapture as he ceremoniously untwisted a plastic sack (the equipment bag), opening up the most crucial thirty minutes of his life.

"Check it! We should charge admission."

Monroe, the schizoid Dominican street hustler who had driven her to Río Blanco, strutted back and forth, keeping a supercilious eye on the laid-off sugarcane workers who had ambled over to witness the tryout. That morning he had been hawking factory art at tourists; now he was George Steinbrenner.

The plastic bag held one can of lemon soda and a neon-green lady's golf glove. Alberto forced his left hand into fingers already split down the seams.

Cassidy stared. "What is that?"

"Local version of a baseball mitt," Monroe told her.

Alberto had brought along a smiley voluble fellow in his forties wearing slacks and a Hawaiian shirt, introduced as Señor Gómez.

The town pharmacist.

Local version of an agent.

"You are extremely privileged to see Alberto," Sr. Gómez began in grievously overcooked English. "He is part of the great tradition of excellent ballplayers from the Dominican Republic. Because God gave sugarcane a growing season of six months. Six months of beautiful sunshine! Six months of nothing to do but play baseball! God gave us the talent of Alberto Cruz as one of His finest blessings."

Cassidy glared, peevishly uninterested. Tibetan monks often enter meditation with the ringing of a bell. Now she clapped her hands two times, signifying she and Alberto and his teammates straggling down the embankment were entering the purity of ballpark space. It didn't matter that the field was bald and spiritless and looked like it had been raining stones—ballpark space exists between the white lines all players carry with the same precision inside their heads. It is quite possibly the only true universal—and those who are not in it, who are still concerned with cheap sales jobs, should fuck off.

First thing, Alberto ran the sixty yards in less than six seconds. The big, lithe strides would have made him a track star in any American high school. He went out to deep center and worked up to the long throw, making it to the plate five times dead on. She watched the flight of the ball. Told the catcher to let it drop and looked for the high quick bounce.

Then she picked up the old splintered bat, heavy as a two-by-four, and fungoed them out—long rayon skirt, pink cheeks, flying braid and all— with that tic she has of licking the fingers of her left hand before plucking the ball out of the air and giving it the small sweet toss, knocking out a pattern of grounders and flies with a practiced cadence that doubled the admiring crowd.

Kitchen chairs were set out and boom boxes, so merengue carried over this unusual dance between scout and prospect, her quick bat answered by his quick feet, the fluidity of his beautifully muscled frame matched by the elegant sinewy power of hers.

Alberto dominated the game against a ragtag bunch of Haitians from a rival sugar town with speed and power, even a hint of artistry. Good instincts on the base paths, such as they were. Cassidy hunkered down under the Dodger cap and shades, notebook and stopwatch in hand, locked onto Cruz, trying to look into the future, beyond this undernourished crew to major league competition.

When he stroked his third four-hundred-foot home run, she pulled out the cellular and punched in the number for Raymond Woods's private line.

He had been sitting in his office, looking out at a hundred thousand square feet of Bermuda grass monitored by a vacuum chamber drain-line matrix microprocessed moisture control system.

While she had been sweltering in motionless ninety-degree heat, perched on rotting concrete steps layered with political slogans beneath a palm-frond roof that was dried to a crisp. Half-naked boys scampered in the rafters as her executive assistant, Monroe, snarled at them to go home and play with themselves.

" . . . *And* where *are you?*" *Raymond had asked with legendary cool, over the long-distance crackle.*

A beer right then would have been excellent.

"—What did you tell me, Ray?" she insists, continuing on. "I said he's fast, great arm, above average instincts for the outfield, going to be a .300 hitter and above, and nobody else was on him. What was your response?"

Raymond doesn't answer.

"*'Twenty thousand dollars.'* That's what you said. And that's what I did, even though, if anybody else found out about him, he would have been worth a hundred. That's why we closed the deal so fast, and screw Jacinto Rincón, and you know it."

The long pause. Raymond reaching deep into the mental cooler for that ice-cold calm.

"I told you something else, but you forgot. I said, *'This kid better be able to play.'*"

"I didn't forget."

He's opened the door, looking past her now, across the busy office.

3

Papa's is at its crowded, comfy best when Cassidy walks in that night, wearing tight black jeans and a navel-revealing aqua sweater, carrying her dog.

Marshall Dempsey *springs* off the barstool.

"Hiya, gorgeous!"

He can do nothing less than *spring*—an Australian hardbody tight as a basketball.

"I was praying to see you." He kisses her cheek. "God is good. Take my place, sit down."

"Keeping it warm for me?"

Cassidy settles gratefully beneath the faded awning that covers the bar, furled at the edge like a sail.

Big Tyson lays down a desiccated cork coaster that smells as if it crossed the ocean in a frigate.

"I have a new craft-brewed honey-wheat with notes of raspberry from Spokane."

"Bring it on."

"Right now you'd drink motor oil, is that what you're saying?"

"Tyson, I appreciate your offer to share your blah blah blah honey-wheat."

Tyson goes away.

"One must show respect," suggests Marshall.

Cassidy mutters, "*Artiste.*"

"How was your day?" Marshall asks in his Aussie lilt.

"I need a hot bath and a full-body massage."

"Then what for the love of Christ are we doing here?"

"Trying to regain our humanity."

"What does that mean?"

She strokes his boy-soft cheek. "I don't know. Who are you?"

Marshall smiles, puzzled.

Cassidy studies his face. It is a face you cannot fail to appreciate, unencumbered, barely twenty-eight, you can still see the Irish in it; along with the black-roots-bleached-out spiky hair and nose pierce there is a stubborn young optimism, based on nothing, really, except the day-to-day pleasure of being in that body, getting it to do new tricks. A world-class surfer in Sydney, now a high-priced personal trainer in LA, Marshall works Cassidy out twice a week. When they had begun sleeping together last July, he had felt, touchingly, he had to make it clear "the occasional good-time bang" would not affect their professional relationship.

"Whatever it is, love, it couldn't be worse than having to listen to a certain wife of a studio head go on about her boob job."

"She finally had it done?"

"Will do. She's mad at *me* because the pec dec doesn't do it."

"Big news flash."

"I've been telling her there's nothing for it but surgery."

Big Tyson brings the ale. Cassidy takes a sip off the quivering foam.

"Nice."

Big Tyson goes away.

Nat King Cole is singing "Smile."

On the next barstool a woman is saying, "*. . . That's a great performance. Hitchcock could . . . come on . . . I've never seen a bad performance. He was a master.*"

"Well, *my* guy," says Cassidy, setting down the glass half-done, "could be in trouble."

"Which guy?"

"The young man I found in the Dominican."

"You had your hopes on him."

"Still do."

"Which is it, girls or drugs?"

"Weirder. Someone's sending threatening notes to the stadium. The notes say if he doesn't pay money by February first, they'll kill him."

"Who is? Why?"

"Nobody has a clue."

She drains the rest.

"The boy's a rookie, is he not? Still has to go through spring training and make the cut? Well then, that's ridiculous. What do they think they can get from him now?"

"*I love Rebecca,*" the woman on the next barstool is saying. "*No, Hitchcock is . . . Plus, you know what? He was a master at putting the right actor in the right role.*"

Cassidy sighs. "Someone thinks he has money."

"Or maybe they've got something so bad on him they figure he'll bloody well *get* the money."

"Marshall, I looked at him with my eyes. No *way* he's bad."

Big Tyson comes by to take the empty.

"Let's be real," Marshall says reassuringly. "The Dodgers can't be taking it all that seriously."

"Here's the problem."

Like the prow of the ship on the beer logo, the first brew has already cut cleanly through the sea of horseshit Cassidy finds herself, on a day-to-day basis, swimming under or, at best, through.

"The problem is—even if nothing happens—the problem is, it puts a spotlight *on Cruz* and a spotlight *on me.* Which neither one of us needs. I'm worried about his emotions, he's raw, doesn't know how to separate what's on and off the field. And meanwhile, Raymond's pissed at me for going down there in the first place, although, obviously, if I were a guy, none of this would even be an issue, they would be all, 'Way to go. *That took balls!*'"

Tyson sets down a fresh ale.

"What did I tell you?" he interrupts with the irritating condescension of one who is sober. "You were sitting on that exact same stool when you got the call. What did I tell you at the time?"

"That'll be fifteen dollars and seventy-five cents."

Marshall laughs.

"I *said*"—Tyson points emphatically at the bar, an oversized gnome in a wool beanie—"'*Cassidy . . . leave it.*'"

"Oh, bull!" she exclaims. "Why don't we rewrite history?"

Edith struggles. Cassidy puts her down on the sawdust-covered floor.

Tyson, "That dog better not shit."

"She only shits on beanies."

"—Because that's what I said," Tyson insists. "'*Cool it! It is not your bag. People are going to get pissed.'* Just like when I said, 'Cassidy? Don't *jump off a radio tower.'* Was I wrong?"

Neither of them answers.

"Was I wrong?"

The woman on the adjoining stool says, "Big Tyson is never wrong. Wrong about what?"

"She goes and jumps off a freaking radio tower."

Disgusted wave of a chubby hand. Three silver rings.

"What kind of radio tower?"

"You know those tall things with a radar thing on top."

"It shoots out microwaves?"

"I dunno about the freaking microwaves," says Tyson. "Ask her."

The woman cranes around to have a look at Cassidy. She has two-tone hair, probably because she is habitually too looped to know the difference: a yellow bowl that goes halfway down the bangs, the rest bleached cotton-white. She is wearing a soft pale dress made of something like angora. A brown-skinned man with Asian eyes, with whom she has been discussing the films of Alfred Hitchcock, is reaching out from an adjoining barstool and stroking the dress.

Cassidy gives the lady a friendly tip of the glass.

"It was a fourteen-hundred-foot FM radio tower. Probably *was* shooting microwaves."

She swallows the rest of the beer.

"You jumped off it?"

"Yes."

"Why didn't you die?"

"I had a parachute."

The woman nods seriously as if this made sense. It is hard to tell whether she is aware of the man stroking her dress.

"People do these things?"

"I did it once." Cassidy smiles blankly. She would like to go home.

"That's how we met." Marshall has intervened, leaning across Cassidy with a wink. "It was the ultimate adrenaline rush, I'll tell ya."

"You two jumped together, holding hands!" the woman cries, delighted.

"Not me." A shiver passes through Marshall's tensile frame. "I may be dumb, but I'm not stupid."

"We had a mutual friend who was killed on Bridge Day," Cassidy says, hoping to wrap it up. She teases a folded twenty from the inside ticket pocket of her jeans, which are tightly sucked against the bone of her hip. "That's when a bunch of people get together and jump off an eight-hundred-foot gorge."

"We met at the funeral," Marshall explains. "The funeral was in San Francisco."

"You must have been sad."

"It was sad."

"He was a good guy."

"Do you know?" The woman smiles beneficently beneath the bicolor bangs. "I think that is so romantic. In a *very* special way."

Shadow Lane is south of downtown Laguna Beach, four blocks from the ocean and less than three minutes from Papa's. Most of the houses are hodgepodge makeovers of summer bungalows built in the thirties and forties, but the little number Cassidy rents hasn't been too messed with and retains a rustic charm, from the Dutch door on forged-iron hinges to the redwood floors and beams; the ocher squares with orange-flower patterns around the fireplace claimed to be original Malibu tile.

Cassidy turns left into the kitchen as Marshall goes right into the living room, picking up the remote and punching in MTV before turning on the lights, the two of them flowing through the house with the careless intimacy of partners whose bodies and psyches have been worn to a smooth fit by the repetitive wave action of hundreds of workout sets over hundreds of hours, weaving in and out of each other's limbs and mental space. Bottles of Corona are in their hands and they share a covert cigarette as Cassidy moves through the living room, picking up the week's residue of filmed glasses and Fiestaware plates with toasted crumbs. The expectation of sex curls through the air.

"I just have to make one call."

Marshall waves.

She dials Dulce at home.

"How is Alberto? I intend to burn his butt on the mountain tomorrow. Can I talk to him?"

"He's not here."

"Why not?"

"He's at a club. In Glendale."

"Doesn't he know we have six days left to get him in shape for winter workout?"

"He knows."

"Then why is he out dancing?"

"He is eighteen years old."

Cassidy exhales into the phone.

"Do you want me to send Carlos to get him?"

"No. Listen. Sorry I called so late."

As pliant as she is with Raymond, Dulce does not hold back with girls: "You are too attached to this kid."

"Not true."

"Alberto will be on time for workout tomorrow," Dulce tells her. "Or he won't."

Cassidy hangs up. Marshall is sprawled in a chair watching a pink Cadillac speed across a desert. Inside, a male ska band is wearing high heels and black lingerie. She clicks off the remote, then sneezes four times in a row.

"You're stressing."

"Allergies."

"I know you. Miss Intensity. So the kid went dancing."

"He's got to make it, that's all."

"If you're pushing him the way you push yourself, I feel sorry for the lad. Sometimes with my clients I'll say, You're doing fabulous, skip a workout, go get a massage. They love me for it, think I'm God. And you know what? Next time, they're a hundred percent more focused."

"You are a God," teases Cassidy, offering her hands. She braces her feet and pulls all two hundred five pounds of him up out of the chair.

"Well done."

But instead of proceeding directly upstairs, he remains standing still, head down, seeming to contemplate the way the red nylon wind pants bag over his untied basketball shoes.

"What do you need?"

"I need a drink!" he answers brightly, and grabs a bottle of Gordon's gin off the mantel.

"You won't get far with that."

"Why not?"

"Look what's in it, genius."

He lifts the bottle. Instead of liquor, the bottle is stuffed with twigs.

"Shit! Well, what the hell's the *point?*"

"It's my little altar from the DR."

Laid out on the mantel, on top of a nice piece of plastic lace she had found in a dry goods store in San Pedro de Macorís, is a collection of small trophies: a wooden crucifix, a miniature bag of woven straw with red tassels, a plaster Madonna and child, a house made of cowrie shells, and the merengue tapes which are there as a cosmic joke because afterward, when she had gotten home, she had discovered, like Raymond's phony cubano cigars, she had purchased a stack of fakes. The liners were real but the cassettes were blank.

"What's this crazy thing?"

Marshall has picked up a gourd dressed like a female in an intricate webbing of sequins and beads. Two arms of twisted cloth curve to its hips. There is a round mirror at the navel and, sticking up where the head should be, a plume of orange feathers.

"It's a vodou charm. I watched it being made. The mirror is like a TV station that sends out messages of what's going on inside."

"What *is* going on?"

"That's the mystery."

Cassidy is unscrewing the cap off the Gordon's gin bottle. An unnamable essence—like eucalyptus oil, rosemary and red chilies—penetrates their sinuses.

"Wow."

"They call it Mama Juana."

"No joke."

"You put liquor inside and let it soak and the spirits in the wood are supposed to make it ten times stronger."

"Wish we had some now," says Marshall.

"We don't need it now."

Giggly, carrying fresh Coronas, they squeeze hip-to-hip up the winding staircase to the bedroom. She leans against him, weakened, intoxicated with the unbearable proximity of his smooth young hunky body, one layer of T-shirt, one pull of drawstring, away. Her fingertips snake eagerly beneath the shirt to stroke the warm obliques, solid as the slippery muscle of a deep-sea fish; a trophy fish, cherished for its conquest, like the mementos on the mantel.

Later, candles everywhere and heavy incense, on Laura Ashley bed-clothes twisted up with a blue and gold Bruins blanket, it isn't sweet Marshall Dempsey that gets her there, not even sweet Marshall in a bikini thong with a six-pack of abdominals tired Atlas would envy, no, after too much habitual straining, it is a trick of mind: tonight, a replay of the leap off the radio tower—a rickety elevator jerking up, gloves frozen to the metal struts of the platform, a billion stars, a moment of abandonment and then six seconds of purified terror, treetops rushing at you a hundred miles an hour, a force of panic so primitive just the recall of it jolts the heart like an amphetamine popper—that does it, until she is able to go ahead and Marshall follows, and eventually they roll apart, sated, figuring it had all gone pretty well.

4

By 6:30 a.m. the following morning the grande percent latte is in the cup holder and the Explorer is rolling east on Laguna Canyon Road, headlights on. In seven minutes it reaches the on-ramp where Cassidy, roused from hibernation mode, finds the 405 moving fast, comfortable passing distances, a relief to be driving with commuters who, like she, are freeway professionals, cooperating in a team effort to get to the office without tragedy.

Marshall had left the cottage at six to meet his first client at the gym. Fifteen minutes later, Cassidy pulled out in the Explorer. The shadows of the flame trees had barely begun to shrink beneath the rising sun when already Marshall was gone from her mind; she had forgotten how they said good-bye or if they'd made a plan to see each other. It didn't matter. In a day or two their workout schedule would swing by and round them up again with the tedious dependability of an Orange County Transit Authority bus.

Cassidy checks the rearview mirror; not kind to those tiny fissures like fault lines that run vertically above the upper lip. You can forestall the aging of the body, but not the face. Do the cheekbones, plump as Rogue Valley peaches, the blonde bangs and wraparound sunglasses on a rawhide leash still pull it off? Are the small gold hoop earrings too plain? She has never gone in for makeup or a lot of ornamentation, maybe because when she was playing ball you had to look Spartan (although the Bruins secretly wore mascara), but recently she has begun to wonder if the Revlon counter isn't in her future, and if those threads of ivory at her temples aren't really pale, pale gray.

Last night was good, she can't complain, but there's a failure at the heart of it, a clanking in the engine that doesn't go away; an empty sound she's heard before. Even in high school her tightest girlfriends were on the softball team and the boy athletes, at best, treated her like one of them. Women don't seem to trust a female jock and men don't stick around. So you concentrate on playing ball.

That worked fine until she fell in love.

She had a contract with the Colorado Silver Bullets. There was still a shot (astronomically long) that she could be the first woman in men's ball since Toni Stone covered second base for the Indianapolis Clowns in the Negro Leagues in 1953. Pedro warned her, but she walked away, for a moody cop named David Stohl.

It had been what she called her "numbnuts period"—dating lifeguards and firemen and guys from the sheriff's department. Stoli was a wild man—owned a Harley—they had some wicked times in Rosarito Beach, but she truly believed this would be it: teaching softball clinics in the summer, a white picket fence around a Spanish fixer-upper in Encinitas. At LAPD games, for the first time in her life, she found herself cracking beers with the wives in the beach chairs, happy to be part of the family.

Then David Stohl took off and Cassidy went on a six-day bender, something she hadn't done since her twenties—was told she wrecked her car and smashed a drinking fountain somewhere with a bat. When she came to she discovered he was still gone, along with a big chunk of hope of fitting in anywhere.

Someone ripe as Marshall gets you going for a while, but how can you keep it up when you don't feel responsible, not even for your partner's pleasure? You know he will take care of himself (just like you)—all that is required is to mirror his ardor for his own body. How long can you keep faking it, as if the accident of winding up on the same coordinates in Southern California were enough to justify a kind of life together—Sunday brunch at the Cheesecake Factory, driving to Snow Valley for a day, partying at Papa's, training for the marathon, skateboarding on Venice Beach with your dogs?

Dawn colors clouds of steam billowing around the Arco refinery. Elysian Park, on the other side of downtown, where Alberto Cruz had better be waiting, ready to take the mountain, is at least forty minutes away. A warning flood of red taillights, and Cassidy enters ballpark space, despite six cantankerous lanes of traffic—deciding that today they'll work on concentration, the hardest skill for an impatient young fielder to learn, how to focus on a hundred fifty pitches every game. They'd do visualization exercises, the one where you *observe* everything in your room; she'll talk about relaxation, effortless effort, letting it flow; she'll teach him to take four pitches in the cage, in order to see the ball really well on the fifth — By the time she stops thinking about where Alberto will resist and where he will understand these things, she is at the entrance, heading up Elysian Park Drive between rows of fifty-foot palms.

She has driven the last thirty miles with no other awareness.

The Explorer pulls into the parking lot. Alberto is waiting in the deep shade, throwing up stones and fungoing them carelessly with a stick. His eyes are clear, he's ready to learn; no reason to come down on him for staying out last night.

He doesn't, after all, ask if she had gotten laid, or if it changed her life.

Today's turns out to be an inspired workout, excellent attitude and good communication.

"You're doing fabulous," says Cassidy, echoing Marshall's advice. "Let's go to the mall."

It is a ten-minute drive from Elysian Park to the Glendale Galleria shopping center, a good place to buy Alberto shoes and teach him something about American culture, should he make the minors and find himself in Great Falls, Montana, starving for a pizza at ten o'clock at night.

We are not talking the America of wheat fields and tractors. Or skyscrapers. Subways. The Metropolitan Museum of Art. We are pulling into a salmon-pink parking structure where a nervous kid is directing traffic so badly the Explorer almost creams a teenage mom pushing a stroller. The young man shrugs. The girl, spaced on a Walkman, shrugs also.

Not his problem.

Not her problem.

Hey. Not a problem.

Cassidy guides Alberto between the yellow lines of a pedestrian crosswalk. Approaching from the opposite direction is a mix of middle-class Asians, Hispanics, blacks and whites carrying shopping bags, equally disoriented by the afternoon glare and the universal question: *Now where in heck did I park that car?* Cassidy feels a thrill of achievement. This *is* America, after all.

She opens the glass door to the mall and plows ahead but Alberto has disappeared. Panic attack. Back outside she finds him standing right where he was, out on the sun-drenched sidewalk, shaking his head and laughing.

"What's the matter?"

He giggles, searching for words.

"For me a dream," he manages finally. "A dream. For me."

Cassidy grabs his hand and pulls him inside, like leading a colt over a dance floor. Everything that glitters catches his eye and causes him to halt, all bollixed up in the feet, while shoppers dodge around him. They can scarcely get past the California Terrace food court, with fountains and brass railings, windsurfing boards with rainbow sails decking the upper reaches over neon waves of blue, without Alberto swerving toward the garlicky stench of Panda Express, stumbling at the knock-out cinnamon-sugar punch of Cinnabon. Then there's Hot Dog on a Stick with its surreal tanks of bubbling lemonade and high school girls in striped tunics and tall hats buzzing in and out of candied clouds of steam.

"What do you think?"

"Sweet."

Alberto grins and slaps her five, thanks for delivering all this amazing shit to him.

Cassidy keeps them moving up escalators and down ramps, wondering what goes on in the kid's head when he sees stuff like the window of FAO Schwarz—all that whizzing and whirring, sparkle Barbies and LEGO Ferris wheels—and outside the store a huge bronze bear, big as a church.

How does it feel, when work is a hundred-year-old sugar mill and home is a shack near a sewage trench with pigs in the backyard, to find yourself in a completely fabricated environment, where the trees are fake and the sun, through arched skylights, is a shy and tentative guest?

She remembers the darkness inside the mill, no electric lights, weak illumination filtering through cracks in the roof: a vast, pitch-black space filled with moving bodies and the hulking shapes of a complex assortment of antique equipment. Black faces slick with sweat looked up at her with tired amazement. She stared back with equal intensity, slowly panning every man: those hollow eyes, those grizzled cheeks, a yellow bandanna much too cocky, cleft palate, bald head, stupefaction, middle age—searching for the good face, the face of Alberto Cruz.

Now Alberto Cruz is here, gaping up at a fairy-tale clock with exposed gears, passing folks sitting down and resting their feet who are spooning ice cream from paper cups and basking in the idea of an old-fashioned small-town square where good community behavior prevails, due to a satellite police station with friendly western lettering, someone's shirt on a hanger, homelike, behind the storefront glass.

Cassidy would like to know how you make such a psychological leap, monitoring Alberto's every reaction from the corner of her eye, when, as they head toward Mervyn's, the young man starts making *click-click* sounds with his tongue and the answer becomes clear:

Babes.

Forget the big abstract questions.

Alberto is cruising the babes.

Japanese babes in butt-skimming skirts, plastic mules, Prada bags and attitude.

A gothic babe, black hair, chalk skin, purple lips.

An African-American babe wearing a backwards leather cap and a shirt cropped to show off the ring in her navel, walking like she knows something.

Alberto swivels to watch her melt down the escalator.

Oh God, thinks Cassidy, snatching him from a collision with a planter, I will teach this kid to order a hamburger and see the ball off the bat, but I will *not* have a conversation about condoms. Let the coaches handle the rigors of the male anatomy, and welcome to it.

They reach McDonald's.

The rookie eyes the counter where a Latin guy his age warily checks the gangsta in the bad threads.

Alberto tries the dazzling smile. "*Hola.*"

"*Hola.*"

"*Por favor, me puede ayudar con el menu.*"

"*Tenemos una buena oferta—*"

"We are doing this in English," Cassidy interrupts. "My friend wants to practice his English."

"Sure," says the kid, puffing up. Eighteen months out of Chalchuapa. "So, what do you like?"

Alberto studies a grid of photographs showing eight different Extra Value Meals while fiddling with the plastic heart containing the Virgin and Christ.

"I like two."

"Two what?" prompts Cassidy.

"Two *hamburgesas*."

"*¿Con todo?*"

"*Con todo, por favor*."

"Go ahead. Say it."

Alberto balks, prideful, not wanting to make a mistake.

"Two Cheeseburgers Meal."

They grab some stools. Two more teenage moms have found each other, feeding bottles to their babies. Alberto eats slowly, watching them.

"You don't want to go there," Cassidy says.

"No. I don't." He crumples the wrapping. "I know what I got to do."

"Which is?"

"Do real good in spring training. Impress the people, show them I can play ball."

His eyes stray over the corridor where shoppers graze; then return to Cassidy with quiet purpose.

"I got to do my best. Do what the coaches tell me. I got to speak with the Americans, try not to worry for my mistakes in English. I got to know I gonna be proud of myself one day, one day, I gonna have a great conversation. I got to stay away from drugs. In my village, when they know I going to the United States, they say, 'Why you not go to New York and sell *manteca*—cocaine?' Some people, they like baseball to get them off the island, but they no want to *play* baseball. I no understand that. They want to go to New York and make money. I have one friend, he is dead right now. He selling, got a lot of money. Car. House. In two years he is dead. Somebody shoot him. I know a ballplayer, Vargas, he was real good. He play in the major leagues one, two years, but he never make it because he swallow cocaine, and they catch him in the airport in Puerto Rico. Why he not worry, I might die for this?"

"I know Vargas. He was talented. But not as smart as you."

"My mom? When I leave, she cry. I got to do these things for my family. Things are very bad in my home after the hurricane."

Alberto is unusually still, fingers clasped on the counter, resolve coming off his body in waves. Only the butterfly eyebrows seem to rise in an uneasy question.

"I worry for these letters, too."

"You haven't gotten any more?"

"No more."

"That's good. My boss says not to worry. You just play your game."

Cassidy pushes the tray away. It is beginning to smell like something dead.

The store of choice is Champs, where young men can be outfitted like their favorite sports heroes in Official Merchandise. Alberto is tall enough to put his nose into the folds of the garments hanging from the racks suspended off the ceiling, lost in the sensuous pleasures of hooded cotton sweatshirts, boxer trunks, mesh shorts, polyester warm-ups in oxidized green.

Cassidy has wandered over to the baseball section, marveling how they get eighteen dollars for a T-shirt with a blurry picture of Ken Griffey, Jr., when the commotion begins.

It starts with a guy in work boots and jeans who says, innocuously enough, "Hi. Mind if I have a look at that?"

Alberto is handling a gym bag. "No problem."

The guy opens the bag and finds a batting glove inside.

"How'd that get in there?"

"I put."

Immediately he reaches into a back pocket and comes out with a badge.

"Police. Step to the wall."

"What I do?"

"Don't hassle with me, dude. Just turn around."

In the heartbeat it takes Cassidy to cross the floor, Alberto Cruz has been locked in handcuffs.

"What's going on?"

"Police activity. Stay back."

Store people stop what they're doing. Customers gather.

"I do nothing!" says Alberto.

Cassidy: "The young man is with me."

The cop is mouthing into a walkie-talkie.

"I said, he's with me."

"He's with you," the cop repeats. He seems incredibly tired. Disheveled hair, rings beneath the eyes. Physically, midsize and unremarkable.

"My name is Cassidy Sanderson. I'm a baseball scout with the Los Angeles Dodgers. This young man is one of our prospects from the Dominican Republic."

Apparently the officer hears this kind of thing from tall blonde women in the Glendale Galleria all the time, because his tired expression does not change.

"The lieutenant will be here in a minute, ma'am."

He is keeping Alberto at arm's length with fingers just touching his back, making certain the boy stays face-front to a wall of athletic cups.

"What are the charges?"

"He hasn't been charged with anything yet, ma'am."

Reinforcements arrive. A pair of brawny security guards with guns and a couple more undercover guys also wearing work boots who, in fact, look funnily alike—the same black hair, dark circles and double-shift exhaustion, like brothers running a failing restaurant.

The lieutenant, a blow-dried job in a better shirt, studies her business card and listens to her story, explaining that nevertheless the suspect will need to be questioned on suspicion of shoplifting.

"That is total horseshit!" Cassidy shouts, realizing, too late, she is exiting the Zone on a pair of Saturn rockets. "He was not shoplifting!"

"He put a batting glove inside a gym bag."

"So?"

"Why would someone do something like that?"

The first cop still maintains the feather-light touch on Alberto's back.

"He didn't walk out of the freaking store with the freaking glove," Cassidy says, hoarse with frustration, "Which, by the way, he can get by the dozens. So what is this? Harassment?"

Behind the lieutenant's bleary eyes something finally clicks.

"Piazza's on a streak," he allows.

Cassidy isn't buying: "I am really looking forward to when the general counsel for the Los Angeles Dodgers calls your supervisor."

When they are finally walking toward the exit Alberto says simply and without anger, "They think I am American black."

"I am ashamed that happened," Cassidy replies with heat. "It's not always like this. Not everywhere."

They push through the doors into lukewarm air and an eye-stinging shaft of setting sun. There, in plain view across the walkway, are two more cops—bicycle cops this time, wearing shorts—poking around the Explorer. But these two have probable cause. The alarm is sounding and the lights are flashing and the driver's window has been smashed to nothing.

Swearing lavishly, Cassidy trots over and identifies herself as the owner. She blinks off the alarm.

"Stereo's still there," remarks one of the officers, a woman with excellent rectus femoris musculature. "Aren't you glad you have an alarm?"

Cassidy peers inside, heartsick. "Not a great day at the mall."

Alberto puts a large warm hand on Cassidy's shoulder, then squats against a pillar to wait it out. While clipboards are brandished and questions asked, Cassidy's attention becomes increasingly drawn to an ominous object resting on the front seat in a litter of broken glass. She reaches through the empty space where her window used to be and gingerly picks it up.

The woman cop whistles. "Well, that's funky."

The thing appears to be a Barbancourt rum bottle, you can see the lettering underneath the red cloth in which it has been tightly wrapped. Lashed to the neck with hundreds of turns of black thread are two pairs of scissors, open wide. Dangling off the bottom on multicolored strings is a bizarre fringe of razor blades that flash like silver teeth.

Her partner says, "What is it? Some kind of punk thing?"

"Gang thing?"

Cassidy holds it very carefully. It spooks her in a deeply primitive way. Unlike the whimsical gourd with the belly-button mirror on her mantel, this bizarre construction is definitely broadcasting on an evil wavelength: the shape of the bottle like a human body. Meticulous tiny stitches in the cloth. The yawning jaws of the scissors, or are they supposed to be a woman's legs pried apart? And the sinister razors, swinging free—are they supposed to cut her up?

Alberto is on his feet, moving forward with a look of astonishment.

The woman cop puts on a pair of rubber gloves.

"We better log this in."

Carrying the bottle steadily to avoid being nicked by the twisting razor blades, she slips it into a Ziploc plastic bag, then packs it away in the panniers on her bike.

The cops leave a copy of their vandalism report and pedal off. Cassidy uses a sweatshirt to sweep the glass off the seats. It isn't until she and Alberto are back in the Explorer ready to pull out that she says finally, "They don't have stuff like that in Glendale."

"It come from Haitian people."

"You've seen that kind of thing before?"

She starts the engine.

"Lots of Haitian people living in my village. To them it is a religion. We call it *obeah*."

"What does it mean?"

Alberto's looking straight ahead, stroking his mustache.

"We got to pay."

They sit for a moment, smelling exhaust fumes.

"They follow us. They want the money bad."

Four cars are lined up behind them, waiting for the spot.

Cassidy puts the Explorer in reverse.

"You know what today is?" She backs out. "February first."

Two months before, she had stood outside a sugar mill of rusted sheets of corrugated iron, holes in the roof open to one hundred years of rain, and heard the voices of the dispossessed and dead. Now, three thousand miles away, she is sitting in a parking structure listening to the rumbling of cars as they clamber over metal gratings.

But the voices are not distant. Somehow, they are here.

5

This time Raymond Woods doesn't fool with it. He calls a meeting in his office with security consultant Mark Simms, the LAPD detective on regular assignment to the team.

Simms is a large man with a ponytail wearing a gray pinstripe suit and purple snakeskin boots, who maintains this greaseball image because when he is not on duty at a game—surveying the locker room for theft or alleged rig-watching by female sportswriters—he is working narcotics. Cassidy first met him during the "Fungus Fandango," when a star pitcher had reported his cleats missing, only to have them surface several months later for sale in a collector's magazine, prompting one TV commentator to observe that twelve hundred bucks seemed a lot to pay for athlete's foot.

When the "Fungus Fandango" turned out to be an inside job, Simms was called upon to give a lecture on security—how to prevent slippage of officially licensed merchandise, such as an entire rack of jackets that never made it from the truck to the locker room. Mail fraud. Phone fraud. Player impersonators, like the guy who walked into a car dealership, identified himself as a Dodger, asked to test-drive a car, and drove off with a sixty-thousand-dollar BMW.

Extortion is pervasive, the chronic lower back pain of sports crime, Simms explains; if the vodou bottle had been *laid* on the hood of the Explorer rather than hurled through a smashed window, he would have taken note and gone back to surveilling crack dealers in Panorama City.

"—But an act of violence occurred," Simms tells Alberto, who is sitting in a chair in the corner of Raymond's office, bouncing so hard on the balls of his feet that he gives the impression of running in place sitting down, "Somebody broke glass."

Winter workouts have begun at the stadium for players in the Los Angeles area, and Alberto is wearing clean cleats, stirrups, blue pants, a

blue cage jacket and a Dodgers cap of soft new wool, having
been called to the office from the field. Cassidy almost gave him a
hug of pride when she saw him in uniform for the first time. But only
guys can do that. So she had touched his shoulder and said, "Major
league."

"How good's his English?"

Simms has insolently addressed the question to Raymond, who keeps
both big palms flat on the oak. The legendary desktop is empty. Not even
a pencil cup. For a moment nobody says anything, posed like a snapshot
of today's multiply divorced and reblended baseball family: ethnic ten-
sions and global reach and high-stakes corporate anxiety around the
money sitting in the corner chair.

"Good enough," Raymond replies. "You can talk to him."

Simms removes a small pad from his pocket.

"I'm going to take a crime report," he says. "Standard PIR."

"Is it usual?" Alberto asks.

"Usual?" Simms smiles.

Cassidy notes that Simms smiles often and not always with warmth.

He takes Alberto through the preliminaries with slow professional
deliberation: birth date and place of birth, address in the United States
(Dulce's), how long he has resided there, any idea who would want to
hurt him or threaten him for money?

Alberto shrugs. "I don't know."

"The notes say you did something—"

Alberto jumps out of the chair. "I do nothing!"

"Calm down, take it easy," Raymond admonishes. "Everybody's on the
same side."

Alberto sits, shaking his head.

Simms goes on: "Who knows how to find you in the United States?"

"Mi familia."

"And the pharmacist," Cassidy remembers suddenly.

Again Simms smiles. "'The Pharmacist'? What's that, a handle for a
drug dealer?"

"He was the advisor to the family when we made the deal."

Simms: "Did this pharmacist get money?"

Alberto nods.

"Maybe," Raymond suggests, "he didn't think he was getting enough."

Alberto makes the slow dismissive finger wave.

"He like a father."

"Señor Gómez," Cassidy recalls. "Río Blanco, DR."

Simms writes down the name.

"What about your family, Alberto? How do you get along?"

"No problem."

"No jealous brothers who think maybe *they* should be playing ball in the United States?"

Scoffing, "No way. They *happy* because they know I gonna take care to them."

"What about your pals, the guys you used to hang with?"

Alberto shifts uncomfortably. "They ask me for things. When I sign. They think I rich. People want to be friends. They tell you, 'I need two hundred pesos to fix my house, my kids are hungry . . .' People think, you are a ballplayer, you are a star."

"So nobody comes to mind who might be angry or upset that you got signed?"

"Maybe. I don't know."

Cassidy says, "What about those Haitian guys?" She has been thinking about it the last two days. "The team I saw Alberto play against. Rough trade."

Simms: "Which team is this?"

"From a town called Las Lomas."

"Who are they?"

Alberto shrugs. "*Brazeros.*"

"Sugarcane workers."

"Any one specifically?"

"The pitcher."

"Know his name?"

Cassidy and Alberto shake their heads.

"But he was Haitian and pretty out there. He wasn't wearing a shirt, just two strands of beads crossed over his chest, like ammunition. And he was smoking a cigarette."

Simms chuckles. "On the mound?"

"Can you picture it? The crisscrossed beads, the cigarette? He was upset when I said we were just loaded with pitchers right now."

A less-than-pleased look from Raymond.

"*What?* He must have been fifty years old! They threw rocks at the windshield when we left."

Simms writes quickly, pleased to have a theory.

"Let's say they do have a grudge. These are poor people," Raymond points out. "How could they get all the way to the United States, find Alberto, and follow them to the Glendale Galleria?"

Simms: "They have relatives. They send a message to this young ballplayer—we're going to make trouble for you if you don't pay."

Raymond looks doubtful. "Is there a large Haitian population in Los Angeles?"

Nobody seems to know.

Simms stops writing and looks at Alberto.

"It must be somebody in your culture, or who knows your culture very well, to be messing with this vodou-type stuff."

Alberto swivels his head impatiently. If anybody else in the room had tried it they would have ruptured a disk.

"I do the right thing. I give these letters to the organization. The organization say not to worry. They gonna take care. But they not take care. Now this happen and we got to pay."

"Detective School, Day One: Never pay a blackmailer."

"Then I go home."

"Alberto—"

"They could hurt his family," says Cassidy. "That's what he's saying."

"Let's go back to when you both were in the Dominican," Simms says smoothly. "We're looking for a link. Who else, besides your family and people you know in town, were you in contact with when you signed?"

Alberto's hyper breathing slows. He scratches at a sideburn, forces himself to think. Only his feet keep tapping the floor.

"Pedro Pedrillo."

"The Latin American scout? Okay," says Simms, and plunges into an increasingly troublesome string of questions: How long has Pedro worked for the Dodgers? How long has he known Alberto? What is his relationship with Cassidy? Does he have financial problems?

"What's this got to do with Pedro?" Cassidy interrupts.

"That's what we're going to find out."

The smile.

Simms folds the notebook.

"This is what I'm going to say to you, Alberto." Then he says it: "Pay close attention to your surroundings. Strange cars in the neighborhood. Late night phone calls. If you or your friends think there's anything suspicious, let the police know immediately. Do you understand?"

Alberto nods.

Simms gives him a card.

"This is a special 800 security number Major League Baseball set up for players and umpires. You call this number, you get a cop, twenty-four hours a day."

"Thank you. I can go?"

Raymond: "Go."

Mumbling, "*Adiós, señorita*," Alberto is out of there.

Through the open door Cassidy waves to Doc Ramsey, a locker-room attendant who had been sent to escort Alberto up from the field to make sure he didn't get off the elevator on the wrong level and wind up in a terrifying pitch-dark warren of laundry carts and floor waxers. Nice to see guys in uniform around the office again.

"Good kid," Simms remarks. "And he's young."

"Eighteen years old. Could go all the way," Cassidy says encouragingly. "Good bat. Fast. We have hopes for him at spring training, don't we, Ray?"

Raymond isn't interested in discussing Alberto's tools just now. He is standing with arms folded. Bigger than Simms and a couple of restive steps ahead.

"What do you think, Mark? Does this make sense? Why would anyone go after an unknown like Cruz?"

"How much money you say these kids get?"

"Eight hundred a month. Plus the signing bonus."

"It's a clumsy attempt," agrees Simms. "But shouldn't be that hard to nail it, we're looking at a relatively small window of time. Alberto signed on Friday, Cassidy left on Sunday. Right?"

Cassidy says, "Right."

Simms waits. "So what happened in between?"

"In between?" Suddenly she feels warm. "I stayed overnight in the pharmacist's house. The next day I went to a ball game in San Pedro de Macorís."

"Alone?"

Offhand, "With a guy."

"What guy?"

"This guy from LA I met in the Miami airport." The business type who kept buying drinks. "I ran into him again in the DR. We went to a ball game, no big deal."

"Does this guy have a name?"

"Joe."

"Do we know his last name?"

"I don't remember."

She becomes aware of Raymond staring at her.

"We were together maybe a total of six hours."

"The next day you left?"

"The next day I left."

Simms is done with it.

"In my opinion, we're dealing with someone who had to have known Cruz down there. Could be a grudge, could be a lark. Hit him up, see what happens. Pretty typical. We'll check out these names and the post-box address. Which means dealing with the Dominican authorities, which, by that time, we'll all be dead."

The detective wraps his right arm around his own head and under his jaw and cracks his neck with a sickening *pop!* so Cassidy and Raymond both flinch.

"But whoever is doing this is here in the United States," she says. "They followed us. They crossed the line. They broke glass."

Simms, again talking to Raymond over her head, "Does she want protection?"

"No, I don't!" snaps Cassidy. "But I'm worried about Alberto's family and also about Dulce."

"Dulce, the secretary, Dulce?"

"Alberto's been staying with her."

"Rampart Division will send extra patrols by the house."

Cassidy objects. "Dulce should know about this."

Simms gives the smile. "Let us handle it."

Cassidy: "She has two children."

"I hear you."

"He hears you."

Raymond moves Cassidy toward the door.

Dulce looks up from her desk. "How'd it go?"

"I've had better days at the dentist."

"Why did they want to talk to Alberto?"

Cassidy hesitates. Not an easy call. She can't tell Dulce about the extortion threats. She can't risk Raymond finding out she had gone against the chain of command one more time.

"They were concerned about some adjustment problems, but they think it will work out once he gets to Vero Beach."

"I am also concerned. It happens so many times."

"What does?"

"They get homesick." Dulce's voice catches. "These boys, they are just babies."

In the garage, in the side pocket of the black duffel bag (squashed flat beneath a twenty-pound bag of dog food), Cassidy finds the brochure for the Gran Caribe Resort the businessman named Joe had given her at the bar in Miami. His company had a controlling interest in the Gran Caribe, he explained, and if she had any free time at all while she was in the Dominican, she was more than welcome to stop by.

"It's a four-star resort, rated number one in the Caribbean," he told her.

For a four-star fuck, she had thought.

She unfolds the glossy pages. On the cover a man and woman ride a white horse across a beach, she with breasts spilling out of a bikini, he bare-chested. Inside they play tennis, dine by candlelight, sail, get massages on a patio decked with bougainvillea. Then you see them back in their room—tropical florals and ceiling fan—looking at the sunset, drinking wine and contemplating yogic acts of pleasure in the private Jacuzzi.

The man in the pictures has dark curly hair and a soft open nice-daddy smile. You can imagine him modeling five-hundred-dollar cashmere sweaters with three or four kids piling on his back.

Joe was dark-haired too, strong good features, similar creases around the mouth, but he was a loner and his smile was taut. Maybe that is why, when he dropped her off abruptly after the game, she ultimately did not make the move; something, she had sensed, too complicated there.

Beneath the logo for the management company, Omega Development International, he had written *Joe Galinis* in amethyst fountain pen ink.

It takes one phone call to reach his office on Olive Street in downtown Los Angeles.

6

Two weeks later an assistant calls back and leaves a message that Mr. Galinis would "definitely love" to see Cassidy again, could they meet at a party at his attorney's home in Studio City?

The assistant faxes a map showing a tangle of roads going into the hills, but Vista View comes up too quickly to avoid a screeching left turn, the traffic behind Cassidy continuing to trample past like a mad steeple-chase that will stop for nothing. The signs for Vista, Vista Drive, Vista Point and Vista Terrace are all obscured by foliage or have been bent into the darkness by car crashes, but finally she finds the driveway, her ears popping as it curves up through a majestic gate.

A valet opens the door of the Explorer. Cassidy swings her brown suede heels to the ground and takes a moment to steady herself with the familiar acorny night scents of the California chaparral. A Rolls-Royce and a catering truck are parked in front of a triple garage. A Mercedes coupe pulls in and a lady in a vanilla suit pops out, linking arms with a bulky guy with a beard, slip-sliding in tandem along the cobblestone drive, passing Cassidy as if in a decathlon in which dinner at Harvey Weissman's house is just one more grueling event.

High heels are a problem on the smooth rocks. It does take determination to make it to the door. Picking her way carefully, she remembers meeting one of her idols, an Olympic skating champion, at a multimillion-dollar house like this. Cassidy had followed her career with awe—such athletic jumps, such incredible flow—envying the Olympic spotlight. By the time they had met at the party, the skater had become an international celebrity. She had been wearing thirty thousand dollars worth of jewels and a pink Chanel suit with high heels. She still radiated that magical quality, she had achieved greatness, she was turned out like a princess, but all the guests could look at were her thighs. Thick, muscular, developed thighs.

"Dyke jock," said someone in the crowd.

Harvey Weissman's house is a remodeled ranch with eastern pretensions; white clapboard, pine trees, pots of chrysanthemums on flagstone steps leading to a shiny green door held open by a young male server in a white jacket to the clear notes of chamber music being played on an amazing sound system, and the buttery perfume of puff pastry on the rise.

"This way, ma'am."

The server gestures formally down a hall illuminated by picture lights over gilt frames. Inside the frames are oil paintings of ladies with parasols Cassidy believes she has seen before, leading to a kind of crossroads from which she can view a succession of living rooms decorated in high English style, a profusion of wing chairs and sofas in scarlets, gold, evergreen, cream, like a bouquet of winter peonies, fires blazing in three or four separate hearths. The amazing sound system turns out to be a live string quartet wearing black tie and playing Haydn.

Another server brings champagne on a round silver tray, handing Cassidy not a paper napkin but a cotton square bordered with lace. She walks through the rooms looking for Joe Galinis. Ninety-eight percent of the women are wearing black. The men are dressed in piercingly conservative business attire. Cassidy notes she is the only one with bare shoulders, the only woman wearing a nude spandex slip dress with an espresso-brown lace overlay. And nobody else seems to have gone in for a French twist, either.

Joe is nowhere. Cassidy accepts another glass of champagne.

She takes up a corner position, trying to distract herself by observing the number of oversized insect pins made of rhinestones, and how many of the older women sport identical doe eyes and the same diminutive cheerleader nose. The server comes through with a tray of tiny cherry tomatoes, centers roto-rootered out, rosettes of cream cheese piped in. As the minutes tick away, cucumber slices with dollops of salmon mousse appear, and skewers of Thai chicken. Her feet are swelling inside the high heels like the pastry around the mushrooms *en croûte*.

Softly as a pair of snowflakes, an elderly couple has drifted beside Cassidy, she wearing a black knit suit with gold braiding, he a white shirt, striped tie and brown jacket, oversized glasses big as a diving mask. They introduce themselves as Mr. and Mrs. George Ellis. Cassidy fingers the lace napkin, wondering how she is going to get through this.

"We've just come back from Turkey," Mrs. Ellis announces in a quiet, underpowered voice. The effort of speaking seems to rock her back on her heels. She is willowy, with the body grace of another era, when girls were taught correct posture and how to set a champagne flute on a mahogany table (fold your cotton square into a triangle and place the glass on top).

"It's tiring," Mrs. Ellis says, "all that packing and unpacking."

Cassidy pictures leather trunks and brocade carpet bags.

"When did you get here?" she asks.

"Just this afternoon."

"This afternoon! You must be jet-lagged! How do you even know where you are?" Cassidy exclaims, regretting an unconscious reference to the lady's swimming pearly eyes.

"We've just come down this afternoon from *Santa Barbara*," Mrs. Ellis explains steadfastly. Then, "Who are you with?"

Oh God, thinks Cassidy, she's looking at my thighs.

"Joe Galinis, but he's not here yet."

Mr. and Mrs. Ellis exchange a questioning look.

"The developer," recalls Mr. Ellis.

"Oh, yes."

"Unusual young man," he goes on. "Bright. Greek."

Cassidy: "I didn't know he was Greek."

"His dad was first generation. I remember him from the California Club. The Greeks work hard. You have to admire a self-made man."

Mr. Ellis aims his diving mask glasses more precisely at Cassidy. She can see double reflections of herself, exaggerated as cartoons.

"Have you met Harvey?"

"Not yet."

Mrs. Ellis, rocking back: "Harvey is a rare bird."

Mr. Ellis: "It *is* rare when you get good food, a lovely setting, a good cause and good company. Harvey makes it look easy, but it's not. I'm impressed by people who know what they're doing. My father was an inventor, maybe that's where I get it from. I'm an inventor, too."

"Really," says Cassidy. "What's the next big invention? The next big thing?"

Mr. Ellis: "Well, forget the electric car."

The Ellises turn out to be an attraction and Cassidy finds herself introduced to two other couples, including the lady in the vanilla suit, "a big supporter of the Music Center," whose dorky husband, she says right off, hates musicals.

"He used to direct television, now he directs me."

"In what way?"

"The way men do."

"I've never even heard of a woman baseball scout," comments the other man.

"Edith Houghton. Scouted for the Phillies in 1946. My dog is named after her."

"Well, I'm an Ivy Leaguer, I went to Harvard, which doesn't mean a damn thing in the aerospace industry—"

He laughs, CEO of the largest employer in Southern California, paisley handkerchief peeking out of a double-breasted suit, not a care in the world. ("I'm interested in making airplanes and exotic weapons," he had said.)

"Nevertheless, I was a Harvard man, on the football team, and when I went to school, athletes were *scholar* athletes. We don't have *scholar* athletes today. Now Joe Galinis is an interesting guy—"

"He's going to be an interesting *dead* guy," says Cassidy, "if he doesn't show up soon."

"Joe has a lot on his plate."

"Probably hung up at the mayor's."

"The mayor's what?"

"The thing at the Bistro."

"—Did you know Joe played soccer?" the CEO goes on. "That's how he went to Stanford."

"On a scholarship?"

The CEO nods.

"Not possible," counters the vanilla suit. "We're talking San Marino banking money."

"I thought he was from the Midwest."

"I like Joe," Mr. Ellis remarks suddenly, and instantly everyone agrees.

"Charming man."

"Staunch promoter of downtown."

"Well for heaven's sake, he got the public money flowing."

Cassidy, curious, "How?"

"He was able to manipulate the pieces. To get a direct cash subsidy from the city to build roads and streets and utilities."

"Once he was able to deliver the hotel, it was a done deal."

"Everybody wanted a convention center hotel but it wasn't economically justifiable. Joe took the risk."

"He is not risk-averse."

"Oh, no."

"He's done quite well in foreign countries, as I understand."

"Well, *this* hotel will become a gold mine, if they turn downtown LA into an entertainment zone."

Cassidy: "What does that mean?"

Red wine suddenly jumps across the vanilla suit, huge streaks of it like blood-red comets.

"Soda water," advises the CEO's wife.

"No," says Mr. Ellis. "That's a common mistake. Take it right to the cleaners."

The husband: "Couldn't you be drinking white?"

The server appears with napkins.

"What's an 'entertainment zone'?" pursues Cassidy. "You mean like theaters? Don't we have enough theaters downtown?"

"No, dear," says the CEO's wife (she's the one with the tortoiseshell headband). "It means a restricted area that would be created especially for legalized gambling."

"Legalized gambling? In downtown Los Angeles?"

"The bulk of the money would go to the schools."

"That's what they say."

"It would not altogether be a bad thing," smiles the CEO, "to own that hotel."

The evening has reached a ravenous peak, the sense of security and belonging escalating to a giddy high, whatever notes still missing from the raucous conversation filled in by the string quartet's slightly hysterical "Night and Day." People are shouldering each other good-naturedly on the way to the buffet, no longer afraid to make eye contact or share a generous smile, at the same time scoping out those going by with oversized white plates jammed with corn soufflé, *haricots verts*, pasta salad, relishes, rolls, salmon fillet and turkey and roast beef carved by a chef at a copper warming tray. Despite the extravagant display of plenty, there seems to be an undercurrent of anxiety: will there be enough for me?

Cassidy peels off from the flow and finds herself in a tiny sewing room done all in red chintz. Although a fire whips in a brass grate, the air is cool and undisturbed and the poufy love seat inviting. She slips off her heels for a moment, rubbing her feet on a needlepoint rug set over a peg-and-groove floor, gazing at a collection of folk art on the coffee table. There are Navajo pots and African masks, a llama made of woven reeds, polished stones in an obsidian bowl, and a spirit bottle, like the one that was thrown into her car, only this one is dotted with red sequins.

She stands up so quickly her knees jam the table and she stumbles over the rug.

"Whoa there."

A man lunges across the room to steady her arm, a big man with flying tufts of white hair.

"Thank you."

"Are you okay?"

She is stuffing her feet back inside the shoes, which have shrunk two sizes. "That thing just freaked me out."

"Which?"

"That." She points to the razor blades hanging off the bottle, splayed on the table like a rusty skirt.

"I imagine that's what it's designed to do."

"Where do you think he got it?"

"Who?"

"Harvey Weissman, it's his house, right?"

"Actually the house belongs to First Fidelity, but don't tell anyone. I'm Harvey." He extends a soft damp hand.

"Oh, I'm sorry—"

"Not a bit of it."

Harvey Weissman is his own being, you can tell. He looks more like a rich successful artist than an attorney, a hulking man in a wide-lapel English suit that flaunts a shocking-blue iridescent shirt and yellow tie.

"It's an artifact from the Caribbean. A client of mine does a lot of business down there."

"That wouldn't be Joe?"

"As a matter of fact, it would be Joe." He appraises her. "And you must be the goddess."

He brings his face toward Cassidy's (a face like a puppet's, deep creases between the bulbous nose and round protruding cheeks, eyes behind wire-rimmed glasses squinched into a smile by all that pressure) and kisses her cheek.

"Your other half called from the car. Late as usual. As you know, he can be a royal pain in the ass."

"I don't really know him at all."

"Well, I've been Joe's lawyer for twenty-two years. We have a long and mostly profitable history." Harvey winks. "Joe is older than me but he dyes his hair."

He takes her arm and guides her into the hall, where the woman in the vanilla suit is emerging from the powder room, giving no sign of ever having spoken to Cassidy. The stains look worse, watery streaks of magenta.

Cassidy murmurs, "I am so glad I didn't spill that wine."

"You don't have to worry about this crowd. They don't come to these things if they don't know how to take care of themselves. See how they all home in on George Ellis?"

The Ellises are seated on a couch, plates upon the dinner napkins delicately spread across their laps. Like giving a good dinner party, Mr. Ellis is saying, it is also not an easy thing to write a good poem: "Poetry is like a differential equation. It has a lot of information packed into it," he decides, while others stand or squat around them, trying to fist wineglasses and silverware, one man cross-legged on the floor at their feet.

"Why?"

"Well, the Ellis Foundation, as you know, is the largest contributor to the arts in the west. Old, *old* California oil money. Once, over lunch, I convinced George to give a building to CalArts. He was prepared to make a contribution." Harvey chuckles. "He ended up donating a building."

"You must be good at what you do."

Harvey waves dismissively.

"It's a great party, Harvey, but I'm leaving. If you see Joe, tell him to call me."

"You're miffed. Is it love or sex? You can tell me. Attorney-client privilege."

"It has to do with something in the Dominican."

Harvey scuffles behind her with a stoop-shouldered gait down the hallway with the paintings.

"Joe told me all about you."

"What did he say?"

"He said you were a fabulous original."

Cassidy pauses, giving Harvey the opportunity to tip his glass toward the paintings in private toast. He has a way of cocking his head so one eye peers out with a mischievous gleam, hinting at a shared knowledge, an exotic landscape of sexual secrets. Cassidy holds the look, acknowledging she's been there.

"So how was the weather?" he asks suggestively.

"Fine, except for the hurricane."

"I heard it rained."

"It did, but it didn't matter. I signed my ballplayer."

"So all in all, happy memories?"

"Do you want to see my scrapbook?"

Harvey laughs.

"Joe will fire me if I let you slip away. Love your updo. Now come on," herding her back toward the party, "this is the big time. You know about that, hanging out in the major leagues. These are all high-stakes players."

"Is Joe a player?"

"One tough competitor. Learned in the street."

"Takes no prisoners?"

"It isn't so much that, it's pride."

"What, exactly, is his game?"

"This is the downtown community, and what we're doing here, besides raising money for the Museum of Contemporary Art, is *insisting* that in the year 2020, when the population of Los Angeles has increased forty-five percent—that's the size of three Chicagos—completely Asian and Hispanic, and the sprawl goes all the way out to Palm Springs, *downtown*—site of the original pueblo, don't forget—will be the geographical, cultural and economic center of it all. And we're gonna own it. There's the artist, he's the bait."

A tanned, amiable fellow wearing a denim shirt.

"Do you believe that man is in his seventies? South Beach boys, keep you young. That's his agent."

Bronze shaved head.

"There's a famous author. You've read her books."

Big-bosomed, big hair, professional makeup job, gripping the crystal handle of a handbag with a hangdog look.

"Pissy, because nobody's paying attention to her. Well"—he takes Cassidy's arm—"we want her money, so—"

"Don't—"

"I'm going to show you how to work a room. Joe is a master at this. Now, touching is important—"

Harvey drags Cassidy toward the unhappy author.

"—Get your hand on the shoulder. But with women, actually, waists are better because it's less likely that you'll come in contact with real flesh. You give a friendship hug. Every woman, no matter how independent, likes a hug, but it's subtle. The hand goes around the waist—"

"Don't make me do this—" Cassidy pulls on Harvey's forearm, soft as a pillow.

"—and there's a little squeeze, a friendship squeeze. And it's—'How ARE you doing? I haven't seen you since—'"

"Harvey, no. I'm embarrassed."

"You're upset about Joe."

"I need to talk to him."

"He'll be here. He's bringing his daughter, did I say? Nora. Have you met Nora?"

"We met in the casino at the Gran Caribe."

"A free spirit. Sometimes too free. She did a stint at Treetops, I got her in. The two of them will make an entrance, you watch. Hungry?"

"No, thanks."

"You're not hungry, you think Joe's a cad, but you're sticking around. And you *still* won't tell me what it's all about?"

"Harvey, have you had much experience with extortion?"

Harvey's eyes stop smiling.

"I did once. Yes. I can tell you the advice I usually give: Never pay. Never pay an extortionist."

"You big adorable thing!"

Cassidy had seen her coming out of the corner of her eye, a young attractive person who had made herself conspicuous by *not* wearing the regulation black dress, *not* smiling, *not* paying attention, giving off nothing but a superior detachment that must have taken all her concentration to affect.

"Hi, Nora." But she is pointedly ignored, so Cassidy, fed up with non-chalance, gives Joe's daughter one good slug on the upper arm, good enough to feel bone.

"Hey!" Nora cries out, forced to stop and also to pretend it doesn't hurt, "Cassidy!" then she has to kiss the she-jock because she's already kissed Harvey. "I'm sorry, it's my fault, my baby-sitter conked, we've been running late all night."

"An entrance, I told you," Harvey says. "Look at this," making Nora twirl so Cassidy can get the full benefit of her loose black wavy hair, the beautiful fringed shawl she holds over a black beaded camisole, the long animal-print skirt of georgette and silk slit up the thigh. She's tiny, but toned. Probably Pilates. Her chest is piled with necklaces of amber, silver, shell and stone. "Terrific."

"How are you?" Nora asks.

"Good. Working."

"You *look* good." She fingers her beads.

"Where's papa?" asks Harvey.

"Somewhere. Working the room."

"Told you," says Harvey. To Nora: "What are you drinking?"

"Perrier with lime."

He signals a server as Nora says, "Gee, it's great to see you again."

Cassidy cannot help searching her delicately angled face for clues to something Harvey mentioned. Treetops. Some kind of bad-kid home, she remembers from *People* magazine, somewhere like Utah? Colorado? Children of celebrities go there. Free-spirited, all right. So what was it? Acting out? Learning disabilities? Smoking marijuana? Alcoholism? A major depression? The skin is pale and fragile for a twenty-something; and what about that habit of looking away, wet-eyed, nervous? One thing: although the words are effulgent, Nora's facial expression has not lost its chill reserve, a sign to Cassidy that at the very least none of the warm and fuzzy things she has said has been true.

"Harvey taking care of you?"

"He's introducing me to the downtown crowd."

"What you have here, basically," remarks Nora, taking in the guests at the buffet, "is the white man holding on by his fingernails."

Harvey spots Joe in an adjoining room.

"There he is."

Half a dozen guests, male and female, are waiting uncertainly, like fish bobbing up and down in a current, apparently for the opportunity to speak to Joe Galinis, who is standing with his back to the fireplace, talking with a disheveled-looking older woman in harlequin glasses.

Cassidy pauses at the threshold, watching how, with his ramrod posture and a now beguiling smile, he holds the attention of those even in back of the room; they want something he's giving off, as if being touched by the magnetic force of his self-assurance could cause their own fragmented spirits to line up and be whole.

She had felt it too, first thing, when they had met like war correspondents in the anarchy of Terminal E in Miami.

Every flight to Latin America and the Caribbean had been canceled or delayed. Rain was coursing down the slanted glass and the light inside the mammoth terminal seemed dimmed. Electronic ciphers with dancing letters spelled out exotic destinations—Lima, Santiago, San José, Costa Rica—above the gates which were arranged like spokes in a glittering karmic wheel.

As Cassidy charged forward, the sign that said "Santo Domingo" disintegrated into a scramble of dots. Passengers who had been in line for boarding, defending their positions like Green Berets, surged around the counter in an unruly mob. She couldn't even get close. Joe Galinis had simply folded a magazine and turned purposefully away.

Cassidy had grabbed the sleeve of his blue blazer. "What's the problem?"

"The flight to Santo Domingo has been delayed two hours."

"Oh, crap!"

"Life is a cabaret."

"Tell me about it."

He had given her the scan.

"You just got in from LA."

"How did you know?"

"I saw you getting off the plane."

Tell me another.

"Besides, you're wearing a Planet Hollywood jacket."

"I got it in London," she snapped, a lie. "You were on that flight?"

He nodded. "I fly a lot. But that was bad."

"The worst was having to sit next to a waitress from Gladstone's 4 Fish."

"You mean Gladstone's up on Pacific Coast Highway?"

"Been there?"

"A million years ago."

"Well, the waitress is going to Aruba, so she has to put her German shepherd in a kennel. The German shepherd has a terrible skin disease, so she's obsessing about whether or not they'll remember to put on his tea-tree oil."

"Tea-tree oil?"

"Finally I said, 'Sister—we all have to leave our dogs.'"

"Amen."

Cassidy had run a wrist over her forehead in a self-conscious way, hoping to check the guy out from underneath the cover of half a dozen silver bracelets. They had, after all, been speaking at least twenty-five seconds longer than necessary.

But the ploy hadn't worked.

Unexpectedly she had found herself looking directly into his eyes, which she discovered were intensely bright—not blue-bright, but shining with a transparent light like water, shining with aliveness, curiosity and warmth. It had been startling to find something so complete. Slowly she lowered her arm, not breaking the look, entranced by a strong feeling of familiarity that was totally irrational.

She is five foot ten, he three inches taller, fair physical condition, tennis and racquetball, looked to be late forties but with a worn worldly sense, mileage on him, someone who carried a lot. Olive skin, black curly hair cut aggressively short, heavy eyebrows and a long, beautifully proportioned nose; that's what was arresting about the face: large, classical proportions. Fluid body movement that showed some arrogance—an attorney or maybe a corporate VP, she had thought, wearing comfortable funky old jeans with the nice blue blazer that had gold buttons plump as Roman coins.

She had gazed toward the windows streaked with steam. Despite torrential rain, some clouds had cleared from a corner of the sky, creating a patch of cerulean blue punctuated by a white three-quarter moon like a sticker.

"What are we supposed to do?"

"I'm going to have a drink."

Her eyes had come back to his. "Without me?"

He laughed uncomfortably.

"The truth is, I'll be on the phone the next two hours."

"Hard telling the truth."

"I try to avoid it. Nice to meet you."

She watched him go, calculating her losses. Forget the annoying stimulation down below. She needed to make some calls. Do something about her blood sugar. Caffeine or alcohol? It was a toss-up.

A line of thirty people waited for the phones. She picked up her bag and headed into the main corridor, smack into the intersection of every culture in the western hemisphere, a perilous swarm of humans pulling luggage carts. Trekking mindlessly, she glimpsed the blue blazer fifty yards ahead, moving at a jaunty clip.

Suddenly it stopped at a door marked Admirals Club and Joe pulled out a credit card.

Now two real possibilities were put into play: finding a phone and having a drink. Sprinting ahead, smacking people with the flying bag, she reached the door just as the lock buzzed open.

"Hi. I realize this is kind of lame, but could you sneak me in?"

"It's supposed to be for members only."

"Please. It's a zoo back there."

She couldn't tell if he was being ironic or was seriously concerned about upholding the corporate policy of American Airlines when he said, "I really shouldn't do this."

"Suck it up," Cassidy had replied.

Their eyes meet across the room.

"Cassidy!" as if they hadn't seen each other since lunch. "Let me introduce you to Hazel Porter-Gaines, wife of the British consul—"

The warm smile, long outstretched fingers impatiently inviting you in.

"It's the consul *general*," corrects Mrs. Porter-Gaines. Dandruff has collected on her plum damask Chinese silk dress with frog closures and puffy sleeves. The harlequin glasses would be terrifically hip had they not been the real thing, what the lady's worn for sixty years.

"Forgive me. The British consulate is one of our greatest friends, downtown."

When she turns to answer someone's prickly question about the IRA ("We don't get involved. We serve the Queen"), Joe says,

"Cassidy."

He has a way of breathing her name so that it sounds like the announcement of spring.

"How *are* you?"

"I'm well, Joe, how are you?"

He looks good, really good, a little fuller in the face than she remembered, but with that same simmering fire and desire, limpid hazel eyes with sable lashes, glistening hair, aura of accomplishment, wearing a charcoal nipped-waist suit the way a lion wears its skin.

"I was so glad to hear from you," he says. "Glad you could come."

"It's good to be here."

"Have you said hello to Nora?" he asks. "Where is she?" fretfully scanning the room.

"Don't worry, she's fine."

"I'm not worried. I just like showing her off." Joe fixes Cassidy with a smile. "What's going on with you?"

"Winter workouts. Getting ready for spring training."

"Any more trips to the Dominican?"

"Not real soon. How about yourself?"

"In town for a while. I usually get down there once every few months, but since we broke ground on the sports arena, I've been crazed."

"I heard you're responsible for that."

"You make it sound like the Vietnam War."

"I have mixed feelings."

"It's going to save downtown."

"I like plain old-fashioned ball fields. I like Dodger Stadium."

"Dodger Stadium is a relic. They'll have to tear it down or sell. The world," Joe says mildly, "is one big sell." He sips some Scotch. "How's the phenom working out? You signed him, right? He's here?"

"Oh, he's here."

"Is he turning out as well as you'd hoped?"

"He'll be fine as long as he plays his game."

"You sound tentative, and somehow I don't think that's you."

"We have a situation, Joe."

"How can I help?"

She hesitates. "That bottle from the DR you gave Harvey, the one with the razor blades—where did you get it?"

"Gee, I don't remember, one of those little markets on the street?"

Somebody's pager goes off.

"Is that you?"

"I think it's me."

Fumbling in purses and jackets.

"Is it me?"

"No," says Cassidy, "me."

When she comes back from the phone Joe is still standing beside the wife of the consul general, admiring framed portraits of Harvey Weissman's Cardigan Welsh corgis.

"—Oh yes, well, we could never have a dog because we moved around so much. The Queen has five of them, so I suppose they've become quite fashionable," Mrs. Porter-Gaines is fussing on, "and just this morning someone asked if I like corgis, what is this, some kind of a *thing*?"

Cassidy interrupts, "Excuse me, thank you, but I've got to leave."

"What's wrong?"

"Emergency at work."

Joe looks at his watch. "Now?"

"Unfortunately."

She heads out through the gallery.

A pianist has taken the place of the string quartet. Guests have gathered around the baby grand, listening to someone who sounds a lot like Robert Goulet singing "Falling in Love with Love." It's the CEO—back straight, eyes on the second balcony.

Joe catches up. "Wait. Can we talk? Just for a minute? Look, I'm sorry, maybe I should have apologized for that first date at the ball game."

"Was that a date? Getting lost in a hurricane, getting ripped, ending up soaking wet and completely covered with mud?"

"In the Dominican, that's the senior prom."

It stops her. She laughs.

Gently, "Tell me what's wrong."

"My kid's in trouble. My player, the one you met, Alberto Cruz."

"What kind of trouble?"

"I don't know, but they've got him down at the Glendale police station."

"Probably his car was towed."

"He doesn't own a car."

"Is this the 'situation' you were talking about?"

"It might be related, that's what's freaking me out. Two weeks ago someone broke the window of my car and left one of those awful bottles, exactly like the kind you gave Harvey."

"But that's incredible."

"It's a threat, to scare Alberto. They're trying to blackmail him."

"Why?"

"We don't know. They'll kill him if he doesn't pay."

"What are you saying? With some kind of curse?"

"No, Joe, give me a break, they've been sending notes to the stadium. This is real. The cops are involved—I've got to go."

"Can I call you?"

She feels Joe's hand on her waist, hot through the tight layers of lace.

"There was never any reason you couldn't."

He releases her. She hurries down the flagstone steps. Three valets in red vests prick up their ears. She takes quick breaths of woodsy air. The CEO's big-chested baritone soars confidently from the house. *Falling in love with love is falling for make-believe—*

The Explorer rolls up the driveway, misted over in the windshield, roof splattered with those irritating little berries.

Car wash city.

7

It is a low-slung building on a leafy residential street, unobtrusive as the phone company, but still, Cassidy doesn't like police stations. They reek of failure.

Too many times she was busted in high school for racing her Kawasaki 100 down Main Street and brought to the Ashland police station, feeling sour and stupid because now she had to face the inevitable boring consequences: the "disappointment lecture" from the coach, suspension from the team, tears of grief from her mom whom she would have to end up comforting. Things would die down and she'd do it again. Mindless. A death wish at age seventeen. No wonder she has a headache just passing through the door.

The headache had begun inside her left eye, reaching like a pulsing wire to the back of the brain where paranoid scenarios are going off like fireworks. For example, the police department is just a few blocks from the Glendale Galleria where Alberto had been retained by plainclothes officers for allegedly shoplifting a batting glove. What if those sad-eyed cops at the mall had beaten the crap out of her best prospect? What if this arrest becomes the rationale for Raymond to ship Alberto back to the Dominican, and Cassidy to start a new career stacking cartons at Sport Chalet?

Although it has taken less than fifteen minutes to speed over here, the brassy warmth of Harvey Weissman's fireplace is worlds away: she has exited the heaven of privilege and arrived in the underground realm of bad luck. Perhaps they try to get rid of the bad luck by disinfecting the lobby with some kind of acid wash several times a day: she has never been in such a sterile space. Gray floor, gray sofa made of a plastic material you would not want to set your butt on, the usual forlorn trophy display. She can spot the photo of the team the police department sponsors in the Babe Ruth League from across the room.

A young woman with a ponytail is appealing to a tired but sympathetic female desk sergeant behind the bullet-resistant plastic.

"We cannot enforce something without orders from a judge," the officer explains slowly, and apparently not for the first time.

Overweight, short-chopped hair, worn lipstick, worn smile, the sergeant is old enough to have grown children. What is she doing here, eleven-thirty at night?

"I don't have the papers—"

An open folder, documents spilled across a narrow shelf. The young woman fingering through them, not seeing, not hearing, in a state of walking shock.

Cassidy bullies past. "Excuse me—"

"I'll be right with you," admonishes the desk sergeant from her stool on high, like a teacher who knows that you know better. To the blonde woman, "Have you ever had a court order *brought in here, signed by a judge?*"

"That's the transcript from the day the order was made."

Cassidy rubs her bare arms and fidgets with the back of the French twist, finally pulling the whole thing out.

"We can't enforce it," the sergeant is saying.

"She's two and a half years old—"

"I know. I'm with you. Trust me, I've been through it myself . . . Just a moment."

The cop frowns over the mother's head at Cassidy, who stops shaking her hair out like a horse.

"Can I help you?" she asks disapprovingly.

"I'm here for Alberto Cruz."

"For Alberto Cruz—what?"

"He paged me. Said he was here."

The sergeant checks the computer. Cassidy stares at a cluster of white blossoms embedded in the inch-thick plastic. Shots were fired.

The young mother turns to Cassidy.

"When he took her and disappeared for three weeks, I thought *that* was bad."

She gazes down at her papers without hope.

"I'm so sorry," Cassidy murmurs.

"We've got Alberto Cruz. He's in jail."

Cassidy exhales long and hard. She's got problems, too. Like, *jail?* It certainly has that rock-bottom sound. What the *hell* is Alberto doing in *jail* when he should be at Dulce's house, asleep in bed, in a deep alpha state, fast-twitch muscle fibers rebuilding like crazy for tomorrow's workout?

"What are the charges?"

"He was taken in on a felony."

"What did he do?"

"All I can tell you is he was booked for assault with a deadly weapon. Bail has been set at ten thousand dollars."

Cassidy stands there, as immobilized as the traumatized mom. Slowly she becomes aware of both women watching her curiously, taking in the espresso lace slip dress and the black satin evening bag with pager attached.

"Are you Mr. Cruz's lawyer?"

"No—"

The doors open and Joe Galinis walks in with such authority all three turn to look. It is more than a surprise to see him, not only because his elegant personage is in striking contrast to the sterilized sofa and smeary glass of the waiting room—but because the influx of such wealth and confidence seems unthinkable in a holding station meant for losers.

"What are you doing here?"

"You left, so the party was over. Did you find out what happened?"

"They booked Alberto on a felony charge."

Joe does not reply but produces a thin leather case from an inner pocket. His deft olive fingers slip a card through a slot in the bulletproof divider.

"What are the circumstances?" he asks.

The lady sergeant examines the card.

"You're an attorney?"

"I would like to know what probable cause the officers had to arrest Mr. Cruz."

"Again, sir, are you his legal representative?"

"No, but I'm sure it's late for all of us, so can we just cut through this?"

Joe is half smiling in a condescending way. You can see the sergeant's aging face go cold and congealed.

"Then you're *not* his legal representative?"

"I am a *very concerned* friend. Ms. Sanderson represents his employer."

Cassidy says, "I can get a lawyer on the phone—"

The cop cuts her off. "The attorney of record can pick up a copy of the arrest report tomorrow." Crisply, "This young lady was first—"

But the young mom isn't listening. Her eyes are watery. She is wearing cutoffs and a sweatshirt with a picture of a California mission. Souvenir of a trip down the coast.

"He can go ahead of me." Tears break loose and roll. "That's all right."

"No, ma'am, it is *not* all right," the sergeant replies angrily. "You've got to stop letting men roll over you."

"Oh, kiss my ass," mutters Joe.

Cassidy whirls toward him. "Cool *out.*"

"This woman just *said* it's okay. And *I'm* the insensitive male? I resent that."

The sergeant turns his card over. And over.

"What gives you the right?" she says evenly. "Because you have a fancy car out there? Because your name," squinting dismissively, "is *Galinis*? What's Galinis? Is that supposed to make me jump? Because believe me, I can tell you, we have a lot more important names coming through those doors every day of the week."

Joe struts forward, finger jabbing.

"You want Mr. Cruz's legal representative?" raising his voice. "No problem. We'll call the general counsel for the Los Angeles Dodgers and the mayor of Glendale and three council members I happen to *own,* and wake them up and get them down here and see why a young black ballplayer with no criminal record has been locked up by the police and the police say, 'No comment.'"

Cassidy says, "Joe? You can leave now."

She gives him a little shove on the chest. He grabs her hand, for a fraction of a second, so quickly she cannot be sure he really did that, pressed her fist against his heart.

The mom, perking up, "He's a baseball player?"

"*Joe?*" says the cop, liking it now. "What kind of car *is* that?"

"A Bentley."

"Well, it's parked in a red zone."

"Is that a problem?"

"Not for me." She picks up the phone.

"Please," says Cassidy. "Move the freaking car."

Joe lifts his head and takes a deep breath. When his gaze comes back to the sergeant, it is level and contained.

"This will be addressed," he promises, and walks out the door.

"How do you know a baseball player?" asks the mom.

"I'm a scout with the Dodgers," shrugging as if to acknowledge the whole thing is absurd and, yes, she should be selling condos in Maui. "Alberto is one of my prospects. Eighteen years old, been in this country a month."

"He must be psyched. The majors."

"I think the biggest thing to him is getting his underwear back. Are you a fan?"

"I *love* the Dodgers! Been taking my daughter to Dodger Stadium since she was *born*! What position does he play?"

"Outfield."

"Another Raul Mondesi?" yawns the sergeant.

"Alberto could be Raul."

"Is he *hot*?"

"Let's see, ladies, are we talking about his bat?"

Slowly, through the glare of champagne, vodka, two fat glasses of sauvignon blanc and a wall of static created by Joe Galinis, Cassidy reawakens to the magic of baseball, which is always present and always beside us.

"Raul ended the season at .306," rattles off the mom, "when he was Rookie of the Year. He had, like, eight triples? Are you saying this kid, right now in *this* jail, is on *that* level? God, that is so exciting!"

"Yes," she says emphatically, "we think Cruz has that kind of potential. I need to see him, now," showing her game face, as full of equanimity and respect as she can make it.

"He's only a rookie." The mom appealing to the cop. "Give the kid a break."

The sergeant stretches, arms overhead. The heavy bosom just about splits the uniform.

"You want to see him, see him. But not your date."

"He's not my date."

The sergeant smiles with tired cynicism. "I'll tell you what. For once, let's win the pennant."

"Thank you."

"Good luck," calls the mom, the joy draining out of her face as she leaves the serenity of ballpark space for her useless papers and stolen child.

Cassidy walks back and gives each of them her card.

"Box seats. Call me."

She follows a brown line on the floor of the police station around a corner, past an ominously padlocked refrigerator, to a door out of a forties prison movie—dirty banana-colored paint, a metal grate, faded red lettering: NO GUNS BEYOND THIS POINT. The door swings open and Cassidy glimpses a three-hundred-pound bald jailer wearing rubber gloves.

She realizes with a nauseating chill where Alberto has been. He has been in a holding cell, in a foreign country, with a bunch of diseased, deranged drug addicts and violent felons. Her anger at whatever reckless behavior got him in here shrinks at the sight of the jailer. Anybody's balls would shrink. The blank expression. The rubber gloves.

But Alberto flies into the interview room like an enraged demon, slamming both palms against the Plexiglas divider and then—one, two, three—on all the other walls, as if to curse every direction that brought him here. Cassidy flinches with each smack but waits until he throws himself into the chair and folds his arms, kicking at something, muttering, "I don't believe it! How you believe this happen?"

His voice comes out all squawky through the microphone. He is wearing his club attire—leopard-print velour shirt, two gold earrings in one ear.

"What happened, Alberto? Did someone come after you? Were they threatening you again?"

"It happen because of Carlos Guevera," spitting the words.

Cassidy writes the name on the back of a receipt from Sizzler which she had found in her purse.

"Who is Carlos Guevera?"

"He come every night to the disco."

"Do we know this guy? Does he have a job?"

"Yeah, picking up girls. He try with one girl, name Lucy. He put his hand down her dress."

She writes that, too. "Is Lucy your girlfriend?"

"She a girl."

"Okay. He hit on Lucy and—?"

"I hit him with a chair."

Cassidy takes a long moment to deliberately hook a strand of hair behind one ear.

"Let me get this dialed in. A guy says something dumb about a girl and you try to kill him with a chair."

"He lie."

Alberto is becoming even more tightly wound, fingers digging into biceps, legs twisting like rope on a winch.

"He lie about the things he say."

"Like what?"

"He call her 'Baseball Annie,' say she love Latino players, all she want is to have babies with the big-league guys. He say, 'Do you know where she go on dates? The men's room at the Union 76. The gas station outside the stadium. They meet her after the game.'"

"Sure, they fill up the tank before they go home."

Alberto kicks at the wall, almost kicking himself out of the chair.

"He jealous. He lie."

"It doesn't *matter* if he lies."

And now *Cassidy* springs up and slams the Plexiglas with an open palm, as if to cuff his soft young head.

"You're going to let this lowlife bring *you* down? You're a professional ballplayer at the beginning of your career! Do you want to blow it completely? Do you want to get sent home?"

She remains standing, long-legged, one spaghetti strap fallen off her shoulder. Her hair, unclipped, has turned stringy and lank, and those dark circles that seem to afflict everyone in the division have crept inevitably under her eyes.

While the goodness in Alberto's face seems to have collapsed beneath a heavy mask—a hurt indignity—new for him, and sad to see.

"You no have to talk to me like that, like *mad*—"

"—Get used to it," Cassidy is rolling on. "The hard stuff has just begun. The girls, the drug dealers, the hangers-on—they all want a piece of your smile. I guess you have to see it for yourself, maybe, I don't know, you have to fall into some shit. Okay. You fell. You let some jerk-off get your pride, you weren't thinking."

"What the coaches gonna say?"

"They'll say"—she spreads her arms, exasperated—"*'Don't do it again!'* They know your talent, they're on your side. Look, it isn't the first time in history a player gets into a fight. You have a great future, but if you can't fit in, if you don't have the right attitude, you won't go anywhere. When it comes to choosing between two guys, who do we want? We want the guy who will make the club click, and not the troublemaker—so next time don't get involved, call the police, do you understand?"

"I know this is bad for me," says Alberto. "And my family, too."

Cassidy sinks into the single metal chair, a weight of dread on her shoulders like a pair of spectral hands. It's held her down before, this sadness, sometimes so deep she's wanted just to give up to that death wish and drown. Alberto's staring at an empty corner, rivulets of sweat gleaming at his temple. She aches to reach him, pull him to safety, but he is on the other side; completely separate from her.

The door to the interrogation room creaks open. A draft of air and Joe Galinis edges into the smarmy yellow light.

Cassidy sees his reflection and stands.

"How did you get in here?"

"Some guy threw up in the lobby. Everyone was going ballistic so I just walked on through."

"This isn't funny, Joe."

"A homeless man spitting blood? Not funny, no."

He is behind her, close. She holds his look in the Plexiglas.

"A real cowboy, aren't you?"

"I've learned not to wait until someone opens the door."

His fingers trace the skin where her strap has fallen loose and lift it gently into place. He puts his lips against her ear and whispers, "Fuck the police."

"Remember Mr. Galinis?" she manages.

"*Here's* the man!" says Joe, buoyant, loud. "How *are* you, buddy?"

Alberto looks blank. "I don't know you."

"Yes you do," says Cassidy. "I was with Mr. Galinis when we ran into you after the ball game in San Pedro de Macorís. We gave you a ride—"

"Oh, yes. *Sí.*"

Alberto breaks into the radiant smile: you see it, you remember the universe is good.

"We have fun!"

"We really did."

"The last time we were all together was in the Dominican. Now we're in California . . ." Cassidy shrugs like an awkward host.

"The modern world," comments Joe.

"Well, it was pretty strange how you and I got together down there," she reminds him. "It was the day after I signed Alberto." She turns to the rookie. "It was Saturday, right? I'm driving back to Santo Domingo with that crazy guy, the jeep breaks down, and all of a sudden, here comes Mr. Galinis, completely out of nowhere, moseying down the road."

Joe: "There was only one road."

The road tunneled *straight through miles of cane ten feet high. They could have been in Iowa under a big blue sky except for thick swirls of white and yellow butterflies that crisscrossed the jeep with mad intensity.*

The cane was planted right down to the edge. There was no shoulder and pedestrians walked complacently alongside vehicles zooming by. Monroe, the runty little driver, almost took out three barefoot girls in braids and cotton smocks carrying five-gallon containers of water on their heads.

"Slow down. You almost hit those girls."

"Fuck 'em. I hate rush-hour traffic."

Monroe's uncle, an older gentleman they called the General, owned a car rental company in the city. Monroe's claim to fame was that he had driven a cab in New York and picked up a punchy, aggressive Bed-Stuy accent to match.

"How does a person like you get to be a baseball scout?" he wanted to know.

"It's a long story."

He was peeling down the wrapper of a granola bar.

"I mean, how many you fuck?"

"Ballplayers?"

"Whoever. Whatever it takes."

"Uh-huh. Let me ask you something. Would you talk that way to your sister?"

"Yeah." Monroe pushed the bar into his mouth. "She's a prostitute."

They sped past mongrel island ponies clipping at grass. Inbreeding and starvation had left them emaciated and dazed. One had a plastic bag tied to its back as a saddle.

Cassidy slouched with arms crossed and legs stuck out. She would have liked to jam her boots right through the rattletrap floorboards. She was being driven seventy miles an hour down a one-lane road in a grotty subtropical country by a putz.

Or maybe this would qualify as baseball legend—alongside, say, Hugh Alexander who worked for the Indians, White Sox, Dodgers and Phillies and scouted Darryl Strawberry. The story goes that as a young man Hugh got his hand mashed in the gears of an oil rig. He wrapped it in a pillowcase and drove fifteen miles alone in a pickup truck to a Native American doctor who gave him a couple of shots of whiskey and cut the hand off with a saw. After that, he said, nothing in life could scare him.

Like spending ninety minutes in a car with Monroe. When Alberto Cruz became an All-Star, Cassidy vowed, she was going to call that sportswriter and contribute her own colorful bit of scouting fucking lore.

The road dipped to the east and they glimpsed the ocean, slate blue with low serrated swells. The far horizon was ruffled with a ridge of flamingo-pink cloud.

"Where's Hurricane Gordon?"

"Don't worry. He's out there."

The jeep died. It was quick. Sputtering, slowing, a mass of steam.

They pulled over, half into the cane, and opened the hood. Black hoses were spitting hot water like snakes.

"Fucking piece of shit. This happens to me all the time."

"Great, then you can fix it."

Monroe stepped away from the jeep. Cassidy waited with hands on hips, a warm gust from a passing truck pulling at the hem of her long skirt.

"I can fix it, no problem," said Monroe, scuffing around in the dirt until he found a piece of rusted iron rebar. Then he gripped it, hauled it back, and smashed the front headlight. Glass popped all over the road.

On the second backswing, about to smash the other light, Cassidy grabbed his wrist and pressed so hard with both hands Monroe's fingers turned crimson and he was forced to release the bar.

She kicked it away, panting, sweat running freely down her ribs.

"Your uncle would not be pleased."

"*Fuck my fucking uncle. He's not standing here with this fucking piece of shit!*"

Monroe was hopping around and rubbing his wrist, glaring with a scattered machismo Cassidy had seen before in kids too hyped and disconnected to make it through nine innings.

"*Don't mess!*" he warned, staggering back, trying to weather the waterspout in his brain.

They were nowhere, surrounded by three hundred sixty degrees of fields, a blanket of flatness that had contrast and depth only because of the shadows cast by clouds, deep pools of jade in the wavering acres. Despite a roaring blue sky the unbroken landscape was stark; without the texture of the moving clouds it would have been pitiless. Far from the turmoil of life in the capital, they were suspended in a rural isolation reduced to two elements: sun and sugarcane. Here there were no shantytowns. Not even a melon for sale on a chair by the road.

A black Range Rover passed, stopped, and then backed up to where Cassidy stood. The window lowered and a white American face leaned out and grinned with smug pleasure.

It was the man she had met at the airport.

"Hi," said Joe. "Can I buy you a drink?"

In the interrogation room in the Glendale police station, the three of them have been trading stories, more amused now, more relaxed, about what happened later that night, after Cassidy had left with Joe for an afternoon by the pool at the Gran Caribe, after they had gone to the ball game and met up with Alberto as it started to rain and they all hustled into the Rover.

"I said, 'What's the plan?'" recalls Joe, "and you said, '*Why do you need a plan?*'"

They laugh.

Cassidy: "Good question."

"You let me drive your car!" says Alberto. "We laughing because I cannot decide which I going to buy when I get to the majors, a Range Rover like that one or a BMW Z-3 like James Bond."

Cassidy: "I say the BMW."

"I never drive such a rich car. It was great."

"Except for when we clipped that horse," says Cassidy.

"*Pobrecito*," echoes Alberto, shaking his head. "Poor horse!"

"He was okay," says Joe. "Your nose took it a lot worse."

"Woke me up," says Cassidy, "flying off the backseat."

"You give to me such a good time. I feel so great. I just sign with the Dodgers . . . Everybody think I big guy . . . Man"—looking around—"everything different."

But in a way not so different. The substance of Joe's body behind Cassidy's, the heated smells of sandalwood and bay leaf and new wool and lilac and sweat, fill their tiny half of the room to abundance, the way the inside of the Rover had been ripe with the astringent scent of Mama Juana and the spice of limeberries crushed beneath their muddy shoes. They had driven those lightless roads for hours, drunk and happy, celebrating the future of a promising young man, his fortune wheeling just as wildly as it has tonight, the charge inside the Rover as combustible, all of them jammed together, inexplicably, airtight.

They hear sirens, paramedics coming for the homeless man. Suddenly the party's really over.

"So who are these assholes," says Joe gravely, "and why are they trying to blackmail you?"

"This has nothing to do with that," answers Cassidy. "He's here because he got into a fight over a girl in a disco and hit somebody with a chair. When the lawyers get into this, I'm toast."

Alberto: "I very sorry that I make trouble for you."

The door jerks open and Detective Mark Simms comes in, wearing jeans and a T-shirt with a couple of gold chains, a half-smoked cigar between his teeth.

"Hello, Alberto. Cassidy. You're working late." He takes in the dress. "Dedication. Beyond the call of duty, but appreciated."

Cassidy folds her arms. "We were at a museum event."

"Would you excuse us, sir?"

"No problem," says Joe, newly energized and tense. He cocks a finger toward Alberto. "I'll make a call."

When the door closes Simms begins: "Let me explain why I'm here. As the LAPD detective assigned to Major League Baseball, I was notified of your arrest. Can you tell me what happened?"

"I fight."

Simms sits in the metal chair, hitching it three times toward the glass, a move he has obviously made in this room a thousand times.

"With a thing like this, you don't want it staying wet too long."

At first Cassidy thinks he is talking about the case in some kind of obscene police code, then notices Simms rolling a cigar between his fingers appreciatively.

"Genuine cubano," he explains.

"I tried to buy those in the Dominican. Where did you get it?"

"A Hollywood madame."

Cassidy leaves, depressed. She knows nothing about the world.

Isabel Street is deserted and heavy with mist as if someone had taken a spray bottle and tried to revive downtown Glendale. Cassidy comes down the steps to find Joe leaning against the most princely car she has ever seen, a weighty verdant-green convertible with cream interior — long, with a stately and determined stance.

"Are you okay?" he asks.

"Tired. Look, Joe, what was going down with Alberto, that was club business. It was nice for all of us to be together shooting the breeze, but you really had no right to be in that room."

"Let me make it up to you."

"How," she says in a voice going husky, "are you going to make it up to me?"

"What if I told you how to make the felony charge go away?"

"I'd be interested."

"What's so funny?"

"Nothing. Go ahead."

"Okay, you call the owner of the club and get him to agree to a civil compromise."

"Which is?"

"A way of not going to court. You pay for damages, the felony charge is reduced, they cite Alberto out on a misdemeanor. It all goes away. No big deal."

"How did you come up with that?"

"I called Harvey."

Her fingers lightly drum his jacket lapel.

"Our lawyers would have thought of it tomorrow."

"I know," he says, "but this is tonight."

They stand still in the empty street. Neither wants to leave the other's shining eyes.

"What can it do?"

"The car?"

"Of course," she says. "What do you think I'm talking about?"

"Zero to sixty in six-point-something."

"Fast."

He makes a cup of her hands and drops in the keys.

"Any way you want."

LAPD Detective Mark Simms exits the lobby of the police station, eager to relight the cubano, but slows in the doorway when he observes Cassidy Sanderson sliding her hands up the chest of the guy in the expensive suit, all the way up around his neck, and they kiss, a gum-crusher, no kidding around, then manage to pry themselves apart long enough to maneuver into separate doors, she's driving, then the Bentley disappears, leaving a slick trail in the dewy dark.

Simms mouths the wet cigar and makes note of the license plate.

Habit.

8

The Bentley Azure convertible whispers past City Hall and follows a row of old pink brick apartment buildings down Broadway. Behind
the crystal windscreen the damp air puffs discreetly at Cassidy's loose hair.
The motorcar handles like a cloud.

She hits a button on the CD and they are suddenly enveloped in the
climax of a grand Italian opera—oceanic bass and sweet soprano, lush
brocades and golden tassels instantaneously made almost visible by the
pure rich clarity of sound.

"Got any blues? Muddy Waters, B. B. King—"

"I've got jazz."

He punches up a trio playing "Waltz for Debby" and Cassidy sum-
marily punches it off.

"What is this, a V-8?"

"Three hundred eighty-five horsepower and don't ask me anything
else, that's all I know."

"What's the fastest you've ever driven it?"

Her eyes are on the freeway entrance a couple of blocks ahead.

"A hundred thirty, going out to Vegas." He studies her profile. "You are
actually licking your lips."

"You offered. No taking back."

He smiles but unconsciously crosses his arms.

Protection. At a hundred thirty.

They stop at a light along a cheesy strip of discount stores and bail
bond storefronts. A red Trans Am pulls up beside them, hip-hop pummeling. The tinted window rolls down and a Latino guy calls, "Do you know
how to get to Pasadena?"

"Take the 134 east," says Joe, pointing ahead.

The guy cracks up laughing along with his pals, about seventy of them
crammed into the backseat.

The street is empty, harsh white light spoking out from the barred windows of the bondsman. Cassidy counts the remaining seconds until the light goes green. It isn't just the music that is pounding in her chest.

Both cars start to roll, grille to grille, then without effort, without even seeming to accelerate, the Bentley vaporizes as, incredibly, Cassidy cuts the guy off, hits the westbound ramp at sixty and puts a half mile between them by the time Joe recovers enough to say, "Are you out of your mind?"

"Didn't mean to scare you."

He doesn't answer.

"Are you mad?"

"No."

"You're nice to let me drive. Just like you let Alberto."

"I live to serve."

"Go ahead. Put on your music."

"No, thank you," says Joe. "I'm in your hands."

She smiles.

"Is that what you like? Power over men?"

"I don't have power over men."

He raises an eyebrow skeptically.

She answers, "Come with me to work one day."

Her palms slide up and down the hide-covered wheel.

"So what does a car like this cost?"

"Three hundred, plus change."

"Three hundred *thousand*? I am totally intimidated."

"I fell in love, what can I say? Isn't that what it's all about? Passion?"

"If you can afford it."

"To me this is the most beautiful car in the world. I wanted to surround myself with beauty, no matter what the cost. But now I realize I was wrong."

"Why?" asks Cassidy, glancing at the side mirror. Behind them the freeway is empty and the emptiness keeps piling up. They're cruising at ninety.

"Well, it turns out," says Joe, "I had no idea what beauty was until tonight. Only now, with you in the car, is the beauty complete."

A slow blush starts at the base of her throat and mounts to her cheeks.

"It's that virginal quality."

She sputters laughter.

"Yes, Joe, I am a virgin."

"I believe, underneath, there's a lonely girl. Want some heat?"

An insinuating warmth radiates from the driver's seat like a hot bath at warp speed.

Does it vibrate, too? she wants to say, but that would be a dyke jock thing.

"Are all scouts as involved with their players as you seem to be?"

"You get attached, to varying degrees."

"What is it about Alberto?"

"He's talented. A good kid. Alone in this country—"

"Such the big sister."

"It's my job."

"No, I can tell you're really concerned about him." Joe lowers the back of his seat an inch. "Who do the police think is behind the extortion threats?"

"They say it's a grudge. Someone looking for reflected light off the star."

"A pal from back home who didn't make it?"

"It's after working hours, Joe."

They don't speak. For several minutes the flat light-grid of the San Fernando Valley strobes by.

Finally Joe yawns. "How far do you want to take this?"

"The ocean."

"Really? Way over Topanga?"

"Why not? You have to be somewhere?"

"Uh, no—"

"I want to drive this thing over the canyon."

"Fuck! I just remembered. I have a meeting in the morning—"

"Should I turn back?"

"Never mind—"

"No, it's silly, if you—" She starts to sneeze. And sneeze. Six times in a row.

"Allergies?"

He presses buttons.

Seven sneezes. Eight. "What's that going to do?"

"Filter the air."

"Joe, we're in a—convertible." Ten. "Do you have tissues—?"

Swollen-eyed, blinded with tears, she reaches over and gropes the glove box open.

A pistol falls into Joe's lap.

She swerves. Out of nowhere a sixteen-wheeler blasts by with a horn like a freight train.

Cassidy veers to the right, almost hits a Volvo.

"Watch out!"

She compensates. The Bentley centers itself.

"What is that?"

"A Beretta."

He has put the gun back in and snapped the glove box smartly.

"Why do you need a Beretta?"

"Protection."

"From what?"

He thinks about it.

"I know this is going to sound somewhat corny, but I believe it's true. Our lives more than crossed in the Dominican. Our lives changed. Mine did. Since the first time we met, I haven't been able to stop thinking about you."

"Why didn't you call?"

"I had some things to sort out. I'm still not sure. I still don't know. Except that you're different. No woman has ever done this to me. How many guys get a hard-on driving by Dodger Stadium?"

"Not nearly enough. Should I turn off here?"

"Yeah, sure. Go for it."

She coasts down the freeway ramp onto Topanga Canyon Road, a curving mountain pass black as pitch. She takes the first hairpin at forty, a rockfall of stones stirred loose in their wake from the invisible shoulder of the hill.

"Easy. I like my paint job."

The heat brings out the same rich smell as the supple leather seats of the Range Rover when they had driven those endless looping roads, unable to see beyond their headlights in the intensifying rain. The Rover had the same walnut veneer console; she remembers how it felt to be up high, as if they had been in command of all the roads in the Dominican.

A car comes down the opposite direction, slopping over the yellow line. Cassidy hugs the canyon wall so branches whip the door.

"Don't worry. I'm on it," downshifting so the tires chirp. "So why the gun?"

"I'm going to take a very big risk here," says Joe.

"You're already letting me drive."

"I'm going to tell you something. In confidence, okay?"

"You got it."

"I've been getting blackmail threats as well. The same as Alberto."

Cassidy glances over. His fingers flex the top edge of the door. His black hair glistens with perspiration; full of contradictions, perplexingly attractive, and fierce—a flameless, smokeless ferocity.

"Oh my God, Joe."

"That's why the gun."

"What do they have on you?"

"Nothing! I don't know! We've had some problems down there, I thought it was another government crook on the take, so I paid."

"You *paid*? How much?"

"Thirty thousand dollars. So far."

"So *far*?"

"The notes kept coming. I kept paying."

"Harvey said you're never supposed to pay a blackmailer."

Alarmed, "When did he say that?"

"At the party."

"What did you tell him?"

"Nothing. I was talking about Alberto, but I never even got to say—"

"Look," interrupts Joe. She can see dark sweat creeping at the armholes of the suit. "It is very, very important that Harvey never finds out anything about this."

"He's your attorney—"

"My life is complicated. Harvey can't know."

It is still dark but pickup trucks have begun to appear on the road, laborers going to the job. They slow through Topanga Village, the buried heart of hippie culture, horse corrals and slipshod weathered structures overgrown with plants, where Druids and fairy-worshipers still dress their children in crowns of flowers during rituals in spring.

"You know, these spirit bottles—"

"Don't talk about that."

"There's something that brought you, me, and Alberto together. Once. Twice. Why?"

"You're giving me the chills."

"I don't know who or what it is, but frankly, I don't like it. Less and less. Or more and more. All I know, we have to stay together. You're the only one I can talk to about this. We have to trust each other."

Cassidy turns into a lookout, braking at a dented guardrail. She cuts the headlights and there is nothing but black and the silence of the canyon. In an hour there will be light and birdsong; now, in darkness, coyotes hunt and owls cry.

The top goes up, *swoosh*, and the locks go down, *swoosh*, and Joe and Cassidy touch lips.

She forces herself to slow down, to savor the untying of the tie, the opening up and pushing apart of the jacket and the white dress shirt, off his shoulders like the wings of an angel, drinking from the pool between the small bones, then both of them clawing gracelessly along the pleated panels of soft hide in order to do this thing; skins hypersensitive, even the featherweight brush of his tongue causing her to cry out from the unendurable actuality of being with this man, the real mass and weight of him, then the goal between her hands, unbearably unmysterious.

Finally, Joe sitting up in the backseat. Cassidy on his wide-apart thighs, dress half down, half up, a twisted cummerbund of spandex and lace. Their ankles scrolled together.

Now she has it where she wants it.

"Oh do it."

The first time they had touched had been at the bar in the airport. *"You know what I think?" "What do you think?" "You have Swedish hands." "Swedish hands?"* She'd laughed and hidden them under the table. *"What do you mean?" "They look like they could handle a pitchfork. Or weave some incredible sweater out of raw sheep's wool."* And the back of his hand brushed hers as he passed along a drink.

Now his fingers are enslaving as they compress the tendons of her wrists, forcing them, in the last unbinding moment, to hold their arms straight out together: a double crucifixion; throats exposed, and blood-red fists.

9

One week later. The phone rings at dawn. A male voice with a foreign accent says, "Wake up. You know what you have to do."

"Who is this?"

"Your trainer, gorgeous."

Cassidy rolls over. Her heart rate has skyrocketed.

"You scared me."

Marshall chuckles. "Usually it's the other way round. See you at the gym."

Edith jumps on board, jiggling the bed frame. Cassidy hangs up and rests a hand on her heaving breast, waiting for a resting pulse to return. She does not want to leave that warmth. She does not want to work out. Right now she would be content to float like a fetus in salty sleep until noon.

Waking up in a rented cottage in Southern California can itself be a shock. Too much seacoast light. Whose Picasso poster is that on the wall? Why a map of old Laguna Village? What is going on with the pile of pillows and blankets and mismatched sheets on a pine bench in the corner and exactly how long have that earthenware rice bowl and those wooden chopsticks been sitting on top of the TV?

Edith and Cassidy stare eyeball-to-eyeball for a vacant moment as she makes an effort to bring up the task of the day: she has to make sure Travis Conners gets there *this afternoon* to see a kid named Brad Parker play. It has rained during the past week and she hasn't been able to get Travis down. But the big western regional meeting prior to the June draft is coming up and Parker is Cassidy's top pick. She's feeling a lot of pressure to claim him now.

Do something right.

She reaches for the electronic personal organizer and scrolls down to

Pierce High School and the home phone number of math teacher and baseball coach Jack Hughes.

Coach is on his way to school, says his wife.

"Are you calling about Brad Parker?" she wants to know.

"Why do you ask?"

"The Astros called last night."

Cassidy tries diversion: "Is the field playable?"

"The field is fine."

"And Parker's on the roster?"

"You'll have to ask Coach," the wife says firmly.

"There are other kids to look at besides Parker."

Good try. There aren't. Not on this team. No one else averages 13.5 strikeouts per nine innings. She calls the high school, identifies herself as a scout for the Los Angeles Dodgers, asks a grumpy front-office secretary if she has the lineup for the varsity baseball game today and, Great, isn't it, they didn't get rained out?

"Oh," says the secretary, perking up. "You must be calling about Brad Parker."

Not a good sign.

Cassidy swings out of bed, more anxious than ever for Travis to see the right-hander.

She had liked Parker early, good curveball with good spin on it, pitched a shutout the first time she had seen him, in command all the way. His dad had been a high school champion javelin thrower, you can see where the body is going. Travis will like his self-control, the way he thinks ahead, and the way he handles pressure — *Forget the hitter, just you and me out there playing catch.* Parker could turn out to be an important find, a solid blue-card prospect for whom Cassidy could receive major credit down the line.

She pulls sweat shorts over a lizard-green leotard and laces up the cross-trainers. She should feel good. The lawyers worked out the civil compromise deal. Cruz got spoken to by Raymond Woods and sent back out to winter workout. If he stays away from trouble, and with a strong report on Parker, she will already have improved her percentages for the year. And tonight she has a date with Joe, a real date, a fancy society dinner on the Pier. In a tiny bathroom she turns a corroded tap and a weak stream of water releases the smell of algae from the drain. She brushes her hair and braids it, watching a soulful face.

Then why the emptiness?

The kitchen is vintage sixties. Pots and pans hang on a brick wall over a built-in stovetop. The stainless steel oven has a round window like a porthole. Cassidy stands in the center of the linoleum floor drinking apple juice as consciousness comes up inevitably as the light of day: she and this kid Parker will never sweat together. They are not about to conquer the mountain, the dewy freshness of Elysian Park giving way to spectacular city views. They will never jog together through the daily fires of the athlete's work. With Alberto Cruz she is bonded in a sad and prideful way. With Parker it is different. Parker is a prospect. Cassidy is a scout. In the end, it will simply come down to numbers.

She becomes aware of yakking birds; notices the ferns in the spectacular flower arrangement Joe had sent are dry. Pouring water into the vase from a measuring cup, brown furls crumbling away in her fingers, she acknowledges the chance she had with Cruz may never come again—to imprint on the muscle memory of a young player, like a leaflet fossil formed in stone, one detail, one petiole from the pattern of her own lifetime in the game. The position of his hands on the bat. Striding into the ball correctly. One small thing he can take all the way to the majors.

Hold it. The tears in her eyes are completely out of whack. Letting go of Cruz won't be the worst moment of her life. It won't be the 1984 Olympics, the year she had been training for her entire career, the year they suddenly dropped women's softball as an Olympic sport. Or having to bury your brother, or being told your father, who still ran the marathon at age fifty-eight, dropped dead of a massive coronary on the bicycle path near the stream.

The phone rings. Her heart jumps. Impatiently she wipes a cheek. What now? Marshall wanting her to pick up a tall decaf percent latte on the way to the gym?

She says, "Hello?" to the screech of a fax.

She hangs up as the machine on the counter engages. The digital readout says 6:27 a.m. Raymond sends out weekly scouting reports, but not usually before breakfast. She slips two slices of whole wheat into the toaster and watches as the paper starts to roll.

Her heart jumps again. The first thing to come out of the machine is the logo for Omega Development International, Joe's company.

Oh, this is going to be cool! He must be in the same condition—drifting through his day in the Omega tower, one meeting after another, part of his mind absorbing, revising, politicking, making decisions—the other part, like hers, lost in a daydream of perpetual sex. The card that came with the flowers had said audaciously, "Your breasts are like diamonds."

The fax goes on for seven pages.

It includes the lineup, schedule and player bios of the Colorado Silver Bullets, along with an article about a publicity tour through LA.

The cover letter is not from Joe but from his daughter, Nora:

> Dear Cassidy,
>> Thought you would be interested in this.
>>> Best to you,
>>> Nora

The machine stops. Cassidy gathers the pages that have curled all over her counter. She played for the Bullets more than two years ago, why would she be interested in this horseshit now?

Hey, she tells herself, Nora's just trying to be friends. Then stuffs the whole thing into the garbage. Toast is ready. Edith whines.

Outside in Shadow Lane the California sky keeps expanding with dubious promise from royal blue to pale transparency. Cassidy shoos the dog inside. A briny smell comes up from the beach along with a persistent and habitual regret. Backing out the Explorer she glances up at the weathervane on the gambrel roof. It always seems to point in the same direction. Is it stuck, or has she missed the move?

Marshall says, "I'm here with you."

Standing behind her, pressing close, he puts both hands on her waist. "Again!"

She lifts the bar—twenty-five pounds with ten-pound plates on either side—and, muscles quivering, squats deep into a plié.

"Twelve more. No locking of knees. Tighten up!" He slaps her butt.

Cassidy is snorting like a Clydesdale.

"Find the groove, find the groove," he urges, "find the groove."

The snorts become grunts, the grunts become shouts, and they bellow together—"*Rrahr! Rrahr!*"—like a pair of gladiators, though no one on the StairMasters or treadmills in busy South Coast Fitness Center—a franchise gym in a strip mall behind a Ralph's supermarket—pays the slightest mind. An Eagles disk is playing and there are plenty of distracting TV monitors showing helicopter shots of freeway traffic.

"Everybody's got an exercise video."

Marshall picks up an old argument as they move on to leg curls. "Why not you and me?"

"Because everybody's got one, that's why."

"But look at us!"

He forces her to confront the mirror. They do look sort of mythic. He with the cleft chin, spiked hair and sartorius muscles like flying buttresses; she with cheeks flushed bubblegum pink, sweat-soaked bangs, those beautifully sculpted shoulders and powerhouse quads. He with the macho Aussie accent, trainer to the stars; she with the Dodgers.

"Okay," she admits. "We're buff."

"And we boff." He smiles cleanly. "But not on video."

Cassidy does not enjoy the joke. Does not, all of a sudden, like seeing herself side by side with this young man at all.

"What's wrong?"

Catching her dismay in the mirror Marshall self-consciously covers his mouth.

"Do I stink of eggs? I had an egg white omelet earlier."

"You're fine," Cassidy tells him, "I'm just having a strange day," and straddles the machine, slipping the pin into the stack of weights at fifty pounds.

"Talk to me," squints Marshall, "tell me about your emotions," the by-the-books manner in which he pretends intimacy with clients. "Pushing their buttons," he calls it.

They have an arrangement, no questions asked, she is under no obligation to make a big confession about Joe. It would not be of benefit. She hadn't been exactly thrilled to hear about the lady hand model, whose job it is to hold bottles of detergent for magazine ads, but at least that had explained the deviant-looking pairs of white cotton gloves in Marshall's nightstand.

He is waiting for an answer with a look of concern so fake she laughs.

"What now?"

"You spend too much time with actors," Cassidy huffs.

"Don't get me started."

But he is already started. The ditz afraid of getting old. The TV detective who needs sex, sex, sex ("Bangs like a dunny door"). The actress who made a career fighting aliens before women had biceps ("Steroids").

Usually Cassidy is amused by the Hollywood stuff. Today she finds it intolerable.

Hefting a dumbbell, "Which one?"

"Start with eight. All actors want to talk about is themselves. It's boring. And after a while you feel, what good am I? I'm only a trainer. We've got to move on."

"We?"

"We have a groove happening here, you and I, a consciousness of the physical that I feel is quite unique."

Cassidy performs flat bench flies. Sex with Marshall is like driving a race car in a video arcade game. Level One is a ride in the country, a few tricky curves but navigable, trees and houses going by. Level Two the road comes at you twice as fast and there is menace—roadkill, bridges falling. Level Three is all-out urban warfare, dodging mortar fire and explosions, wrestling the joystick until you die as a result of your own reckless unthinkable acceleration—a meteoric crash, then slo-mo fragments floating on a field of apple green.

Making love with Joe in the Bentley had been like losing your way inside one of those religious paintings—a mysterious labyrinthine path, pear trees and archways, exalted marble flesh martyred by a flight of golden arrows. They had been fearless with each other, belligerent, shameless and harsh; afterward he had thumbed the fiery tears from her cheeks like a supplicant.

They had driven to the beach and watched the sky and tried to pinpoint the moment night crossed into day. The cold sand was littered with bits of Styrofoam and fishing twine, cigarette butts and aluminum poptops, but the easy slap of the waves was a wonder that seemed to unify their lovers' story, from the volcanic shores of the Caribbean to the slope of Santa Monica Bay.

"I've got a guy who says you can make a video for less than five thousand," Marshall is saying. "I told him we'd meet—"

Cassidy grunts, up to fifteen pounds. "Spring training. I'm gone."

"I can get a shitload of celebrity endorsements—"

Cassidy mops her face with a towel. Sweat stains have turned the bright green leotard a mottled sage.

"I don't want to. I don't really care."

She heads toward a multistation. The gym is nothing more than an airless box between a donut shop and a health food store and every morning, just about now, it begins to reek of fry grease and new-mown wheatgrass.

Marshall is following, clearly puzzled.

"How's your piriformis?" he asks and expertly inserts a steely thumb between the muscle layers of Cassidy's left buttock, instant domination that penetrates to one of the most sensitive junctions of nerves in the body.

Pain travels with the speed of light down the back of her leg. Her knee buckles.

She whirls and lands a smart crack across his face.

He stumbles backward, astounded.

"Bloody hell."

"Keep your hands to yourself."

"What is this? PMS?"

Cassidy steps up and grips the handles of the machine.

"I told you," she mutters in the midst of a series of burning abdominal raises, "a very strange day."

Marshall rubs his cheek, considering.

"You'll want to eat a lot of protein," he decides.

When she gets home from the gym, Edith is gone.

Not in the yard and not in the house although Cassidy is certain she remembers putting the dog inside.

Edith is eight years old. She is fixed and does not stray. The pounding starts again in Cassidy's chest and she starts to feel slightly disoriented, as when you have misplaced your keys. She is craving a shower while her muscles are warm, but suddenly it seems a not-very-good idea. Warily she scans the living area—brown plaid sofa, round maple table and spindle-backed chairs—keeping very still as if, in the subtle whisper of air along her skin, she could sense a disturbance. But she cannot sense a thing.

In the kitchen, another pile of papers has collected on the floor.

Another fax from Nora, something off a Web site, pages of citations of books and articles about women in sports. She kicks them aside. The red light is blinking on the answering machine—Coach Jack Hughes full of blustery assurance that Brad Parker will be on the field at three o'clock today. "He's certainly the kid you want to see. I've personally never seen such perfect hitting mechanics—"

Cassidy cuts it off and speed-dials Dulce at the stadium.

Dulce confirms Travis will meet her at the high school. "And I have your plane ticket for Vero Beach."

The moment she hangs up the phone rings again. Startled, she spasms it clumsily as if it were covered with soap.

"Cassie? Uncle Pedro. I heard we got some trouble."

"What trouble?"

Now she's got the receiver around the right way.

"I heard our kid Alberto Cruz got in some trouble."

"He was in jail overnight but no big deal."

"No, I'm talking of this terrible blackmail."

"How do you know?"

"The police have been here."

"The Dominican police?"

"An officer called Molina came to my apartment. I wasn't home. Poor Rhonda thought he was there to tell her I was dead."

"No way!"

"He comes back and explains the situation, about the letters from Nagua, and I tell him, thank you very much but this is a baseball family problem, we gonna solve it like family. You'll be at Vero?"

"Absolutely."

"We'll put our heads together. Doing your homework for the regional meeting?"

"Yes, Uncle Pedro."

"Remember what I told you, write everything down. A speech for every prospect. You gotta get their attention, sell your guys, know exactly what you're going to say. Otherwise, all they'll be doing is looking at your legs."

"Believe me, I'll be wearing pants."

When Cassidy hangs up she hears scratching and follows the sound to the bedroom upstairs. Edith has somehow gotten herself stuck in the

closet. The terrier innocently trundles out and licks Cassidy's leg, probably because she has just peed all over a nice pair of suede boots.

Cassidy worries the door, wondering how the dog could have become
locked inside. The bedroom is the usual mess, no way to know if someone
had been there. She pokes around the stuff on the rattan dresser and
inside the drawers, exasperated, trying to shake a growing unease.

10

By 2:30 p.m. that afternoon the pack scouts have assembled around the metal bleachers on the high school playing field.

It is a narrow, uninspiring vista angled between the tan industrial edifices of the school—rusted chain link, a cinder-block shack, the smell of fine clay dust and of French fries from a Mexican lunch truck. Way out behind center field on an old retaining wall with flaking paint somebody's hung a bedsheet with tilted juvenile lettering: Home of Dolphin Baseball.

Cassidy, in pressed khakis and a plain ivory polo, weaves the gauntlet through a dozen men—tall, Caucasian, heavy-chested, wearing for the most part an assortment of witless polyester shirts and jeans, accessorized with straw cowboy hats, toothpicks, stopwatches. The talk is of two kids who got stabbed in a car, somebody's mom who has cancer, a wicked storm back east.

Coach Hughes, who does not look any less like an air-puffed marshmallow because he is wearing a baseball uniform, inspects a couple of puddles on the infield, making a joke about a wet T-shirt contest which Cassidy gracefully ignores. Squeezing past a bespectacled guy in a sports jacket from an American League team, she says, "Excuse me," and betrays no reaction when he moves aside with an exaggerated pelvic thrust, smirking, "Sure thing. Made my day."

Cassidy is wearing her give-'em-nothing face, a mask of calm impenetrable confidence she has shown to the boys since she was eleven years old.

But it does not mean she is not tense with a low-level outrage that has also, always, been part of the game.

Travis, looking like a rodeo heartthrob in a black Stetson and denim shirt with pearl buttons, is talking on the cellular way back near the Explorer; no need to billboard the fact a supervisor is here.

"Here's the batting order."

Travis skims it. "Hmm."

"Problem?"

"Yeah, they didn't put down the arrest records of the players."

Cassidy's eyes narrow.

"How are we supposed to tell if they're up to the level of Alberto Cruz?" Travis chuckles. "Assault with a deadly weapon, hey now—"

"Here's what's going to happen," Cassidy says. "You're going to give me all this horseshit about Alberto Cruz and then, when he's Rookie of the Year, you'll take credit for discovering him."

Cassidy and Travis stare at each other.

Both in silence.

Both in awe.

Realizing she has called it exactly.

Then: "That Parker?"

Travis has infallibly picked him out of the players gathering around the home-team dugout: four inches taller than the others, Parker is also the one carrying the helmets, checking the scene with an eager smile. A new day. A new game.

"He's not like a lot of kids, think they're doing you a favor," Travis observes.

"You hear talk on him but I know he's not that high on people's lists."

"Talk's mainly coming from the coach?"

She nods. "This program hasn't had a kid drafted in three or four years."

Travis watches Coach Hughes yell at the stragglers to start stretching. They ignore him.

"Clueless."

"The kid's never had instruction."

"This the dad?"

A six-foot-two beefer is headed their way, wearing gray slacks too tight over the glutes and a shirt with floating golf clubs.

"Uh-huh."

"A little early for the hard sell."

"The family wants it."

Lang Parker is already shaking her hand.

"Hello, my friend. Good to see you again."

His square midwestern face has gone to jowls and a bald spot encroaches on the sandy hair. He and his wife, Pepper, run a tree-trimming business and a string of copy shops out in Perris. Cassidy makes the introductions as her beeper goes off.

"Can I use your phone?"

Travis flips her the cellular, nodding patiently at Mr. Parker's pitch:

"First thing you have to know, we're a family of athletes. My dad played football for Notre Dame, I ran track and field. Our girls are into ice-skating and one of 'em might have a shot at the Olympics. She's only four, but that's what they tell me. We are also a religious family, Mr. Conners, and I have to tell you that all along, from the time Brad was six years old, it's been our deepest prayer that our son could go on to pitch for the Dodgers—"

"Guys, I'm sorry," Cassidy interrupts, "I've got to hop back up to the stadium."

"What's the deal?"

"Raymond wants to see me. Now."

"You go along," Lang Parker says. "We appreciate everything you've done, God bless."

Edging toward the Explorer, "Mr. Conners is more than qualified to check Brad out."

Travis's hard features have taken on a reproachful stare. Cassidy knows what he is thinking: she is trying to screw him by leaving him alone with the windy dad.

"Dulce left a message saying it was an emergency."

"Have fun."

Cassidy climbs into the front seat.

She doesn't tell Travis that her friend Dulce had been sobbing.

Or that nobody in the department had picked up, when she had repeatedly tried to call back.

11

Cassidy pushes through the glass doors.

Immediately she can tell there is tension in the waiting area. Nobody is at the receptionist's desk. Phones are ringing and men with attaché cases are impatient to be seen.

Deep within the inner offices secretaries are gathered in groups whispering in Spanish. Cassidy doesn't even bother to stop, buzzing all the places Dulce might be, finding her at last running water over paper towels in the ladies' room.

Dulce stops when she sees Cassidy in the mirror. Coldly, "What are you doing here?"

"You were upset. You paged me."

"Raymond paged you."

"You left the message. What's the matter?"

"Go see Raymond."

"He's not in his office."

"Then he must be on the field."

"Dulce—what happened?"

She presses wet towels against her puffy eyes and hot red cheeks. Water stains the white satin-polyester blouse.

"You are not normal."

Cassidy laughs. "We knew that."

"It is not funny! I feel sorry for you!"

Incredibly, Dulce is shouting. Still Cassidy cannot drop the smile. It is hard to process—this quietly competent, accommodating woman who runs a department full of brash male egos without ever losing her cool, suddenly throwing some kind of theatrical fit.

"You want to play a little boy's game? Well, go ahead and play with the boys."

A deep disquiet turns Cassidy's gut.

"Did I do something?"

Dulce doesn't answer.

Louder, "Do you mind telling me what I did?"

Cassidy lowers the backpack. She had suddenly become aware of the strap cutting into her shoulder.

Dulce stutters. She averts her face and gestures with both hands as if trying to turn off a faucet that had suddenly begun to spew sewage.

"This trash, this piece of filth comes to my house."

"Are we talking about one of Alberto's friends?"

"Not his friend! Who knows *what* it is? A disgusting videotape."

"Oh."

"My mother opens it. She thinks it is a cartoon, it comes in a box, like you get from a video store, with cartoons on it, she thinks it is for my son—"

"Let me guess—it turned out to be adult material."

Fresh tears burst from Dulce's eyes and Cassidy takes a step back. Try to be patient. You can imagine the shock it would be for a Catholic grandma to get a glimpse at the kind of pornography out there today.

"My mother had heart palpitations. My neighbor had to call 911."

Okay, a big shock.

"Is your mom all right?"

Cassidy is holding her ground but mightily disgusted by the thought of yet another conversation with Alberto. *Don't get into fights in bars. Don't get sent to jail. Don't fall in with a bad crowd who would send stupid dirty tapes to the home of the people who are sponsoring you in this country. When is he going to get it?*

"My mom's okay."

"That's good."

Dulce wipes her nose with another paper towel which seems to just about lacerate her skin.

"My husband doesn't want me to work here." She holds her face up, shiny with accusation. "He wants me to quit."

"Well, Carlos is a macho man," says Cassidy with an easy shrug, a joke they have shared before.

"He's right."

Could that be hate in Dulce's hard amber eyes?

"Why should I work in a place where I can't trust my friends? Some people around here, it doesn't surprise me that they would keep me in the dark, I'm only a secretary, but *you* I can't believe."

"Hey," says Cassidy, "I didn't send the freaking tape."

"The only explanation I can see for why you didn't tell me is because you don't have children. You don't have children, you don't know how to feel. Not like a mother."

Talk about free fall. Talk about plummeting a hundred miles an hour.

"Check it," spits Cassidy with a downward jab through the air. Adrenaline-torqued, prancing.

"Maybe it's a cultural thing," Dulce says, smug, arms folded.

Suddenly it *is* a cultural thing, as if they'd never known each other, never gone to lunch, talked about fathers, shared family occasions like first communion for Dulce's little girls, looked out for each other around the office a hundred different ways, gossiped about movie stars and TV personalities, and ballplayers and ballplayers' wives—alliances that had been shyly built over two years, snapped.

An unfamiliar rage tornadoes Cassidy's body.

"What? Spanish women have a lock on having babies? Is that what you're saying? Because if I said that I'd be stripped naked and run out of town. I'm not a *mother*, so I don't know how to *feel*? You have no idea how it feels."

She pulls the door so hard it slams open against the wall and scrapes her knuckles.

Dulce continues to grip her own elbows with a stony expression.

"You knew it was dangerous for Alberto Cruz to be in my house."

Cassidy turns.

"—I mean the danger *to my family* of having Alberto Cruz stay *in my home*. You knew it. You said nothing."

Cassidy remembers how Detective Simms steered her out of Raymond's office. "Let us handle it," he said.

"They specifically told me not to tell you."

"Good!" Dulce throws up her hands. "So you are still a member in good standing of the boys' club."

"Dulce. What was on that tape?"

"It is an atrocity."

Both hands fly up to cover her crumbling face. Cassidy attempts to touch her shoulder, but Dulce pushes past and out the door.

Down in the dugout level a group of minor league kids is waiting to hit cage. They are big, six feet and taller, the bench is too small for all of them but they squeeze together, doing their best to look cooperative in preseason grunge of goatees, pimples, baggy shorts and sagging socks— overgrown adolescence concentrated as ammonia. These are not men yet, don't have the smoothness of men, the knowledge and confidence of men, they can't see beyond their own strike zones, or what their agents put before their eyes—they don't have the global picture, as a man would have, like Joe. Cassidy strides past with *"Hihowyadoin?"* but none of them will meet her gaze. Only in baseball is the quaint custom preserved of looking you in the chest, not the eyes.

Even during a three-second pass-by Cassidy cannot resist checking out the hitter—looking to make Double A this year by the way he's trying to hit the cover off the ball. All that separates her from the deadly arc of the bat is a rope curtain. She registers again how instinctual it is, the swing, how brutal, forceful and primitive. The hitter steps and connects. Sound explodes in the enclosed space.

When the regular season starts this corridor will be closed off and heavily guarded, but now there is free passage from the cage to the bull pen where the sun glares off the smooth blue walls as if they were sheet metal.

"Just throw soft," a pitching coach is saying—white hair, skinny legs, buttless—but even soft you can hear the whistle on the ball. A few spectators lean over the seats. A video camera. The omnipresent dad.

Cassidy opens the gate to the playing field and enters ballpark space. The red dirt track is mealy from three days of heavy rain. Skirting wheelbarrows and sandbags, she makes the long walk toward first base, where, on a patch of dry between orange stanchions, half a dozen two-man teams play catch. Raymond and LAPD Detective Mark Simms, both conspicuous in civilian clothes, have pulled Cruz out of practice, talking to him close and low. He gestures, dismissive, impatient to get back on the field, but they keep him shouldered in.

Cassidy goes forward and backward at the same time, impelled toward the tight little trio while simultaneously drawing what comfort she can from the stories of empty seats, a buffer against the dread of getting there.

It goes way back, this profound security of being on a diamond, to being carried by her father through a crowd of giants dressed in white, over the green grass. She was high up, safe, part of him and the exhilaration and privilege of being the one for whom all that benevolence came radiating from the fans. Astride his shoulders, she would wave unabashedly. Or throw on the track with her brother Gregg, who, at eight, was destined to be a star. He had a crew cut like his dad, and Smoke's strong, flexible body and a serious focus you don't see that young. His fine boy's cheeks were usually scarlet, wet with perspiration or hose water. He owned first base, mature, taking care of business. Cassidy was the little sister with an arm, freakish and cute, a pregame sideshow attraction.

They lived in a run-down blue Victorian on a hill (before it was designated the "Historic District") in Ashland, Oregon (before real estate prices tripled). The casement window in Cassidy's old room had been generous—not like those energy-efficient sliders Maggie put in after Smoke died and she remarried and turned the place into a B&B—big enough so children could climb right through to the airy secret world of the back-porch roof.

Cassidy always remembers the irony, that Gregg had been doing her a favor for once, gathering leaves from the rain gutter for her doll's soup. There he was, poised at the edge of the roof in tendrils of trumpet vine, late summer light showing through the hot red membranes of his ears. Too good a target. Cassidy—strong enough at four to ride a two-wheeler and sock a ball—had slid confidently down the shingles and popped him into space. A delicious sweetness burst from the base of her tongue. She never forgot the illicit taste.

Games, all kinds of games, were a way of life in the Sanderson house—poker, pickle—arguments resolved by contest. If you won the toss, the race, the mumblety-peg, rope swing, thumb wrestle, breath hold, sit-ups-per-minute, if, in water polo, you drowned your sister, then you had made your point, and you were right.

The game of baseball was the creed by which they lived, the stadium their personal and public shrine. Maggie would be down there making jokes with the ushers, and Smoke would be signing balls, and that's who they were in 1964, that family, moving through that moment in time.

Later on, when things went bad for that family, the only place that still made any sense at all was the ball field, and that's why Cassidy came to live more and more within the white lines, where events are orderly and nothing happens that cannot be explained in a book of rules.

The men look over, guarded, as she joins them.

Simms says, "We have a situation."

Raymond says, "Let's talk about this," and leads them into the empty dugout.

It can be a thrill to sit on the same comfortless hard cushions as the multimillion-dollar stars, but Alberto refuses, putting one foot, then the other, up and down on the step like he's doing aerobics. Raymond and Simms have assumed the spread-leg stance, two spans on a bridge; only Cassidy sinks onto the bench.

"What's going on?"

"Alberto got another threat."

"Does this have to do with the videotape?"

"You heard."

"A little, from Dulce. But she was too freaked to really tell me." Cassidy looks questioningly at each but no one wants to speak. "What was it?"

Finally it falls to Simms.

"A dead woman laid out on a cot in a shack. We're assuming this is in the DR. It looks as if someone beat out her brains with a baseball bat. There are candles and bottles and crap all around her like they've made some kind of altar. Human skulls. Crosses wrapped in chains. A man wearing a ski mask rubs the body with what looks like blood. Then, basically, he ejaculates."

"Is this supposed to be real?"

Raymond snorts and looks away.

"The film?" Simms gives her the blank cop blink. "Yeah. It's a *real dead woman with her head beat in*. And there's a message, which I'm not at liberty to quote, but it's basically the same as the notes."

Cassidy: "Alberto, have you seen this?"

Alberto has been looking at the field and muttering in Spanish.

Simms answers for him, "He wasn't able to identify the victim."

Raymond: "Kind of hard when she doesn't have a face."

"They beat her up as a threat?"

"Looks that way."

Cassidy whispers, "Guys, it's ten thousand dollars. Why don't we just freaking pay?"

"Against policy."

"That's just stupid—" But she stops, thinking of Joe, and then because Alberto's head is bent and tears are falling to the ground in two pale columns.

"*Chico*," she says softly, and starts toward him but Simms blocks the way.

"Tell us about it, Alberto. You'll feel better."

"*Him?*" says Cassidy incredulously. "He has nothing to say."

"Let Alberto answer."

"We're all on the same side," the scouting director puts in.

"How I play? How I play with this?" Alberto pounds his forehead.

Cassidy: "It's not your fault."

Simms: "Here's how: You tell us who talked to you, who pressured you, put you in this position."

"I know nothing!"

"Drug dealers have the power." Alberto is bent over. Simms has a hand on his back. "They make you do things you don't want to do. They start small. Threaten your family. It goes from there. But you know what? We can take the power. You and me, working together, we can take the power away."

Simms's hand, hovering, tightens into a fist.

"Somebody don't want me to play ball. That all I know."

Alberto straightens, wiping his eyes.

"Screw 'em," Raymond says suddenly. "Get out there."

"For real I can go?"

Raymond jerks a thumb toward the field. Alberto is gone.

Simms cocks his head at Raymond. "Why did you do that?"

Raymond replies, "He's a good kid," and Cassidy wants to hug his big bear chest.

Simms: "I didn't say he wasn't good, I said, Maybe they got to him. Maybe they said they'd kill his mother and rape his sister, so he sticks a bunch of cocaine down his throat, delivers it to Los Angeles, swears he'll never do it again. Then it's, Too bad, sucker, we've got this on you, pay or you're history."

Raymond considers. "I don't think so."

"You don't."

"I have pretty good instincts about these boys."

"And I've been working narcotics seventeen years."

Simms scrapes one muddy boot on the step.

"No question in my mind, when we get to the bottom of this extortion thing it'll be about drugs. Has to. Nothing else that big could be at stake. Besides, you've got a whole new drug route going through the Dominican. The Colombian drug lords used to be in bed with the Mexicans but that ain't happening because the Mexicans started taking the business, so the Colombians went to the DR—it's a joke down there. Security is so lax they've got people at the airport fixing the X-ray machines. And they've penetrated this country so now Dominican drug traffickers are operating the east coast all the way the hell up to Maine."

"That's not Alberto."

"This town of Nagua, where the notes allegedly came from—?"

"Did you find out who owns the post office box?"

"We're working on that. It's the biggest port of export of illicit cargo on the island—I'm talking human illegals as well as heroin and cocaine—because of its geographical location. Say that's circumstantial. But this tape. I gotta tell you"—Simms shakes his head—"it's a similar—technique—if you want to call it that—we see drug dealers using to influence the common folk all across the Caribbean. Those spirit bottles, like the one they left in your car, that can be a legitimate religion, I checked it out, but the dealers use them for intimidation."

Shadows have been thrown across the infield. It has become chilly in the dugout, Cassidy's hands are cold and stiff. The kids are playing pepper, Alberto among them. Their shouts echo percussively in the empty bowl, while underneath, like a drone, come the scraping of shovels and the thrum of a riding mower.

Raymond: "Alberto needs protection."

"Yes, and frankly? I have concern for the other players. I would recommend removing him."

"No!" says Cassidy, jumping up. "If you're talking about sending him home, you *can't*. This is his shot! You wouldn't back off a starter who got the same threats, you can't just back off Cruz because he's a kid and he's cheap. *Raymond?*"

Raymond steps out of the dugout. They follow into the brightness of late afternoon. Farther away, where the sun hits the outfield, small waves of heat are steaming off the grass. At their feet are deep squooshy puddles in which float fat pink worms.

"Raymond," begs Cassidy, "we brought him here. We made a commitment."

Raymond looks at his watch.

"What if we got him out of LA?"

"That would help."

"We can ship him out to Vero early—"

He and Simms are walking away.

"The victim—" Cassidy is running after them— "can't anyone down there identify her?"

"Down exactly where? We don't know if it *is* the DR, we don't even know how she was killed."

"You said she was beat up with a baseball bat."

"I said it *looked* that way."

"She's covered with mud," Raymond explains.

"Like a human balloon covered with mud. You've seen the Thanksgiving Day parade?"

"Mark!"

"In scientific terms, okay? The body is bloated from lying out in the open," Simms says, "and parasites have begun the natural process of decay. We're going to have a hell of a time even coming up with cause of death. The country was hit with a hurricane. There were mud slides and floods and God knows what. She could have been killed a hundred different ways. Hard to make a determination when you can't examine the body or the scene."

Raymond has been thinking. "So it's possible these guys—jealous rivals, drug dealers, or whatnot—found some messed-up body and said, This is cool! Let's drag it to the house and use it to terrorize Cruz?"

Simms: "Told you they were amateurs."

Raymond shakes his head. "Seems a little out there."

"The lab is on it."

Cassidy has been walking along with a brisk gait, as if she were simply an interested spectator.

"Could you really know the cause of death if all you have is a tape?"

"It's been done," says Simms, impatient now. "We're already into the high-tech stuff, sent the tape to the top guy in digital forensics. Also, to a special unit of the FBI."

12

Cassidy has been waiting on the sidewalk outside the club level for twenty-five minutes, nodding hello to every publicist, account manager, receptionist, community relations person, human resources assistant, gardener, archivist and interpreter going in or out of the stadium, while pacing back and forth in front of the entrance like a demented troll on a cuckoo clock.

Finally Joe appears across the parking lot at a lope, tall, one hand outstretched, head bent at an apologetic tilt. The sight of him only tightens her gut.

"I apologize for keeping you waiting. Some guy made me park way over there."

"Tall gentleman in a golf cart? Resembles a large grasshopper?"

"We had words. The whole place is empty, I don't get it."

"No one does."

Joe is wearing one of his million-dollar double-breasted suits, pale chalk stripes on navy, a silk satin tie. The discreet ovals of the sunglasses seem aggressively small for his face, as if wanting to make a statement about the character of the decisive nose and lean cheeks, that they are unrepentant. The glasses are jet black as his hair, although now, in the sun, she discovers reddish highlights. Was Harvey Weissman serious? Does he really dye it?

"This is what I mean about Dodger Stadium."

Joe has hands on hips, looking at the blue facade.

"It's an understatement."

Cassidy pulls a bottle of spring water from her backpack.

"—See, that's what I call 'thin' construction. No masonry, no concrete—all metal. Typical of the early sixties, but not enough great stuff going on. It's not . . . entertaining." He squints. "More like the back entrance to a warehouse."

The water is lukewarm. She closes her eyes and chugs half.

"It fries me when people want to put Dodger Stadium on the National Historic Register. The building is a shrine, I know, it creates memories and a sense of pride—but you can't say it's architecturally significant." The ovals come back to Cassidy. "Did you want to go home and change?"

"Sorry," glancing down at her mud-stained khakis, "I meant to. I was going to. But something's come up."

Joe looks perplexed. "Do you need to cancel?"

Just then the clubhouse attendant, Doc Ramsey, strolls by with a wave. Out of uniform, wearing a cardigan sweater and wire-rims, he looks like an affable librarian. Who doesn't miss a trick.

"We have to go someplace and talk."

They trudge up a rise through the empty parking lot where the Bentley is a small and arbitrary object in three hundred acres of sun glare.

They get in. The doors seal shut with a heavy exhale.

"What's the problem?"

Joe's tone is suddenly cautious. They haven't touched. This is hardly the reunion Cassidy had been imagining in the shower all week.

"It has to do with you, me and Alberto."

"You have a very unusual face," says Joe. "It can take all kinds of light, did you know that?" He's leaning away from her, slumped against the door. "But go ahead."

Her hands are clasped over her stomach as if to contain the ache in her bowel.

"I think I know the reason for the blackmail notes and I hope to God I'm wrong."

Joe is still.

Her throat closes up. She has to get the water bottle out.

"Remember how we talked about, when we were driving, Alberto clipped a horse? I don't think it was a horse and I don't think he clipped it. I'm afraid it was a person. A woman." Her voice almost evaporates. "And she died."

Cassidy sobs once, clamps a hand over her mouth.

Slowly Joe sits up. He strokes her hair, then the strength seems to go out of his arm.

"What makes you think that?"

"The blackmailer sent a videotape to the house in LA where Alberto is staying."

"They know where he lives?"

"They must. They've been following him."

Her eyes skim the palm trees at the far edge of the property, focus on a metallic haze going all the way out to the desert.

"What was the tape?"

"It was a female, bloated up and covered with mud so she couldn't be identified. I didn't see it but they said her head looked like it was bashed in with a baseball bat. They don't really know how she was killed"—her voice hits a note of hysteria—"she could just as well have been run over by a car—"

"Shhh. Calm down. Where is the tape?"

"The cops have it. I was just in there. It makes perfect sense, Joe, that's what ties us together, we were all in the car, that's the reason they'd—"

"Okay."

"There was another threat on the tape, like, if you don't pay, this will happen to you. Or your mother or your sister, I don't know. They may have no idea this is the actual woman we killed."

"First of all, *we* didn't kill her—"

"We certainly were in the car. And we certainly were drunk. That's going to be the closer." She rubs her scalp at the temples. "Am I crazy? Could this have really happened? Could he have killed someone and left her in the rain?"

"If anything, it was a tragic accident," says Joe thoughtfully. "It was pitch-dark, a blinding downpour, you couldn't see a thing. You don't remember?"

"I was out of it."

"We hit something. We did a three-sixty—"

"All I know is waking up on the floor of the backseat, staring at a little plastic dog that was under there, and realizing I was swallowing my own blood."

"Let me reconstruct this as best I can. I wasn't thinking too clearly myself."

Joe speaks slowly. His eyebrows knit, eyes shut.

"Alberto wanted to see what happened. I said, Forget it, we're in the middle of a hurricane. He got out anyway, out the driver's side, and I stayed in front. When he came back he looked like he'd taken a shower in his clothes. He said he'd hit this pony but there was nothing we could do, it ran away into the field. The left headlamp was gone to hell but basically the car was okay, so I dropped him off somewhere, some relative's house, and drove you back to the resort."

"Is that why we didn't sleep together? Was I really gross?"

"No, darling, you were a delightful drunk."

"Is that a joke?"

"Let's say neither one of us was at our best."

A sense memory comes back to Cassidy: the stinky wet floor mat against her cheek. She can see, in macro close-up, a small plastic Dalmatian that must have belonged to Nora's daughter, lying on its side. It had a smile.

Joe is shaking his head. "I'm still not convinced this woman, rest her soul, has to do with the extortion. How did they know it was us in the car?"

"Somebody saw the accident."

"There was nobody out there and nothing but cane."

"We don't know who was out there," Cassidy replies. "It was dark and pouring rain."

"Why didn't they threaten you?"

"*Me?* I don't have money. He's the big league player. You're the rich American. I'm the girl."

"If he really did this, if it's true," says Joe, "we're all fucked."

Silence is a wonderful thing. You can slip into it like a hammock and float.

Cassidy lays her neck back on the headrest. Maybe she'll take a sunbath.

Joe: "Now what?"

"I'll talk to Alberto." She doesn't open her eyes.

"When?"

"I'm leaving for Vero Beach on Saturday."

Suddenly they are in each other's arms.

"She's a person. With a family. What if we killed her?" whispers Cassidy. "How can we live with that?"

"We'll make it right. Whatever we have to do. Even if it means giving up our illusions about a kid I know we really care about."

Cassidy's arms tighten around his neck.

"He couldn't have done such a thing."

"Desperate times."

Desperately poor young boys will do anything to get off the island. Alberto told her that.

It seems they have been sitting for a long time in the open car, the light reflecting off the bowl of Chavez Ravine like a telescope dish. Joe's forehead has become a burnished red. He presses a button and the roof performs a complicated choreography, enfolding them in privacy.

"I have to tell my boss."

"Tell him what?"

"That Alberto killed somebody."

"Not yet."

"Joe, I don't think I can handle this alone."

"You're not alone."

They kiss.

"We're amazing together," says Joe.

They kiss again. They haven't gotten tired of it.

MARCH

13

Two little touches always make her heart sing whenever Cassidy returns to Dodgertown.

One is the baseball lights—white globes hand-painted with jolly red stitching that sit on top of black posts along the walkways winding through the campus-like grounds—playful reminders of why everybody's there, reassuring as a child's night-light in the dark. Cassidy loves those baseball lights. Few things in life have a purpose so plain and yet so completely fulfilled.

The other is the Hall of Fame, a corridor in the administration building where great moments in Dodger history have been captured in a series of massively enlarged period photographs. How can she pass Jackie Robinson's imperial face, or "Roy Campanella tags Spider Jorgenson out as Billy Cox looks on," without an uplifting sense of hope?

Especially when outside the sun is bursting with the sweetness of a perfect Gulf morning—tamer than the Caribbean, more luxuriantly moist than California—lulling you into a pregnant balmy state of mind, dreaming what is to be born; while inside this cool dim passageway the fecund breakfasty reek of coffee and warm maple syrup and the clatter of good-natured talk still breeze from the dining room as Cassidy moves along in a pleasant wash of greetings from members of the far-flung Dodger family—Triple A coaches and Vero Beach administrative assistants, big-league starters, sportswriters, publicists, legendary scouts, Sandy Koufax himself—all of it, all of them, new as spring.

And waiting at the far end of the corridor, backlit in the doorway like a ghost at the end of that dark tunnel in an out-of-body experience, is Pedro Pedrillo with arms open wide.

She hurries to his strong embrace, breathing in the reassuring cedary scent of cigars.

"God, I'm glad to see you."

He plants a kiss on her hair. "Come on, we got a lot of boys to see."

As they walk outside she asks, "How was the drive from Miami?"

"Boring!" Pedro complains. "You drive and drive and what do you see? Nothing. A lot of green. But Rhonda is happy to make a visit to the grandchildren."

"Do you have pictures?"

"Sure I got."

He pats his briefcase. He is wearing a tropical weave Panama hat and a blue satin Dodger jacket (so is Cassidy), and the moment they hit the gusty paddock where a crowd of fans has gathered on the other side of a yellow rope waiting for autographs—now turning eagerly to see if these two are worth something—they both affect the baseball man's stare: a look of pure disdain that refuses to make eye contact, aimed just above the shoulder at a higher cause than you.

"Seen Cruz?"

"Not yet." Cassidy unfolds a training schedule.

"You talk with Hoot about him?"

"No."

"He's not playing his game."

Her stomach goes bad.

"Why?"

Pedro's stare sharpens toward the playing fields. "We gonna find out."

Suddenly from behind them comes the rhythmic tromp of cleats as a squad of minor leaguers in crisp blue shirts and clean white pants trots out of the clubhouse to the batting cages while the fans call out to the coaches, some of them retired big-league stars.

A twenty-something with wavy blonde hair down to her skimpy lingerie shorts rubs up against a white-haired grandpa who used to play for Boston.

"Will you be my coach?" she purrs.

"Sure." He winks and signs a faded baseball card older than she is. "I'm a great coach."

Cassidy says to Pedro, "It's the uniform."

They thread their way through the crowd, past the Old Lady in the Lawn Chair who calls out familiarly to players by their numbers, "Hello, Nine. How's that new baby?" and the Cat in the Hat, a lost-looking young woman wearing six or seven Dodger caps stacked on top of each other, and the Pear, universally despised not only because of his pin head and wide mushy hips but because of the fat loose-leaf folders filled with multiple cards he aggressively demands to be signed, for profit at trading shows.

The leather-skinned security guards, who have been eating baseballs for breakfast the past forty years, keep a close eye on the Pear.

"What exactly are you hearing about Alberto?"

By his silence Cassidy recognizes Pedro has already heard a great deal, in the locker room, the strings, in certain bars and pasta joints in town she doesn't even know about, casual talk among coaches and scouts filled with richness she as a woman will never have access to, and that's the way it is.

"Don't make me find out at a staff meeting."

Pedro considers this. Finally, as they near the field, he reluctantly explains that some of the coaches do not believe Alberto has the "maturity" to play in the major leagues.

"He comes here with a certain buildup. So the coaches are maybe a little disappointed."

"What do they say?"

"They say, 'I know you told me about this guy but what I *hear* and what he *is* are two different things.'"

"He has the tools," Cassidy objects.

"He does have the tools, no question, but he is not making the adjustment," Pedro replies steadily. He has had a long life in this game.

"Adjustment to what?"

"Being a professional. Living in the United States."

"Do they have any idea the kind of pressure he's under?"

"Hoot says he talks about how he is worried for his family. The mill is gone in the storm and there are no jobs. And naturally, aside from those things, he is concerned about making the cut, the same as every kid."

"It isn't only that—"

"They heard about the blackmail letters but you can only take it so far. They ain't gonna care about his problems until Alberto shows to them the kind of ballplayer you and I know he can be."

Cassidy struggles with it. She promised Joe she would tell no one about what Alberto might have done. But Pedro is here beside her now;

even while they are talking business, she can feel the power of his belief in her—a belief that got her through the bad years and brought her back to the game, and most likely would not falter now if she confessed to the bewildering ache in her heart over this boy.

So she tells Pedro about the accident and the woman on the videotape and he keeps striding along, head up, eyes straight, no reaction, as if they were talking free agents and draft picks.

"Alberto's got to be going nuts inside. If he really killed her, Uncle Pedro, this isn't about a kid with an adjustment problem, it's a serious mess and Raymond will go through the roof, this will go straight to the top—"

Pedro squeezes her arm. "Don't get yourself upset."

"I'm very upset—"

"We don't know nothing."

"That's what Joe said."

"Who is Joe?"

"The guy I met who owns the car we were driving in. He has to be kept out of this. You can't mention his name."

"What do I care about any kind of *Joe*? I care about *my kids*. I don't believe my kid could do what you say."

"Well he sure hit *something*, big enough to send me flying, almost break my nose—"

"He says it was a pony, I believe him."

"You believe him."

"Cassie, I been looking at boys almost thirty years. I'm not always right about where they end up, but with Cruz, I know he's got the good face. You know it, too. You saw with your eyes."

"Then why do these people, whoever they are, say he did this?"

"You're very nervous right now. When you're nervous, you don't sleep, your mind goes all over the world. You think Alberto hit this poor woman and someone saw and now they want money. I think you are putting two things together that don't belong. Alberto could not live with this on his shoulder."

"He didn't hit her?"

"No, I will bet money she was killed in the hurricane, like you said, and now some bastard wants to blame this tragedy on our boy. They got these scams all the time in the Dominican—"

Cassidy remembers the blank tapes and switched cigars.

"—They're trying to scare him so he'll pay."

"Then we have to prove he's innocent."

"We don't have to prove nothing. Relax, the police gonna figure it out. A reporter who was interviewing me one time said, 'The way you care for these boys is like a priest.' I laughed. I said, 'It is my job to get them to the church. The rest is up to the Holy Father.' Come on, we gonna understand a lot more when we see Alberto play."

Scrimmage is in progress as Cassidy and Pedro sit on the bench next to Hoot Hawkins, an African-American outfield coach who played three years in Triple A until tearing out his knee. Hoot is holding a stopwatch and making notes next to players' names on a roster with a very sharp pencil. Two other coaches stand at first and third like sentinels in their blue jackets, arms folded, expressionless, surveying every player in the shrewd unblinking crossbeam of their stares.

Cassidy watches, motionless as the rest. There is a way the pros watch ball and it has to do with becoming a rock, a slow process of petrifaction that takes place over twenty-five or thirty years of sitting on narrow bleachers, in windy biting springs, in drop-dead summers and cold wet falls, and never once giving anything away. Cassidy has learned not to hunch the shoulders in frustration or twist the hips in joy, certainly not to jump up and shout, "*Get in the game!*" even as it becomes increasingly difficult to retain the demeanor of a chunk of anthracite while watching with distress as Alberto Cruz takes three strikes in a row and goes down without lifting the bat.

Nobody says anything.

Alberto stalks out to right field and stands there practicing the swing as if he were all alone in the world.

Hoot makes a note on the roster in tiny handwriting.

"Ted Williams used to do that," Cassidy remarks casually. "If he had a bad at-bat he'd swing away out in the field, try to get it right."

Hoot takes a small metal pencil sharpener out of a pocket, not seeming to hear.

Meanwhile, because he is preoccupied (apparently talking to himself), Alberto fails to notice the dugout is waving him over. Therefore he is out of position when the ball is hit. Cassidy could close her eyes and see the rest: see him charge the ball and try to pick it up like a shortstop, see him make the superhero throw to third instead of hitting the cutoff man, see a straightforward play become a 'tweener that doesn't do anybody any good.

"Reaction time is bad," mutters Pedro.

"Who? Cruz?" Hoot grinds the pencil with deliberation. "Yeah."

Yellow curls of wood fall slowly to the grass. Twenty other prospects are showing their stuff and it is impossible not to get caught up in the drama of the ticking clock as they move toward the end of spring training and the weakest are eliminated, a few more every day, sent to the farm director's office for a fatherly talk and a plane ticket home. Cassidy's attention goes to the third baseman from Placentia, California, seventh pick in the draft. To the Filipino catcher who drove in 21 runs in 11 games. She slides a bound scouting report from her backpack and becomes engrossed in matching stats with the faces of kids she hasn't yet seen—surprised to find practice suddenly over and Pedro down the first base line talking to Cruz.

"I can play better," Alberto is saying in Spanish when she joins them.

He shakes hands with Cassidy, brushing her briefly with his eyes, then lowers his head.

"We know you can," Pedro assures him.

"Concentration," Cassidy prompts. "Mental toughness. Remember how we talked about that?"

"Yes."

A warning siren starts to warble in her head. Alberto Cruz does not look like a prospect. The Midwest kids, the California kids, are pumped up and confident and Alberto's shoulders are slumped. He hasn't gained weight, in fact in the week or so since she's seen him he looks even thinner, as if that spirit bottle had worked its evil magic. She has the real and terrifying sense of life force slipping away.

"All right!"

Pedro claps his hands and Cassidy knows he has seen it, too.

"Tonight we gonna take you out to dinner and have a good meal and relax and talk about what's happening and what's gonna happen. You are too good a player to let the pressure get to you."

Alberto ventures a look at Cassidy. There are hollows beneath his eyes.

"Great idea," she agrees vigorously.

The squad is trotting off to the indoor batting cages.

"Later," mumbles Alberto.

They watch his skinny butt blend in with the flashing whites of the departing troops.

Pedro: "I don't like the way he looks."

"He does not look good."

"Hoot said he collapsed on the field."

"No! What happened?"

"He fell down."

"I mean, what *happened*?"

"He got dehydrated. Electrolyte imbalance. What's the matter?"

"That's exactly what happened to Gregg when he got sick the first time."

"It's not the same thing."

"He fell down on the first base line and couldn't breathe."

"Stop it now." A hand on her shoulder. "Cruz has the stomach flu. It's not the same."

They walk through the quiet industry of the camp.

"Do you realize Gregg's been gone almost twenty years?"

"Can't be."

"Right now he'd be retiring from his major league career . . ."

"Not your brother. He would have gone to college, gotten a couple graduate degrees—"

Cassidy takes in the sunny fields.

"No," she says softly. "He would be here."

Six diamonds. Batting practice and bull pens. Running and stretching. The ancient crack of leather on ash, the timeless cries, *"That's the baby! Good hands! Good hands! Look at that! OH, what a play!"* sometimes one squad in a circle rolling on their backs, sometimes jogging by in twos and threes, occasionally the whole parade, two hundred young men in one long spread-out pack lapping it around the big green, all of it working from a deep sense of tradition like a fine old military academy.

Pedro takes a deep breath off the fresh breeze: crushed grass and salt spray.

"Some things haven't changed since your dad and I were here for spring training. We used to rent two little bungalows way back in there—"

At the edge of the camp you can see a patch of shady residential streets.

"I remember that bungalow. I was five so Gregg had to be nine. He played with your Carlos and Migue. Was Esteban even born?"

"He was a baby."

"I have a vague picture in my mind of you and Rhonda and my parents doing the cha-cha on the patio."

"Oh, sure. Those were good times."

They walk in silence. Cassidy takes Pedro's hand.

"I miss them both so much."

He squeezes her fingers. She returns the squeeze gratefully.

"Don't worry, your dad and your brother are up there right now, playing catch, and your dad is yelling, '*Concentration should be effortless!*'"

Cassidy wipes at her eyes.

Outside the clubhouse the crowd of autograph seekers has grown thick. The Dodgers face the Mets at Holman Stadium in half an hour and the Pear is holding up the line by shoving card after card under the nose of Hideo Nomo, who is applying great mental toughness in his resolve to ignore a tightening circle of belligerent Asian camera crews.

Someone is calling her name, high-pitched and sweet, the voice of an angel.

"*Cass-i-dy! Cass-i-dy!*"

She looks down. There, at her waist, is an eleven-year-old girl.

"Would you sign my baseball card?"

"Don't worry about Cruz," says Pedro. "We gonna straighten him out," and hurries toward the clubhouse.

The girl squints up at Cassidy, one eye closed against the sun. She is wearing a T-shirt that says L'il Sharpshooters.

Cassidy squats, looking for the small face beneath a bill of kelly green.

"You play softball?"

"BobbySox League."

"Where?"

"Springs, Nevada. I followed your career, I read about you on the sports page. How you became a scout."

"Really?"

"You were always my favorite player."

Cassidy takes the silky still-fresh card in her hand. CASSIDY SANDERSON, it says on a banner across the bottom, Colorado Silver Bullets. She looks at a photo of herself in red and gray: bent at the waist and low, glove down, both hands well out in front of the body, eyes focused on the hop, textbook breakdown position. Long body, precise angles, all in motion. The quads are tight, and the cords in her neck. She remembers the feeling: indestructible.

"Which do you like better?" asks the girl. "Softball or hardball?"

"I love softball. But hardball is the game I wanted to play. What about you?"

"Softball is good for me," she pronounces matter-of-factly.

Amused, "What position?"

"Center field. I'm small but I'm fast. Our team made the playoffs, but we lost the last game by one lousy little run. We tried too hard."

"Trying too hard is just as bad as not trying at all."

It's Coach Dad, standing behind his daughter, wearing the same kelly-green shirt and shorts but with a carefully groomed brush mustache. Cassidy has to remind herself not all these guys are assholes.

"Your team deserves credit," she says. "Tough to have a loser in a situation like that."

She signs her name.

"When I grow up," says the girl with assurance, "I want to be like you."

Cassidy pauses in reply. Coach Dad pipes up with how he's always been a Dodgers fan, there's a rookie he knows from Nevada they should keep an eye on, and it's great to get away from the snow. Cassidy finds herself in another place entirely, entranced by the girl's pure blue eyes. Clear as the sky. No static. No history. No pain.

She used to be that little girl, wearing a baseball cap with a long ash-blonde ponytail down her back. Back then there hadn't been a softball league for girls (not enough girls for a team even in junior high), so there she was, holding her mother's hand on the sideline, waiting to try out for boys' Little League.

She had been taken to her brother's games since she was a toddler, penned inside a portable chicken fence while Smoke had coached and Maggie worked the hot dog stand. She had grown up biking and skateboarding with her brother's friends, and when she was seven she and another girl, D. J. Reed, spent the summer playing baseball with the dirty-faced ripped-in-the-knees neighborhood scrappers. You didn't need anyone's *permission* to play, the game was out there like open territory to be claimed, democratic as America. Besides, they needed the girls to make up two teams.

But during that tryout every one of those pals from the neighborhood was on the field shagging flies and running bases except Cassidy, who kept close to her mother, knowing something was wrong. The coach, a rooster-ish opinionated little man with the sideburns of the day and a big mustache like Li'l Sharpshooter's dad, had been yapping aggressively that it was league rules—girls were not even allowed to pick up a bat and try. "She'll get hurt." "How would it look?" "These boys are here to play a serious game." "You don't understand." "There's a reason we have regulations." "She doesn't have the skills. She'll slow down the play—"

And Cassidy had felt ashamed. For herself and her mother (why did Maggie have to wear those overalls and Swedish clogs?), as if, by simply walking out onto the field, they had committed a repugnant act. Girls, she realized, must be pretty worthless, even loathsome compared to boys, who were unquestionably entitled to everything—even the scrawniest, most spastic, weak, dumb and talentless among them.

Then it got all mixed up with Gregg. After he was diagnosed with cystic fibrosis at age fifteen (they had thought it was asthma), everyday playfulness in the Sanderson family gave way to a state of siege. Strange machinery and odd routines moved into their lives. Brown bottles of enzymes. Vaporizers. Inhalers. Oxygen delivered to the home. At that time, before lung transplants and gene therapy, the life expectancy for a person with CF was eighteen years of age. It was unthinkable that Gregg, a star athlete, Smoke Sanderson's son, might not live to see his twentieth birthday, but twice that year he was hospitalized with infections and the chest physical therapy he needed at home every day consumed the family. Smoke's initial stoicism eroded, giving way to a hard, impenetrable anger; once he stopped the car in the middle of the hospital parking lot, said nothing, got out, and walked ten miles back to the house. Maggie marched around to the driver's side determined to take control. Instead, she put her forehead down on the steering wheel and sobbed.

Gregg was the one who said, "Come on, Mom. I haven't been dealt the worst hand."

It was Gregg who insisted Cassidy was good enough to play with the boys, even though she was his annoying little sister. When they chose up sides, he'd always pick her first—a feeling of specialness Cassidy has carried to the ball field ever since.

Eventually her parents filed a legal complaint with the National Little League.

Cassidy was put on the roster.

"My son could be a professional ballplayer," the father of a twelve-year-old once told Maggie. "Your girl is taking a spot on the team."

She was teased, booed, boob-tagged, ignored, slashed with a razor blade by the catcher's girlfriend, hit by the pitcher, put out in right field or kept on the bench. She once hit a triple that won the game and the coach yelled, *"Don't look at the ball, look at the coach!"* She took the punishment with nothing but an abiding, blue-eyed stare. It hadn't been until much later, with Gregg and Smoke both gone, that she had been sitting on a barstool in Papa's and seen a story on ESPN about the all-women Colorado Silver Bullets. She had called Maggie up at one in the morning and said, "Mom, there's a chance I can play baseball," and she and her mother both cried.

"Work hard," she tells L'il Sharpshooter. "Never lose the feeling of happiness."

They say in sports you always play for someone. Mom or dad or coach. Cassidy's eyes follow the girl and her father into the crowd as another mix of faces comes to view, farmland faces with white skin, turned-up noses, strawberry hair, tank tops showing fleshy arms—4-H kids, cowboys, ski team, stoners—the memory of taking the field for the Grizzlies high school intramural softball team, of not even having to turn around to know Gregg was in his usual seat to the left of the plate, but to feel him in her chest reverberating with the cheers, to understand for whom she'd stuck it out.

She played for her brother, for all the reasons you would suppose, but also because in those spring days, when you could open any window and smell apple blossom flooding the valley, she had not yet known to love her own gift.

14

Late that afternoon Cassidy goes for a run on the track that follows the perimeter of the camp. Only a couple of players are out there; most are wiped after a week of nonstop pressure, back in their rooms cooling out for a western barbecue the O'Malleys are putting on tonight. On the second lap, on impulse, she veers out the gate toward the neighborhood where thirty years ago the Sanderson and Pedrillo families rented houses on the same street.

Pedro had been right about the drive up from Miami, all you could see from the interstate were factories and malls and flat open land. Turning off Route 60, past flimsy motels and fast food drive-throughs with cartoony playground equipment, you wind into the town of Vero Beach. The scale of things suddenly goes conservative and small and you find yourself driving more leisurely, as if slowed by the heavy southern air, peering down shade-tunneled residential streets where life seems contained and known.

Cassidy jogs through a high-end section, raw stucco redos with luxury cars in the driveways, working up to a seventy-five-percent effort, crushing beneath her feet tiny round flowers from the buttonwood trees that line the avenue. She passes a municipal park where half a dozen little kids have gathered around a tall thin good-looking young man who, despite the nondescript tank shirt and baggy shorts, must be a Dodger, one of the young lords from behind the gates.

The light has gone weak, the tropical air taken on a chill. Only one old guy is watching the children in the park, from way up in the empty bleachers, a bearded grandpa wearing white. The Dodger has an arm around a paunchy eight-year-old, squaring him to the plate, hands on his, bringing the bat back together and whipping it around—*extension*—then having to hang on to the kid so he doesn't go flying down the third base line with the force of real, big-league power.

In a flash as she goes by, Cassidy recognizes the player is Alberto.

He could be kicking back in his room. Doing extra work in the cage. Instead he's out there coaching kids he'll never see again. She thinks about the packs of boys in the Dominican—boys everywhere—from the airport to an empty field outside Micheli Stadium where they had been mimicking the game in progress with gloves made of cereal boxes; boys with no place else to be except in the heat of the developing play. Far from home, her kid is giving something back, even to these working-class children of Vero Beach.

Does that mean he is incapable, also, of the most ruthless abandonment?

She continues down a funky block of pink duplexes and white single-family homes with scalloped metal awnings from the forties. There's the little market with its damp sawdust smell where she stopped when she first hit town, thirsty, compelled to buy a Coke and half a pound of fat cooked shrimp with hot sauce for four bucks; sensations teased from the edge of memory by shelves full of huge sacks of rice, boiled peanuts in cans, gumbo and grits, biscuit mix and homemade pies.

It is the women's world of spring training she remembers, a safe and secret club created by the wives. First thing in the morning, she would put on a bathing suit, then walk through this exotic fragrant hush to Rhonda's, holding Maggie's hand. Mother and daughter were like tender lovers, then, faces always close, gazing into each other's eyes. TO: MOMMY, FROM: CASSIDY, she'd write on drawings of rainbows and hearts—quick sweet kisses on the lips, reading books by flashlight and falling asleep with an arm over Maggie's neck, in absolute trust that nothing in this world would ever separate them.

By nine a.m. the Dodger wives would have gathered at Rhonda's bungalow in their swank terry cover-ups and gold lamé mules, young soft willows like Miss Americas in the swimsuit competition. There would be cigarette smoke and the antiseptic scent of lemons for their Bloody Marys, noisy shoptalk sharp as the men's. It was an alternate baseball world, a sorority of fierce loyalties, where Cassidy, at five, felt accepted and in bliss—playing in the backyard pool all day, receiving special favors from the queen bee herself (awe-inspiring in high heels and a cocktail apron) because Rhonda and her mom were (equally as mysterious) "bosom buddies."

She will never find the house, but it is good to think of Rhonda (stout now, a thick curve to the back of her neck), an eternally reliable geyser of love. When Cassidy was ultimately torn from her mother's arms by Gregg's illness, Rhonda was there, not in Oregon but inside Cassidy's self, radiant as she had seemed in childhood. Even now, running in downtown Vero Beach, out of the expansive shade through hot, depressed back streets—pool halls and rib shacks—she can invoke the power of Rhonda's unconditional care, as present as it had been when they had encountered each other four months before, in the bathroom of the apartment in Santo Domingo, the day after she had arrived from Los Angeles.

Six in the morning *and Rhonda was already dressed in a skirt and blouse patterned with irises, gold necklace and gold loop earrings, lipstick in hand at the ready.*

"My God, preciosa, what happened to you?"

Cassidy had been barefoot and in cutoffs, staring hopelessly into the mirror, the tissue around her left eye swollen up like a donut.

"Something bit me."

Rhonda opened a cabinet to reveal shelves of American brand-name medications.

"Whenever we go back I stock up. Pedro says I'm crazy, but see—we have an emergency."

"Where is Pedro?"

"He got a call about an infielder. He had to leave this morning while it was still dark. To drive to Barahona," she said bitterly, "to look at boys in the heat."

"He's not coming with me to see Alberto Cruz?"

"He said he was very sorry. He said he wanted to see your face when you watch that boy hit."

Cassidy smiled painfully.

"He left directions."

Rhonda put her big concerned face close to Cassidy's and patted on cortisone cream with the detached care of an artisan.

"We could have such a good life in Miami. But what can I say? I'm only the wife."

In the kitchen she made Cassidy a packet of ice wrapped in a dish towel, then picked up a knife with an amber handle and began to slice small jasper-green passion fruits.

Cassidy sat down near the window. The Caribbean sun was already hot, softening a flowered sheet of vinyl that covered the table. The air was sultry and laden with dust. Over the rooftops she could see—with half her sight— the ocean turned brown by the approach of the hurricane, big floats of sea- weed tossed in the rough surf.

She pressed the cold rag to her eye.

"I remember that knife. You had that knife in Vero Beach. I remember you cutting avocados."

"Time to get a new knife."

"Time to get out of the kitchen."

Cassidy expected a laugh but Rhonda only glowered and punched the button on a small TV. A variety show had come up, young men in tuxedos playing merengue under hot red lights.

"Spring training." Cassidy was pushing the enthusiasm. "You and my mom were making guacamole. For the boat."

"It was fun on that boat. My boys and you and your brother, rest his soul—all together. Unusual in those days."

"You mean Cubans and gringos?" Cassidy said. "I guess. My dad al- ways talked about how close you were, going back to the Hollywood Stars."

"Remember the manager, Bobby Bragan?"

"I've heard about him. I wasn't even born."

"That guy was one hundred percent crazy."

Rhonda had smiled and Cassidy recognized she was there, she was going to tell the stories—an astonishing turn grown-ups sometimes take when suddenly they give you something they have unequivocally denied. She settled her elbows on the vinyl cloth covering Rhonda's kitchen table, happy to be enfolded again in the pleasures she felt as a little girl in the kitchen of the bungalow with the baseball wives.

"I remember one game"—Rhonda was talking about the Hollywood Stars—"it might have been at Wrigley Field. I know it was against the Angels because we hated them. If we lost to them it was the end of the world. So in this game we were behind and I guess Bobby Bragan didn't know what else to do. He sent the first hitter up to the plate, then took him out before the pitcher made the first throw. Sent the second hitter in. Pulled him out before the pitcher could throw. The third. Fourth. He did this nine times.

Nine pinch hitters in a row before the first pitch! *I thought the pitcher was gonna tear his throat out. The fans loved it."*

"You could get away with that stuff."

"Oh my Lord, they used to drink whiskey in the stands! They used to get into fights, but not like today."

"Like the time my dad punched out the ump?"

"Well," Rhonda said quietly. *"That was different."*

She was twisting halves of passion fruit on the cone of a glass juicer.

"No, no," Cassidy enjoined. *"That was famous. My dad started it off with a double. Then Pedro hit a single. Right? A bloopy little single down the line."*

Rhonda didn't answer, pouring orange-pink juice into a tall glass with ice.

"It was a close call at first," Cassidy went on. *"You could argue the call. Perfect opportunity for Bobby Bragan to come storming out of the dugout, screaming and tearing his clothes off."*

"He only threw down his hat."

"My mom told me he tore off his shirt and was unbuckling his belt when the security guys—"

"It was the hat."

Rhonda wrapped a napkin around the bottom to catch the condensation and handed the glass to Cassidy.

"So Bobby's arguing with the ump," Cassidy went on, less certainly, *"and the ump is yelling, 'He's out!' and my dad punches the umpire in the nose. Fourteen-day suspension, hundred-dollar fine."*

Rhonda had been watching Cassidy with folded arms.

"That's not the way it happened."

Cassidy shrugged. *"Family legend."*

"You left one part out. The ump was, yes, very frustrated—maybe he had enough of Bobby's tricks—but it wasn't just that he was yelling, 'He's out!' He was screaming, screaming so everyone in the bleachers could hear, 'He's out! The nigger is out!' "

Cassidy exhaled a long breath.

Rhonda stared with calm brown eyes. *"That's when your dad walked over from second base, taking his time, you know the way he was, and did it. The man didn't have his mask on, he was a big man, he went down like a bull."*

"So that's why."

Why even-tempered Smoke would get mad enough to punch out an ump, and why, thirty years later, Pedro would confer on Cassidy the gratitude he perhaps could never adequately show her dad.

"There were great Cuban players—light-skinned as you—but we didn't rate. They thought of us like hired labor. 'Watch out for Spanish niggers. They'll stab you with a knife.'"

"Pedro never told me this."

"Of course not. It's not a thing that makes him proud."

A humiliation he didn't want to share when she had asked if the gift of Cruz had something to do with Smoke.

"When this happened," Rhonda said, "Pedro and Smoke hardly knew each other. After that, Pedro always loved him. We were out in California less than one month. I remember because I had morning sickness with Carlos. Your mother was saying, Never! She would never lose her figure!"

Rhonda clucked her tongue and spread a slice of toast with guava paste. One year later Maggie Sanderson, cheerleader, basketball player, supplest of them all, would be fat and pregnant.

And game after game Smoke would approach the mound with a laconic Minnesotan ease and deliver smoothly for six good innings, comfortable throwing fastballs, curves and sliders on any count. His niche was a likable consistency, with a killer move to first. Cassidy never thought of him as a raging libertarian but she could see how the reflex to right a wrong fit a simple sense of justice in her dad, for which she had never felt, until that moment, such quiet pride.

"Your mother is well?" Rhonda was saying. "Give her my love."

Cassidy sipped the fresh passion fruit juice, unlike anything she had ever tasted, sweet-tart and fragrant as a gardenia, the essence of a subtropical dream. The skin stretched over her eye was throbbing and she felt the pulse of it again—the drive to find Alberto Cruz—deep inside her body memory, strong as the very first heartbeat; the result, she suddenly understood, of a most extraordinary conception—a friendship between two men.

Rhonda looked up from whacking an egg. "What time is the game?"

"Pedro said three."

"We better get out of here and rent the car."

Cassidy peered at a clownish reflection of her swollen eye in the toaster, as if a fat drop of mercury had acquired her face.

"I don't think I can drive."

"I'll take you to the doctor."

"No time."

Rhonda frowned. "Pedro wants you to see this boy."

"I know."

For a moment both women were silent.

"How far is Río Blanco?"

"Two hours. You know I don't drive."

"I have to get out there." Again Cassidy looked at her watch. "Where can we get a car and driver?"

"I know where," Rhonda said resolutely. "We'll ask the General. He lives next door. He has a big car business. His office is just down the street. Pedro despises the General. But Pedro isn't here."

She whipped the eggs so hard they turned to lemon foam.

The sun had been *abundant in a way it never is in Los Angeles, soaking through the leafy mahogany trees of the Gazcue, a middle-class neighborhood of houses enclosed by pastel walls. After the first block Cassidy was feeling peculiar, from jet lag and heat. The sun assaulted the neck and shoulders, reflecting off the sidewalk and scalding the ankles.*

At the corner they faced a careening river of vehicles, mostly crashed-in Japanese sedans driven with euphoric abandon—since there were no lines on the road and certainly no crosswalks, why worry yourself? Cassidy tried to sense the rhythm and failed, stepping off the curb just as Rhonda yanked her back. They pushed on through a heavy, palpable torpor, the only Caucasians on the street, although the citizens of Santo Domingo paid them no mind. Peddlers were staked out all the way down Calle César Nicolás Penson, selling cigarettes and candy bars from wooden boxes. A vendor with amazing biceps was whittling the skins of oranges into perfect spirals, spraying the air with fine droplets of citrus oil.

They passed boys sprawled on the hood of a car. Nurses in white uniforms at an outdoor café. The baseball Garden of Eden had evaporated by the light of day. Cassidy could not find the spirit of greatness in the jaded expressions on the street; all she could see was the lack of it.

Finally they reached the ocean and a strip of high-rise hotels. A bony horse pulling a rickety black hansom cab with an unseen driver and unseen travelers passed slowly through the traffic. The peculiar feeling of misdirection Cassidy had felt when they stepped into the sweltering street resolved to the powerful knowledge that this moment, in this city, was exactly where she must be. Her life in Los Angeles, so full of bluster and importance, had receded to a speck lost in the sky as she stood bewitched by the sight of the shiny black wheels of the hansom cab, threaded with orchids, shimmying as they turned.

Rhonda continued past the posh Hotel V Centenario—where the air-conditioning in the sexy gambling casino was probably set at tantalizing flash-freeze—to a suffocating wasteland the size of a city block surrounded by a chain-link fence, in the center of which there was nothing but an ancient Volkswagen bus without wheels. Strange, Cassidy had thought, gazing across the Malecón, where brown surf hurled against an outcrop of volcanic rock, prime real estate for a broken-down taxi and car rental company.

The General had been sitting at a card table in the shade reading the morning edition of Listín Diario, a cell phone and a can of Coke nearby. Rhonda made the introductions and he had risen, tipping the visor of a Licey team baseball cap, shaking with a dry thick hand and courteously offering each lady one of two folding chairs (the office), where Cassidy perched politely in a rose T-shirt and black-flowered rayon skirt Rhonda had strongly suggested that she wear, instinctively responding to the signals coming from the General as clearly as the laser beam of Faro a Colón; masculine signals reinforced by a .45 automatic pistol stuck into a belt just behind the right hip.

"Do you always carry a gun?" she asked.

"I was in the military."

The General smiled and his brown cheeks dimpled, long rugged creases that surfaced like a reminder of the younger man—reckless and brash—no thought, no reflection, no doubt. Even though he seemed the harmless abuelo in a pink-and-white-striped shirt, brown trousers and sandals, playing dominoes in the shade, Cassidy recognized an inflexible constitutional authority that comes of being born to a jackpot of gender, race and class: all the right cherries lined up in a row.

"How do you like my country?" he asked.

"Very nice except for the bugs."

"We don't got bugs."

Cassidy lowered her sunglasses so the General could see the swelling.

"We don't got bugs," he repeated.

Armed or not, the General was getting on her nerves.

"Do you have cars?"

"Of course we got cars!" He leaned back and laughed.

Cassidy hadn't seen any cars in the empty lot. A couple dozen Haitian oil paintings were hung on the chain link, stylized scenes of marketplaces and religious epiphanies. A runty Dominican in an undershirt was haranguing a well-dressed European couple, "Are you Christians? Look at this beautiful painting of our Lord!"

The General's sideline. Art.

Rhonda was going on about how she and Pedro had known this fine man for years—neighbor, businessman, loving grandfather. The General returned the respects in a meaningless flirtation that nonetheless made Rhonda's moon cheeks turn pink. There are dances to be danced but it was eleven thirty-five and easily a hundred degrees.

"What will it take," Cassidy cut in, "to get me to Río Blanco and back?"

"Pedro was going to drive," Rhonda explained, "but he had to go to Barahona to see an infielder."

The General nodded seriously. "Always the search."

"We need your help."

"It would be a privilege."

For three hundred dollars.

The General clapped his hands and the runty salesman trotted over.

"This is my nephew."

"Whatzup?" Not just in English but in an accent wide as the East River.

"You're from New York?"

"I'm from here but I drove a cab in New York. Spent time in Miami," he added proudly, as if it were a graduate degree.

"Monroe knows the countryside." The General clapped his nephew's bare clove-dark shoulder. "He is a good man."

Good at hot-wiring cars, Cassidy thought, wondering how else they were going to get one, and if she should really drive off with this sleaze, a grown-up version of the street boys at the airport. She recognized exactly where Monroe was from: hustling and getting high. Not because of the buzzed hair or the enormous baggy pants held up by a green plastic belt; it had been in the eyes, filmed over, not clear. The eyes sat on you like two oily brown-orange moons.

She was still thinking about it while Monroe went off to get the car, while she and Rhonda and the General stood in an awkward row on the scorching sidewalk.

"What would we do without the General?" Rhonda had purred with a coy smile Cassidy wasn't positive had not been returned by a wink. "You know our friend held an important position under President Trujillo? A very difficult time," she added.

"I liked it better under Trujillo."

The General had been rocking back and forth on the balls of his feet. A thick gold bracelet swung on his wrist. A heavy ring of keys swayed off a pinkie.

"Really?" Cassidy asked. "Why did you like it better?"

"There was more discipline."

Three hundred dollars and the relentless sun were making her testy.

"Trujillo," Cassidy said, "was a dictator who killed a lot of innocent people."

The smile faded from Rhonda's coral lips but the General had remained unmoved.

"People always die from one thing or another," he had observed. "The enemies of Trujillo, they died faster."

Monroe pulled up in a blue Isuzu jeep. The General continued to rock, knees buckled and groin thrust forward, self-stimulation showing in a hard mound.

Cassidy stared at his smug, bronze face in disbelief.

He gave her dimples.

15

The Coast Grill is deceptive.

Low-slung, with a narrow red-and-white-striped canopy, it looks like one of those classic Atlantic fish places that have attached themselves to the end of a pier like a mollusk; been there forever, weathered and cozy, a comfortable safe harbor for the rain-soaked traveler or the mature affair, where the barkeep knows how to blend up a pretty good whiskey sour.

Maybe, forty years ago.

Today the Coast Grill has a gift shop that sells china replicas of itself, along with dish towels, recipe books, candles, lighthouse earrings, fish kites and Indian River grapefruits, shipped anywhere. In the lot, where Cassidy parked the rental car about an acre away, the preferred automobile is a Cadillac. In the cavernous series of dining rooms, lit by flickering "kerosene" lanterns, the preferred dinner jackets for gentlemen are robin's-egg blue. For ladies, anything in the Easter palette.

All in all, thinks Cassidy, striding past tables of gray heads, the perfect place to take a nervous kid from the Dominican.

Pedro is waving. As she joins them in a booth Alberto cannot suppress an eighteen-year-old male smirk.

"You look good."

Cassidy is wearing a short sleeveless black wool dress, black hose and black square heels. Her hair is loose.

"Thanks," she says. "So do you."

Alberto seems to shudder. He has on chinos and a black knit shirt. His cropped hair is glistening. As usual he cannot sit still in a chair, stretching and yawning, leaning back with hands clasped behind his head. At the next table there is a birthday party, a bouquet of Mylar balloons. Through the strings of the balloons, through the chatter ("*I saw such beautiful gowns in Singapore—*"), one wide-shouldered old geezer in a marigold-yellow suit is staring openly at the three of them.

They are handed menus the size of newspapers. Alberto shuffles his feet and diddles the red tassel as Pedro translates one hundred fourteen ways to broil, poach, grill and bake a wearying selection of Gulf seafood.

Cassidy says, "I saw you coaching those boys. That was a generous thing to do."

Alberto shrugs. "We having fun."

She pours another glass from the cold pitcher of draft. "What was going on for you out there on the field today?"

"For real I play much better than you see."

"That part's okay. Everybody has a bad night—"

"I know what's going on." His eyes are earnest. "Here I play against thirty outfielders—big guys, they have good coaches. All they lives, they play with good conditions. I know I can't go Double A or Triple A with those guys. I'm going to play rookie ball, I got to be real."

"Realistic."

"When I take that pressure off of myself, I can play my game."

Pedro: "Son, you're right, you only got one problem. You are all tied up in a knot. You got to work with the *brain*. Because the body's gonna do what the brain tells it."

"I have to work on my concentration."

"It's not just that," says Cassidy. "It's what you carry with you. What you dream about at night."

She looks meaningfully at Pedro.

"My dream is to play in Dodger Stadium." Alberto laughs, believing he has given a good answer.

"We know you got pressure," Pedro goes on, "with guys like that looking over your shoulders."

Cassidy: "Like what?"

Pedro nods toward the bar.

"You see that bodyguard?"

White hair and clipped white beard, a reddened, weathered face long past fifty. Gold chain, white nylon windbreaker, white slacks. In the midst of talk and motion, the crisp impassivity of the man provides a lesson in focus. Although his look seems aimed nowhere in particular, you can tell by the calm deliberate way his slender hand picks up a glass that he maintains a honed and disciplined balance between stillness and, should it be required, action.

Cassidy blurts, "I saw that man in the park."

"The organization brought him down from Port St. Lucie to keep an eye on Alberto."

"Isn't that a little paranoid?"

Alberto is drumming the table. "The letters are coming here."

"What letters?"

"The same."

"Blackmail letters?"

Alberto nods.

"They followed you *here*?"

Cassidy is hoping that pure logical deduction will reduce the panic in her gut. If someone in Los Angeles who had been sending stuff to the stadium wanted to send something else to Alberto, it would make perfect sense to send it to Dodgertown. Of course they would know he's at spring training, it's in the paper, for God's sake.

"The letters were sent from Los Angeles?"

"Florida," says Pedro. "Sent from here. That's why."

Again he indicates the man at the bar, who is taking a measured sip of orange juice.

Cassidy scans the room of senior citizens with alarm.

"Nothing to do. Someone put bad magic on me. *Obeah*," Alberto explains.

The waiter brings a basket of fried shrimp.

"Come on," scoffs Pedro, "you don't believe in that stuff."

"Before I don't believe, but now I don't know. I feeling weak like a baby. I go on the field, I can't do nothing."

Cassidy comes back to Alberto's hollow eyes. "Are you eating right?"

"The trainers say I'm okay. I eat great. The food here is great. But I no gain weight. My roommate he give me these cans? These supplements?" Alberto shakes his head. "My stomach no good."

Cassidy, impatiently, "If you fail here, Alberto, you go home."

He scowls. "Nothing gonna help. Someone put the magic."

"Only if you think so." Pedro bites a shrimp.

Eyes downcast, "I think the bad luck start when we run over that pony."

Cassidy takes a breath, absolutely dazzled.

"We all know it wasn't a pony."

The waiter brings a loaf of white bread on a wooden board and three tomato salads, barely deiced.

"It was not?"

"No."

Alberto laughs again. "What you talking about?"

"I'm talking about the woman on the tape the cops showed you in LA. That's what we hit, not a pony. Somebody knows and they're trying to blackmail you."

She holds back from saying, *You and Joe.*

Alberto's face retains the trace of an uneasy smile.

Pedro: "This is serious. The Dominican police have been to my house. I don't need that kind of trouble."

Alberto's eyes grow round and his hands go to his chest.

"Why you look at *me?*"

Cassidy: "You're the one who hit her."

Silence.

Slowly, so there can be no misunderstanding: "You were driving the Range Rover."

Alberto slowly hunches forward until his forehead comes to rest on the table.

"Yes, I drive."

His words are equally measured.

"That is true. Mr. Galinis let me drive."

He straightens up and stares at them full bore.

"But not when we hit the pony. Then it was Mr. Galinis. He drive."

He looks between Cassidy and Pedro.

"Why you not believe me?"

Cassidy's heart is pounding. "That is not the way it happened."

Pedro: "Don't disrespect the lady. She was there. She knows."

Alberto's dark brown eyes pin hers.

"You were sleeping. How you know?"

"That's my recollection. I can't say I really *know* . . ."

Alberto, triumphant, "Right! *How you know who's driving when you are sleeping drunk in a car?*"

The seniors are singing "Happy Birthday." The almond-crusted pompano arrives.

"Calm down," says Pedro. "We are in a restaurant."

Alberto's tapping with a knife. "I don't believe this happening. Someone put the magic."

"Don't tell us about magic—"

"Cassie, is this true? You were passed out cold?"

"I'm sorry about that. Really sorry. Can I just crawl under the table now—?"

Alberto, at the same time: "—Right away you don't believe me! How I can prove this? How I can go up against the American guy? What I can do? You know what happen to me if I go back? I go to jail or this woman family probably gonna kill me—"

Pedro, "You're important to the organization, we gonna do everything we can—"

"—Sure, and I supposed to play tomorrow, like nothing?"

"That's right." Cassidy, hard. "You have to play."

Alberto stands angrily. "How I play when this is going on?"

"Then don't!" Her hand slams down, jiggling glasses. "Forget everything!"

"It was an accident. We gonna straighten it out," says Pedro. "We gonna help you. And your family, too."

"What you know about my family?"

"They are suffering," Pedro replies steadily. "Sit down."

Alberto swipes the air.

"Right! My nephews go to Santo Domingo, live in the street. Where my mother is, they got no water. Everybody sick. *I* here." He punches his own chest. "*I* supposed to save their life."

"We know. We understand—"

The man in the marigold jacket, who has been eyeing them all evening, elbows his wife.

"Are you a Dodger?" the old man shouts.

Alberto turns. "Yes, sir."

"You look familiar."

"Thank you."

The wife produces a clean new baseball and permanent marker—as standard in Vero Beach purses as photos of the grandkids—which are passed knowingly around the table to Alberto.

"Sign it 'To Dr. Wessendorf, Best regards.'"

Alberto scrawls something. Dr. Wessendorf gives a one-finger salute and the boy runs for the door.

The bodyguard slips off the stool and follows.

Pedro continues to eat. Cassidy finishes another beer. It tastes like soap.

Pedro says, "He is not in control of himself."

Cassidy folds her hands like a schoolmarm. It would be good if she didn't start throwing things here.

"He has a lot on the line."

Pedro chews with deliberation. "The Dominican police wanted to know if he's involved with drugs."

"That's what the cops said in LA. That Alberto might be caught in the middle of some drug dealers." She shrugs stiffly. "I don't know. What does that have to do with anything?"

"You never saw him getting high?"

"We drank some Mama Juana—"

Pedro groans.

"—but that's all."

"I try to talk to you about your drinking—"

"Uncle Pedro, please. Don't you think I'm sick about this? I was in the car, I'm the one responsible for him—"

The waiter asks if they want coffee. No, they don't.

"He is almost a grown-up man. You are not responsible."

Cassidy puts her head in her hands.

"I don't like the police," says Pedro, "but maybe they are right. We are a poor country, everybody takes from us. They build big resorts with gambling casinos, and it's a gold mine. For who? Americans, Germans and Japanese. What do *we* got? Where's *our* politicians? In bed with the Mexican drug lords. I'll tell you one thing," he warns. "You see the big rich ugly houses of the drug dealers in the towns like Nagua, you see them with the gold watches in the cafés." He gives the slow contemptuous finger wave. "Over my dead body they not gonna get in *our* business."

He signs the bill.

"I'm gonna go down there and ask some questions about Cruz."

"Go where?"

"Río Blanco."

"Be careful."

The idea seems to strike him as absurd.

"It's my territory."

He slides around awkwardly and hefts himself from the booth and through the busy restaurant and out to the street where a Town Car is waiting to take him, Alberto and the man in white back to Dodgertown.

Cassidy walks down the boardwalk.

That Alberto is lying to save his family makes her heart hurt. She knows what it's like to go out in the world and be the one who has to win it for the folks back home. It leaves you standing alone, leaning against a railing, watching floodlit waves break against the seawall.

Damn her stoned-out brain. She struggles to remember. While she was groping the filthy floor, mesmerized by a little plastic dog, was Alberto out there drenched in rain, staring at his crime, watching his future wash away like watery blood? Did he panic, run, leave a stranger dying by the road?

Then lie like a teenager to put the blame on Joe?

Can terrible events melt even the good face? If so, what do you find underneath? An animal grimace fixed on escape with the indifferent eyes of a killer? Even Pedro had been shaken by the possibility; he did not want to see the opportunist in Alberto, so he's off to indict the conquerors—builders, drug dealers, capitalists, smugglers, sugar kings, the European sex trade in the north—who have seized on island boys for centuries, forcing them to labor in their own personal gold mines.

A spit of salt spray chills her despite the tropic breeze.

The words hit with another meaning.

Gold mine.

They had also been Joe's words, when he had been talking about the hotel in the Los Angeles sports and entertainment center.

Another hotel for which he had put together the financing.

She understood when he said "Gold mine," he did not mean regular hotel profits, heads in the beds, but what would happen to his investment if down the line the city did make downtown an "entertainment zone," where gambling would be legal.

The Los Angeles hotel would have a casino.

Just like the Gran Caribe.

Cassidy hears laughter and turns from the rail. The party has drifted out of the restaurant onto the sidewalk, silvery balloons and the elderly birthday girl wearing a corsage, stoop-shouldered Dr. Wessendorf patting someone on the back. A warm bath of voices reminding her that she is alone.

They had been in the Bentley outside Dodger Stadium, at a loss as to what to do on their suddenly disconnected date.

"I've seen where you play," Joe said at last. "Let me show you where I play."

They had driven slowly in rush hour traffic through Chinatown and Pershing Square to the deadened corners of the old industrial sector of downtown.

"This is the future," Joe said.

Cassidy, in the business of futures, caught his excitement.

"We're coming up to the Convention Center. A beautiful piece of architecture designed by I. M. Pei's firm, but it's in the middle of no-man's-land. Not a neighborhood without character," he added judiciously as they passed stately prewar office buildings with zigzag fire escapes and decorative swags, plastered with For Sale signs. The only moving figures in the abandoned cityscape were the most homeless of the homeless, unrecognizable as upright beings beneath sculptural piles of rags.

"The multipurpose arena will be surrounded by a promenade of City Walk–type shops. The hotel will be to the west. We need a great convention center hotel," Joe went on. "It will be economically fragile for a while, but if LA grows the way we think it will, the hotel will become a gold mine."

He had spoken with the polish of an orator about a thirty-screen movie palace, about "density and mass" that would tie the new development into the USC–Coliseum–Exposition Park area . . .

Cassidy remembered, *Gold mine.*

They passed a gated barbershop and a liquor store layered with gang signs and skulls as Joe brought to life the vision of a new power structure, Latin and Asian, that would emerge from the shards of the white-dominated eighties; a three-hundred-million-dollar West Coast South Beach, Florida, that would be, in color, music and sophistication, in sync with the new ethnic beat of Los Angeles.

They turned onto Tenth Street, where a huge comic-book warrior had been painted on the brick-walled factories and flophouse hotels so everywhere they looked he seemed to be aiming a laser gun, at them.

When they arrived at the site she was surprised at how subtly the structure fit. It was skeletal, the caissons that go down to bedrock were in, and the footings and foundations, beams and columns that you could see formed an ovoid superstructure curving around to end abruptly in space.

They went into a trailer and signed out badges and hard hats, and crossed the street to the entrance where dusty-faced workers with lunch pails were streaming home.

"Just walk in like you own the place," Joe said.

A path of wooden planks led to the lobby—a floor of concrete—where Joe pointed out the sloping columns that supported the sloping roof, how the building was a series of curves, the prow of it an ellipse, conceived in strata—offices and restaurants, decks, concourses, private clubs—stuck in layers to the round arena portico. They stepped around piles of steel beams, squeezed between generators, wheelbarrows, hoses and wire. He held aside a curtain of black plastic and she stood a foot away from the edge of the stadium, looking down a hundred feet to the jam-packed event floor. Rakers wrapped with steel wire swung from massive skyhooks on ten-story cranes, and the blown-out chaos of work in progress, like detritus from an explosion, was littered everywhere. Joe pointed toward the cross-trusses on the roof. "Look at it on this plane," he instructed, tilting his hand until she could make out an octagon of steelwork in the middle: "That's where the scoreboard will go."

It was easy to imagine the lights on and seats filled, the scoreboard alive and blaring, cartoon characters and corporate logos pulsating, to claim the very center of the action.

"Want to climb to the top?"

They spiraled up several tiers of concrete steps until they reached the highest level. The deck was open, a thin wind blowing through the scaffolding because there were no outer walls. It was precarious. Empty elevator shafts dropped several stories down. "Don't lean on those," Joe warned of the wooden barricades. "They're not always bolted."

He showed her the unfinished spaces that would become private suites and took her before a sweeping unguarded opening which was to be the multistory windows of an exclusive club: humidors for your cigars, a cellar for your wine.

Joe was in a delirium of optimism. High above factories and parking lots and private homes, everything was possible: *Big impact. New skyline. Disney concert hall. Hire people from the inner city.* He waved at where the hotel would eventually go and turned and kissed her with such passion that she laughed, then pressed her up against a pillar with his fingers between her legs and they might have done it standing if a worker hadn't scuffled by with a screaming vacuum that was sucking up a stream of water as he carelessly pulled along an electric cord.

Back in the Bentley, Joe sorted through two dozen invitations—screenings, benefits, gallery openings, dinner parties.

"This is my life," he mused. "Keeping everyone happy."

They made two quick stops—a reception for a Republican senator in an Italianate villa behind the Chateau Marmont and a fortieth-birthday party for the wife of one of Joe's partners at the Four Seasons. The downtown crowd filled both, a cold crowd, Cassidy was discovering, where the women wore the same smart no-risk black dresses she had seen at Harvey Weissman's and turned away after a limp sentence or two; the men refused to meet her eyes, no smiles, no flirtation. Joe had seemed perfectly content to keep introducing her over and over to the same icy indifference, and she just kept on drinking chardonnay.

"We're running late."

He checked his watch for the millionth time, agitated, as they waited for the third or fourth parking valet of the night.

"Nora will be beside herself."

Cassidy hadn't realized Nora was part of their mandate to keep everyone happy, but in any case, they had failed.

It was past eight when they pulled up to a hacienda on North Doheny Drive. Joe had gotten out and gone thoughtlessly ahead, so by the time Cassidy walked through the curved doorway, he and his daughter were already in the foyer, arguing.

"Sorry we're late, go and change," he was saying.

"I'm not going. I have to look at the language in a tax proposal."

"Fine," said Joe. "Send me an e-mail."

He took her hand. She pulled away, twitchy and quick.

"What's the matter with you?"

"I'm not being—I never even got dressed!" she said irritably.

In the low-ceilinged stucco room with tiled fireplace and wrought-iron candelabrum Cassidy felt acutely claustrophobic and wanted to flee, as if the evening's elegant express had taken a wrong turn and ended up in a 1940s horror movie.

"I'm not dressed, either," offered Cassidy, still in her work khakis.

"Oh," said Nora, "look at that body. You always look fabulous."

She had started to pace.

"Got your faxes," Cassidy said. "About the Colorado Silver Bullets."

"You're welcome."

"That's a lot of information to research."

"It's what I do at four in the morning, when I can't sleep."

Joe had been staring at Nora's feet. "You got dressed as far as your shoes," he observed.

Nora stopped and gazed down at the spike-heeled gold silk sandals with rhinestone buttons, incongruous with her size four jeans, as if she were surprised to find herself wearing them.

"What do you think?" she asked, suddenly coy.

"'Fuck me' shoes."

"Excuse me, Dad, but this is the nineties. Now they're called 'Fuck you' shoes."

They both laughed—a laugh so minimalist, so knowing, so dry, so hip, it scarcely existed beyond a few screw-nosed sniffs. Then, like a vapor, it was gone.

"I thought this event was important to you," Joe was going on with an unpleasant edge. "You at least could have called me in the car. Cassidy and I could have made other plans."

Cassidy flinched.

"Was this the fancy dinner?" she asked, still trying to help out. Trying to target the reasonable part of Nora, which kept whirling past them in a blur, like a child on a schoolyard merry-go-round.

"It's a fund-raiser for Children's Hospital," Joe answered, "on Santa Monica Pier. My daughter's on the board. She's worked very hard. I don't get it," he said, arms akimbo and thumbs hooked on his belt, clearly exasperated. "Come. Be with us. I want you to go."

"No."

"Well it doesn't make a damn bit of sense for us to be there without you—"

Cassidy wished he would lighten up. He looked a lot older in the creepy yellow light.

Nora raised her eyes. In the gloom the blacks were huge. "The trouble with my father," she began tremblingly, "is he has to control everybody's life, and if—"

"It was inconsiderate and *rude!*" Joe shouted as Sophie, Nora's five-year-old, ran down the staircase squealing, throwing herself into his arms. She was wearing a flowered nightgown over heart pajamas, three different necklaces of pearls and beads and a sparkling tiara. Tucked beneath one arm was a large stuffed duck.

"Ready for bed?" asked Joe.

Sophie inclined her tiny nostrils like a butterfly sensing the wind and judged the currents in the room precisely.

"I want HER to put me to sleep!" pointing emphatically at Cassidy, whom she could not possibly have remembered from a five-minute encounter they'd had on the beach at the Gran Caribe.

But Cassidy felt as if she'd won the lottery as the child flew across the Mexican pavers on bare feet, wrapping her arms around Cassidy's waist. Without thinking she had picked her up (all forty fragile pounds) and held her close, a perfect fit, whispering stupid things into her soft rosemary-scented hair like, "Want to come home with me?" and Sophie nodding obediently.

Now the black Atlantic surf breaks vigorously across the spotlit jetty as Cassidy remembers the feeling of being bereft when the English nanny came and took the child away, Nora giving orders with arms crossed tight, all twisted up like her wrought-iron candlesticks—how could she not want to hold her own daughter? And hold her. And hold her.

They left Nora alone in the foyer and drove pretty much in silence to the Santa Monica Pier. But when they had gotten out of the car Joe looked tired. "We don't have to do this," he said.

Cassidy did not reply. They walked to the edge of Palisade Park, a high bluff overlooking the ocean. Excruciatingly bright crime lights jaundiced their skin, made the park look flat and ominous.

They watched the kaleidoscoping lights of the Ferris wheel on the Pleasure Pier, as it used to be called. A huge green-striped tent had been pitched in the parking lot for Nora's event, squatting on a layer of hot white light like a flying saucer.

"They'll raise a quarter of a million dollars for the hospital tonight."

"And Nora doesn't want to be here?"

"I don't know. Probably angry at me for some reason."

"Or me."

"Nah. Why should she be?"

"She's incredibly possessive of you, Joe."

"It isn't you," Joe said. "It's complicated." He sighed. "Her mother is an alcoholic. She lives in New York. Nora inherited a whopping problem with addiction. Her teenage years were a series of freak-outs. Sometimes I think we're still in them," he added ruefully.

"How old was she when you got divorced?"

"Fourteen. And *defiant*?" He shook his head. "She was doing things . . . I'll never understand. Totally out of my experience."

"To get drugs?"

"They're born, they're beautiful, then they tear out your heart and put it through a meat grinder."

"Well," said Cassidy lightly, "I wouldn't know."

"There comes a point, like tonight, when all of a sudden you have no idea who they are."

He stared at the ocean, genuinely at a loss.

She took his arm. "I'm sorry."

He seemed surprised by the sentiment and pulled her close.

"I'm so fortunate." He kissed Cassidy's cheek. Then, "God was looking out for my girl. She got herself into a program and she's been clean and sober seven years and seven months."

Cassidy hesitated. "You're sure?"

"Of this, I am sure." Joe put a warm hand over Cassidy's. "When she was pregnant, she finally came back. She'd been on the street, she was sick and scared and wanted to come home. I took her to our church, St. Sophia's, and made her get down on her knees and swear. She had to stop the crap, then and there, for the sake of the baby. She no longer had the option to destroy herself. She got her head on straight, went back to school, *with* the kid . . . She's not a stupid girl. She knows if she blows it, the car, the house in Beverly Hills, the full-time nanny—they're history. She's off drugs," he said, drawing up, "I'm sure."

"She was lucky. Sophie is gorgeous."

"Sophie is my angel."

"Is there a father in the picture?"

Shortly, "No."

The Pier was throwing off a pearl-pink glow of Victorian excitement, suggestive thrills to be had in the speed of modern machinery or in the gaming parlor, twirling rides and lose-your-shirt arcades, still drawing lovers from deep in the city to come out to the ocean and take a chance.

Joe could build his monuments, and stand on top of the world. His daughter could adorn her feet with gold. But Cassidy had known, of all the treasures she had been shown that night, Sophie was the only one worth having.

Now her skin is tacky from salt and cold, shoulders tight, as she turns from the Atlantic and passes through the birthday guests lingering beneath the lit canopy of the Coast Grill. The parking lot is still half-full. She walks between the Cadillacs and Oldsmobiles, in and out of pools of darkness, to the rental car at the far end.

She has unlocked the door and the keys are still in her hand when a black man—lithe, youngish—rolls out from under the car, slashing with a knife, aiming low. She jumps back, the keys fly, the door pulls open, a momentary shield against the attacker. She slams it forward against his oncoming forehead but rebounds against another man waiting right behind her who pins her arms. She bellows with rage and stomps his toes with her heel—"*Hey!*" someone shouts, "*Hey, you!*" At the reflexive release of his fingers she gives him the elbows, hard, he lets go but then it's two on one, dragging her over the concrete and holding her down. She resists with all her arm strength but one of the men is able to grip her wrist, pressing so tightly the blood vessels burst, and push her clawing fingers into open space, while the other quickly and efficiently slams the car door on her hand.

16

Cassidy becomes aware of lying on a gurney. Under two blankets. Inside a circle of closed white curtains.

A male voice says, *"Knock, knock."*

The curtains fuss and pull apart and a short man wearing a jacket and tie comes through.

"Cassidy Sanderson? I'm Sergeant Nathan Allen, Detective Division, Vero Beach Police Department. Mind if I talk to you?"

Her throat is dry.

He perches on a stool, stubby hands loose in his lap.

"I'm the detective on call. The road officer asked me to respond because of the incident that took place outside the Coast Grill this evening. Could you please tell me what happened?"

For no particular reason she seems engaged by the polka dots on his tie.

"Feeling no pain, are we?"

In fact the Demerol is making everything smooth and beige and sweet as a coffee ice cream shake.

"Okay." He appraises her. "But I'll need to talk to you after you're discharged. We need a statement while your memory is fresh."

With effort she brings up a shoulder and wipes her lips on the hospital gown, leaving reddish drool. "I was jumped."

"I know," he says, interested. "You sustained what is called 'great bodily harm.'"

"So did they."

The detective sits back and the stool creaks.

"So we should be looking for a couple of crippled black guys?"

Her answer becomes a slow-motion fall over a cliff.

She is wearing her own dress again. After the hospital gown the satin lining feels sumptuous, caressing her hurting body as she walks slowly but unassisted out of the ER.

"It's not that bad," she says of her left hand, elevated in a sling inside a hot pink cast (what was she thinking?). "There was a time in my life when I got into a lot of accidents. In six months I totaled the car four times."

"Drinking?"

"Being crazy, being a kid."

"God watches out for children, huh?"

"Most of the time."

Detective Allen steps along patiently at her side.

"I once went through a plate glass window. Dislocated an elbow during a game," shamelessly boastful, even now.

"What kind of game?"

"Professional women's baseball."

"The Colorado Silver Bullets?"

"Right."

"You play?"

"Used to."

"Why not anymore?"

She smiles. "I'm old."

"No way. You've got good years left. I can see 'em."

"Sometimes the price for continuing is just too high, know what I'm talking about?"

"Yes," he says. "My marriage."

He holds the door. A restless wet tropical breeze assails them and Cassidy begins to shiver in the sleeveless dress. By the time she slides into the front seat of the unmarked tan Ford her teeth are chattering. Detective Allen reaches into the rear, picks up a blue nylon windbreaker with POLICE in block letters on the back, and drapes it over her shoulders.

A Christmas tree–shaped air freshener dangles from the mirror but the interior still smells dusky and male, and she has a stoned sense of being on a high school date with a nice guy from the tennis squad—smart (he'll become an ophthalmologist), but likes her too much, is too short, driving his mother's car.

In eleven minutes they are at the Vero Beach Central police station, a spiffy blue and white building barely seven years old, with a clean lobby that has a gumball machine and lots of notices about community this and that. Detective Allen waves to a desk sergeant behind a wall of dark glass and punches a code into a box next to a steel door. They enter a corridor and then Cassidy finds herself in a tiny soundproofed room.

"Can I get you some coffee?"

"Please."

"*Latte?*"

The door seals shut before she can answer. Cassidy isn't sure whether Detective Allen is joking or not, but suddenly none of it seems very funny.

The room contains a table and two chairs, one straight-backed, the other, unaccountably, a Barcalounger. There is no space for anything else. She looks at her reflection in the smoke of an obvious two-way mirror and a thousand movie clichés clutter her mind. One cheek is swollen, contusions on the neck and forehead, hair a mess, clutching the windbreaker over bare shoulders like some kind of strung-out prostitute they dragged in on a raid.

Stop. That's the way they want you to think.

It is hot in the interrogation room and already Cassidy has begun to sweat. She throws off the windbreaker, finds a hairy old elastic band in the pocket of her backpack, and pulls up a neat ponytail. Then, of all things, lip gloss. Funny what you fall back on.

Detective Allen returns with two black coffees and a slew of artificial creamer packets.

"Starbucks, we ain't." Nicely.

"No problem."

Cassidy stirs the noxious powder as cheerfully as if it were 9 a.m. and not three in the morning, time to take another Vicodin from the hospital pharmacy.

Although her hand is already throbbing she intends to put off that next pill as long as possible. She cannot allow her selective attention to be compromised. She has to stay focused on what she is going to say.

There is a slogan lettered above the door in a funky old women's locker room at UCLA:

Pain is temporary but Bruin pride is forever.

Pain is temporary.

Forever is a long time.

Passion, where is that?

Detective Allen is fighting with the Barcalounger. Something is preventing the back from straightening up—turns out to be a Barbie doll stuck in the seat. He fishes it out, tosses it into a box full of toys.

"When we have to interview a child victim," he explains, settling in.

Cassidy says, "Oh, shit."

Detective Allen has a watchful, not unattractive face with a hip brush haircut that stands straight up like two inches of new lawn. Cassidy's age, lifts weights, needs to work on his abs. Palomino coloring, intelligent pale blue eyes, gold on blond, likes the sun, she figures, when he doesn't have to work nights. He rubs his hands on his knees in a self-conscious way but does not appear to be the least bit tired or distracted. Rather he seems enormously enthusiastic, like the tie with dancing polka dots and the white shirt with wide navy blue stripes, echoes of Carnaby Street. Cassidy can smell the starch.

They go through the standard questions. Place of birth. Residence. Employer.

"You're a scout for the Dodgers?"

"That's what they tell me."

"Cool."

"Usually."

"Why? The male-female thing? Please. That's old. We've had women officers on the force twenty years."

Cassidy shrugs. Sighs. Watch out. Don't feel too comfortable.

"Would it excite you to know that I own a Ralph Branca baseball card? He was the pitcher who—"

"Bobby Thomson hit the home run off when the Dodgers lost the 1951 pennant. Why Branca?"

"I don't know. I think I was using him as a bookmark. Somehow my ex-wife missed it when she threw out my baseball card collection."

Cassidy giggles. "Sorry. Not funny."

"Are we ready to get into this?"

She nods.

Good-naturedly, "So. Who *were* those guys?"

"I have no idea."

"You've never seen them before?"

"I don't think so."

"Can you describe the assailants?"

"Dark skin."

"Can you be more specific? African-American? Hispanic?"

He is writing on a yellow pad.

"I couldn't tell."

"How old?"

"Maybe in their twenties?"

"Can you describe any facial characteristics? Beards, mustaches, birth marks, scars—"

"It happened fast. I never even saw the second guy."

"Height?"

"I know the one who grabbed me was shorter than I am and that's five ten."

"Weight?"

The kinetic memory comes up, accurate as always, of the depth to which her elbows penetrated his ribs.

"Small muscle mass."

"You mean he was thin?"

"Undeveloped."

"But strong?"

"Average strength. I hate to sound like John Wayne, but in a fair fight I could have taken him."

She says this to psych away from the pain tightening around the fingers of her left hand like a wrench.

"You tried, though. You fought back."

"I went by instinct. Maybe it was dumb."

"Instinct is always right."

"My instinct was to kill the fucker. I'm sorry. The assailant. Whatever you call him."

"The fucker."

She laughs but her lungs hurt.

"Cassidy, what do you think they were after?"

"My backpack?"

"Did they take anything?"

"No."

"Did they attempt to steal the car?"

"Maybe. I couldn't see."

"What did they say?"

"Nothing I could make out."

"Did they perform or threaten any sexual acts?"

"No."

She raises her hand. She lowers it. If it were to sprout flames right now she would not be surprised.

"Why did they hurt you?"

"Because I fought back? Why do *you* think?"

"Don't know yet. One thing, you got lucky. Would have been a lot worse if they hadn't been interrupted by some people coming out of the restaurant."

"Is one of them a Dr. Wessendorf? Huge guy, yellow jacket, looks like Big Bird?"

"They're witnesses, I can't release their names."

"I'd like to tell him thanks . . ."

She is drifting off to sleep. Coming back, she hears, ". . . Do you have any enemies, Cassidy?"

"Do I?"

"Do you know of anyone who would want to hurt you?"

She is sweating so freely it must be fever. It is roasting in the tiny room. Even Detective Allen's cheeks show pink.

"An old boyfriend? Someone associated with the Dodgers? A pissed-off fan?"

Cassidy experiences brain lock. Nothing inputs. Nothing outputs.

"Are you all right?"

"Let's just finish this."

"Okay, go back to the one who rolled out from under the car. You got the best look at him, right?"

"Young. Thin. Maybe five eight."

Pain is temporary. She searches for something to focus on. Detective Allen's lips. Pale strawberry-colored lips. Sucking black coffee from a white paper cup.

The lips say, "You said he had a knife. What kind of knife?"

"I don't know anything about knives. It was a knife. Scary. Boom."

Suddenly she is greatly impatient, a hundred percent irritated.

"What were they wearing?"

"I can't tell you. It was dark, it was fast."

How many times does she have to say it?

"Any colors stand out in your mind? Jackets? Chains around the neck? Athletic shoes?"

"Don't remember."

"It may come back."

Detective Allen is fingering the material of the sleeves of his shirt.

"I want to be thorough because it seems they were lying in wait."

"Does that mean anything?"

"It could mean a tougher sentence, but more to the point, if they were waiting for you, we better find out why."

Her stomach is starting to feel sick.

"I think it was—just random."

"Could be. We've had two attacks in that parking lot this year."

"Looks so peaceful around here."

"We have crime, same as you—lesser numbers because we have a smaller population, but it's the same proportion as LA. You look ill. Let's call the club, get you a ride."

"Don't wake everyone up. I'll take a cab."

Cassidy stands. Detective Allen steadies her arm.

"One thing I wanted to ask—"

"Sure."

"Why was the guy slashing at the ground?"

"He was going for the Achilles tendon. They do that when they want to bring you down. Real fast."

She sucks air. "Where's the bathroom?"

Compared to the interrogation room the rest of the place feels arctic. Cassidy stumbles past empty desks and bulletin boards covered with "Wanted" photos, pushes a door open, gropes for a light, makes it to a stall, and throws up.

When the nausea recedes she swallows two pills. Her face in the mirror is milk white.

Nate Allen is standing in the middle of the room now, snapping on a shoulder holster that contains a startlingly large Glock nine-millimeter. This must be a hallucination. Near-empty before and quiet as a country pond, the police station is suddenly Emergency Central. Uniformed officers have materialized from nowhere, checking earpieces and walkie-talkies. Several hustle by in POLICE windbreakers.

"I have to go," the detective says crisply. "The desk officer will get you a ride."

"Thanks."

"We appreciate your cooperation."

If Cassidy had her wits about her she might have seized the difference between the shy-seeming neb of five minutes ago and the law enforcement professional. A crucial difference: of who, exactly, maintains control, this balmy, savage night.

17

The following morning Cassidy takes the first flight out to Los Angeles, where she continues to avoid everyone associated with the organization, betting that a crime report on an unsolved assault will live and die in the computer of the Vero Beach Police Department.

She has never actually been to the beach where Joe lives. Like many exclusive California coast communities, all this one will show you from the road is butt. The houses face the ocean, backsides careless and shoddy. The only way to get beyond a hodgepodge of garages and Dumpsters and ten-foot-high fencing is to have access.

Cassidy wedges the Explorer behind the Bentley and climbs out to the smell of burning charcoal briquettes and the lazy drumroll of surf. Immediately she starts to sneeze. Even when the air is clear, it's not. She presses a button on a call box and waits for the door lock to unclick. Nothing happens so she presses it again. Finally she unlatches a gate and follows a narrow passage around the side of the house, leather huaraches soundless on the sandy tiles. Maybe she should not have worn white jeans, white stretch-lace shirt. The hot-pink cast sticks out like a cooked lobster claw.

From the beach it is a different story. Who cares about the miles of houses crammed together in the dusk—a lavender sky is fast dissolving to a beltway of stars, and beyond the empty dunes the ocean belongs to you.

She hesitates in front of Joe's modernistic beach house wondering what it's supposed to be: stark spaces, I-beams painted white. Slowly a motif emerges, frames within frames, but clearly the house, mostly hidden by an opaque wall, was designed to hold back more than it reveals. All she can see of an inner courtyard are suggestive shadows of a citrus tree playing across a pair of glazed doors like etchings on Lalique glass—a translucent mystery the passer-by may choose to explore, or continue on.

Inexorably her fingers reach toward the bell and the doors swing wide on chrome hinges and Joe is there in the brownish-amber light, wearing faded jeans and a pink polo shirt, holding a glass of wine.

"Sorry. Come in. Didn't hear you ringing. I was on the phone."

She forgot about his physical presence and dark sparkling hair and how it feels to get close enough to press against his rough cheek in a hasty kiss, his hand light on her shoulder as he guides her past a small reflecting pool.

"What is this?" he asks of the cast.

"I was jumped in Vero Beach."

"You're kidding. Why didn't you tell me?"

He slides a glass panel open and they step into the living room. Two simple sofas, slipcovered in white, face each other across a low wood table in a stain of tangerine.

"I am telling you," Cassidy says. "That's why I'm here." She sneezes again. "Welcome to LA."

"What happened?"

"They broke my hand."

"Who did?"

"Two guys in a parking lot."

"My God. What else?"

"Nothing really. A couple of nasty bruises."

She indicates the purple.

"Cassidy, this is outrageous."

"I've had worse spills off a mountain bike."

He hugs her but she seems to resist.

"I'm sorry, does it hurt?"

"Not anymore."

He peers into her eyes as if searching for something else. She seems so self-contained.

"Let me get you some wine."

Eric Clapton Unplugged is playing on a sound system so exquisite she can feel the vibration of every guitar string. She follows Joe into the kitchen and says, "Whoa."

"Whoa, what?"

"Kitchens tell a lot."

"And?"

"Do you have a thing about submarines?"

The small space has been fabricated entirely of stainless steel—cabinets, sink and stove. The floors are limestone. There are no windows. Seafoam light filters through a wall of glass blocks.

Joe smiles painfully.

"Submarine," he says. "That's kind of fascinating."

Inside the refrigerator there are bottles of wine, green Perriers, fruit salad in a crystal bowl and a four-pound jar of Kalamata olives. He scoops some into a bowl with a slotted spoon.

"What's the idea behind this house?"

The briny herb-scented olives taste the way fresh seawater smells. Joe spits the pits rapid-fire into his palm.

"What do you mean?"

"Somehow it doesn't seem like you."

Cassidy has put her elbows on the surgically gleaming countertop.

"That's ridiculous," says Joe.

"I pictured you in some place darker, more traditional—"

Joe busies himself with the cork.

"—More like Harvey Weissman's."

"That's why I like this house."

"Why?"

"Because it isn't dark. It's all about the natural light."

He fills a glass with Pinot Grigio. The bowl frosts over.

"You like keeping secrets."

"Not really."

"It's not about the *light*. People don't buy crazy houses because of *light*. I mean, I'm sure this house isn't crazy—"

"That's all right."

"—So what's it about?"

"The house?"

"Yeah."

"Greece."

"Thank you!"

Resigned, "There's a Greek expression. *Odessia*. It means 'the great desire of going back home.'"

"You wouldn't know you were Greek until you opened your refrigerator."

"The Galinis nose? Hard to miss."

"Your nose is beautiful." She lazily draws a finger down the hard straight line of it, tapering to a pleasant point in balance with the high square forehead and long face. "I didn't know you were Greek. Until some old lady told me at Harvey Weissman's party."

"You knew," Joe says shortly. "Come sit down."

"What's this?"

She lifts the aluminum foil off the corner of a large roasting pan that is resting on the stove, releasing the scent of cooked olive oil, garlic and oregano.

"Lemon chicken. I made it for you."

"You made this?"

Crusty chicken breasts surrounded by soft thick rounds of potato, the rich scrapings in the pan all caramelized and dark.

"Hungry?"

"I will be."

They return to the living room and face each other on opposite sofas. The wine is clean. She could drink a lot of it.

"Tell me what happened in Vero Beach. Start from the beginning."

It takes a while because Cassidy seems to feel it is important first to communicate exactly what was wrong with Alberto's *ballplaying* that alerted her to the depth of the problem. So she does a lot of talking and demonstration there in the pristine living room of drop-step, crossover, catching mechanics and release, during which Joe gets up restlessly and changes the CD several times—to blues and finally jazz—as they work their way through the Pinot Grigio.

"They didn't go after Alberto because he had a bodyguard. Instead they delivered the message to me. Joe, a man was hiding under my car, he tried to slash my Achilles tendon with a stiletto—ever see a stiletto in real life?"

"I've had a gun held to my head in my own driveway. Not here. When we lived in Cheviot Hills. When Nora was a baby. She was asleep in the car seat."

"The reptilian part of the brain takes over. The most primitive response."

She sips the wine. It might be glass number three.

"Then another one grabbed me from behind. I never saw his face. Everything was wrong. Out of balance, out of myself."

Her heart is racing. Nausea spiraling up. *Their hands press her wrist. Her ankles scrape the asphalt. They're dragging her. She's pinned.*

"Come sit here."

In the dark reflection of the glass she can see her chest flushed pink, self-containment split open like a fig.

"Let's get some air."

Joe has jumped up and unlocked the sliding panel. When they are outside he tells her to relax and breathe.

He says, "You're safe."

But she does not feel safe because above the enclosed courtyard there is nothing but sky, a disturbing lack of context—dark possibilities of the unseen, and the sea air only bringing back the wet tropical night in Florida.

"This is bad. I'm sorry. I didn't think it would affect me—"

He snorts, "Not *affect* you? Who was the genius who told you back in 1984 you were the Bionic Woman? Which redneck coach, because I'd like to find him and blow his brains out."

"Don't yell at me, Joe."

"I'm not yelling!"

He jams his fists into his pockets. "I feel like shit, that's all, it makes me nuts beyond belief that A, this happened, and B, you had to go through it alone."

"I wasn't alone. I had Detective Allen."

"Oh," says Joe. "That's good."

She breaks away and sits on the edge of the reflecting pool. She takes four breaths from the diaphragm. *This isn't real. The attack is over. Say something. Distract yourself.*

"He asked me to identify 'the assailants.' I said I couldn't. Not the most creative lie, but I'm not the world's best liar. Detective Allen was really very nice. It was a cute police station. Maybe I should move to Vero Beach and teach gym."

"What do you mean, you lied? You knew who they were?"

"I know they were Dominican."

Joe sits beside her on the cold stone.

"How?"

"Their bodies. The stiletto. Words they said in Spanish and the way they said them."

She studies his face, impenetrable, looking for a clue in the shadowed eyes, wide-set creases in the cheeks, that might reveal the brutality it would take to gouge earth, to raise buildings, to survive the constant pummeling of below-the-belt local politics. She can't see it in the dark. But that doesn't mean it isn't there.

"I didn't tell Detective Allen about the extortion threats. That this was their way of suggesting to Alberto that he pay. Maybe he'll find out from the organization. Maybe he won't. I made the decision to play it out."

Cassidy feels chilled, a consequence of the flashback. Goose bumps have risen on her arms.

"Hold me."

Joe puts his glass down on the edge of the pool. She leans into the heat of his body.

"Alberto said it wasn't him. He said that when we hit her, you were the one who was driving."

Joe's body slackens.

"That's really disappointing."

"What?"

"That Alberto would come up with something like that. Those are seriously dangerous charges. If it were anybody else I'd be outraged. I'd have Harvey on the next plane. The trouble is, I like the kid. He's a good kid, his career just got royally screwed. I can understand why he'd lie. Okay, fine. We gave him the benefit of the doubt."

"Were you? Driving?"

She expects him to sit up and throw her off. Instead he laughs, the dry hip laugh, so conscious of itself.

"That's a joke, right?"

"I have to ask."

"No. No you don't have to ask." Now he does gets up, pushing her away. "Don't you know me? Haven't we made love?"

"Yes, of course—"

"Then you should know the truth."

She comes up behind him, puts her arms around his waist, and lays her cheek between his shoulder blades.

"I'm sorry," she says. "So torn. I feel so guilty. I never should have let him get into that car—"

"Honey, there will come a point where you just can't save him."

Joe turns around.

"I know you want to." His voice breaks. "That's because you're so good. So good."

They cling to each other with relief. Their fingers stroke each other's temples, eyelids, cheeks—savoring the reassurance that they're both still there.

"No, I'm not so good, no, please forgive me. That was such an awful thing to even ask you—"

"Oh," big ironic sigh, "I should be used to it by now. The developer is always the bad guy."

Teasing him with little kisses, "Sure, and nobody ever paid anybody off, or ever did anything underhanded or illegal, to get the entertainment center built?"

Joe is smiling at her fondly. "No."

"No?"

"We settle it like Greeks."

He cocks his head in a secret way that makes her feel it with a jolt down below.

"There's a famous story. Two Greeks were having an argument over who owned some olive trees. You know how they resolved it? They burned the olive trees down."

"That's inspiring."

He draws her closer.

"What you need to do is fall back and trust someone's going to be there for you."

"I don't know who that person would be."

He kisses her throat. There are hazards. The edge of the reflecting pool. The sand. Chaise lounges under the stars, folded towels on each, the scent of orange blossom from the trees in containers. The living room—sofas, rug, why not the polished stone hearth?—and, of course, the staircase, which quickly becomes littered with their clothes.

On the second floor, a mezzanine overlooking the first, a half dozen oil paintings seem to float in silver bodies of light. The paintings are grotesque. Abstract lines and tortured human figures disappear into eerie mists but certain loud exaggerated features remain—ears, mouths, muscle, sores—that seem to shout for attention, refuse to melt, like gold teeth in a crematorium.

"What is this?" Cassidy breathes.

"An Irish painter named Francis Bacon. I began collecting him when I was in college."

"You knew his paintings would be valuable."

Joe says simply, "He moves me."

Cassidy shudders. "People with their souls hanging out."

"Well put."

"For a jock."

"Our insecurity is showing."

Cassidy moves away and stands, barefoot and in underwear, before a scene of crucifixion in which the martyr's skin is peeling away to show gristle and white rib.

"I remember this," she says softly.

"You've seen it before?"

"No, but I feel like I have, it's what you were talking about when we were driving in the Dominican. There was a horrible dead cow on the truck ahead of us."

Joe is hooking a finger in the champagne-colored lace of her panties.

"*What* was I talking about?"

"*This painting.* Whether it was when we were with Alberto or not, I can't remember, but we were looking at this cow carcass tied up on this truck and you said something about how it was crucified and it was so beautiful."

Joe caresses her neck. "Could I have been more pretentious?"

She keeps on staring as he tugs her backward by the G-string into the master bedroom where the walls and built-ins are finished in honey-colored sycamore, a warm contrast to the cold stainless steel below.

"I like this a whole lot better than downstairs."

"They each have their moments in time," Joe allows, pressing a remote that brings Stan Getz into the room.

The bed faces the ocean at the same height as the tops of the Manila palms. Opening the doors to the terrace just a slice brings the steady blow of the sea. Joe sits on the edge of the white linens wearing nothing but the pink polo shirt, a frank raw erection looking straight at her from between his legs.

"Wow," he says. "You have really good posture."

Cassidy flops from the waist, giggling.

"Let me see that, turn sideways."

She complies.

"So is this what the babes in the gym look like?"

"No."

She raises a leg to his shoulder and pushes him down with the sole of her bare foot.

"They're toned. I'm in shape. They fantasize. I'm it."

She climbs on top. Wrestles off his shirt. Luxuriates in his well-developed barrel chest.

"You know what we should do?"

He is naked above her, supported on his hands. Her pelvis is arching up, hot, too hot, willing to say yes to anything.

"—We should get married," says Joe.

"We should?"

"Yes, and for a wedding present, I'll buy you a baseball team."

She laughs exorbitantly, to the point of hysteria, like a crazy person.

"Who says I can't? Who says you can't? Be the first woman manager in the history of the game? You don't think I mean it."

"You mean it now."

"It doesn't matter."

His fingers are warm and their skins don't pinch and pull.

"Here," she breathes.

"Like this," he whispers. "Wait—"

Together they keep changing. Aware, then unaware. Lost, and then, like dripping pebbles, found.

A handful of wet pebbles under a burning olive tree.

MAY

18

The Dodgers win at Colorado, 6–4 with Raul Mondesi going two for four, a double, a homer and three RBIs. Cassidy listens to the play-by-play in the car, announcer Ross Porter's voice pure and strong all the way from Denver. It is comforting, like hearing your dad talking in the den. Between the warm-up and the wrap-up Cassidy is able to cover three high school games and two hundred miles, seeing kids she has already seen once or twice before, a dedicated effort to track every last possibility before the big western regional meeting.

This is it, fish or cut bait, when the West Coast scouts present their top prospects for the June draft. The pressure is severe, each man on the line to sell not only his prospects but his own expertise. If you stumble or hesitate, all that preparation flies out the window and you look—the worst thing possible for a baseball scout—indecisive.

Besides, if Cassidy messed up in a room full of male competitors, all that would remain would be two gold earrings and a forty-nine-dollar Ironman watch. Maybe not the watch.

The last bit of business of this long May afternoon is another visit with Brad Parker, the right-hander she had brought Travis down to see, whose family lives all the way out in Perris.

An outpost of suburban blight on the lip of the desert, it takes Cassidy an hour and a half on baking freeways to get there. She has made the trip so often she is known by name in two different Denny's and rejoices at the rows of battle-gray KC-10s lined up at March Air Force Base because the sight of them means she is almost at Cottonwood Gardens—a dusty-pink-walled tract—and can stretch that lumbar spine.

"I brought you my mom's recipe," she announces, walking through the unlocked front door and into the kitchen as if she were a member of the family. "Cranberry-walnut-pumpkin loaf."

"Aren't you a dear!"

Brad's mom, Pepper Parker, is setting out a welcoming snack, cheese nachos, cans of diet soda and carrot sticks. The nachos are topped with mild chili peppers, just like at the ballpark, and served in square paper containers with gingham checks she buys by the hundred.

Overweight, with ash-colored hair all puffed and multiple pierces up the earlobes, wearing turquoise bicycle shorts and matching sleeveless blouse, Pepper, plus twenty pounds, is exactly who she was when she left Des Moines with baby Brad to follow her brawny high school impregnator to the Camp Pendleton Marine Corps Base. From there it was a drive up the 215 to a starter home and a gig as an assistant manager in a twenty-four-hour copy shop that grew into an empire of three, plus the tree-trimming business.

Pepper is a world-class baker of Christmas cookies, as Cassidy had discovered inside a heavy almond-scented tin last winter, who continues to be fascinated by Maggie Sanderson's creative notion of using her own talent for baking to turn the family home into a B&B. Of course Maggie and her new husband, Stan, the retired marketing man from the Bay area, took it a couple of steps further by enshrining Smoke's Pacific Coast League memorabilia in what used to be the dining room, renaming the house where Cassidy and Gregg grew up the Hollywood Stars Inn and Baseball Museum. Pepper still has the brochure Cassidy brought back from a visit in December stuck to the refrigerator with a koala bear magnet.

"Thank your mom so much and tell her we'll have to stop by. Next time we're up in Oregon. We've got that camper out there," Pepper says wistfully. "I imagine we'll be getting *it* going around the same time we get that fish tank fired up."

An eight-foot-long, two-hundred-gallon empty casket of glass remains on the floor against the dining room wall.

"Someday," Cassidy sighs in agreement, as if it were her dream, as well, to replicate a living coral reef just minutes from Riverside.

"Has Brad heard from any schools?"

"We hope next month."

"Promise to call me when you get those envelopes?"

"Oh, absolutely."

"I want to get a jump on the competition."

Pepper looks toward the door. "Lang and Brad'll be here any minute." She checks her watch and makes a decision.

She sits down across from Cassidy.

"I want to share with you, in all honesty—and we both know there's other interest—we're sold on the Dodgers."

"My supervisor was real pleased when he saw Brad pitch."

Pepper's darkened eyebrows arch hopefully. "Lang said he really had his stuff that day."

"When it comes to the draft, it's going to be tough, but I'll do my best. You know I believe in Brad."

"He adores you. Thinks you're cool."

"*Cool?*" Cassidy laughs self-deprecatingly. "Anything that works."

"So . . ." Pepper taps the index card with the recipe against the oak table and stares at it for an anxious second or two, "if Lang seems to be giving you the runaround, it's just his way—"

"I know. Listen, I want him to always feel free to ask questions."

"What I'm telling you is . . . between us, and I probably shouldn't say *anything* . . . when the time comes, we want to make a deal."

"I hear what you're saying."

For the next twenty minutes, until the dad and prospect show, Cassidy sits with Pepper Parker and talks about brownies. Great brownies from the past, orgasmic brownies of the future we can only imagine. Dense or cake-like, does it really work if you use mayonnaise? Yes or no on the question of walnuts, chocolate chips, and various toppings of coconut, frosting or mini M&M's—why *do* women crave chocolate?—and let's sneak a Snickers from the freezer right now!

It is the hardest and most crucial work she has done all day.

On the morning of the western regional meeting Cassidy takes a long run on the beach, turning south at the Laguna lifeguard tower, the rented cottage quickly lost in the mishmash of pastel houses and red tile roofs that clings to every curve of the brooding coastal mountain range.

She is going for broad external focus, calmly taking it all in, but it is hard to keep her eyes on the horizon. Several times she has caught herself with head down, spacing out on the toes of her running shoes rhythmically chugging the wet sand. She has had to make a conscious effort to loosen the jaw, relax the shoulders, keep the head up for max oxygen intake, and concentrate on rehearsing the promotional spiels Pedro had insisted she write out on behalf of her prospects, but it is difficult to concentrate on signability and bat speed when all she can think about is Joe.

She had woken up dreaming they were making love. The bedroom, dormers bending close and rectangles of trapped sun, had felt like a slow oven on all night, her body the source of heat. Even the outside world seemed fat with desire, animated in tropical colors: the crowns of the palm trees lemon pinwheels of light, three black crows crying over and over the same primitive note.

Release me.

"When you are a physical person," Marshall once said in a burst of postcoital eloquence, "you become addicted to the physical, driven by the physical, wanting to get back to the feeling of playing ball, searching for that level of intensity like *Wow!* and *Holy shit!* It can become almost sexual, sometimes you can't tell the difference. It's hard to separate, doesn't matter, all you know is that you're hungry for it."

For example, today is Wednesday, and according to their no-surrender training schedule, Cassidy and Marshall should be running together, six miles on the beach. But he is up in Vancouver training one of his bratty male movie stars on a film, which is a good thing. They might otherwise wind up in bed from 8:35 to 8:45 a.m. — not on the schedule and not where Cassidy wants to be with Marshall — but she might, in this current state of aroused aggression, be driven to it; an impulse buy, guilt-inducing as a walnut bear claw from Scandia bakery in town, and just as sticky.

She turns around and heads back north. The tide is rising, forcing her to run on soft sand, harder on the hamstrings, so she angles down a ridge and sprints through the water. The pink cast came off last week; her left hand is beginning to throb inside its brace.

Since the assault she has been shadowed by wild thoughts: that out in the open like this, someone is watching her through the scope of a high-powered automatic rifle. Unexpected objects make her jump, like the brown padded envelopes and FedEx boxes she finds on her doorstep from Nóra—signed jerseys she'd bought at auction, paperbacks on how to coach your kids' Little League team, a silver cable bracelet from Neiman Marcus, whole sports sections from the *New York Times*—with sad little Post-its that say, *Let's have lunch!* and *Thinking of you.*

Despite her paranoia, no more threats have been received by Alberto or Joe. Hopefully they have left the fuckers behind in Florida. Nobody from the organization has called to interrogate her as to why she didn't tell Detective Allen about the Dominicans in the parking lot, or that Los Angeles developer Joe Galinis has been a target of the same extortion.

Find the groove.

When he becomes transfixed with that tragicomic stare of longing, Joe will go down on his knees and caress her ankles and say, "I adore you."

Should she marry the adoration? The privilege? Should she be a trophy? Be a star? Walk into the life she had lost when she lost the shot at the Olympics and a big endorsement deal: beautiful clothes, exclusive gyms, a gracious home with a dazzling pool, looking good, plastic surgery, always sitting in the skybox seats? Joe seems to want to give her everything—including her own baseball team (was he serious?). Still, she has a kind of power over him; something she has never felt with any other man.

Find the groove.

Out here in the open it is difficult to pretend that moment didn't happen—when she had seen Joe naked and exposed, or nearly so, kicking a soccer ball in the waves with Sophie—and the feeling overwhelmed her, strong enough to override everything else.

The bite of salt spray brings it back, watching Joe from the cliff outside the perimeter of the Gran Caribe as he lost himself in the game with Sophie, discovering his capacity for tenderness although he tried to keep it hidden in a cove.

The clouds *that had been skidding freely all morning had drawn together and changed character from impertinent white to iron gray, forming an ominous tower in the eastern sky. The fringed fronds of the king palms were stretched out like pennants on a good-sized wind. At poolside the band played to rows of empty lounge chairs. A half dozen young Italian men were clustered around, wet hair, wet legs, wet shorts, smoking cigarettes and drinking piña coladas by the pitcher. The barman stood idle. A towel boy was swinging his keys. The resort felt disconcertingly empty, Disneyland on a rainy day. Cassidy passed a table of Japanese who seemed to be the only other guests, puzzling out the Western dinner roll; one was sawing at it* *with knife and fork while the others watched. Two of the Italian boys were kissing with their tongues.*

The front desk manager advised Cassidy to look for Sr. Galinis in the casino, just beyond the restaurant.

The casino was vast as a supermarket, cold as a morgue, filled with rows of glaring adult toys blinking and chirping to no one. Cars made of light-bulbs rotated above hundreds of digital slot machines; the sugar towns still didn't have electricity, but here in the citadel of sugar the lights were on and the air-conditioning howling twenty-four hours a day.

"Who is there?"

A man (not Joe) had risen quickly from a video game table upon which he and a woman companion were apparently doing work. There were coffee cups, printouts, a couple of piles of Dominican bills. In the underwater glow their faces looked green, but Cassidy recognized the imperious bearing. The man was the General, who had rented her the car.

"¡Señorita!"

The General clasped Cassidy's hand in both of his.

"What a pleasure! How are you? My nephew said everything went well?"

"Very well. We had a little problem with the jeep—"

"I am so sorry."

The young woman extended her hand.

"Nora Galinis."

"You must be related to Joe."

"I'm his daughter."

Even in the strange neon light the resemblance was powerful. Dark hair. Aegean cheekbones. And the same defensive pride.

"I was just looking for your dad."

"Were you?" The daughter held the other woman with the freckled nose and sun-bleached hair in silent commanding scrutiny for as long as it had taken to perform the necessary calculations.

"He gave me a ride when the jeep broke down."

"I hope it was no inconvenience," said the General. "Did you find your player?"

"Signed him. Over and out."

"Congratulations. The lady is a baseball scout!" cried the General, dimples twinkling.

"Do they have women baseball scouts?"

"They do now."

Nora's smile had become childlike. "I wish I could do something fun like that!"

"You already have a big job," crooned the General, patting her wrist. "She runs her daddy's hotel."

Nora's head dipped bashfully. Cassidy marveled at such machismo. First Rhonda in a swoon and now this Los Angeles mogul playing the ingenue.

"I was wondering where your dad might be."

Nora checked a gold watch with heavy overlapping links.

"At the beach, naturally. He's got my daughter, Sophie, and we have to make a plane."

She had begun to gather up the money on the game table.

Cassidy asked, "How do you two know each other?"

"Luis owns a taxi and messenger company."

"Oh right," said Cassidy, putting it together. "Your nephew told me that he also drives for the big hotels."

"Everyone is in a panic to get out because of Hurricane Gordon," Nora was going on. "Yesterday we were booked. Today you could shoot a cannon through this place. Luis had to come up with an entire fleet—"

"Even one ambulance!"

"—Some very funky," Nora agreed, patting his wrist in a familiar way. "To get our guests to the airport."

"Monroe right now is driving to the airport, a hundred times, back and forth like a cockroach!"

Cassidy appreciated the image.

"We were thrilled Luis could help out."

"Always a privilege, Señorita Galinis."

They climbed the black-carpeted stairs and exited the casino, exchanging frigid darkness for savagely dense humidity. The General shook their hands in turn, nodded respectfully, and left. No erections, Cassidy noted. This was business.

Cassidy and Nora had climbed into a golf cart parked in a tiled courtyard. As Nora twisted the key and stepped on the pedal Cassidy could not help watching her feet in black patent leather sandals with tiny white daisies stitched along the straps. She had never seen such refined feet, long *and white with square scarlet toenails, soft as a pair of snowy ermine. By the time Cassidy's feet come out of sweat socks and athletic shoes they look like crumpled paper cups.*

"I do not manage the hotel," Nora was quick to clarify in a markedly less cordial tone, swinging the golf cart onto a service road. In the daylight her face had looked fresh as a high school kid's. "I am not the person who puts a Godiva chocolate on your pillow."

Cassidy was thinking it would have been really great if she had been wearing her bimbo cap. It is pink and in sequined silver letters it says B-I-M-B-O. Too bad she left it home.

"I'm vice president of the resort corporation but"—jabbing at the air like a politician—"I have an M.B.A. from Harvard!" Nora laughed, then kept talking. "I have to say that or you'd think it's nepotism. Although most people would not identify my father with the Gran Caribe."

"I thought he ran the place."

"That would drive him nuts. He has no patience for the petty day-to-day. He's always been like that. He wasn't the kind of father who would sit on the floor and play games. He'd take me to a construction site and let me drive a bulldozer, or to his office and show me reports and memos that were way over my head, and explain what was going on. His big thing was, 'Always look at the big picture.' His office was up on the twenty-third floor. I'd look at the view from the window. It was big. No, no," she said, her hair in a snarl from the wind, "once my dad puts a deal together, it's on to the next. He's a visionary, really."

As they skirted the complex through low-lying gardens she pointed out oranges, tangerines, tamarind, yucca, casaba, string beans and a saffron tree loaded with red pods.

"It was funny. We had to promise the environmentalists the Gran Caribe would be self-sustaining. What do they think? Please. We still have to get foie gras from somewhere."

Cassidy once knew a girl like Nora Galinis, her roommate freshman year at UCLA. Cassidy had been on full athletic scholarship, playing shortstop for the Bruins and training for the 1984 Olympics; Andie Bigelow was Connecticut money, not deigning to date Jewish men because "yid boys are all short." Mysterious and intimidating, Andie shopped at Saks and had her nails done—stuff Cassidy dismissed as for old ladies—and kept her distance, undoubtedly afraid the she-jock was a lesbian. After one semester

Andie moved to an apartment in Beverly Hills, where, it was rumored, she was kept by an Iranian jeweler.

Nora, too, wore the brittle gloss of a much older woman (she couldn't have been more than twenty-eight), prematurely trapped in an aging woman's fears—dark hair deftly highlighted with auburn, thin angular shoulders and narrow hips inside a little white suit with a fitted jacket woven in a provincial floral like a fancy tablecloth. But the suit, for all its deftness, hung off an undeveloped frame, and Nora Galinis, a Greek princess living on who knows how many hundreds of thousands of dollars a year, looked as if she were starving.

"They gave us a hard time—"

"The environmental people?"

"The government. The politicians. My dad won." Nora shook her hair until the wind and forward motion tangled it up in her face. "Nobody beats my dad. He's the smartest, most competitive man in the world. When he wants something he locks on like a low-flying missile and nothing stops him, trust me—"

"I believe it—" Cassidy began, but her voice became lost in the roar of the ocean as they suddenly crested a hill and stopped beside another golf cart on a bluff overlooking the beach, a wide crescent of black sand between huge dramatic formations of dark charcoal lava boulders. On a calm day it would have been an enchanted hideaway, but then, before the storm, the black cove seemed a cauldron of tempestuous power.

Below them the Caribbean Sea, mad luminescent green, was throwing twenty-foot swells against the black rock towers, spraying fine shimmery mist through sea grape and wild sage. One lone pelican was gliding across acres of multilayered inky cloud through which the sun presented its last pale yellow rays, aimed, it seemed, at two figures weaving just as madly through the foamy shallows—Joe Galinis dribbling a soccer ball with his five-year-old granddaughter against a surf slope of molten gold.

He must have been one hell of a soccer player, she remembers thinking, in control, graceful as a dancer, he trapped it, floated above, teased with a fusillade of naked feet, then popped it off the instep high into the air as Sophie shrieked with laughter. All of this bare-chested, a shining compact competent torso, strong good arms extended, linen trousers soaked to the knees while the child raced around him, sprite's body corkscrewing with joy, hurling herself with great crescendo into the obsidian mud.

Cassidy followed Nora down a trail to the beach. The little girl abandoned Joe and ran toward her mother, who held her at arm's length until a middle-aged nanny, who had been sitting on a blanket, came to wrap her in a towel.

"I booked us on the last flight out," Nora told her father. "It wasn't easy."

"Can I wear my sparkle shoes on the plane?" Sophie wanted to know.

"Yes. Get her out of that wet suit."

"Will do," sang the nanny, English, wearing an awful caftan.

Joe shrugged into a shirt and smoothed his hair.

"You've met?"

"We've met," Nora answered bluntly.

"Are you leaving, too?" he asked Cassidy.

"I can't. I've got to finesse a visa for Alberto Cruz. In fact I need your help."

"We'll drive to the capital tomorrow."

"Dad, it's crazy to stay. We're supposed to get hundred-mile-per-hour winds."

"Propaganda," said Joe. "We'll only see the tail end of it."

"Cassidy could fly out with us. I can scrounge another ticket—"

"I appreciate that," said Cassidy. "But—"

"—Hard to leave paradise," Joe finished.

Nora looked back and forth between them, realizing her calculations had been flawless.

"Enjoy," she said at last, removing the sunglasses in the silvery dusk.

Her large dark eyes were full of pain.

"Watch out for my father," she had added with attempted nonchalance. "He won't always let you win."

The enchantment of seeing him from the bluff in the cove with Sophie made the earth seem to fall away from under her feet. Giddy, she was about to call out over the wind, *I'm in love!*—maybe he would have looked up and their eyes might have met, and everything might have been different.

But she had not called out, and suddenly it seems urgent to remember why—as Edith, having waited in the usual spot for Cassidy's return, streaks toward her, barking and getting tangled up in her legs—and her

ability to recall brings it back with clarity: Nora, it was Nora who somehow got in the way, so the dreamy possibilities of calling down to Joe had
snapped with a sudden shift in perspective, like coming out of this lung-
busting oxygen-deprived overdrive to discover the Laguna lifeguard tower,
a moment ago a matchstick in the haze, is suddenly here—big and round
and present in all its dimension, like the raw ache pounding undeniably
in her smashed bones.

19

Cassidy arrives for the 9 a.m. western regional meeting in the director's room at Dodger Stadium fifteen minutes early. Most of the other scouts have been there since eight, accustomed to getting to the field well before the game.

They fill the awkward spaces around the oak conference desk with a heavy-footed male presence like a pack of steers herded together, hindquarters nervously backing into each other. Computer cases and overnight bags are strewn around. Two fans keep the air moving in the windowless room.

Dulce bustles in with a fresh pot of coffee.

"¿Cómo está, señora?" Cassidy inquires cordially.

"I'm fine," Dulce replies sharply in English, cutting off the possibility of bridging the cultural thing that still divides them.

Just for that, Cassidy chooses not to help her with the string on the pink jumbo-size bakery box, although the Swiss Army knife in her backpack would have sliced right through that baby. Anyway, she thinks, standing back with the men while Dulce reaches into the box and draws out one sweet roll at a time, carefully holding each underneath by its paper, setting out the pastries is a devalued feminine task that she should take pains not to be associated with in this room.

Travis reaches past with a whiff of woodsy deodorant.

"For you." He picks a donut. "Cream in the middle."

"Aren't you nice," says Cassidy, ignoring it.

"What happened to your wrist?"

"Busted it Rollerblading."

"Never heard of wrist guards?"

"I've heard of them."

She smiles pleasantly. It throws him.

"So," says Travis. "How many cards did you ultimately manage to get up there?"

A large white board is divided into columns headed RHP, LHP, 1B, 2B, 3B, C, SS, LF, CF, RF. Beneath each position the names of the top prospects are posted on over two hundred color-coded magnetic tiles, gold meaning first-round picks, blue second, on to green and gray. Even having made it this far is no guarantee: every player on the board now faces one-in-thirty odds of ever playing in the bigs.

"I've got a bunch of greens and gray and three blues, but Parker is the guy I really want."

Travis's narrow eyes seem complacent.

"You like Parker as much as you like Cruz?" he asks.

"With Cruz you're talking phenom."

"Aren't you Miss Confidence?"

"He made Double A, he's in San Antonio, didn't you hear?"

"I also heard he's having health problems."

"Oh, you mean that stomach flu—?"

"No. Something else. Hey, Raymond. What's the deal with Cruz? What's he got, some stomach condition—"

"They don't know," Raymond replies. "Still doing tests. My guess, it's psychological. Adjustment problems. Are we ready to start?"

Cassidy sits down uneasily. Okay, it's not CF like her brother had, but it's also not impossible that Alberto's body's tripping him up, causing him to fail. She wouldn't wonder if she hadn't seen him play, but the distraction she saw on the field, the histrionic exit from the restaurant, seem to fit the picture of a young man who has made a serious mistake; who could perhaps bury it in his heart and in his mind, but whose body would behave according to the guilty truth. The body, Cassidy has learned, never lies.

She finds herself next to old-timer Skip O'Donnell—white hair, glasses, white shirt over a potbelly—who ignores her, complaining as usual.

"I took the kid off the list, he lied about his age."

"How did he think he could get away with that?"

"Thought I'd never ask to see his birth certificate! Well, he sees everyone else lie, cheat and steal." Big sigh. "Baseball's gone to hell in a handbasket."

"It's war," says B. J. Backer without looking up from a laptop.

"It's a slaughter," agrees Skip.

Cassidy takes out her notes, places the knapsack at her feet. She keeps her left hand, in the wrist brace, in her lap. She is wearing loafers instead of Jack Purcells, a light tweed jacket to go with the khakis, a velvet headband in blow-dried straight hair and Nora's silver bracelet. The rest of the guys, in short-sleeved knit shirts mainly blue or beige, jeans, cowboy boots, buzz cuts, could be a bunch of burly in-shape firemen or telephone repairmen, except if you noticed the weighty World Championship pendants and rings.

For them the regional meeting is a milestone in the year, a hassle, a stress, a hot lunch.

For Cassidy, every moment on the job is life-or-death.

At ten past nine Raymond closes the door.

"When you go over a player, stick to his tools, intelligence, does he want to go out and play. When you discuss signability, don't tell everyone what a pain in the ass his father is and whatnot—do you have a good feeling about the parents, can you trust these people? Is there a medical condition, is there an agent? Above all, what is your gut feeling? Be thorough with your comments but stay to the point. Everything we discuss in here stays here."

Randy Elkins, based in Seattle, a soft-handshake feet-on-the-ground type father of three, starts it off with a gold card right-hander. No argument here. Every club in America wants this kid.

"Big strong guy with thick thighs, got a chance to have a plus-plus fastball. Best thing about him is his arm action," says Randy. "I don't think he has any idea what is going to happen to him. To me he's a solid first-round guy, I can't say enough good things about him."

Raymond asks, "Is there school in the picture?"

"Washington State, fifty percent ride."

They go on a bit, then Raymond cuts it off. Logged in. Next.

Patrick Herald, kind of a noir mystery, black hair slicked back and pockmarked cheeks, takes the second gold card, a pitcher from Baldwin Park.

"This kid had arm surgery but solid number one stuff, 91 and 94 on the jugs, power curveball, aggressive on the mound, not a great body, somewhat fleshy, I'm not sure he's a great athlete, but boy, he had some kind of good stuff for four and a third innings. He's going to have an agent and he's going to be a first-rounder. I don't think he'll be there for us in the second round . . ."

Cassidy tries to focus on Roy Campanella's jersey in a Plexiglas box on the wall. They are getting through the gold cards quickly: thirty-five blues until Parker. It will be afternoon before they get to greens and grays. The scouting staff has been seated twenty minutes and already there is a lot of leg shaking and toe tapping and chairs bobbing up and down. This is not a group that likes to stay indoors on a sunny day.

At ten fifty-five Raymond interrupts. "I've got to take a lunch order. Pork chops, halibut, Cobb salad, mixed fruit salad. How many for pork chops?"

At eleven-thirty, to raised eyebrows and head shakes, Skip O'Donnell changes his mind and disqualifies one of his own picks:

"He puts you to sleep, this guy, but every once in a while he'll wake you up with some power. I never did like this guy, he's a dead guy for me."

Raymond: "You don't want him?"

Skip: "He's not much of a competitor. There's something there but I'm not going to fight for the guy. He's played like he's got mono all year."

Bubble gum is being passed along the back row, everyone absorbed in reading the fortunes. Cassidy leans forward. Thirteen cards until Parker. Her stomach is tight. She counters with a deep breath for relaxation, narrowing the focus: internal, rehearsing the speech. The door opens and Dulce slips in, giving a folded yellow sheet to Randy, who is sitting closest, whispering to him to pass it on. When the note reaches Cassidy she is shaken to discover it has her name on it.

Cassidy reads the message and looks up, dumbfounded, but Dulce has already withdrawn.

Whatever calm she has achieved ignites into four-alarm panic. But she is forced to wait while Raymond methodically grills B.J. about a shortstop whose dad is ambivalent about the Dodgers because "he doesn't want the boy to play in the smog."

"Let's start over," Raymond is saying. "Tell me if you want the guy or not, B.J."

"That's a hard one."

"Would you take him in the seventh round?"

"Yes, definitely."

"How much is he worth to you?"

B.J. chews his gum. "Thirty or forty."

"Fine."

Cassidy raises her hand.

"Raymond, sorry, security needs me to take care of something, could we jump ahead—"

"If nobody has any objections."

Which is a way of saying everybody probably has. But they all keep doing what they're doing.

Raymond shifts impatiently on his feet. "Okay, let's go to your top guy."

"Parker," Cassidy says, pointing.

"Do it."

Travis sits up. She doesn't like it, going on with a tight gut, head full of snow.

"This is the guy I really want. I liked him early. He didn't show everything you want to see in the beginning but he's come a long way." She can tell she is going too fast. "Good pitcher's frame, loose, has a quick arm, some deception to the hitter. Throws across his body a little bit. You talk about projecting a player, this guy is starting to put it all together. I think he's got a chance for a good breaking ball. Good mound presence. Confdent."

Raymond asks, "What about signability?"

"Signability is excellent. The parents are very knowledgeable, they'd love him to be a Dodger. If I can get him quickly it will be a done deal. He comes from a good family, not a lot of money, he wants to go out."

"Negatives?"

"He might struggle with his lower half in the future. In some ways he's crude. Never been coached. But he's a good-looking prospect. It's just a question of, what we see in him, others will see, too."

She stops, heart pounding and breathless. Did she throw it all away? Travis's expression is as unreadable as Raymond's.

She gets up, red-faced, climbing over knees and feet to the door.

"Hell of a time to hassle you about your parking space," Randy Elkins whispers kindly.

"Really."

The room waits with a mix of smugness and disinterest, as if Cassidy were being called to the principal's office, speculating, along with the bubble-gum fortunes, whether things will turn out well.

Or not.

Waiting in Raymond's empty office, along with LAPD Detective Mark Simms, is a short amiable man with a brush haircut wearing a double-breasted tan sport coat and tie-dyed tie.

He comes toward her, extending a hand.

"Nate Allen, Detective Division, Vero Beach police department. Remember me?" he asks, altogether perky.

20

"Great view."

Detective Allen goes to the window that overlooks the field.

"You sneak up here to watch the games?"

"Usually I'm on the road."

Simms: "Who has time to sit through nine innings?"

"I know what you're saying."

Allen seems to have materialized as calm and attentive as he had been that night.

"Dodgertown is just down the street," he continues, "but do I ever take my kid to a game? How's the hand, Cassidy?"

"Better." She waits. "What are you doing here?"

"A homicide occurred in Vero Beach the night you were attacked. I need your help in identifying a suspect."

Her heart squeezes.

"You might remember we had some activity when you were leaving the station and we had to cut things short. It turns out a college kid was killed during a robbery. He worked as a clerk in a 7-Eleven. Good kid, nice family."

"Those things make me sick."

"It happened about three hours after you were assaulted in the parking lot. Two gunmen held up the store using automatic weapons. The incident took place less than a mile from the Coast Grill. The suspects fit your description."

"You think it might have been the same guys?"

"They wouldn't have sent Detective Allen all the way to Los Angeles if they didn't think there was a damn good possibility," says Simms impatiently, crossing his arms.

By contrast, Detective Allen seems almost apologetic. "We were hoping you'd cooperate in our investigation. We have the tape from the surveillance camera in the 7-Eleven. I was wondering if you would mind having a look."

"Anything I can do."

Allen opens a briefcase and takes out a videocassette as they wait in silence.

Finally Simms, with the hollow smile: "Are you okay with this?"

"I said I'm okay."

Allen says, "It's grisly. I have to warn you. But maybe you can help us catch the fuckers."

He isn't looking at Cassidy when he says this but she knows it is a coded reference to the conversation—no, interrogation—at the Vero Beach police department, a reminder that when she was injured he was there to help—a cryptic bond between them, like strangers who have passed on a street corner moments before an explosion.

Allen inserts the tape and presses the button on Raymond's VCR and Cassidy's mind goes desperately to the meeting in progress in the director's room, wishing she were back there right now; what had been high drama seems placid and comforting as a nursery song.

The image hits the screen. A high angle behind the counter shows a moth's-eye view of the convenience store. The top of the clerk's head is visible as he sits on a stool, and a time imprint in the right-hand corner of the frame, 2:35 a.m. The sound quality is better than the visual. Country music playing from a radio is distinct, and motorcycles streaking by outside, but there isn't much you can tell about the clerk except that he is African-American, skinny knees crossed over each other as he reads a magazine. The doors open with an electronic buzz, and then it is over fast—almost as soon as the two blurry men are in the picture the boy is standing, moving backward palms up, there are shouts in Spanish then suspects open fire with automatic carbines, a two-dimensional *pock pock pock pock pock pock.* The boy does not fly backward spraying blood, spread-eagled against the yogurt machine—in fact, for a moment does not seem to realize he is hit, then drops like a pile of books.

The men fire at the cash register but it won't open so they keep on shooting, random, manic, scattering boxes of candy, spinning a card display, piercing the glass door of a cooler so it shatters. Then they are out of there but the camera rolls on unblinkingly, looking at the pitted counter, the upended stool; the clerk, lying on the floor, is not visible but a tiny mewing sound goes on for a very long time, forty-six seconds according to the timer, until a couple bangs through the doors, both fat, white and wearing undershirts, the man with a goatee, the woman smoking, barreling straight for the cigarettes until he jerks her arm with *"Oh my Lord sweet Jesus Christ"* in a slangy drawl and the woman startles, not entirely in shock, and Detective Allen shuts it off as the man is yanking her backward out of the store.

Cassidy finds she is gripping a tissue. She doesn't know where the tissue came from, but she is clenching it so tightly her pinkie has gone numb.

Detective Allen rewinds and stops at the first man firing. "We've enhanced the image." He removes a photograph from a file folder.

He slides it toward her.

Cassidy stares at the grainy enlarged face on Raymond's desk. It is not the face of rage or pleasure, but wild-eyed distraction like someone in the grip of a waking seizure.

"Do you recognize this man?"

Her lips are dry.

"Yes."

"Is this one of the men who assaulted you in the parking lot of the Coast Grill?"

"I couldn't positively say. I didn't see their faces. But I know this man."

"Did you know him prior to that night?"

"Yes."

The two cops look at each other.

"Where, Cassidy?"

It is no longer avoidable:

"In the Dominican Republic."

Simms rubs his face as if incredibly bored. He is wearing the greasy gray ponytail and a windbreaker and brown slacks, convincingly as if he had just stepped off a powerboat loaded with cocaine.

"This was last fall, when you went to the Dominican Republic on an unauthorized trip?"

Where did this come from? What is he getting at?

Edgy, "Raymond Woods knew I was there."

"What is your connection to the shooter?" asks Simms.

"Shooter?"

"This man." He pile-drives a thick forefinger against the enhanced photograph. "How do you know him? What's his name?"

"Monroe."

"Yeah, okay, whatever he's calling himself these days."

"There is no '*connection*,'" Cassidy insists, dying to take off the tweed jacket but then they would see the sweat stains in her shirt. "He drove me to see a ballplayer."

"Cruz?"

"Right."

Simms looks disgusted.

Detective Allen shakes his head, concerned, a friend.

"You were alone in a car with this character?"

"I had to get to the game."

"Work is work, I understand—" removing other documents—"but this guy's got outstanding warrants in three jurisdictions—street fights, bar fights, pushing drugs and guns, domestic violence—didn't your dad ever tell you not to get into cars with strangers?"

Simms: "Three jurisdictions?"

"Dade County, New York City, the Dominican Republic."

"That's not a jurisdiction, that's a country."

"Mark, now I see why LAPD has such a reputation for thoroughness."

Simms doesn't even bother with the empty smile.

Cassidy is staring at the sheaf of faxes: warrants in English and Spanish; mug shots of "Monroe Rodríguez," and "Manuel Castro" and a half dozen other aliases—younger, with and without a mustache and/or long hair; forms filled in with Spanish words Cassidy never learned in high school—*robo, asalto y agresión, falsificación.*

"How did you get all this?" she asks. "How did you know it was him?"

"Superior police work," says Allen.

"He means luck."

"Ballistics was able to come up with the fact that the bullets used in the attack were loaded with Berdan primers, of the type only manufactured in the Dominican Republic. We faxed the enhanced photo and fingerprints recovered from the scene to the authorities in Santo Domingo. Turns out they know this fellow Monroe real well. His uncle's a major drug lord down there. They call him the General. That opened it up for us."

Cassidy swallows. "I met the General."

Simms: "You know *him*, too?"

"I didn't say I *know* him. Met him. Once. Twice."

"When was this?"

"When I leased the car. The General owned the rental company."

"One of his many fronts," adds Allen. "He's also into restaurants, malls—or whatever they have down there—prostitution, the whole deal."

He was running a crime syndicate from a card table in an empty lot.

"When did you meet the General for the second time?"

"At the Gran Caribe hotel."

A current runs between the two detectives who make it obvious by not looking at each other.

"Isn't the Gran Caribe kind of rich for the budget of a scouting department?"

"Look, guys, I've got to get back to a meeting."

"Let's just complete the thought. What were you doing at the Gran Caribe?"

"The jeep I was driving in broke down. The Gran Caribe turned out to be close."

She tries to sound bored, too.

"Detective Simms tells me Cruz has been receiving blackmail threats."

Allen's look is pleasantly receptive.

Cassidy tells him that is true.

"Monroe drove you out, saw Cruz play?"

"Right."

"And he knew you signed the kid?"

"He was there. In the room. When we made the deal."

Allen turns to Simms.

"Makes sense, doesn't it Mark?"

Simms nods with eyes closed.

"We're working on a theory, Cassidy, that your pal Monroe—"

"Don't call him my pal."

"—that Monroe is behind the extortion scam. What we've got so far, Monroe sees a kid make the majors. He sees an opportunity. He fires off some half-assed blackmail notes—"

"But why?" she says. "What does he have on Alberto?"—then suddenly afraid she's gone too far.

"Say he's fishing. Fear of violence against the family might be enough to make a naive kid pay up. He's a target because he's made it, that's all. When nothing happens," Allen speculates, "Monroe comes up here to get results. No question the uncle is behind this. The Dominican authorities have been playing cat and mouse with him for years."

"Can I go?"

"Sure," says Simms. "Just one more thing. Communication."

Cassidy forces herself to stay in the chair.

"Communicate."

"Detective Allen is here to solve a homicide. My job is to protect our ballplayers. Now where are you on that?"

"What do you mean, where am I?"

Simms: "It's interesting."

"What?"

"You take an unauthorized trip to a foreign country that's out of your territory. Way out—"

Angry, "That's called *working your butt off*—"

"—You make a dubious connection with a known felon which maybe later goes bad—"

She turns on Allen. "Is this a joke?" He signals, *Calm down*.

"You come back here and immediately there's all this gnarly stuff around the ballplayer. Blackmail notes. Vodou whatever."

"What are you implying? Do I need a lawyer?"

"—You go to Vero and become involved with a violent incident yet you don't tell the investigating officer, Detective Allen, any of the background. Didn't you think it was relevant?"

"I didn't think about it, frankly—"

"She was pretty shaken up," interjects Detective Allen.

"Nate," says Simms, exasperated, "you have to ask yourself, Where is the loyalty of this gal?"

"Where do you think?" Cassidy stands up. "What are you saying? I broke my own hand?"

She shows him.

"Like I said, things go bad. You and Monroe might have had a falling-out—"

"Me and *Monroe?*"

Simms keeps on pounding.

"Why wasn't the very first phone call you made after the attack to this organization? Instead you hop on a plane to LA, like what? Like it was nothing, like you had a Rollerblading accident? It raises questions."

A shock goes through her, wildly paranoid. She used that lie, Rollerblading, with Travis. She finds she is twisting the silver bracelet and stops.

The LAPD cop brazenly leans against Raymond's desk, fingers gripping the edge. He is wearing gross overwrought gold rings on both hands. Part of the costume or the real guy?

"If you have a direct question," Cassidy suggests, "something you want to know, ask."

She lets her eyes go blank, the give-'em-nothing stare.

"Alberto Cruz is potentially worth a lot of money. Maybe, as scouts, you and your friend Pedro Pedrillo—he's the one who found him, isn't he?—are the only ones who know exactly how much. And you also know how vulnerable the kid is right now."

"Somehow," she says, "I'm still not getting it," shooting a look toward Allen, who lowers his eyes.

"In our business, Cassidy, a lot of the time, the perpetrator turns out to be the one who is closest to the victim."

"In my business, Mark, it usually turns out, the bully with the ugly mouth is the one who's scared."

She goes to the door. She opens it. She walks out. Nobody stops her.

21

At four-forty that afternoon Cassidy is still waiting at the top of Elysian Park. Finally the highly waxed hood of the Bentley comes gliding over the hill and swings into the last spot in the shade.

"You'll get those berries all over your car," Cassidy calls.

As Joe strides toward her late afternoon sun strikes his forehead like brass and Cassidy realizes it is all up there—the source of his determination—different from hers. Subtle glints come off the belt and the temple of the black sunglasses, because like everything about him, they are fabricated of expensive jazz, as the creamy soft cotton of the shirt with the mini-checks Cassidy crushes between her fingers, pulling him toward her forcefully.

"You look terrific," he murmurs.

A balmy wind that smells of sage lifts her hair as it falls from the headband.

A gentle kiss.

"Are you okay?"

"No," she says, "I'm not okay. How are you?"

Reflexively Joe checks his Cartier tank watch.

"I'm supposed to be in Century City."

They can see it twelve miles to the southwest, a cache of tiny skyscrapers poking out of the mauvish sprawl that unfurls over the curve of the earth until swallowed up by the glare of the Pacific.

"Oh well, it's other people's money. What's going on?"

"I've been talking to the police, Joe. Or rather, they've been talking to me. Detective Allen, my bud from Vero Beach, showed up at the stadium today along with our security advisor from LAPD. They embarrassed the hell out of me, pulled me out of an important meeting—"

"Back me up. What was an officer from Florida doing in LA? Why were they questioning you?"

"They're investigating a homicide. The night I was assaulted, a kid who worked in a 7-Eleven was shot to death. They showed me a tape from the camera in the store. They wanted to see if I could ID the killer. The killer was Monroe."

Joe shakes his head, not understanding.

"Monroe?"

"*Monroe*, the runty little driver from the Dominican. You know Monroe. He was beating up the jeep when you drove by and picked me up. He works for the Gran Caribe."

"Monroe shot someone?"

"Why is that a surprise? He's a psychopath. I'm almost certain it was him who attacked me in the parking lot. It's him behind the blackmail threats. Him and his bad uncle, who the cops say is the Dominican Mafia."

Two crimson-faced, sweat-soaked joggers have laboriously crested the hill. A man walks by with four Shih Tzu dogs on four leashes.

Joe: "Let's get out of traffic."

"Which way?"

To the east is the picnic area overlooking the stadium, grills and cement picnic tables and skinny baby trees still in their stakes: exposed wide-open space.

Ahead is a trail that leads into thick brush.

Joe coaxes her toward the trail.

"I think this is becoming clear," he says. "Monroe was fired."

"When?"

"After I saw him beating the crap out of that car, it occurred to me he might not be the type of individual we want to employ. I told transportation to fire his ass."

"Did he know it came from you?"

"Most likely."

Doubtfully, "So he *blackmails* you?"

"He doesn't plan it. He doesn't think that far ahead. He comes across the opportunity. Like witnessing the accident."

"You think he saw it?"

Joe shrugs.

"I saw him at the ball game. He must have followed us. He must have hung far enough behind so we couldn't see his headlights in the rain.

Then, after we hit, he drove up, checked out the body, and an idea began to form in his pea brain. He certainly knew who was in the car and exactly how to find us. His uncle probably picked up the plane ticket."

"Do you know the General?"

"Not personally."

"I saw Nora with him in the casino. Talking business. She said it had to do with taxis for the hotel."

"I'm sure it did."

Cassidy waits. "The General is a drug dealer, Joe."

"He is also the only game in town."

"Please."

"You want a guest to go from the airport to the hotel, you have to use his cars, or the guest never gets there," Joe snaps. "Think I like it?"

"Calm down. I don't want to get into a big moral thing. I'm concerned about Nora."

He wipes the back of his neck. "Why?"

"She's the one who has to deal with him on a day-to-day basis. He's a seductive man, in his way."

It takes about three seconds for the pink flush to shoot through Joe's cheeks.

"I take offense at that."

"I didn't mean to *offend* you—"

"She's fine, I told you, I can take care of my own kid. She's doing great, so drop it."

"If I were you I'd find another taxi company. Or start my own."

Joe shakes his head incredulously. "You just won't let go."

"Sure I will. I've got my own drama. Now the cops think the extortion letters have to do with me."

"You?"

"They accused Pedro and me of blackmailing Alberto, can you believe that? I almost came off the wall. Pedro and me. Trying to exploit our own player."

Joe makes a dry exasperated "*Huh?*"

"Yeah, right."

"Tell me this. When you were talking to them, was there anyone else present in the room?"

"No."

"Not your boss?"

"He was in the meeting."

"Not your private attorney? Not general counsel for the organization—"

"No!"

"Do me a favor. Next time a cop wants to hassle you—"

He pulls out his wallet, removes a card.

"—you state that you will not consider any kind of conversation without a lawyer *present in the room*. This is Harvey Weissman's cell phone. Twenty-four hours a day. This is outrageous. Two cops, trying to fuck you both ways."

Joe walks on ahead, kicking at the wild lavender that bends over the narrow trail. A handful of gnats roils against the slanting sun. Cassidy's face is prickly. It is stupid to be taking a hike in business clothes. Her loafers are covered with silky red dust.

Without turning around Joe says, "Did you mention my name?"

"No, I did not."

They walk in silence. The air has taken on an empty heated hum that swells from the woody manzanita and poison oak crowding the hill in a dense impenetrable maze. A lizard startles, or a bird; otherwise they are alone. In the middle of four million people you can still disappear into the shrub forest of the Los Angeles foothills.

But then the brush gives way to a clearing and the trail widens out to a well-traveled path, flat enough to reflect the pinkish light like a coin. Ahead is an amazing surprise: an abstract modern sculpture on silver pilings twenty feet high, metal squares and curves on top of a platform like an oil rig. The sculpture has been positioned on an open rise so that it confronts the towers of downtown.

"Did you know this was here?" she asks.

"No. I'm just flying by the seat of my pants."

They walk underneath the platform and weave between the pilings, but the packed dirt smells like urine so they go out into the sunshine at the edge of the embankment, which cuts away abruptly to a steep slope of decomposed granite and rounded boulders that have fallen and rolled and hit rock and split apart.

Due east, as the hawk flies, is the steadily growing skeleton of the sports and entertainment center.

"I've always said downtown is the heart and soul of LA. If downtown dies, LA dies." He waits. "You realize Alberto has to turn himself in."

"As long as you tell the police that you've been getting threats, too."

"I can't be involved."

"It was your damn car. How do we explain that?"

"You two took it for a ride."

"No way! I'm not going to lie about that."

"I have to stay out of it for now."

"Why do *you* get to stay out of it while we look like two irresponsible children?"

"I have to. Until the financing is in place."

"Give me a break, you didn't just say 'the financing'—"

"Stop acting like an airhead, you're smarter than that."

She spins away. Joe grips her, hard.

"Where you play is one thing, where I play there are no rules. Things happen in the dark. Getting from A to Z is never clear. You sweat? I've got flop sweat. We've dug a hole more ways than one. Most of the money still has to be raised. It's a balancing act right now, a house of cards. From the beginning there was fierce opposition from the city council, people are upset about using the city's money, but we got it, despite a rat's-nest of mayoral politics in which I was one of the major rats. If there were a *whiff* of scandal around me now, public funding would dry up and it's not inconceivable the rest of the project would evaporate, and believe me, none of us would survive it."

Suddenly Cassidy has the shakes, as if her vital signs had plummeted.

"The minute Alberto admits he killed that woman, his life is over."

"I'm sorry it happened, I truly am."

"You can't pretend you weren't there. We all have to share the responsibility—"

"That's where you are wildly incorrect. No, we don't."

"Let's not do anything until we hear from Pedro."

"Please, haven't we given him enough chances—"

Desperately, "Pedro's down there checking it out. Maybe she was still alive. Maybe Monroe came along and killed her—"

Joe is still gripping her shoulders. She has underestimated his strength.

"This is craziness. At some point, you have to make a choice. Alberto or me."

Her body, by itself, resists, jerks away, the leather soles of the loafers slip forward, she pitches back, and for an instant they both scramble without balance at the edge of the canyon until Joe plants his feet and pulls her back up over the crumbling rock.

They cling to each other.

"Monroe is a loose cannon. He could be ten feet away right now. *Let go of it.* We're running out of time."

"All right." Her own voice sounds far away; from a place that is unfamiliar and without hope. "I suppose you're right."

Joe whispers, "I thought we were talking about getting married."

Cassidy nods into his damp shirt.

He kisses her forehead and lets his arms drape heavily around her.

"What I love about you," he says, "is that you believe it matters."

She stands quite still, breathing fast and shallow.

JUNE

22

Brad Parker is drafted by the Dodgers in the fifth round. Pepper Parker shrieks like a car alarm when Cassidy calls to inform the family. The following day a package is delivered to the stadium containing three dozen sudden-death chocolate-chip brownies and a card with a photograph of a lizard hanging upside down. Its green toes suck onto a twig. Its black eyes bulge with shock. Inside they've written, *Can't wait to seal the deal! With deep appreciation, The Parker Family.*

In the lull after the draft Raymond sends Cassidy on pro coverage, scouting minor league teams from San Diego to Salt Lake City, foot soldier in the department's objective to stockpile reports on every professional ballplayer in America. Still, the rewards are infinitesimal. Pedro always says, "The worst player in the majors is better than the best player in the minors," and in fact after nine days of effort Cassidy will only be able to report one or two guys who are *maybe* capable of playing in the bigs.

It is past midnight when she finally turns down Route 133 to Laguna Beach, past thinking, past the numbing buzz of Taco Bell coffee and diet Coke, past even Bruce Hornsby and the Range, cranked up so you'd think the band was right there, hanging in the back with Edith.

A deer runs through the headlights. Cassidy's reaction time is zip. She rolls into the intersection of Broadway and Beach Street grateful to still be alive, comforted by an Englishy compound of white plaster and brick with a red London telephone kiosk out front.

Eucalyptus trees drape the streets in shadow but the drugstore window is afloat with plastic sailboats, sand buckets, shovels, an outsized yellow sun, the effect as artificial and melancholy as the deserted center of the village itself, where solitary fountains play and just one spark of human life remains outside Hennessey's Tavern—half a dozen Asian kids, the last of Disco Night, smoking cigarettes and waiting for a bus.

Cassidy could easily fall into Papa's but bed sounds a lot more warm and fuzzy, and that's about her only thought, drifting like a pink cloud in the mind, as she drives along Glenneyre to Shadow Lane and cuts the engine.

The air is wet, down to fifty degrees, feels good. Edith hops out and makes for the tea tree, gray-green and somber having shed its white blossoms, while Cassidy hauls out her backpack and laptop, leaving the burrito wrapper/highway map gradu for the morning. At the same time, somewhere nearby, a car door closes gently and a male voice calls, "Cassidy?"

She turns, weighted down.

A man comes toward her across the unlit road. She watches dully, slowed by fatigue and a stubborn belief in the safety of her own street despite the vacant bushy dark.

He reaches inside his jacket.

And pulls out a badge.

"It's Nate."

"This is a surprise."

"Didn't mean to scare you."

"Should I be scared?"

"We need to talk."

"After I call my lawyer."

He gives an impatient bobble, a bend of the knees.

"You don't need a lawyer."

She searches the shadow for his eyes.

And believes him.

She unlocks the Dutch door and they enter a settled damp, as if surf grass were growing out of the walls.

"How long have you been waiting in the car?"

"Let's just say, can I use your john?"

She points the way. Turns on the lights. Goes out for the mail. Ineffectually runs water over dishes she had left in the sink.

"Coffee?"

Detective Allen shakes his head. He is wearing a dark blue suit. It is unnerving to have a cop from Florida wearing a dark blue suit in your kitchen at one in the morning. And his face, she decides, is not quite the professional mask he would like it to be. The face leaks worry, around the blondish eyebrows and thin-set mouth.

"This morning we were contacted by the Dominican police. There is some concern for your personal security."

She must be really tired because she was about to make a joke about concern for personal security and Kotex pads, but she has the feeling that even if she did say something incredibly embarrassing and crude, Detective Allen (unlike Travis, for example) wouldn't flinch—he doesn't seem the kind of man who enjoys watching a woman make a jerk of herself.

"You guys should have been concerned in the parking lot of the Coast Grill," she says, jerkily sarcastic instead.

Sure enough, Nate Allen doesn't flinch.

"Are you doing physical therapy for that hand? In your spare time, right?"

Cassidy leads into the living room.

"Listen, I've broken so many bones . . ."

Switching on a pair of lighthouse lamps.

"Cute."

"They were here."

"I like this place. Like a ship." He looks around. "You should be using those window locks. Is there an alarm system?"

"You're looking at it."

They stare at Edith, lying flat with nose between her paws, possessing all the physical menace of a bleached-out bathroom mat.

He pulls over a spindle-backed chair.

"So you, basically, you live alone—"

"I live alone but I'm never home. Because I travel a lot, as you can see. I like you, Nate—I can call you Nate?—"

"Been called worse."

"—but I don't get why you keep popping up."

"*Popping*," he echoes. "Does that mean I'm toast?"

"Here. At the stadium. You really think I'd have anything to do with that scum Monroe?"

"We have to follow every possible—"

"Yeah, yeah."

Detective Allen clears his throat. "You mention that scum Monroe—"

"Can I interest you in a Tylenol and a beer?"

Steadfastly, he shakes his head. She gets up and grabs the backpack. All she wants is to be allowed to go to sleep.

"We're dealing with a political situation that goes back a couple of hundred years, along with some majorly inadequate criminal personalities, " Detective Allen says. "This all didn't start with Monroe."

Cassidy pulls a Corona from the fridge, pops the cap, downs two extra-strengths in a belchy acrid wash.

"Let me guess. It started with his uncle."

She returns to the living room and resolutely crosses her feet up on the coffee table.

"The uncle's a player," Allen agrees, "but corruption is a way of life down there, especially now that drug-trafficking routes are changing, from Mexico through the Caribbean."

"Right." She yawns. "Forgive me."

"In the south they've got countries that produce the stuff, in the north they have the buyers—in between twelve hundred little islands with easy ins and outs. It's a perfect package for the drug lords, especially when guys like the General, who work for the Colombian cartels, are also running the governments. But I'd have to say that money laundering for drug dealing trash is not the General's worst offense. His worst crime, by far, is owning a bad Italian restaurant."

Cassidy chokes on the beer.

"The post office address in Nagua, where Alberto was instructed to send the money, turned out to be a restaurant called Roma 3. I just heard from my Dominican counterparts this morning. They've managed to trace the ownership of the restaurant through some byzantine twists to the General."

Cassidy sits up, alert.

"Evidence the General is behind the blackmail threats?"

"A link."

"More than that!"

Allen rubs the bridge of his nose, observing Cassidy through slightly lifted pale blue eyes.

"Things are also changing inside the DR," he goes on. "There's a young generation of movers and shakers who want to replace the island mentality, get rid of the old system of corruption and get into the twenty-first century—make some money—legit—and spread it around. They come to the US to get educated. The lieutenant in charge of their investigation, Ramón Molina, he and I went to the same police academy in Fort Pierce, Florida."

"He's the one who talked to Pedro."

"Correct."

"And Molina is on to the General?"

"He's a general, all right. They're looking to try him for war crimes. Apparently he personally oversaw the massacre of about ten thousand Indians under Trujillo. Molina is mounting a major task force—assuming he doesn't wind up in little pieces in the trunk of a car. They do that. Torture and kill federal agents. Well, that just ain't gonna fly anymore."

"So you're saying," says Cassidy, with just a little buzz on, *"that's* why I need an alarm system?"

"No," replies Detective Allen. "I believe the danger to you is much closer to home."

She watches as his reserve gives way; the tight features soften, guardedness running out like flour from a sack.

"I'm concerned about your relationship to Joe Galinis."

"What do you know about—"

"We know."

She glares at him.

"You were seen getting into his car outside the Glendale police station."

"I am stunned. I am totally freaked—"

"Spare me."

"—I thought this was America."

"We also know," Allen rolls on, "as a result of Molina's investigation, that the General has been laundering Colombian cocaine money through the Gran Caribe hotel."

The pressure inside Cassidy's skull pumps a few more hundred pounds per cerebral inch.

"—They usually do it through the casinos."

The detective's tone remains even.

"The scale of the money laundering in the Gran Caribe could not be happening without the full knowledge and consent of Joe Galinis."

"But Joe has nothing to do with running the hotel—"

A hard impatient knock sends Cassidy springing to her feet.

"Easy."

Detective Allen goes to the door and says, "Yo."

Two male Laguna Beach police officers wearing heavy jackets are waiting in the lamplight. They exchange identification with Detective

Allen. Cold air sweeps in and Cassidy can hear a police radio from a patrol car in the street.

"I've secured cooperation from the local jurisdiction," Detective Allen explains, "to provide surveillance on your home. They'll be coming by each shift."

"This is an invasion of privacy, I swear I *will* call my lawyer—"

Flashlight beams pierce the foggy windows where the officers have gone around the back.

"We've done a thorough background check, we know a lot about Mr. Galinis. For example, he is currently under investigation for tax evasion."

"Did you also know, and you probably do, he's a great fuck?"

She's said it. The incredibly embarrassing, crude jock thing.

Tired, Allen rubs his face all over like he's taking a bath.

"I'm out of here. Look. I'm staying at the airport Traveler's Inn. If it's an emergency, call the local police." He writes some numbers on a card. "Monroe is still at large. You saw the tape."

He hands her the card, adding, "But I like your loyalty."

She follows him. "Why shouldn't I be?"

"We're developing a strong connection between you, Cruz and Galinis. You and Cruz have been threatened, and you and Galinis have a relationship. That puts you square in the middle."

She sees the hardness in his eyes and wonders if she should be afraid of him.

"But what we don't know is," says Detective Allen, "the middle of what?"

Cassidy fights to hold his gaze.

"Joe doesn't even *know* the General," she says. "I admit he has a chip on his shoulder and he's out to conquer the world, but he'd just never associate with a pig."

"Business is business."

"You don't get it. Joe has to be in control. It has to be his way: elegant. Classy. Knowing all the right people. He collects art. Owns an amazing house at the beach. He and the General have nothing in common, they're not even on the same planet."

"Sometimes it's a very fine line, between a competitor and a killer."

She is walking him to the door. They hear the patrol car driving away. She leans against the jamb with faux insouciance.

"Really, Nate, why all the drama?"

"You're a witness in a homicide investigation. It's my job to protect you."

She watches him retreat into the leafy shadow, as if she were standing in the front door of her parents' house in Oregon after that mythical high school date she had imagined in the unmarked car—Nate Allen, captain of the tennis team, too short and too smart—but the heavy odor of night-blooming jasmine numbs that fantasy like curare.

And the fact that Detective Allen has reappeared, stepping back into the light.

"Which beach?"

"What are you talking about?"

"The house you said Joe has?"

"Near Balboa, why?"

"It's just interesting."

"Why?"

"To my knowledge, we don't have any record of Joe Galinis owning a house at the beach. Good night."

23

Lilac light condenses into fog. Cassidy, wrapped in an afghan, sits on the sofa and observes the marvel of dawn. Officers return and thrash around behind the house. She hears a crackling radio and the unit driving away. She gets up once to let Edith out, then comes back to the sofa and the afghan.

Sleep had been a tease that night, beckoning her under, spitting her out. No dreams, no explicit thoughts she could name, instead a looping ribbon of black that widened to a highway where she rode the air at deadly speeds.

At 5:30 a.m. she was starving, but there was nothing in the house since she'd been gone so long, so she dug some sun-dried tomato chicken sausages out of the freezer along with multigrain waffles and the old Aunt Jemima, a pretty weird combination with bancha tea since there weren't any coffee beans, either.

It's amazing how the traffic picks up, even on a back street like Shadow Lane; the ringing of the phone is muted by some huge-ass truck that seems to be idling with a roaring thrum right there in the impatiens outside the window.

It is Uncle Pedro, reporting on reconnaissance from Río Blanco.

"What did you find out?"

"There ain't no Río Blanco. Everything is gone. Nothing but a big brown lake."

"Gone?"

"Where the little houses used to be? Now they got nothing but islands made of mud."

Cassidy can remember shanties painted lemon yellow, women at a water pump outside the *farmacia*, dusty alleys hung with laundry, strange-looking mongrel dogs, which, like everything else in town, looked as if they had been put together out of spare parts.

"The roads are all washed out with big rocks. I had to go by donkey. Poor donkey."

"What happened to everybody?"

"Many escaped the floods but they don't want to stay. The roof blew off the sugar mill, the company ain't gonna fix. They got no jobs and nothing to eat. A lot of the people went over to a bigger town, El Seibo, so I went there too—"

"Oh, Pedro."

"Well, I wanted to find out. Now I wish I listened to Rhonda and stayed home."

Cassidy, rueful, "She usually knows what she's talking about."

"These families are so poor they think, If our boy plays baseball it's gonna be all right, it's gonna save us, buy us a big house . . ." He waits. The silence is unusual, for him. Then: "When I first saw him, Alberto told me he is eighteen. The truth is, actually, he's twenty-two."

Cassidy falters, "That's not good."

"Tell me about it."

They had signed Alberto, like all prospects, based on the projection of how he would play in four or five years, when the training pays off and he starts to become valuable to the team. By twenty-one he should already have minor league experience. By twenty-seven, if he's in the majors, he should peak. If the age is wrong, the calculations—tools, intangibles, playing time, hitting, baserunning, fielding, overall—are meaningless and the time frame slams down on your knuckles like a loose window.

"How do you know for sure?"

She is pacing. Her pits are damp.

"I went to El Seibo and I found some of Alberto's relatives and people he knew from Río Blanco. Everyone was telling a different story about who was the oldest in the family—no, Alberto, no, his brother—so I start to get suspicious because I know this kind of thing goes on, so I become best friends with the postman there. The friendship cost twenty-five dollars. These are the kind of guys that usually run the black markets because they have connections all across the island, and I am right, last November, this man says he sold a fake birth certificate to Alberto Cruz. It cost the family two hundred dollars—more than they make in a year—but I am lucky, because he said to me that if *I* wanted to buy a birth certificate for any of *my* prospects, the price would only be one hundred fifty. He sells a lot to professional scouts."

"I can't believe it."

"Happens all the time."

"I know, and contracts get terminated."

"Sometimes, if they're good enough, the front office looks the other way. In one regard it's understandable, why Alberto thought he had to do it."

Then Pedro is quiet.

"I didn't see it, either, Cassie."

She is quiet, too.

"Does Raymond know?"

"I wanted first to talk to Alberto. I called the minor league office in San Antonio but they say he is on his way to LA. They're sending him to a specialist for this problem that he has."

Cassidy snorts, "Black magic?"

"They think maybe a parasite in his gut."

She sighs heavily.

"If he lied about his age, what else is he lying about? What else did he think he *had* to do?"

Pedro, soberly, "I know what you mean."

"Joe is very upset, he wants me to force Alberto to go to the police and get this over with. But I'm afraid that Joe is lying, too. Or *maybe* he is, I don't know."

"About the accident?"

"No, something else. It's stupid. Not important. A house he might or might not own. I don't know what to think."

"You're trying to protect them both."

She doesn't answer.

"You can't remember who was driving?"

"No, I can't."

"Then you gotta find out the facts."

"That's exactly what I'll never find out!"

"Remember what I told you, *Always kick the tires.*"

She laughs. He's not kidding. And she's done it. You meet the prospect's family. You sit around the kitchen table, talk, get their background, economic level, a sense of their commitment to baseball, then, as you leave, you pass the family car and check out the tires.

It tells you if they're telling the truth, Pedro would say, if they have what they say they have—or maybe don't have. It tells you how they take care of business, what they think is important — those are the things you want to know because *those* are the things that get passed to the son.

"Does this Joe *own* the house," he's asking now, "or is he making up a story? Is it important? We don't know unless we check it out."

Cassidy continues pacing, head down, staring at the floor.

"Get this: The police actually think you and I might be involved. Can you believe it? Like *we're* blackmailing Alberto because we think he's worth a lot of money?"

Pedro says, "Find out about the house."

Eleven o'clock in the morning, still not dressed, she calls Harvey Weissman.

His voice is cordial. "How *are* you, Cassidy?"

"I need to talk to you about Joe."

"What did he do, I'll break his neck."

"It's not about our relationship. So much. I need to know if he owns some property at the beach."

"I can't discuss a client, that's a breach of confidentiality. Have you asked the man himself?"

"No."

"What are you, shy?"

"I'm not sure he would tell me the truth."

Harvey laughs. "You're calling his *lawyer*, asking for the *truth*?"

"This is something I really need to know."

"Well, property ownership is public information. Go to City Hall and check out the records."

But it's not so easy to figure out which city hall when you don't exactly know which beach the house is technically on, nor, exactly, the name of the street (you could find it if you drove there), so you try to describe it to a clerk who ultimately transfers you to the courthouse in Costa Mesa, but then that's not correct, so maybe the jurisdiction is Newport Beach, and you wind up caught in phone trees of complex and bewildering choices, put on hold, disconnected, until you finally reach a recording that says the assistants at the property records department are all busy assisting other inquiries, but please be patient and stay on the line because your call is important to them.

At 2 p.m. Cassidy downs a frozen diet entree, takes a shower and is grabbing her keys to drive up to Newport Beach before the zoning office closes at three when the phone rings.

"Grizzlies rock!" shouts D. J. Reed.

Hearing that gruff throaty voice instantly time-tunnels Cassidy to the summer of 1970, the two girls riding to Lithia Park on their bikes with a baseball card clipped against the spokes by a clothespin to get that professional *thwick thwick thwick*, and a mental treasure map unfolds of the slopes, slides, swings, wading pool, Japanese garden, patch of sword ferns, where each station of childhood took place. The "boys' ship" and the "girls' ship." Fifteen-person hide-and-seek. Cool woodland and a lively creek, antidote to the hot red dust of the diamond where they'd usually play two games a day, with a break for Orange Crush and Jujubes.

Along with this sweet burst of memory is also a hulking dread and an almost physical need to get off the phone and run.

"D.J.! Great to hear you!"

"Had to call. Had to take the shot."

"It's great."

"Is this a bad time?"

"No."

"Well, you know, it's been a while."

"How's the team?"

"Finished first in the conference."

"Congratulations."

"My girls didn't take to losing. They were crushed by our first loss, I had to tell them the biggest learning lessons are the losses, not the wins. Takes more of an athlete to go through a loss."

Wistfully, "How is it being head coach?" thinking of the simple pleasures of small-town high school sports, kid-size problems, manageable goals, team breakfasts, caring for your girls, going to their plays and choirs and water polo games, and oh those green, green leaves of Lithia Park.

"It's amazing to think I hold enough respect to be a mentor. Gained a lot more confidence in myself. And you?"

"Fighting the fight."

Excited, "You know who I ran into at the mall? Patty White. She's got three kids and one more on the way."

"She was tough. What'd she weigh, about one-fifty?"

"Weighs a lot more now. Remember when we had that plan? We were going to allow Patty White to have a breakaway lane and whichever one of us was closest, we were going to demolish her—"

"And Melody Wolf gets whomped instead."

"Old Melody, man, she had no fear—Patty's going for the layup and Melody's right behind her and she just *tramples* her and they both go sliding across the floor and Patty gets up and Melody stays down and the ambulance comes and she tore part of her knee . . . We planned it from the git-go and the wrong person got injured."

"Good plan."

"So what'd we do? Put horse manure on Patty's car."

Cassidy laughs. "I forgot about that."

"Well, look. I'm sure you're busy. I just wanted to call."

"That was nice."

"June eleventh."

"Yes, I know."

"Are you okay?"

"I miss him every day, so this is just . . . another reminder . . . about how long I've been missing him."

Damn D.J., making her throat ache, draining her resolve.

"Doing anything special?"

"No, not really. Maybe take a walk along the beach," she lies. As soon as they hang up she's going straight to Papa's.

"Jim and I went up to the cemetery. There were lots of flowers on Gregg's stone. Isn't that nice? Red ones. Grizzlie red."

"Always."

"Gonna call your mom?"

"I saw her at Christmas."

"Well."

"We don't make a thing about it anymore."

Because Maggie has already entombed the memories of her son and husband in the Hollywood Stars Inn and Baseball Museum.

Eleven o'clock Christmas night Maggie was still in the kitchen, filling tins for tomorrow's breakfast muffins with an oversized spoon, no drips, when Cassidy, restless, grabbed another bottle of Oregon gold from the refrigerator and walked into the darkened museum. It was overheated and smelled of cat food. She pulled the chain on a floor lamp and a soft yellow glow filled the room.

There were Gregg's baby pictures and trophies on a shelf, and Smoke Sanderson's intimate life on display inside specially made oak cabinets: letters from a baseball camp in Kansas, his Pacific Overseas Air Force Command patch, dog tags, a photograph taken with a swami, his violin, soft black leather cleats, a thick jersey with an H in the center of a black and red star, a telegram care of the Hollywood Plaza Hotel in which the young pitcher was fined twenty-five dollars "for the use of abusive and profane language, which you will remit immediately or stand suspended," his high school diploma and a Louisville Slugger bat; his boyhood mitt, brown as an acorn.

Cassidy tapped her fingers on the glass that separated her from him. She could hear his voice, garish as in an old film clip, coaching first base: "Cassie! Be the one!" standard chatter to the kid at the plate, but after Gregg died it carried a special message she alone could hear. At the clap of his hands she was alert to his sadness, at the sound of his voice the force of his hope—that she might be the batter who would turn the game. That she would be the one to grip the opportunity. To heal his grief. To change, everything.

She sat in an easy chair and swigged the brew. The house was quiet. Their type of guests tended to go to bed early. A sweet baking scent blossomed through the doorway and she listened to the dishwasher thrumming along. Display cases glinted in the lamplight, artifacts sealed in time. She couldn't touch any of it.

D.J. is saying, "I still think about Gregg every day. He was like my brother—only better than my brother."

"Get out of here, your brother's *way* cool."

"Not when you had to live with him," says D.J. The throaty voice goes even more husky. "I love you, kid."

"I love you, too."

24

It is early for Papa's, that harsh twilight when daytime alcoholics who have been at the bar three, four hours are working on winding it up for the time being and the evening regulars have yet to settle in. Golden light layers the streets. It is the hour when choices can still be made although most people will choose to go home. Dry cleaners and grocery stores are busy and there is plenty of traffic but none of it (the hometowny routine) seems to have anything to do with Cassidy.

In the last hour she has left eleven messages for Joe, alternating between his beach-home answering machine and an increasingly hostile secretary who has repeatedly said Joe is at a city council meeting and cannot be reached. Nevertheless Cassidy has continued to call, like taking a hammer to a steel door just to savor the bone-ringing futility of it.

The pub at this hour looks rudely exposed, someone caught in the middle of a yawn, showing speckled tongue and worn fillings. Cassidy does not like the daylight on the smeared red tables nor the stink of disinfectant coming from the rear, remembering with a bitter jolt the gambling casino at the Gran Caribe, carpeted in black and freezing cold twenty-four hours a day—no matter what the heat or humidity outside, escape to the dark ice womb was always available. There, the General had put down a coffee cup and smiled with satisfaction. There, unlike at the sugar mill, we no longer had the need for human sweat and rusty apparatus. There, in that postmodern refinery (if Detective Allen is correct), computer-driven slot machines turn pure white powder into a jackpot of gold.

At the moment the only other folks in Papa's are three drunks doing Wild Turkey with Coors Light chasers. The female of the trio is one of those lank toughies who looks like she's spent the last sixty years riding horses in the sun.

"The cops were following her," she is saying in a loud smoky voice, "and she like fell into the driveway like, Oh fuck they can't do anything to me now I'm in the fucking driveway—and her son Christopher was home in the house."

"What'd he do?"

"He left." Deep laugh. "Didn't want any part of that situation."

Cassidy continues to the last seat at the bar where she can stare at the dead-fish aquarium. Why would anyone construct such a thing? What could be more melancholy than dried-up seahorses, shriveled to the size of paper clips?

Big Tyson slaps down a coaster and a menu of microbrews.

"How are you?" Cassidy asks in a hollow voice.

Big Tyson doesn't answer. The heaviness in the shoulders slumped beneath the leather vest tells her he's sunk into one of those Tysonian depressions, the cause of which probably goes back to some bad window-pane during his Stanford undergraduate days, when he was a physics major living above a garage in a single room papered with blacklight posters, traveling in a beat-up Toyota Corolla to every concert the Grateful Dead ever gave, dropping acid and trying to climb on stage to blesh with Jerry Garcia. But the freakiest, he once confessed, was tripping out when he worked nights at the Stanford University nuclear reactor.

That is why, when he gets like this, Cassidy leaves him alone:

Because watching Maurice Tyson set down a Pilsner glass of honey ale thirty years later, squarely on a coaster, without a tremor, without a spill, without blowing up the western coast of the United States, is an awesome and deeply spiritual experience.

"Thank you" is all Cassidy chooses to say.

The woman is signaling for the bill. *"I've got a crush on you,"* she sings, a warped Etta James.

Tyson frowns and picks up the phone.

"I'm calling a cab for you people."

"What for?"

"Take you home."

"What for?"

Tyson dials.

"We're not drunk!" says one of the men, jowly, gold-rimmed glasses, white short-sleeved shirt and bolo tie, indignant.

The others chorus, "Sober enough to drive!" and "What's your problem?"

"I don't want the responsibility," Tyson says quietly, continuing to talk into the phone.

"Let's go."

The cowboy queen scrapes her keys and cigarettes off the bar. The keys are attached to a rawhide braid and the pack of cigarettes fits into its own hot-pink leather purse with a twist-snap catch.

"Mellow out," suggests Cassidy. "Take a ride."

The woman turns. Her rheumy eyes are rimmed with black and her hair is lacquered auburn.

"You know what, honey? I can fucking well drive a car."

Cassidy slips off the barstool. Her body feels like it is filled to the brim with very unstable, highly flammable rocket fuel.

"You know what, asshole?" Cassidy replies. "You could kill somebody."

The woman plants her heels, hands on hips. For a stringy old broad she looks fairly strong. Cassidy gets ready to block if she whips those keys around.

The woman fixes Cassidy with a deranged stare.

"I have a son who died in Vietnam."

Her pals are saying, "Let's go, Ricky."

"No! I'm on this bitch."

Cassidy's nails are digging into the nearest barstool cushion, through the worn plastic to the crumbly foam.

"Bring it on. Bitch."

Big Tyson steams around the bar like a robot activated to life, fingers clutched, all but red laser beams shooting from his eyes.

"Now," he tells the woman, "I have to ask you to leave."

"Up yours," Ricky says.

"Watch it," cackles one of the geezers. "She kicks."

"Let's all chill," Tyson says. "Nobody's going to hurt you," trying to move her backward by taking a step forward. "Nobody's doing anything."

Cassidy: "Want me to call 911?"

"You know what you can do?" Ricky croaks.

Cassidy retires to the end of the bar, taking herself out of the action.

Tyson is bigger than all three of these goons. She picks up the glass but her hand is shaking.

"Girls like you," Ricky says, "fuck niggers."

Cassidy pushes down so forcefully on the rung of the stool in an effort to get to Ricky fast enough and hard enough to knock her to the ground that the stool flips backward and she is off-balance as she scrambles forward, recovering lithely but abruptly shouldered back by Big Tyson's big torso. The blow snaps her neck and takes her breath away.

Ricky shouts, "*All right!*" and her companion announces, "I gotta go pee-pee," shuffling off as if it were halftime in his own living room.

Tyson looks at Cassidy. "Do me a favor? Answer the phone."

"Do not let that trailer trash get into a car."

"Trying my best." Tyson gives up a tight smile. The small yellow teeth are not his best asset.

As Cassidy moves behind the bar she becomes aware of several things: pain in the ribs, throbbing fingers, a squat Croatian in the doorway yelling, "Somebody vants a cob?" Ricky's hoarse coughing mixed with sickening seventies music that has been blaring the whole time, *Come on! Take the money and run!*

"Papa's!" she spits into the phone.

"Is Cassidy Sanderson there?"

"Speaking."

"I have Joe Galinis calling for you."

Why not? The universe is perfect.

In an instant he is there: "Cassidy!"

The announcement of her name as bright as ever.

"Where are you?"

"In the car. My secretary said you were ballistic. What's the matter?"

"Everything."

"First of all, are you okay?"

"No. I'm not okay. Everything is blowing up. It's meltdown, Joe—"

The line goes dead.

"What are you doing here?"

Mary Jo Martin, the sportswriter, who usually never makes it before midnight and always wearing a conservative blazer and slacks with a belt, always in a tiff about some editor or newscaster messing with her stuff, has materialized on the buying side of the bar. She is backlit by a burning wedge of sunset through the open door which hurts Cassidy's eyes, so it takes a moment to adjust to the new, unexpected, daylight Mary Jo: sweats, no makeup, looking like a radiant vision of herself, as if she'd just been turned into an angel.

Mary Jo says, "I just sold my screenplay. For half a million dollars."

They stare at each other. The phone rings.

"That's going to be my agent."

Cassidy picks it up.

Joe: "I'm at a pay phone now. We can talk."

Mary Jo: "My agent—"

Cassidy turns away, squeezing up her eyes so Mary Jo recedes like an actress in a harness being cranked back into the wings.

"—I was on my way to the site. I didn't want to have this conversation over the air—shit. This was not a good idea. There's going to be jackhammers. Wait a minute. Shit."

"Joe? Can you hear me?"

"Yes."

Something is different in the bar. The drunks and the cabdriver are gone and the music has changed to Terence Blanchard's soothing horn. Cassidy is trying to talk loud enough but not too loud, the effect a punching rasp. Tyson is squeezing past to take care of some professional surfers, more pumped than usual, who have gathered around Mary Jo. Ignoring their raucous greetings Cassidy takes the radio phone into the women's bathroom and hooks the door.

"Joe, I have to ask you a question."

"Ask."

"How long have you owned the house on the beach?"

"The beach house? *What?*"

"Who was the architect? Who was the contractor? How long did it take to build it?"

"I'm sorry. I'm lost."

The background fills with the roar that words make when they accelerate through the ozone layer into space.

"You said the house reminded you of Greece."

"Yes?"

"So did you build it? Custom? Or did you buy it from someone else, who's also a fanatic about *the natural light?*"

Someone's knocking on the bathroom door.

"I don't know what your problem is. The architect was a young guy named Jason Kilbourne, a disciple of Richard Meier. The house is six years old. Okay? Now what the hell is going on? Did you talk to Alberto about going to the police?"

"No."

"I thought we agreed that you would."

"I would if I were sure."

"How can you not be *sure?*"

Someone's getting cute, going *rat-a-tat-tat* like a woodpecker.

Cassidy screams, *"I'm in here!"*

"You have no idea how many lives and livelihoods you are placing in jeopardy," says Joe over what sounds like a semi thundering by, "by clinging to this nothing kid. I just don't get it, but there's not a lot I can do about it right now, I'm standing in a phone booth at the corner of Eleventh and Flower—"

Alone in the bathroom, Cassidy says quietly: "I don't know who to believe."

Despite the noise, she can hear Joe's breath, quick and close.

"I've always tried," he says at last, "to understand what the world is really like, the world outside my own head. The real world, the pure world, that's beyond our vision and the limitations of our own psychology, everything we carry with us, how we grew up. Sometimes you get a shot at it."

"I have no idea what you're talking about."

Cassidy looks at herself in the silver-stained mirror and waits.

Joe: "Do you want me to say I love you?"

"Do you?"

"Yes. You sound surprised. I mean, by your silence, I'm guessing you're surprised."

"People who love each other don't lie about stupid things like beach houses."

Joe's voice rises with helplessness. "What is this crap about the beach house? Jesus Christ."

"The cops are investigating you. They know a lot of things—"

Cassidy slides down the metal divider between the sink and toilet until she is sitting on the filthy bathroom floor. Disinfectant or no disinfectant, there are shards of toilet paper, hairballs, a tampon applicator, a couple of bright yellow capsules someone dropped on the way to hypnotic sedation.

"—including the fact that you don't actually own the beach house."

Mocking, "They *know* this?"

"There's no record of it, okay?"

Another truck roars by whatever half-demolished corner Joe is standing on, a tiny figure watching the gargantuan construction of his dream. Tears well up as if the very same dust had stung her eyes.

"If we can't be honest with each other, there's no point."

"There *is* a point, but never mind. I care about you, of course I want us to be honest. I had a reason, but okay. The house belongs to a friend of mine. Her name is Alicia Morgan."

"Alicia."

Cassidy stands up and jams her hip into the corner of the towel dispenser.

The knocking starts again.

"I've known her a long time. She's in Europe for a while—"

Cassidy says nothing.

"See? I knew you'd be upset."

"Are . . . you . . . still . . . involved?"

She kicks the metal divider, once for every word.

"No. We haven't been for over two years."

When she's made a few good dents, she stops.

Joe is pleading, "Sweetheart, please, this is all so out of proportion—"

"Do not disrespect me now."

She presses the END button.

The bathroom door springs open. Three pissed-off girls are waiting, a skinny one in bell-bottoms, one with pierces up the nose, one a hairdresser with teased hair.

"About time."

"*For what?*" asks Cassidy, and the skinny one takes one look at her and decides to slip inside and lock the door.

She walks into a full-swing Papa's evening. After-work regulars are clustered at the bar and the Mary Jo *OhmyGoddoyoubelieveitthisisinsane!* contingent has spread to three tables. It's wild, it's a party, and it's going to get wilder, but to Cassidy the scene seems muffled by a peculiar silence and a vast psychic distance.

She puts the phone back behind the bar and ambles past the pool table where unaccountably she picks up the yellow, hefts it in her good right hand, crow-hops and throws it low and hard at the wall. The heavy ball fires through the cheap wood paneling like a meteor, demolishing the plaster and flying clear out the other side.

Two of the surfers cueing up, who might, had they moved one step to the left, be on their way to South Coast Medical Center for a brain scan, look at Cassidy without saying a word. Then the long-haired one, Skyler, goes to the hole and rubs a finger around the splintered edge. They can hear a diminishing *crack-crack-crack* as the ball bounces down the alley.

Skyler says, "Fresh."

25

Cassidy, Joe and Alberto left Francisco A. Micheli Stadium in
the Range Rover and drove through a warren of unlit streets in the old colonial section of town—shuttered windows, Romanesque archways, a church
with ruined tile walls—then suddenly found themselves on a dark country
road, a dead cow swaying off the back of a pickup truck in front of them.

"Can we please lose the cow?" asked Cassidy.

"Sure," said Joe, taking the very next turn. The road forked several times
across the cane fields, bumping downhill to a marsh. The headlights poked
through climbing philodendron and swung around to a stucco house
painted acid green. Despite the isolation, the doors and windows were
barred.

"Where are we?"

Alberto answered, "Yo no sé."

"I think you could say we're lost."

At the ball game they had eaten soft orange cheese cut into wedges and
ground meat steamed in banana leaves, and peanuts and chips and a
steady flow of rum and Cokes from vendors whipping flasks out of their back
pockets. It had been a while since Cassidy had been drunk on rum: a slow,
steep ascent.

The game was a blur of spectacle played at a tempo meant to savor each
moment, the stadium announcer rooting unabashedly for the home-team
Azucareros like the troublemaker in the back of the class—a blaring raspberry for the ump, a shout of despair on a strikeout, a maniacal laugh on a
double play, filling every lull with a sonorous refrain, "Siempre, Coca-
Cola."

"Who is this guy?" Cassidy shouted.

Joe said, "Our modern concept of God."

A CRACK!, a gasp, but the towering hit went foul, continuing to rise

with incredible grace in a slow perfect Euclidean arc, the spinning white
ball reaching its zenith against a jet-black sky, then falling gently, inevitably, into somebody's outstretched cap.

Now the rum was making Cassidy spin out in the motionless car. She
drew her legs up beneath the long skirt and held on to her knees. Lizards.
Hibiscus. Rats. Orchids. Wild ginger and oregano. Small charred bones in
a pile. An egret stalking the edge of the swamp. The green house impaled in
the headlight beam, scalding white as a lamp on an examining table.

"Whoever lives here," she observed, "has a lot of water."

Five-gallon containers were hanging off the roof like tassels.

"No," said Alberto, "that to keep the devil away."

"Wrong turn, no problem," said Joe, immediately shifting into reverse.

Just then the security door, heavily meshed as a liquor store in South-
Central, creaked open and a cadaverous-looking old man with sunken
cheeks of dark sienna, wearing an ancient black suit, stepped into the headlight beam.

"I know this place!" Alberto said suddenly. "This guy is a Haitian
guy—" and he was out the door, haranguing the old man, "You tell your
friends, they lose. I win. I play for the Los Angeles Dodgers!"

Cassidy was beside him, pulling his arm. "Back in the car."

Alberto was still angry at the Haitian pitcher who had cursed them after
the tryout.

"I no got bad spirits. They got the bad stuff. Who care for obeah? We no
believe it. We say junk!"

The old man fixed Cassidy with golden eyes. He must have been ninety.

"Do you have a problem?" he asked in English.

"No. No problem."

"This young man, he has a bad thing on him?"

"No, no. We're fine."

"Come inside."

"No, thanks."

Joe charged up behind them, rolling down his sleeves against the swarms
of biting mosquitoes.

"You can't stand here," pushing Cassidy through the door, "you'll get
malaria."

Inside it was wondrous. The walls were dusky colors, tomato and sage,
with huge skulls and crossbones painted on them in thick primitive black

lines like cartoon pirate flags. Embedded in the dirt was a wooden cross draped with chains and studded with white candles. Behind that, a child-size chair had a broken doll and a real human skull bound to it with rope. The skull wore a Panama hat, and a pipe was inserted backwards between its jaws.

On a large red table there were thousands of ritual objects in fetishistic clutter—champagne bottles, rum bottles, ram's horns, cigarette packs, rocks, sticks, tiny rocking chairs, plaster saints, rusted knives, scrolls of paper, rattles, bells, drums, funnels, scarves, plastic hands, fans, feathers— wrapped in twine or knotted ropes or padlocked chains or ribbon—snared and bound, to capture, trap, punish or dispel.

Joe asked the old man, "Who are you?"

The old man answered, "I serve."

He shimmied a hand toward the objects.

"These are the powers of Bawon Samdi."

"Junk," Alberto spat.

"Look what we have here," wheedled the boko priest as if amusing a child, and he lifted the bottle of Gordon's gin that had been stuffed with pieces of dry twig like grapevine kindling.

"What is that?" wondered Cassidy, with a peculiar feeling of having arrived at a strange altar at which she had been expected.

"Mama Juana."

The priest pronounced it so slowly she could see the red sores floating on his gums.

"You put any liquor inside, any liquor you want, and let it stay for three days and it becomes five times stronger and gives to you special powers of love."

Suddenly he gripped her wrists.

"They call me the Black Panther. Give me a kiss."

She pried off his fingers like growing vines.

"Dlo kler va koule devan ou," the old man said, a blessing. "Clear water will flow in front of you."

Holding up the Mama Juana to the dashboard light she could see a pale curling unctuous river of essential oils that had leached out of the medicinals into the gin. Watching it twine the dark herbs and rise to the *surface like thoughts, like dreams, Cassidy became lost in the tiny forest of stalks and leaves trapped inside the crystalline world of the bottle. The heavy saturated liquor stamped an acrid burn in the back of the throat like pot, like sinking in extreme slow motion into the mother herself, giving up consciousness in her many arms.*

Joe was driving. She clenched the thick curly hair at his collar and pulled his head back so his throat was exposed.

"You're turning me on but I can't see."

She released him. The road had been a tunnel of black, their route a maze that curved and connected in incomprehensible patterns. The stadium, heads of dolls in bottles, Río Blanco and the sugar mill, were floating points that shifted and changed with every turn.

Cassidy, so good at maps, had left all markers behind.

Some people *were talking about being afraid but it was hard to tell who because their voices kept fading in and out like the sound on an old-time radio.*

"Baseball is all about fear."

An interesting theory. She'd have to discuss that with Gregg.

" . . . The hitter . . . facing the enemy."

Yes, she'd heard that one and also about—

"All my life. Major league ball."

Afraid of getting hit by the pitch? She laughed. You never get up thinking I'm not going to hit the ball—

"It is very funny—"

Lots of times I've—

" . . . little dribbler . . . checked bunt . . ."

See, but I get up there and I want it.

"This is kind of embarrassing to confess, but I once had a pissing contest with a boy and almost won."

She was hanging out the window of the speeding car throwing up without discomfort, leaving nothing but a trail of weightless confetti on a wet wind.

The darkness had yielded the Colonial Hotel, a motor court by US standards, perched on the ocean. The place looked closed for the night. A few cars were parked in the lot, desultory spikes of light shooting up the peach-colored walls.

"Wait a second. I own a fucking hotel," Joe kept saying as Alberto directed him to park in the shadows.

They had found a perfect grove of coconut palms. Joe and Cassidy got out, instantly enveloped by a warm humid breeze and the ripe apricot smell of copa de oro. Everything was blowing. A light rain off the ocean.

They walked through the palm trees to a small crescent beach on an inlet where high waves were falling. They kissed and the kiss became insatiable. Slowly Joe sank to his knees in the sand and she followed, finding his lips, entangling her fingers in his hair.

"You taste like bread and coffee and sugar," she whispered, tasting each again and again, lost in sensation, nothing but warm wind and knowing hands. She wanted to roll in his flesh like a dog.

Joe said, "Kamaki."

Cassidy giggled. "What?"

"'Fish in a barrel.' The way we were on Santorini, the island of my youth, the girls—"

"Excellent!" shrieked Cassidy. "The girls of your youth!"

"English girls. Tourists. My cousin had the record for the most in one summer. Fifty."

"Fifty!" Cassidy laughed so hard she couldn't see through the tears.

Alberto remained in the shadows, staring at an iguana which had been looking at him for the last eternity. With the approach of the storm the ocean was crazy, the darkness beyond the hotel filled with endless thundering concussion.

"Alberto!" Joe called. "Remember this! You have to be kamaki."

He got up and strutted.

"We don't know how to do it," he confessed to the boy. "Women teach us."

Alberto smiled slowly.

"Sí?"

"Oh, sí. Here is a beautiful woman. Look at her. Read her mind. She doesn't want us to miss beauty. We're just butterflies, you and I, we transform the beauty of the universe into physical energy and then we get it back in a flashing moment of ideal happiness. We want it to last, to repeat, to be forever—"

He knelt behind Cassidy, gathering her hair over and over like a male courtesan, sometimes slumping completely forward as if momentarily black-

ing out. Cassidy had stayed easily upright, supporting his sloppy weight against her back.

The last thing she remembers, she had been invincible.

Edith is barking, that sharp warning yelp that goes along with hurtling herself at the door and sliding down on her nails.

Cassidy gets up from the sofa, tying the belt on a lavender terry bathrobe. Four years ago her color was lavender. What are you going to do?

She expects it to be one of the Laguna Beach cops, but through the peephole sees that it is Joe.

She checks her watch. 10:35 p.m. The patrol car must have just made its ten o'clock check. She opens the door.

"Can I come in?"

She waits, arms folded. Joe is wearing a black unconstructed linen jacket and drawstring pants, no shirt, his contrite face no less handsome in the zinc yellow porch light.

"Let's not throw it all away."

He pries her arms apart and takes her hands. Reluctantly, she steps into a stiff embrace. Then Nora moves out of the darkness and follows inside.

"We came to say we're sorry," she says.

"We are?"

Cassidy pulls away. "What are you doing here?"

"We're here as family," answers Joe.

Cassidy looks at them together—Nora's jeans ripped artfully at the knee, shocks of thick black hair like her father's, and a fierce entitlement they both possess, completely self-created, without lineage or crown.

"Anybody want a beer?"

"What do you think, Dad, could you handle a beer?"

"Sure, I'll take a beer. Thank you for having us in your home."

"Did I have a choice?"

She distributes Coronas and they sit on the secondhand plaid-and-maple furniture in front of the Malibu tile fireplace.

Joe suddenly doesn't seem to know what to say. He smiles oddly and scratches at his chest hair.

"What I want to express"—bowing his head, pinching the place where his heavy eyebrows knit— "... Look. It's silly to be upset over who owns the title on a beach house—"

Cassidy's leg starts kicking.

"I'll tell you anything you want to know about Alicia."

"Three facial surgeries," supplies Nora.

"I don't care about Alicia."

"I know how you feel," says Nora. "I was jealous, too, at the beginning. But really, they're just friends. She gave him the house because she's living with an art dealer in London. Truth."

Cassidy's leg keeps kicking.

"So those paintings in the house aren't yours, either. They belong to Alicia's friend, the art dealer in London."

"They're mine."

"At this point, Joe, why should I believe anything you say?"

Joe gets up. "Let's go."

Nora, "Wait, Dad, hold on—"

"Why? This is hopeless. She won't talk to me. She hangs up on me." The finger jabbing angrily, "I shouldn't let you get away with that."

"Then don't. Then leave."

Nora grabs her father's arm. "Stay. Talk. Work it out. She's good for you, Dad, better than the neurotic gold-digging cunts you usually go out with."

"You shut up," he tells his daughter.

"*Me?*"

Joe is on his feet, facing Cassidy.

"I've had it up to here, but I'm going to try this one last time, because all I want right now is for this whole ugly thing to go away. I offer this in Alberto's best interest, so try to see it that way. Let's be brutally honest. He's a kid with potential who has about a one percent chance of ever playing major league ball. You know the stats better than I. He's cheap Latin labor, there are hundreds like him, and he's already got some strikes. Bad attitude. Run-in with the cops. You told me yourself, he's not on his game. You want him to be a star, but what does he really want? I'll tell you: a new home for mama and a hundred channels. I'm not being racist, I've spent a lot of time down there. So why don't we cut to the chase? I can write a check right now for more than he would ever make in baseball."

"If? Say it. If?"

"If he does the right thing and turns himself in. I'll get him a lawyer. I'll pay whoever we have to pay. This is fixable. Let's be smart and get on with our lives."

Cassidy says, "No."

Joe smacks her across the face.

"You don't say no."

She weaves.

"You don't talk back. And you *never* hang up on me."

He hits her again.

Nora screams, "Don't fight!"

She's bitten her tongue. He's cracked her nose. Blood is gushing in astonishing volume.

All Cassidy can see are pinpoints of light. She is dizzy, listing sideways.

Joe says, "I gave you lots of chances."

She can make him out, blurry, moving to the left. She puts her shoulder down and suddenly releases all the torque in her body in one quick lash that lands him in the jaw.

You can hear it.

"Daddy!"

Stumbling over furniture.

And Nora, cowering and crying like a child.

Cold air blows through the open door. Cassidy hasn't bothered to close it behind them, sitting on the kitchen floor holding an ice pack to the mother of all nosebleeds. She has gone through all the clean rags in the house and half a roll of paper towels. Edith has stolen a blood-soaked dish towel and is lying in the corner, tearing it apart.

You start off hell-bent, don't think about it, just go. Then you get slapped across the face and realize you couldn't even say where you've been, or who was really with you—maybe, to give yourself credit, because the nature of what was there, and who he was, were truly hidden.

You fight it. But now you're back in your own kitchen, where facts are as unavoidable as the streaks on the window and dog hair on the floor.

Joe hit her because in some desperate way, he wanted her to remember.

She was sprawled across the backseat.

Joe had been talking about an old movie where four guys drive trucks full of nitroglycerin through a jungle in a shitstorm like the one they were in.

Cassidy asked, "Why?"

"For money," he replied.

The hurricane was on them. Black rain pelted the windshield with unworldly force. Visibility zero.

Didn't matter. Cassidy was watching the patterns behind her closed eyes, pulsating like pieces of the Bible if verses of the Bible could be reborn as shapes of brilliantly colored glass that could arrange themselves several thousand times a second into arabesques and mazes, mosaics, Navajo zigzags and fluorescent argyle.

They were driving fast when the Rover hit something with a sickening crunch and rolled right over it. There had been a splatter on the windshield like heavy mud. It braked too quickly and lost traction on the rain-swept road but remained upright, taking a lazy sideways skid, spinning, coming to a sudden stop. Their necks whipped and the seat belts squeezed all the air from their lungs. Cassidy's limp body was thrown off the backseat.

Someone called her name.

She said she was all right.

Someone opened the driver's door, the puddle lamp providing an illuminated triangle of seething rain.

The door slammed.

The Rover was still warm and humming, impervious to the shuddering winds, the deafening clatter of the rain on the roof like a payload of pebbles thundering down a chute.

She was lying on the floor mat staring at a plastic Dalmatian under the seat. Pretty soon she couldn't breathe. Her nasal passages were blocked and blood was filling her throat. Drowning, she clawed her way up. She reached for someone to help her.

Alberto turned from the passenger side.

She saw Alberto's frightened face. She saw his hands reach out to help. He found a roll of paper towels. One by one he tore them off.

"Lie back. Here is water."

He found a plastic bottle.

Joe pulled the door open, climbing back into the driver's seat and ramming the gearshift all in one motion.

"Seat belts on?" he asked briskly.

In the front seat Alberto obediently clicked his belt.

"What was it?" he asked.

"One of those ponies," Joe told them. "Wandering loose by the side of the road."

"Is it hurt?"

"It's dead."

He jerked the wheel around and pivoted cautiously in the slick mud then rolled ahead slowly, fighting to stay on the road.

"They'll skin it and string it up like that cow on the truck. Did you see? It was like a cruxificion in a painting."

"Who will?"

"Whoever finds it."

Alberto said, "We should go back to that hotel—"

But Joe did not seem to hear.

"The three of us?" he said. "We have died to the world."

Crumpled wet paper towels like roses were scattered all around. Cassidy struggled to keep her head up, trying to look ahead in the dim light from the instrument panel. Those polka dots of red on the windshield—were they crusted dead mosquitoes—or long clots of blood stuck to the outside of the glass, resisting the rain?

"What do you mean, we have died?" murmured Alberto, sounding scared.

Cassidy is sitting alone on the cold kitchen floor, rocking back and forth, surrounded by a garden of red-stained paper towels.

Alberto was in the passenger seat.

She saw his face: worried because she was hurt; in pain because she was in pain.

The good face.

26

"And who are you waiting for?"

"Harvey Weissman."

"And what is your last name?"

"Sanderson. Two other guys already asked me the same question."

"I see. Thank you, Miss Sanderson."

The security attendant bows and leaves. Cassidy sits there smelling the lilies which swoon from a silver stand on a scroll-legged library table as big as a Ford Expedition. It is amazing how the scent can fill the vast main lounge, twice as long as a fifty-foot pool, she would estimate, coffered ceilings maybe twenty-five feet high. The paneling is the color of oak logs which have been lying around the bogs of England for a couple of centuries until having attained the deep rich brown of truffles soaked in brandy.

A grandfather clock strikes the quarter hour. We are in a different time, California Club time, not the time of the ordinary world. Here there is no hint of traffic out on Flower, the Central American marketplace along Broadway, no sense of Chinatown or Dodger Stadium just minutes away. Inside this Beaux Arts clubhouse, hidden away without canopy or sign, shoulder to shoulder with bank buildings and corporate towers, beats the hushed heart of downtown Los Angeles. In these private rooms money only needs to whisper. Even the cool cathedral air seems to have been resting undisturbed since the boom of the 1920s; a stillness so profound the sound of one page of a newspaper being turned by a gentleman seated forty feet away crackles as if put through an amplifier.

Sweat forms like dew along Cassidy's inner thighs from the effort of keeping her feet flat and long legs pressed together—an attempt to stay buoyant on the down-filled cushions of the couch. She is wearing a blue blazer over a short paisley wrap skirt, which doesn't help. At least Harvey told her to dress. Her exasperation has grown to bursting with each insulting security check.

Finally Harvey Weissman appears across the carpeting. From her low angle sunk into the couch his six-foot frame appears even larger than life, or maybe it is the dapper two-button seersucker suit, oxblood bow tie, and navy silk pocket square. The light of the manor hall suits him. It cherishes the pudge over the cheekbones and the upturned crinkles at the corners of the eyes, the ageless advisor at ease in the corridors of power.

"Have you had a look around?"

"I was afraid I would get arrested."

He leads her down the great hall, which goes on for a city block, carved sideboards and flower arrangements spilling out of urns, and explains who did the Western landscape paintings and where the pink and gray marble came from (Morocco) and what it is called (*gris perle rose*).

"You know a lot about this place."

"Joe is the expert." His tone is nasty. "Joe can tell you everything about it. For example, the club was built in 1930 but they didn't admit women as members until 1987. Until then, females were not permitted to enter through the front door. '*Manhood, wealth and energy.*' That was the criteria for membership."

"I go for the manhood part."

"Don't we all. See this—?"

Harvey taps a framed list of prospective members and their sponsors, who are, in several cases, the mayor or the cardinal.

"You have to be *approved*."

"It's the same thing at my gym," Cassidy sighs. "You have to be able to put at least fifty bucks a month on MasterCard."

Harvey smiles for the first time.

The main dining room is carpeted in deep cherry and probably seats five hundred within those same fecund-brown paneled walls, beneath some spectacular silver candelabra. This afternoon there are just thirty guests for luncheon scattered across the immense space, drone males in gray suits and one or two heavyset women dressed like senators.

Their table, oceans apart from the others, is set against its own window overlooking a fountain.

"Thank you for seeing me."

"Keep your voice down," warns Harvey.

"I know Joe's a client and you—"

"*Just keep your voice down.* There are *rules.* Decorum. No writing allowed. No doing business. If they see you using a cell phone, they will stop you."

Cassidy casts a look at the killer white-haired waiters dressed in dusty black.

"Do they let you order a drink?"

They both have martinis. Ketel 1, double olives.

Cassidy entwines her fingers around the stem of the glass in a ladylike manner and says more quietly,

"I appreciate you talking with me about Joe."

"Joe is no longer my client."

Gone is the hearty host. Harvey is wearing his four-hundred-fifty-dollar-an-hour game face.

"But you've been Joe's lawyer twenty-two years—!"

"He put me in an untenable situation."

Cassidy takes a quick sip of the drink. With martinis, the chill and delicate bouquet can turn into warm motor oil, fast.

"He told you about the blackmail."

"I can't discuss what he said."

"But he's not your client anymore."

"An attorney cannot do anything or say anything that would be adverse to a present or former client."

"Then why are we here?"

"I think I've just explained the rules."

Cassidy nods, understanding that she will have to lead in this particular dance.

"Joe was getting blackmail notes," she begins. "He didn't know what to do so he paid. Even though you told him, *Never pay a blackmailer.*"

"I might have told him that, I might not."

"You said it to me at the party."

"I do have a basic attitude about blackmail. I'm going to tell you a secret, Cassidy. Twenty years ago someone tried to blackmail me because I am *homosexual—*"

He makes the word sizzle with sarcasm.

"—and I told that rancid human being, 'Do your worst. But I'll get you for extortion.' I never heard from him again."

Harvey's eyes, behind the glasses, dart once toward the garden.

"Never pay a blackmailer. If they give you the negative, you can be sure they've got twenty prints. That's nuts. They'll be back in two months."

"But Joe wouldn't listen."

Harvey remains silent.

The white-haired waiter puts an oval plate of old-fashioned seafood salad in front of Cassidy, pink remoulade and a split hard-boiled egg. Harvey is having fruit.

"Can I get you anything else, Mr. Weissman?"

"Yes," says Harvey. "Lunch."

The waiter hides a smile and withdraws.

Harvey stares at the plate.

"I've been on a diet since the age of three, when they told me it wasn't baby fat."

Cassidy says, "He told you about the accident."

"Whatever he told me was adverse to the company and to his partners. Because of attorney-client privilege, I couldn't tell the others, so I had to resign as his attorney."

"You just left him hanging?"

"No," says Harvey. His knuckles rap the white tablecloth. "I advised him to hire the best lawyer in the DR, fly down there, and throw himself on their mercy."

"Is that what he's going to do?"

"I have no idea. He was more worried about his father."

"He's never talked about his father."

"They gave him a fancy title, called him an 'engineer,' but the truth is, he was a plumber. His dad used to work here."

Cassidy looks toward the vaulted ceiling. The acres of air make you feel like a bottom-feeder.

"*Here*," Harvey emphasizes, "*this club*. Joe's dad came over working in the engine room of a ship, then he got a job fixing pipes at the California Club, where he worked for, I don't know, thirty, forty years. You didn't know this?"

Cassidy shakes her head.

"Joe goes out of his way not to give this impression, but he's the son of the hired help. He still lives here."

"His father?"

"*No no no,* dad and mom live in Glendale. Above us"—Harvey gestures with a melon ball at the end of a fork—"there are floors of suites, like full-service Park Avenue apartments. Members live here. Joe lives here. It's his primary residence."

"So the beach house—"

"Beach house, smeach house. His legal address is the club."

Cassidy looks bewildered.

"Joe's parents were uneducated Greek peasants. I don't know if we can say the word 'Greek' out loud." Harvey looks around with furtive irony. "We couldn't say 'Jew' until 1991. Joe grew up watching the rich guys come through the front door. The thing you have to remember about Joe, he's an insider who knows what it's like to be an outsider. He eats with the mayor and his father is proud. He appears at all the right parties, makes generous political contributions, knows all the council members by first name and they take his calls. He doesn't make a big thing of it, but he's on the board of directors of the Greek Orthodox church, St. Sophia's Cathedral. He paid for a new parking lot, five hundred thousand grand. *That's* for his dad. Every year, on Father's Day, he goes out to Glendale and his mother makes a gourmet Greek meal and you gain five pounds—trust me, I've been there—and Joe plays five games of backgammon with his father and they have a shot of ouzo. This, to Joe, is what it's all about. Bring shame on his father? I think Joe would rather be dead. By the way," says Harvey, "it's also against the rules to cry."

He gives her his blue pocket square, insisting, "Take it, it goes with the whole scene. See? Martinis. Silk? Very nice."

"I'm sorry to embarrass you."

"*Nothing* embarrasses me, kid. But I did want to throw your boyfriend through the window."

"You know I was in the car." She waits. "Along with a prospect for the Dodgers named Alberto Cruz—"

"I don't know about any car and I don't care what his name is."

"I was drunk. Passed out in the back."

"Now you're telling me you all were drunk—*oy vey!*" exclaims Harvey, but it is a poor imitation of surprise.

Cassidy waits. "What did Joe say about me? Forget the legal stuff."

"He said he cares about you. Surprised?"

She shrugs and blots the mascara that has collected in the corners of her eyes with Harvey's pocket square.

"He does. It's this deep ambivalence he has, it's some kind of mental hang-up, a self-destructive streak. All his life he's wanted to be accepted by the people he despises. See why I understand this man? Joe will invariably concoct a situation in which he forces you to choose — it's a test, *Am I worthy? Do you love me enough?* He did it to me when he told me things he should *never* have told me, which he *knew* would create problems: conflict of interest, obstruction of justice . . . It wasn't a big topic in law school before Nixon, but now we have to be aware. The more I would become involved, the more I could stumble into possible obstruction. And, I have a duty to his partners. So I had to fire him as a client. Never mind that his company was my second-biggest account."

The waiter brings the bill. Harvey signs it.

"No tipping, either. Did you know the club used to sell its own brand of cigarettes?"

"All I care about in this equation is Alberto Cruz."

"Then it's easy. Call the police. Tell them what happened. You're the witness. Cruz is off the hook."

"It's not so easy."

"Of course not."

"Do you think I can trust him?"

"Joe?"

She nods.

For a moment Harvey concentrates on scraping together a small pile of crumbs.

"Joe wanted to know his options. I said, Your options are the following: Get a criminal lawyer. Confess to — whoever you need to confess to — and hope she doesn't become a threat."

"A threat?"

"Lawyers work with logic trees. *If* this, *then* that . . . Okay. I told him, *If* she is in fact a threat, *then* your choices are: Pray it will go away. Turn yourself over to the cops. Or kill her." He waits. "I was kidding."

"What did Joe say?"

"I can't tell you what he said."

Harvey flicks the crumbs so they explode across the table.

27

Speed and music. Music and speed. It helps to have the windows down and the radio blasting to match the furor in her heart. It makes no sense, going there, and that feels *great*, just *great*, like hitting the drinking fountain with a bat when that bastard David Stohl walked out, over and over until the pipes separated and water geysered weakly in defeat; stupid and *great*, like doing a backflip, drunk, on a neighbor's trampoline on the Fourth of July.

What I love about you, he said, *is that you believe it matters.*

She laughs out loud. No, darlin', no, it freaking doesn't. Haven't you proven it to me? That attachment—to another person, to work, to love, to sports teams or ideals—just isn't possible anymore, at least not until the financing is in place? Maybe the human heart is outdated also, or just too dumb to get it, and it's absolutely pointless to believe that it has any effect on anyone, anywhere in the world, how one individual chooses to live within the white lines.

She hasn't been this angry since her father died.

The garage door is up, the Bentley parked inside. She steps over a carton with some painting stuff in it, angles past an overturned bag of potting soil and a couple more paint cans rolling loose on the floor, hits the button to close the door. Good, he's home, she thinks, and we can finish this.

The rear door to the kitchen is open. A plastic bag from Buy Rite drugstore is on the stainless steel counter.

"Joe?"

She notices the cordless phone has fallen on the sandstone floor and replaces it in the cradle.

A covered roasting pan sits on the stove. She peels the foil-back—lemon chicken that looks as if it has been sitting around for a while—hard and congealed as the now less-than-tender memory of the first night they spent together in this house, when she came back from Vero Beach, the night she'd had a flashback of being attacked in the parking lot by Monroe. Fear had driven them together like an aphrodisiac. Night had come and the square spaces of the house were lit like facets of a lantern on a boat moving out to sea, their love-making locked-together, frantic and close, as if they'd shared a berth on what they had known would be the start of a dangerous crossing; fogbound, cold black water sluicing underneath the belly of the ship.

Who was that man, who stroked her thighs and hips so tenderly for so long afterward, who wanted to marry her and promised the world? Was he someone who had made an irrevocable mistake, drenched in guilt, scrambling for a way out—or a master manipulator, lying to protect his interests, assuming Cassidy would give it up for him, even give away her kid? *Did he love me at all?* seems a woefully pathetic question, but as she stalks the crisply aloof house it stuns her that she doesn't know, is lost, perceptive apparatus crashing down around her like a shattered radio dish—tower, wires, sparks and flame.

"Joe?"

In the living room a late afternoon breeze sucks the gauzy white curtains out of the open sliding panels, a sticky after-the-beach breeze that makes you want to take a shower and lie back on the white slip-covered sofa with a pitcher of margaritas.

"Hey. It's Cassidy."

She looks at the stairs but something stops her from going up. It's the breeze; forceful, sweeping in through the open kitchen door and out toward the beach, blowing her hair in the same direction as the curtains. That flapping sound—she peers out at the courtyard—is a newspaper that has been—here's the trail of pages—lifted off the coffee table and swept outside and trapped against the chairs and orange trees, fluttering like a flock of wounded birds.

The doors have been open for a while.

He's gone for a run on the beach.

She walks out to the terrace and slides into a banquette built into the wall, behind an oval table made of stone. They'd had breakfast there that morning, bagels, tomatoes and feta cheese, which she had thought endearing at the time.

Above is a twenty-foot-high portico with a roof of open gridwork, so the diffuse afternoon sun is forced into sharp rectangular shafts, hitting the limestone floor in a precise geometry of burning squares.

This elegant composition in shadow and light brings to mind a keen and merciless people, the Mayan Indians, who, Cassidy had learned on a scuba-diving trip to Cozumel, constructed a pyramid so that at a certain hour of a certain day the steps would cast a zigzag shadow, the feathered serpent-god. She had been spaced on blue agave tequila and Lomotil at the time, but she has not forgotten the story of the snake, and the deadly ball games that took place in the ruined arena—mathematical intelligence and blood sacrifice—a savage passion to control the sun. Inside the pyramid, if you were not too dehydrated to climb a million undulating steps, was the hidden heart of their belief: a small dank chamber that contained a golden lion.

There is intelligence everywhere you look in Joe Galinis's borrowed ocean house. Now, in daylight, in the way the open girders frame the sky, the bend to the arms of the slatted aluminum chairs, the house wants to show you what it's really about, how money has been put to *aesthetic* purpose, to engage the minds of the most rarefied designers, give them freedom and then possess their ideas. Even the most numbskull San Marino commodities trader, hauled out here for Sunday brunch with the wife and kids, would have to respect the purity of a Richard Meier–style house at the beach.

The more Cassidy watches the shadows of the orange trees play over the grid of sun, the more she can see the translucent paradoxes in Joe Galinis. He had been dressed for work that morning in tobacco slacks and a cobalt-blue-and-white-striped dress shirt, ribbed silk tie with diamond patterns. In profile he had looked Macedonian, bejeweled.

But inside his soul was a dark secret chamber where a shining lion had been corroded by shame.

She takes off the sunglasses. Without the polarizing lenses the marine-white walls jump to a level of incandescence that is painful. As the sun sets, the grid of light is creeping down the wall. This might have been her home, had she surrendered to its measured spaces. She gets up restlessly to unlock the front gates and see if she can spot Joe's tight, short-torsoed body moving along the beach.

The phone is ringing.

She turns back and peers inside through yards of blowing curtains. On the mezzanine above, the Francis Bacon paintings float, disemboweled body parts in fields of gold.

The phone rings.

It rings and rings in the blowsy empty house.

It rings inside the fillings of her teeth.

"Hello?"

"Southcoast Security. We have a report your garage door is open, ma'am."

"It is? I thought I shut it."

"It's open, ma'am. I have a patrol car outside."

"Thank you—"

"What is your password, please?"

"I don't know the password."

"Your name?"

"Cassidy Sanderson. I'm the cleaning lady."

She hangs up.

Twenty-five seconds later two security officers wearing earpieces, nightsticks and .38s enter through the kitchen.

"Stay where you are, please."

"Don't shoot. I swear to God I closed the garage door."

They don't answer: burly males with shaved heads, Hispanic, completely without humor.

"Can I see some photo ID?"

Cassidy takes out her wallet.

"Do you live here, ma'am?"

"No."

"What are you doing here?"

"I came to see Mr. Galinis."

"What is your relationship to Mr. Galinis?"

"Friend."

"Was Mr. Galinis expecting you?"

"No."

"I see."

Well, it's ludicrous. Of course he doesn't see. She forces herself to choke down complete out-of-control frustration. This is exactly the kind of twisted, inexplicable situation that can get out of hand if you buy into their paranoia.

Stay cool.

Stay centered.

Use what you've got.

"Do you guys, by any chance, follow the Dodgers?"

No reaction. Then,

"Yo, Carlos."

The second officer has successfully sniffed out the one thing in this windswept room that is out of place—a Polaroid photograph half-stuck under the cabinets, apparently blown across the floor.

He shows it to his partner who raises his eyebrows and motions to Cassidy.

"Can you identify this man?"

She looks at the picture.

"That's Joe!"

"Mr. Galinis?"

"Joe Galinis, *goddamn it!*"

It is Mr. Joe Galinis, shoved against the glass brick wall of the kitchen, his face a sickly Polaroid yellow because somebody's hand is holding a gun to his head.

Then, all at once, all three spot the Campbell's soup can that has been set in the center of the stainless steel counter like a piece of Pop Art, a ransom note tucked underneath.

$2,000,000 *or he dies. We will call you.*

What a loser. Monroe hasn't even bothered to disguise his first-grade handwriting.

"Know anything about this?"

Cassidy, dry-lipped: "It's complicated."

Carlos: "I guess."

He looks at her, unsettled now; his close-set eyes so young.

28

This is how it went down in the front office:

People were hyped, transistors on, the Dodgers about to face the Pirates at Pittsburgh. If they won and the Rockies lost, the Dodgers would move into first place—cause for the traditional ice cream party in the "ice cream area" in the front office and the first hopeful turn of the season. But all of that seemed to Cassidy as foreign as a festival in Istanbul. When Dulce saw her coming, she scuttled away like a crab, joining the other assistants in the dim reaches of the filing stacks. Rumors were rampant. People knew something was up, most of them betting it was Cassidy Sanderson's career. You don't assemble two detectives, three attorneys for the Dodgers and a special agent from the FBI in the scouting director's office to talk lowball hitters and career trends.

Cassidy put her game face on and walked the gauntlet.

She opened the door to find Raymond staring right at her with both big palms flat on the empty desk, the others (including Allen in the dark blue suit and Simms, wearing Adidas) posed on window ledges and chairs with cups of coffee, legal pads and absent smiles.

It didn't get any better.

During the next hour and a half she made a statement in which she admitted to taking an unauthorized trip to the DR, to being drunk in a car along with a newly signed prospect and an American developer who later became her lover—who, she stated in a barely audible voice, to the best of her knowledge and recollection, was driving the Rover when they hit an unidentified female, apparently killing her, and who, without informing Ms. Sanderson or Mr. Cruz of the severity of the accident, drove away from the scene. The developer, before he disappeared, an apparent victim of a blackmail scheme turned kidnapping, repeatedly tried to manipulate her into putting the blame on the boy.

That was fun, saying that to a room full of men.

Afterward, when the investigators left, Raymond asked her to stay.

He closed the door. Cassidy drew up her feet cross-legged in the chair, not her usual posture in Raymond's office.

"I'm just going to go for it," he told her. "I feel like a piker. From the day you went down there you kept me three steps behind when we should have been on the same page. I should have *known* you were taking off, I should have *known* what was happening with Cruz, not hear it through official channels. Damn, you get the shit beat out of you in Vero Beach and I'm the last to know? You should have come to me in every instance, and you didn't, and that hurts. I feel like my faith in you has been abused."

"I'm very, very sorry, Ray, it's totally my fault. I thought I was taking care of everyone."

"You did a hell of a great job with Cruz."

"I got him to the game."

"No you haven't. With all your shenanigans, you've made it doubly hard."

"How is he doing? I tracked him down at the USC Medical Center. I left a message but he didn't call me back."

"He had some kind of tropical parasite. The infection went to his liver. They had to do an operation, but he's all right, he'll be fine. Physically. But that's not all there is to it."

"I realize that."

"He has to make a statement to the police. Then there's the fiasco with the birth certificate—"

Raymond heaved up and for an instant his bulk blocked the daylight.

"—*Then*, he has to play!"

Blushing, "I know he has to play."

"I *trust* your evaluation of a prospect. If I didn't *trust* you, then you and I could not be in business." His voice had left the cool reserves. "So would you please explain exactly what it is that keeps *you* from trusting *me*?"

Standing in front of an empty oak bookshelf, dressed according to code in forest green plaid shirt and pressed slacks, Raymond appeared as frustrated as a gifted African-American principal in an all-white school, fed up with the racial crap that keeps him from doing his job.

Cassidy saw it, and the faint gleam of sweat on his forehead.

"I do trust you. I wouldn't want to work for anyone else. You do a great job in player development and you've more than once stepped up for me. And I'm grateful."

Raymond sat back down at the bare desk in the empty office. Clearly, he was moving in or out of there at any moment.

"I guess I'm disappointed all around. Disappointed and disgusted." His hand formed a soft fist. "The Dodgers are family. That's what makes this club different, and to me that's not a bunch of public relations horseshit."

"Me, either."

"Well, now we can kiss our little family good-bye."

"What do you mean?"

He swiveled away and looked out at the field.

"The rumor is the O'Malleys are going to sell."

Cassidy's body went limp in the chair.

"Not possible."

"Another reason everybody's nuts around here. Peter wanted to build that football stadium and the city council wouldn't come through. I think he was disillusioned . . . There's a lot of reasons."

"I can't even process this—"

". . . a solid franchise," Raymond was saying, "but that's all we do," earnestly, "see, *we do baseball*, and it's becoming so as one baseball family can't hold on anymore against the big diversified corporations that have TV networks and newspapers and whatnot to absorb the bottom line."

"What's going to happen to everybody?" Cassidy wondered out loud.

"Nobody knows," Raymond answered. "Depends who the buyer is."

Their eyes met.

"People say baseball's slow, the players are overpaid . . . Hopefully the buyer will be someone who can go all out to promote the game."

"Sure."

"Cultivate the younger fan."

"Right."

"Better in the end." The phone rang. "At this point the intention to sell is not common knowledge. So don't go trading in it."

"I wouldn't!"

"See? I'm trusting you with that."

He spoke for a few minutes, hung up.

"They don't want you to leave yet. You're getting a police escort home."

"That'll be new."

"They're putting you under protective custody. Apparently they believe you yourself are in sufficient danger, with all this horseshit, they don't want you to leave your house."

The Dodgers lost.

No ice cream, either.

29

Cassidy makes sure to keep several steps ahead of Detective Allen going up the steps so she can get to the attic bedroom first—to whisk a bra off a doorknob, sideswipe the curling edge of a braided rug into place, block his view of the intimate mess on top of the bamboo dresser by standing in front of it, fists on her waist.

"It's just a simple tape recorder. Plugs into a phone jack. Can I set it up here?"

"Anywhere you want."

She removes a pile of laundry (at least it's folded) from a wooden chair. Detective Allen places a small black tape recorder on the chair but it totters in the scooped-out seat. Cassidy offers a crocheted pad. Still totters. He finds some magazines on the nightstand and positions them on the seat, pad on top, then the tape recorder.

"Impressive."

"Pick up the phone."

A red light goes on and the tape whirs. Cassidy hangs up. The machine stops.

"Incoming calls will trigger it as well. Come downstairs, I've got something for you to sign."

Detective Allen jogs energetically down the winding staircase as if he's lived in this cottage all his life, having traded the bad news suit for a pair of jeans and, apparently, contact lenses for gold-rimmed glasses. The stairs wheeze. He needs to lose those ten pounds.

He opens a briefcase on the dining table. Cassidy peers inside, curious to see if there is a gun, but instead she spots an empty shoulder holster, headphones, a second tape recorder, personal organizer, screwdriver, airline tickets, a roll of antacids, maps, a science fiction novel, yellow pads, legal documents. Handcuffs.

"This is called a one-party consent. You give us permission to tape-record your conversations."

"What about whoever I'm talking to?"

"They don't know they're being recorded and you don't tell them."

"Isn't that a violation of somebody's rights?"

"Certain rights are waived under a criminal investigation."

"Like me being able to come and go from my own house?"

"You agreed to protective custody."

"Protective custody sucks."

"Hasn't even started yet. Wait until day twelve."

"I'll go insane."

"Feel free to have another conversation with your attorney. As far as I'm concerned"—a pen snaps out between his fingers like a knife—"we've been over this."

His condescension irks her and she signs.

"Is Joe now considered a criminal?"

"Joe is a possible kidnap victim as well as a suspect in two separate cases involving laundering of drug money and vehicular manslaughter."

"Why 'possible' victim?"

Allen is unplugging the receiver from the kitchen phone. He substitutes a Y connector and reattaches both receiver and headphones.

"We're still not clear about the circumstances surrounding the kidnapping."

"They left a photograph for God's sake."

"That's what bothers me. It's a little too neat."

"You mean, like, 'Hi! I've just been kidnapped'? Did you see the expression on his face? He knows as well as you do they cut people up and stuff them in the trunks of cars. They could be torturing him, and do you care?"

"Look, it's a theory."

"Okay," taking breaths to slow the sudden drumming of her heart, to annhilate the images of what they could be doing to Joe right now. "What's the theory?"

"Let's say the alleged kidnappers were lying in wait. He parks the car, they approach at gunpoint, take him into the house, leave the note. I'm fine to that point. But then none of the neighbors sees him leave. Nobody hears a thing. Even though the houses are close together and everyone's got a high-tech alarm system, including Joe. He doesn't hit the panic button, makes no attempt we know of to resist—which means he had to have walked outside and into their car *cooperatively*, then they leave the garage door open with a Bentley parked inside—"

"They didn't leave it open."

"No?"

"Joe did. He kicked the carton with the paint cans in the way so the door would automatically pop up. That's why it didn't stay closed when I closed it."

"Pretty fast thinking for a high-stress situation."

"That's Joe. Quick on his feet." She grabs a bag of pistachios off the counter. "The open door was a call for help. And I walked right through it. Don't you think that keeps me up at night?"

She offers the bag to Allen.

"People have been wondering how you got in," he says, cracking one. "What you were doing there at that particular time."

"Man, I answered all these questions in Raymond's office—"

"You did."

"But?"

He shrugs. "I don't know. I don't know how you really feel about the guy."

He works the shell apart carefully.

"Excuse me, but am I the suspect here?"

"No."

"You think I helped Joe escape? Is that why I'm imprisoned in my own home?"

"You are under protective custody because Monroe knows where you work and probably where you live. He's already beat the shit out of you once. You're a witness to the shooting in the 7-Eleven as well as to vehicular manslaughter in which the driver of the car, Mr. Galinis, has disappeared. Two unstable individuals, one target. It's a no-brainer, Cassidy."

"Okay, so what's the drill?"

Allen snaps the briefcase shut. He takes a couple more nuts and shakes them in his hand like dice.

"Monroe has sent a message with that ransom note. He wants to communicate. We're going to communicate. He calls. The red light goes on. You hear his voice. *'Hello?'* Your first reaction will be to stress. But the key is to be patient and control the situation. The guy is dangerous and crazy. He shot a kid in cold blood so we know he's the type to pull a weapon, show he's a macho man. Right now he's under pressure. The uncle is impatient. The extortion thing hasn't worked out so great, so he's kicked it up to kidnapping. He figured Cruz is too protected, so he's gone for the big kahuna, but he knows that could mean greater risk. When you talk to him he could be agitated, possibly high, possibly verbally abusive."

"How do I know he's not just looking for a parking space in Beverly Hills?"

"Stay with me. We want Monroe to talk. He ain't gonna spill his whereabouts, so just try to have a casual conversation. Anything you can get along the way. For example, we have a good case on the 7-Eleven but a confession would be icing on the cake. You ask open-ended, common-sense questions like, 'Back in Vero—what happened? Why did it go wrong? The cops have been asking around. Word is this clerk was killed and your name popped up. They're looking for you. I don't want to be associated with this kind of thing—clear my mind for me—what went down? The clerk pushed the panic button or what?'"

The phone rings.

Cassidy jolts. Detective Allen slips the headphones on.

"Just answer it like normal."

"Hello?"

"Cassidy Sanderson?"

"Yes?"

"This is Pamela Benson of the *Los Angeles Times.* I'm calling from the sports desk. I cover the Dodgers and—"

Detective Allen, listening through the headphones, raises his eyebrows, *Go with it.*

"—I was wondering if I could ask a few questions."

"Ask."

"There's a rumor you quit the scouting department."

"Quit? No," says Cassidy as normally as possible. "Just taking a leave of absence."

"In the middle of the season?"

"So what?"

Detective Allen makes a cutoff sign at the throat.

"The rumor is you couldn't hack it. The pressure was too tough."

"Who told you this supposed rumor? It wasn't Travis Conners by any chance?"

"I can't reveal a source."

Detective Allen's hand is sawing back and forth.

"We both know what it's like for women," the sweet young voice goes on. "Still a man's world. Sometimes it's easier just to bail—"

"No *way*. Not *ever*. And you tell whoever came up with that steaming piece of horseshit to respect the game of baseball. I don't care if they respect me, but respect the game."

She slams the phone down, strides to the refrigerator and pulls a beer.

"I assume you don't want one of these?"

Allen shakes his head.

She hooks the bottle under an opener mounted on the wall and yanks it hard so the cap goes flying.

"You'll get the hang of it," Detective Allen sighs.

30

They let her run on the beach with one of the officers from the Laguna Beach Police Department. Edith gets walked. The backyard gets watered. The sock drawer almost gets cleaned out, but forget that. Bills get paid. New checks for her account get ordered. It takes forty-five minutes, but finally she prevails in having a seventy-nine-dollar charge she has been carrying for a year for a radial tire she never purchased taken off her credit card.

Hooray.

Late in the afternoon of the third day, during a Padres–Cardinals game, Raymond calls.

"Thought I'd pass along some peace of mind."

"Great."

"I'm giving your territory to Travis."

"Travis!"

The word *dickhead* has barely formed upon her lips when Raymond adds, "I know that Travis can be a dickhead, but the police have been talking to the VPs. There's legitimate concern about the safety and well-being of our personnel. The cops think, basically, you shouldn't be around the players."

"But I'm on all these great kids—"

"It's temporary. Until this settles down."

"There's one," she argues, "Garrett Wright, sixteen years old, incredibly hot left-hander just coming up at Long Beach High—"

"You'll pick up where you left off. We'll be here."

"That's not fair, Raymond, *please*—"

"You've still got business to clean up. When they let you out of there and whatnot, go out and make the sign on Brad Parker. I want to lock that down."

She blows exasperated air into the phone which apparently infuriates her boss.

"*Can you make the sign on Parker?*"

"Yes, I can make the sign!"

Hostile silence.

"Taking your stuff on means extra work for Travis. He's doing you a favor. We're hanging with you, Cassidy, which is more than you've shown us."

She swallows hard.

"Thank you, Ray. That means a lot."

"All right."

Raymond hangs up.

The machine clicks off.

Cassidy thinks about it. After a moment she presses the rewind button. Then she picks up the phone and lets the red light go on, recording five minutes of silence over the conversation with Raymond, thereby wiping it and everything else off the tape.

"What do people do when they're cooped up like this?"

"Play video games. Watch TV."

"How can you stand it?"

Detective Allen is sitting on the sofa typing on a laptop. The locals have been working the other shifts. Tonight it will be his turn to sleep on the living room couch.

"I once saw a woman go through boxes and boxes of family photos. I mean like thousands. She sat in a motel room in Fort Lauderdale for three, four weeks, patiently organizing, meticulously putting them into albums. Nice lady."

"Was she a witness, too?"

"No, it was a domestic violence situation. He ultimately got her anyway."

"The husband?"

"Right."

"But you were protecting her."

"Right."

"How could that have happened?"

"Jealousy is a powerful motivator. Maybe the most powerful of all."

"Tell me one thing. Was the husband in the photographs or not?"

Allen has gone back to the screen.

"I really want to know."

He doesn't answer.

Cassidy sighs and digs into a bowl of Shredded Wheat, the big fat bales, soaked in half-and-half. She has been under protective custody ten days. Another ten minutes and she'll be sucking zwieback.

9:15 p.m. The refrigerator hums.

"What are you doing?"

"E-mail."

"Writing a report?"

"Writing to my son."

"How old's your son?"

"Eleven."

"Plays ball?"

"Infield."

"Good bat?"

"He got hit by the ball, now he's shy of it."

"Needs to work on his confidence. I can show you some drills."

"Cool."

9:20 p.m.

"How do you feel about oral sex?"

"I just got him a BMX bike," Allen answers without missing a beat.

Cassidy gets up from the stool.

"I apologize. When I'm bored, pissed off and going out of my mind, I revert to jock behavior."

Morose, she washes the bowl. The kitchen has never been neater.

"—Now he wants an electric guitar. My ex-wife is not pleased. I don't know what the hell she thinks. He's not going to be a concert pianist."

The keys go *tap tap*.

Then, "Do me a favor?" without looking up, "Don't screw with the tape recorder."

Cassidy fumbles the bowl.

"What makes you think I'd do something like that?"

"Your face is red as an apple."

"It's hot in here."

He stares from the sofa.

"Who called?"

She doesn't answer.

"I asked you a question."

"Raymond Woods."

"Why did you erase the tape?"

"He was relieving me of my duties. It was embarrassing."

"You have relinquished your privacy. You have signed it away. You are not above the law. You're a witness. That's all you are."

Cassidy puts the bowl in the drainer and dries her hands on a dish towel over and over.

"I hear you."

"The problem is, when you do something blatantly uncooperative like that, it makes people wonder if you're conspiring with Mr. Galinis to destroy evidence."

"Think what you want."

"Frankly, I think Travis is a dickhead, too."

She turns, gripping the towel.

"You know what was on the tape, even though I erased it?"

"There's a van parked outside monitoring everything we say."

Cassidy steals a look around her kitchen.

"You better be making that up."

Detective Allen's face gives nothing.

"Aren't you hard."

"Aren't you?" he replies. "I'm just wondering what's behind the mask."

"The Mask. That's funny. That's what my brother and I used to call my mother."

"Tough lady?"

"None of your business."

"I'll tell you this." Allen's body has become immobile as if bolted to the floor. He shakes a finger: "Call your gynecologist."

"*What?*"

"You've already canceled four appointments."

"You shit!" She snaps his bare arm with the wet towel. "How dare you listen to my private calls?"

"My mom died of breast cancer. I have a thing about it."

He goes into the living room.

"They can catch it early now," he adds, not looking back.

7:05 a.m.

A cab pulls up in front of the cottage. A man carrying a gym bag gets out. The morning light is enchanted, you could weave a chain of gold from this light. The sprinklers are on, lopsided, dousing the walk instead of the ivy and maybe that is why—the sprinklers and the light—the man is distracted and does not see two other men get out of a sedan and trot across the street.

"Sir?"

He turns. White, six foot two, a hundred eighty pounds of hard-crafted muscle wearing two-hundred-dollar warm-ups. Does not fit the description of a scrawny Dominican criminal but merits caution.

"Laguna Beach police."

They come toward him, an older guy and a young one, wearing suits, holding up badges.

"What's the problem?"

"Please put the bag down, sir."

"I'm not about to rob the place."

"Put the bag down."

He holds the bag at arm's length, then lets it drop to the wet sidewalk. The young cop flinches.

"Can we see some identification, please?"

"This is ridiculous."

"What are you doing here, sir?"

"Visiting my girlfriend."

Older cop: "Where're you from?"

"Sydney, Australia."

Young cop: "She must be hot."

"In actual fact, I just got off a plane from Vancouver, just a little fried because it was ball-bustingly early, and I've been working three weeks, day and night, on a movie set with a bunch of pathological actors—"

"I get it. The guy is Crocodile Dundee."

"That's right, and you can kiss my autograph. Bugger off."

The police report claims, "Suspect threatened great bodily harm," but actually it is a provocative protrusion of the buttocks that triggers an autonomic response from the officers resulting in the suspect spread-eagled, hands against the wall, as Cassidy pops the top half of the Dutch door open, leans out and laughs.

"What a little milkmaid," Marshall grunts, pushing through the door when the officers finally let him pass.

Cassidy's hair is tousled, knots lifting on the dry air like brittle clumps of hay. She is wearing what she slept in—flannel shirt and boxer shorts—holding Edith in her arms.

"What a grump."

"I fully intend to sue the bastards. Have you got coffee?"

"No," says Cassidy, although the coffeemaker is dripping and the aroma profound.

"That's a joke?"

"No, it's not."

Detective Allen comes out of the bathroom, freshly shaved, tucking a clean shirt into his slacks.

"Who is this?"

"He's a cop."

Marshall plants both feet like he's about to do karate.

"What the hell is going on?"

Cassidy is suddenly quite frazzled.

"Look," she says impulsively, "things have changed. You can't just come here any hour of the day and night anymore."

Marshall scratches his head.

"You needed a team of trained assassins to tell me that?"

Detective Allen introduces himself and extends a hand.

"I take it you know Ms. Sanderson?"

"Well, yes, as you can see she's a bit of a spunk. We've been fucking for years."

Cassidy turns her back. "I refuse to deal with this."

"The baseball team has been receiving threats," Detective Allen says smoothly.

"What kind of threats?"

"Nothing out of the ordinary. The officers are here as a precaution."

"Darling, why didn't you tell me?" Marshall exclaims, implying an intimacy that has in fact never existed.

"You were in Vancouver," blurts Cassidy, as if she needs to be defensive.

"They have telephones now in Canada."

Detective Allen: "I'm going out for breakfast."

"Don't feel you have to leave—" Cassidy suddenly realizes she is still holding on to the dog.

Marshall, "Hell, no."

Allen hesitates.

Marshall puts both hands on Cassidy's shoulders, Edith looking up between them.

"From time to time we go away from each other, but we always come back."

He rubs her bare calf with a running shoe.

"To a place that is always . . . fantastic."

Allen: "The officers are outside if you need them."

Marshall tips his head toward the detective.

"You have something going with this wanker?"

"Grow up."

"Don't trust the police."

Detective Allen picks up his denim jacket.

"Maybe it's my military training," Marshall's going on, "but I've discovered law enforcement organizations in general to be based on secrecy and a particular brand of sadism. Anybody not in their club is fair game. They're cold motherfuckers. They use people. I'd take good care."

"Marshall, that is completely paranoid."

"Well, gorgeous," picking up the gym bag, "it's been a paranoid kind of morning."

3:10 a.m.

The phone rings.

Cassidy's first awareness is of rapid heartbeat, then the weight of the receiver in her palm. Her body has reacted faster than her mind, still lost in a dream instantly cut into jagged slices.

"Whatzup?"

"Monroe?"

"How's the weather?"

"Hot. What about you?"

"Stoked."

Her head clears. She sees the red light.

"Where are you?"

"For all I know your phone is bugged."

"Don't flatter yourself."

"You ready to take care of things?"

"That's right."

"You gonna pay?"

"Yes."

"The price went up. You got the money?"

"Not right now, it's three in the morning—or maybe not where you are."

"I'm with you, bitch. I'm closer to you than you want to know about."

"Like you were in Vero Beach?"

"Hey, how's the hand? I only did the one so you'd still be able to jerk off the team."

By now she is downstairs where Detective Allen, wearing old blue sweats, is standing in the kitchen in the glow of a night light, headphones on, the blanket and pillow she had given him rumpled up on the couch where he slept.

He signals with a finger, *Keep it going,* round and round.

"I'm talking about the 7-Eleven," Cassidy responds. "Where that kid was killed."

"Yeah? Something happened?"

Allen nods, encouraging.

"You know what, Monroe? You are really starting to piss me off."

Monroe laughs.

"I'll see what I can do about the money. Then I want you out of my life."

"I want you to suck my cock—but we can negotiate. Somebody here to say hello."

Shuffling, like a chair being dragged. A soft "*Umph,*" muffled words, close breathing into the phone.

"Cassidy? It's Joe."

Panicked, Cassidy stares at Allen. He signals with the finger, calmly, *Stay with it,* round and round.

"Joe, are you all right?"

"Get the money."

The red light goes out.

Allen: "Where do you keep the hard stuff?"

She indicates. He pours them each a hit of tequila.

"He's okay, he's alive."

The glass is bumping against her teeth.

"You really did not know where he was."

She shakes her head.

"I apologize. I was wrong. I thought you might have planned it with him."

She shakes her head again.

"I wasn't," Allen adds, "being completely objective."

"You don't like Joe."

"My concern is not Joe."

In the silence she can hear the blood beating in her ears.

Detective Allen: "Need a hug?"

She nods obediently. He opens his arms just wide enough for her to step into, compresses her torso briefly like a mechanical toy, then quickly backs away.

Brusque, "You must have a yellow pages."

Cassidy finds it in a drawer.

"What are we going to do?"

"Monroe will call back. It could be soon. He's hooked."

Detective Allen riffles through the phone book.

"I'm thinking next time he calls you arrange a meet in a motel. We'll be watching and listening in the next room—"

Edith, thinking it must be dawn, presents herself for a run.

"—You bring the money, he brings Joe. You'll be wired and wearing a bulletproof vest. And you'll have this little doohickey, on loan from LAPD."

He opens the briefcase and removes a small flat black box on a silver ring.

"Where are your keys?"

She digs them out of her backpack.

"This is a transmitting device. Same principle as the Lo-Jack on your car. See that switch? It activates a global positioning system. Works off six satellites."

She watches with a sense of increasing unreality as he works the silver ring onto the clip that holds her keys.

"You press the button, they get a fix in twenty-four seconds, accurate to one hundred meters."

"I thought I was going to be cozy in the motel."

"The situation could change. We have to be fluid. I promise you, if it goes bad in any way, shape or form, Monroe will not get out of the parking lot."

His glasses reflect the dim light.

"If, when the time comes, you don't feel one hundred percent confident, we bag it. This has to be your choice. Think about it first. We're not talking high school drag races."

Detective Allen hands back the keys, heavy with the unfamiliar weight of the tracking device. She sets them on the table. Just that small jog is enough to cause the black plastic box to split open at the seams. A tiny circuit board and battery spill out.

It is unfunny.

"That won't happen," Detective Allen says.

He reconnects the wires and resets an LED display and snaps the cover.

Cassidy watches in silence.

He picks up the phone.

"What are you doing?"

"Calling my colleague at the FBI."

"I'm going to bed."

"Good night."

She hesitates. "I'm sorry about your mom. I didn't want you to think that I—"

"Don't worry about it."

"I do get checkups. Why am I telling you this? Because I'm so tired I can't see straight. It's just that I don't like doctors, I avoid them whenever possible."

"Not good enough."

"I've had a lot of bad experiences. My brother died from CF."

"My ex-wife had a cousin who died from that."

"Really?" It is rare when someone knows about CF; rarer still to be so matter-of-fact.

"Neat kid."

"I'm sorry."

"Me, too. About your brother."

"Thanks. Good night."

Cassidy is lying in bed with the light on trying not to imagine what they must have done to Joe to get him to plead for his life.

The minutes pass.

She turns her head on the pillow. Detective Allen is standing in the doorway, in his pilled blue sweats, holding something out to her.

A mug of tea.

It is one of her two white mugs with the blue stripe around the lip, ample and hefty and a good fit in the hand; she's had those mugs maybe ten years. A red tea tag clings to the side, fragile and wet. It is after 4 a.m. and cold in the room. You can see the steam in energetic whirls.

Tears fill her eyes.

"What's wrong?"

"You brought me tea."

"It's not a big deal." He sets the mug on the nightstand. "People do it all the time."

She pulls up her knees, wiping her cheek on the comforter.

Detective Allen sits on a chair.

"My ex-wife's cousin, the one who died of CF, her name was Laurie. She was about twenty-five. She was a spitfire. Nothing kept her down. You know, she was a swimmer, so she had this oxygen tank on wheels with a real long fifty-foot tube so she could do laps. She had a lung transplant, put up a fight—"

Cassidy nods. For a moment both are silent.

"Knowing her changed my life."

"That's what people said about my brother."

"Same thing?"

"Oh yeah, people were always saying, Gregg Sanderson, he changed my life. Kids on the team. Kids in the hospital . . . On the cancer ward. He'd visit the little kids on the cancer ward. You know, the bald kids, dragging their own IVs? I couldn't look."

"Hard for even a grown-up to see that."

Cassidy cradles the warm cup.

"My father had to drag me to the hospital, I never wanted to go to visit Gregg, which of course I also felt guilty about. I was twelve, but I'd freak, he'd have to physically drag me through the lobby. It was the seventies. He used to grab my arm and say, *'You're not sick so don't act sick!'* He was an ex-ballplayer, he was strong."

"I believe it."

"God, I remember everything in that hospital smelled like wax beans. And those awful elevators. You never knew what was getting off or on. One time when we got to Gregg's room, there were three or four doctors standing around, along with my mom. Gregg was sitting up in bed wearing no shirt as usual, just a pair of red Grizzly sweatpants—that was our school team—and this macramé choker with one good-luck bead. His hair was dirty, sticking up all over—he was pissed. By then he'd probably lost twenty pounds, you could see the bones in his shoulders. He was a grotty teenager, you know, but maybe from being inside all the time, being sick, his skin was smooth and silky and pale like a little boy's. He was screaming, *'Get out of my room!'*"

Allen smiles. "Get out of my room?"

"Yeah, 'Stop badgering me and get out of my room!' Usually you could hardly hear him because his voice got weird because of the inhalants, but you could hear him then. The doctors were doing their doctor number—*'We have to talk about this—'* *'They miscommunicated to you—'* and my father's saying, 'What's the problem?' and my mother takes him outside and tells him they just told Gregg he developed diabetes, which can be a complication of CF.

"So I'm *inside* the room when I hear this word—"

"You didn't know what it meant."

"*Diabetes.* Yeah. I don't have a clue except I hear my mother saying, 'He's terrified of needles. Now he has to give himself injections, he can't believe this could happen—' And I knew it was bad. My mother pretended there was never anything serious—my dad just got angry—but I *knew* this was bad, what could be worse than having to *give yourself injections*? Terrifying. No way. I'd rather be buried alive.

"So meanwhile Gregg's hauling ass out of bed. *'I'll kill you, I swear, I'll break your neck—'* he's screaming at this very nice doctor, who he manages to ram against the wall, and people in the room are going nuts and my father comes storming back in and picks Gregg up and *throws* him on the bed, and Gregg is jumping up and down and screaming, 'I don't care, I'll cut your throat!—' and my dad's screaming, "Shut up, boy! I'll take my belt to you—""

"Whoa."

"Yeah, and the poor doctor's saying, like, 'Everybody get a grip—' and my mother starts giving orders, as usual, 'Everybody out, just leave him alone—' She tells my brother, 'I'll be back in a couple of hours,' like she's going to the grocery store, and they drag me out and close the door and put me in the community room, where they have a TV that doesn't work and a pile of stupid games, and they leave me there. They did that all the time. Who knows where they went.

"Finally I kind of creep out in the hall and down to Gregg's room and he's in there, crying his eyes out. 'Get out of here,' he tells me. He'd been crying alone the whole time. I climbed onto the bed, he kicked at me, but I ignored him. I wanted to fall asleep and die together."

She sips the tea.

"CF is a genetic disease," she says. "You can pass it along to your kids."

"That's why you never had kids?"

She nods. "Isn't this what you came all the way out to California to hear?"

Allen smiles. His hands are loose in his lap, like they were that night in the hospital.

"Can you always give it to your kids?"

"You both have to be carriers of the gene. There's a blood test you can take."

"So you've had the test and everything?"

"No, I never had the test."

"You *never* had it?"

"Uh-uh."

"Why?"

She blows her nose. She's drowsy now.

"I just never wanted to. I already know."

"You just — know?"

She doesn't answer. He watches her.

"Cold?"

She nods. Even underneath the comforter the chills come and go.

Allen picks up the Bruins blanket.

"Can I tell you something?" He bends close and his eyes are mild. "We're all carriers."

He shakes it out, three, four times, then lays the blanket over her.

31

An FBI agent shows up on the doorstep wearing a gray suit and carrying an orange suitcase. The suitcase detaches into two sections, the top containing a telephone, wires, headset, pinch clips, batteries and tape cartridges packed in molded foam, the bottom a switchboard that will control all calls incoming or outgoing from Cassidy's home. The agent explains he is a hostage negotiator. When Monroe calls again he will coach Cassidy through it, writing her notes on what she should say.

"Never give anything without getting something in return" is the first rule.

Soon Cassidy is on a first-name basis with the officers working the round-the-clock shifts, asking about their kids, eager in her imprisonment to sniff the fresh air of life. It is always easy to talk baseball. The TV is constantly tuned to sports and the cottage is beginning to smell of cardboard pizza boxes and male cologne.

On the first of July the Dodgers score three unearned runs against Colorado and move into first place. Cassidy convinces the copper on duty to escort her to Baskin-Robbins for their own pathetic first-place ice cream party. But the very next day—although Offerman, Piazza, Mondesi, Nomo, and Worrell are named as All-Stars—the Dodgers lose to the Rockies and slip back to second.

She spends most of her time in the bedroom, playing computer games or surfing the Net, lifting, reading magazines. When she thinks of Joe he is sitting on a stool in a bare room, a room still and rich with daylight, like a quiet art gallery. She imagines him looking at her with the same calm, limpid intensity as the first time in the airport lounge.

Monroe's impulsive street-fueled rage is nowhere in the picture.

When Joe does call, the FBI negotiator is of course at a conference for hostage negotiators in Chicago, but a lieutenant from Laguna Beach is there, headset on the moment Cassidy says, "Joe! Thank God! Where are you?"

"Near the freeway—"

The reverberation of traffic is unbearable.

"*Where*, can you tell me *where*?"

"No, I can't, but Cassidy—"

A hundred decibels of live truck roar.

The lieutenant winces and slaps at switches.

"We'll do anything—"

"He's dead."

"Who is? *What?*"

"Monroe is dead!"

Joe is shouting. Maybe it's a gas station at a freeway off-ramp.

"You're free? You escaped? We'll get you—"

"No, you can't—"

The lieutenant scribbles on the pad, WHERE IS SUSPECT?

"Where is Monroe?"

Joe names a motel in Venice.

"He fell asleep. I jumped him. We struggled and the gun went off."

"We're coming to get you—"

"They know about the accident, don't they?"

Still shouting over the barrage.

"I'm sorry—"

"I understand. You did what you had to do. Look, I'm going—"

"Where? What are you talking about—"

"—speak to you."

The motel is a court of squat stucco boxes stained nicotine yellow recessed between a wholesale meat market and a used vinyl record store. An LAPD motorcycle cop and patrol car are already parked, uniforms posted at the doorway of shack-up shack number one, closest to the street. Drawn by the scent of violence, a dark-skinned guy in shirtsleeves (the manager?), three Latina teenagers, a homeless person and a white dude carrying a guitar case stand around mesmerized, whiffing the exhaust-laden air as traffic on Lincoln Boulevard slows down to gape.

Cassidy and Detective Allen roll up in his rented Acura.

"Don't get out of the car, don't touch anything, don't make a fuss."

Cassidy leans out the open window to watch as Allen shows his ID to the cop straddling the chopper whose pants are stretched tight over boulder quads. The cop won't let Allen in.

"That Florida badge doesn't mean jack up here."

Allen doesn't blow, but engages the studbolt in cop conversation until a dark green sedan pulls up and LAPD Detective Mark Simms gets out.

"It's okay, he's with me."

Both detectives proceed to the open door of number one. They speak to the uniform, then stop in the doorway and look inside. Allen goes down on one knee as if sizing up a putt; Simms remains standing. They stay that way, each of them drinking in the scene from a different angle.

Then Allen comes back to the car.

"The guy's lying on his back, looks like he bled out, probably shot twice in the upper body."

"Is it Monroe?"

"Just like his pictures, only dead."

He walks around to the driver's side.

The crowd of gawkers has grown; this is turning into a situation. A bus goes by leaving a hollow vibration in the air. Somewhere a load of pipes spills with an ear-shattering crash.

Allen closes the windows and turns on the AC.

"Gum?"

She takes it.

"It didn't happen the way Joe said. Any close-up struggle over a gun the way he described it would result in stippling—powder burns—on the body, which would be obvious to the naked eye. There was no stippling. At first I couldn't see the cartridges. Sometimes the EMT guys screw up a scene, but there were no EMT guys and that rookie swears nobody went inside. I spotted the two rounds near the baseboard, so I'm assuming they didn't get booted over there, that's the way they were ejected from the gun. A Beretta will do that, kick them out to the right and backwards."

He fires the ignition.

"The lack of stippling on the body and around the wound is a dead giveaway that the weapon was not fired from close up. And the cartridge placement will have a lot to do with this. There wasn't any struggle for the gun. I can tell you this: It didn't happen the way Joe said."

He puts the gearshift into drive.

"Monroe was shot from a distance, most likely just inside the doorway."

"Why would Monroe open the door?"

"He knew the shooter," Allen replies. "Ask me something hard."

32

"Why do I still have to be here?"

Cassidy paces the kitchen, arms crossed petulantly. Two days have passed since the discovery of Monroe's body. The coroner's protocol has confirmed Detective Allen's hypothesis. Monroe opened the door to someone he trusted, and that person blew him away.

"For your own protection."

"Monroe is dead!"

"Monroe had an associate. Who is still at large. And then there's Joe."

"Why do you cling to the ridiculous notion that Joe staged his own kidnapping?"

"There's a link. Monroe gets shot and Joe ankles it."

"Well, you're wrong." Her arms fly up in exasperation. "Didn't you hear his voice? He was terrified!"

Allen's eyelids look droopy. He definitely needs a shave.

"There was no sign of forced entry at the beach house. Nothing out of the ordinary—"

"The photo!" she counters. "The phone on the floor! The receipt in the Buy Rite bag which you said was from two days before—"

"He's still out there on vehicular manslaughter," Allen interrupts. "Leaving the scene, he knows that. The biggest indication he's not acting in good faith is the fact that after this traumatic kidnapping experience, he split. As a general rule, most victims are happy to come home. Do you have something like a Coke?"

Cassidy, surprised, "Sure."

He's never taken her food nor asked for anything before, as if it were important to declare a line between his investigation and the contents of her home.

"So when do I get out of here?"

He cracks the can.

"When we know the whereabouts of Joe Galinis."

"Nate, you have to help me."

"Just hang with it. A few more days."

"It's been *two weeks*. You don't get it. I'm on suspension from my job and every day I'm not on the road, somebody else, probably Travis, is *taking my stuff*. When I get back, you'll see, half my prospects will suddenly appear on *his list*—"

"I'm sorry. It's a consequence of events." To deflect it, "How's Alberto?"

"Fine. They removed an abscess from his liver and he's great, he's going back to Double A. Still the best bat in the Texas League. This is over for me, Nate. I cooperated, I did everything to help you, why can't you help me?"

"Because it's not my decision, Cassidy." He tosses the empty and checks his pager. "This was a determination made by three cooperating law enforcement agencies—"

"Well, I won't! I won't be stuck in here another minute!"

She plucks a saucer from the dish rack and frisbees it so it shatters against the wall.

Allen remains perfectly still. His thin lips tighten. Release.

He raises one finger very slowly. "You get a time-out."

"You've had a hard-on for Joe since the beginning," Cassidy persists, following him to the door. "You don't like him because he's a rich guy who treats police officers like dirt. I know. I dated a cop. Almost married him, do you believe that? He was totally into power. You don't become a cop if you don't need power. So this is your little bit of power. Keeping me here."

"There will be officers outside the house, twenty-four hours a day."

"Bringing me tea. All that stuff. You got everything you wanted out of me to solve your case, didn't you?"

Detective Allen pauses on the doorstep.

"I'm being pulled back to Vero Beach, so, don't worry, I'm out of your hair."

He regards her for a moment in a peculiar way; a look she isn't used to.

Then he says, "Have a nice life."

He leaves. She grabs the remote and flicks on the TV.

The look was pity.

Imprisoned, Cassidy becomes a total sleaze.

She starts going to sleep at two in the morning and wakes up at noon. Her first beer will be around four and after that she keeps a nice buzz going the rest of the night. She makes a big pot of spaghetti sauce and has it for lunch and dinner three days in a row. She has visitors. A couple of scouts. Folks from the bar. A neighbor who wants to know why all the police. After a while she stops taking showers and checking e-mail, even reports from the team. She's long ago given up in disgust her warm relationships with the cops on duty.

It must be around seven in the evening because she's watching the end of the national news when the phone rings. She picks up carelessly. It is Alberto, calling from the Biltmore Hotel in downtown Los Angeles, where the organization put him up during his recovery.

Even through a depressive haze, Cassidy is thrilled to hear his voice.

"How are you?"

"Feeling good. Everything good."

"No more stomach pains?"

"After the operation, I feeling great."

"When do you go back to Texas?"

"I see the doctor one more time, then I go. Day after tomorrow."

"I'm so glad, Alberto. You never answered my messages. I thought you'd never speak to me again."

"I was very mad with you."

"I know you were."

"I think, you're with that guy, what am I gonna do? I know I never hurt nobody."

"I'm sorry. I tried to say I'm sorry. I wasn't seeing with my eyes. But I never gave you up, Alberto. I wouldn't do that until I was sure. Then I was sure. It wasn't you."

"Well, now he gonna pay."

"Joe?"

"Yeah. He gonna meet me at the stadium. We gonna straighten some things out."

"At *Dodger* Stadium?"

"No, the new one they building."

"Joe's *back*? He's *here*?"

"He's in LA but he is hiding out. He say he's gonna turn himself in, but he want to make it up to both of us first."

"You and me?"

"He feeling really bad. He sorry and he want to talk. I am supposed to call you up and tell you to come."

"Where are you now?"

"In the lobby of the hotel. I gotta go—"

"What else did Joe say?"

"Don't tell the police."

"He said that?"

"No, his daughter."

"Nora said, don't tell the police?"

"Yeah, because I not actually talk to him. His daughter, she call me up and tell me all these things. Okay, they say my taxi coming. See you there."

"Alberto, wait—"

He's gone.

Cassidy is shaking as if her body has gone into some sort of shock, trying to instantly purge itself after days of abuse. She drinks a bunch of water. Goes upstairs and picks the cassette out of the tape recorder and pulls out all the tape and comes downstairs and looks around and throws the whole tangled mess into the microwave and gives it fifteen seconds.

That should fry the cops.

She peers through the front window. The cruiser is parked out on Glenneyre. She's going to assume the officer on assignment is sitting in it, reading USA Today. She grabs her car keys and backpack and closes the kitchen door very quietly and steals across the backyard to the garage at the rear of the property. The outside world seems vivid and crowded with sensation. It is cool. From inside the house next door, she can hear someone rattle a drawer and take out a handful of silverware.

The garage door is maddeningly slow. She backs the Explorer out, whips it around and down the alley, glazed with sunset light.

Freedom.

She drives aggressively through the evening grace. The extreme left lane, the diamond lane, is for carpools of at least two passengers, a seventy-miles-per-hour pneumatic tube when the rest of the freeway is at a standstill, and you can get a major ticket if you're driving it alone. But seventy isn't fast enough. Up against someone's rear with no place to go, Cassidy veers suddenly to the right, passes at eighty-five, hops back over to the diamonds.

She punches the CD player. Instantly the wicked mocking guitar licks of Steely Dan fill the interior. *Get along, Kid Charlemagne.* A San Francisco drug wizard on the lam. Martyr to subversive arts. *Did you feel like Jesus?*

Nothing could be further from vinegary pungent Caribbean romance, which is perhaps Joe's intention—to zap her from unknowable dark entanglements to the known. To the 405 and the oil refinery with its swollen tanks and silver smokestacks and great plumes of white steam, day and night a colossus as undeniable as the sports and entertainment center being erected out of the pit like a new Corinth—to jerk Cassidy awake to the naiveté of being stuck in a third world moment that is past and of no interest to anyone when this, *this* is coming at her head on.

Two, three cuts go by. "Haitian Divorce." "Everything You Did."

Finally she accelerates toward a downtown exit, leaving the comforting lights of the city's landmark establishments—the New Otani, MOCA, the Bradbury Building, the spiffy Central Library, the Music Center—and follows the route she had taken with Joe behind the Convention Center into a massive ten-acre construction zone, bumping over potholes, lost in a maze of yellow and orange barricades and flashing cautionary lights, half-demolished buildings, empty lots with curls of razor wire, night air dank with the sewery stench of open pipes.

The "not a neighborhood without character" they had driven through in the Bentley has been meticulously dismantled block by block, barbershops and fleabag hotels gone, the defiant graffiti superhero deconstructed to a crumble of brick. With the streets ripped open there aren't even any homeless, only the gloss of the hindquarters of a rat humping it along a broken curb.

Cassidy plows through a running stream of mud past a scrap-metal yard dominated by a crane. Down Eleventh Street a new order starts to dominate the jumble of demolition: a mural painted by children; thirty trailers crammed together in a provisional city. Temporary parking lots bend around the last property-owner holdouts—disintegrating cottages that have suddenly become gold mines.

She parks in a red zone. The engine goes off and the headlights die. She climbs out of the car. The industrial street is deserted. From the near distance comes the thud of heavy pounding like a pile driver. A helicopter passes overhead.

The five-story ovoid structure, almost complete, rises out of the murk like a space station with its guts exposed—a matrix of ductwork and scaffolding twinkling with interior lights. A guard at the gate waves Cassidy through when she says she's going to the Omega office in one of the on-site trailers. She chugs up the metal steps and yanks the flimsy door. Inside, cold fluorescent lights create a bright manic imitation of day. It is not morning. Supervisors are not hustling through in hard hats. No scent of coffee nor the hot grease of breakfast burritos off a catering truck. Only artificial spaces and dead refrigerated air.

Nora, switching her hips back and forth in a receptionist's chair, says melodramatically, "We meet again."

Alberto looks up from bending over a watercooler. He is wearing a blue nylon track suit that says MISSIONS, the minor league Texas team. Cassidy wants to hug him, feel the strength and comfort in those young satiny arms.

"Are you okay?" she asks.

"Sure. I fine." He gulps water and crushes the cup, leaning back against the trailer wall. Keeping his distance.

"Nice rags," says Cassidy.

He tries to set his face in neutral but he's blushing. "Thanks."

"He doesn't want to be here," Nora observes, still half-rotating the chair; she can't sit still. "He wants to be dancing merengue, right?"

A bushy ponytail is sticking out from under Nora's red baseball cap. Her large dark eyes look like graphic images that have been warped by computer.

"Where is Joe?"

His daughter nods toward the arena. "Inside. He can't be seen by anyone."

"How is he?"

"For a brilliant man, I have to say he has not been thinking clearly."

"I mean, how did Monroe—"

"Oh, they beat the shit out of him."

"Jesus."

"He's basically okay. You'll see. Let's go."

She lifts a set of keys off a row of hooks on the wall.

"What does he want to tell us?"

Alberto answers, "He going to make it okay." Of Nora, "That what she say."

"It was an accident. The best thing for my dad to do is admit it and go on."

She is skipping sideways toward the door and gesturing with her hands with a self-conscious smile, as if the spotlight had just gone on and she forgot her routine.

"I finally convinced him to be smart. He's sorry for all the damage he's caused. He wants to make peace with you guys."

"He owe me a *lot*." Alberto raps his chest.

"He knows. He'll take care of it," she promises, throwing the door open so hard it hits the exterior wall. "Oops."

Cassidy: "How will he take care of it?"

"Let's let him explain."

They follow Nora outside and down the steps, over planks of wood that cover a trickle of raw black oil, then stop at twelve-foot chain link where she uses the key, and continue toward the looming structure, leaving the glistening city and its promise on the other side of the gate.

They walk along in awkward silence. Cassidy aches to touch the boy.

"How's it going, Alberto?"

He seems grateful to find some common ground.

"I playing well, beside this."

"Someone took the spirit off?"

"Oh no," he grins, "I get a *new* spirit."

"Really? What's her name?"

They pass through the gates to the lobby area beneath the thrusting lip of the roof. The superstructure has become more densely complicated since Cassidy was here with Joe—more escalators, Sheetrock, insulation, orange lifts. The girts are in place and some of the metal panels that form the building's skin, kissed by dabs of light from strings of high white carnival bulbs.

"The concrete work in here is beautiful," Nora's saying in a rush. "Sculptural. Almost like clay." All Cassidy can see are dank ramps and unconnected arcing walls. "Straight ahead of you. Keep going."

They pass through an open doorway and find themselves walking across the dim expanse of the event floor.

"This is awesome," grins Alberto, charging in for an imaginary layup shot.

"Welcome to the center of the universe!" Nora shouts grandly, her voice absorbed by the huge space. She laughs. "Say anything! Nobody can hear!"

You can look up and see the wood paneling set into the executive suites. A level of molded plastic seats are in. Exit signs and section numbers. Where cranes and scaffold towers cluttered the arena, now there is a smooth dirt surface waiting for the ice-making equipment, and the basketball floor that will go over it. The roof isn't in but the completed supertruss flies across the dark upper reaches, the scoreboard suspended from cables halfway down from the center like a huge black spider.

Cassidy bends her neck to look up; against the blackness of the night sky she can make out the octagonal framework where Joe had told her the scoreboard would go.

"State of the art," Nora says. "They move it up and down while they're working on it, is that cool? Right now they're putting on the video boards."

The thing is fifty feet across, still lit. You can see corporate logos and scrambled numbers where the digital displays have frozen. You think about the history that will be recorded there. How lives will change because of those numbers.

"So where's Joe?"

"Where do you think?" Nora teases.

"I don't know. He's always late."

Nora laughs. "That is really funny."

"Look," says Cassidy, provoked enough, to the very edge, "what is going on?"

Nora mocks her, "*What is going on?*"

Something unpleasant turns in Cassidy's gut.

"You're using," she says evenly. "Does your father know?"

"Please don't tell him!" Nora whines with scorn. "He'll be so upset!"

Cassidy takes Alberto's sleeve. "We're out of here."

Her boots sink into the newly turned earth. Her ankle twists. Even in the semidark the shape of what will be is undeniable, as certain as the knowledge, in the dark steamy heat of the sugar mill, that it had been a place of violence where people had died. In this pit also there have been deaths, ancient deaths, layered in the buried ruins of the pueblo, indiscernible as fragments of Indian pottery. That is not what Cassidy smells. The stink is excremental, raw. The wet-dug clay of a young grave.

Alberto doesn't want to go. "We got to get this straight—"

"We will. Not now—"

From behind them Nora says quietly, "Screw you!"

They whip around to see the girl bring up her arm and aim the Beretta.

Alberto flinches, big. Cassidy clamps a tight fist on his arm.

"You don't need that," she says. "What's the big deal?"

Nora holds the weapon steady in both hands.

"No big deal."

"Slow it down, Nora—"

Nora is a shape against the ambient light.

"Turn around and walk to the east wall. I'm right behind you."

Cassidy can feel Alberto's breath as if it were her own, quickening in the damp air.

"Go!"

They walk across the arena single file, Alberto first and Nora last. Some huge tread has left zigzag ruts deep enough to trip over and Cassidy stumbles as if she had no coordination in her limbs. *Trust your body,* someone is saying, but her body is absent.

She could duck, roll into the darkness and run. Or execute an elbow jab and knock the gun away. Either one would be a wild, sloppy move and expose Alberto. Nora has the advantage.

"Be cool," she whispers to his back. "Do what she says." Then, "Hey, kid. Friends don't pull guns on friends."

No answer.

"We're doing what you want!" cries Cassidy in exasperation.

Sneering, "*Good girl,*" Nora yanks Cassidy's braid so viciously her teeth go *snap!* and tears sting her eyes.

"If you love your father, don't let him do this."

"My father doesn't have a clue and never has."

"Where is he?"

"Safe."

Cassidy shouts, "*Joe?*"

Her voice evaporates in the cavernous pit. In another minute Joe will come trotting down those concrete steps and the things that passed between them—the gentle pulse of life, their fingers entwined in love-making, breathing into each other's breath—will be meaningless. Joe has set her up, using Alberto as the bait, so he can eliminate them both; a master at manipulating pieces to the end.

Alberto: "What you want? We give it to you, no problem."

"God, are you stupid."

Cassidy pretends her heel gets caught again, stumbling, trying to hide the reach into the backpack, but Nora sees it, screaming, *"Drop it!"* and she does, hard, so everything spills out into the dirt. Pens. Schedules. Swiss Army knife. Tissues. Brush. Wallet. Advil. Dayrunner. Key ring holding the tracking device—the case splits open the moment it hits the ground, battery and circuit board popping out.

"This damn thing. Car alarm," grunts Cassidy, squatting down. "Always breaks."

Nora kicks it out of reach.

"I don't think you want my car going off on the street."

Nora kicks it back.

"Pick up that shit."

Cassidy had seen Detective Allen do it only once, but the kinetic memory has gone into her fingers as surely as if they'd practiced a piano sonata a thousand times. Clean the battery. Reattach the wires. Reposition the circuit board. Program the LED display with the correct sequence of commands. Click the case shut. Toggle switch back on.

Nora sweeps the Beretta across the arena, the entertainment zone, the city.

"This is what you wanted my father to give up."

Cassidy watches the gun, remembering what Detective Allen said, that it kicks shells out to the right.

"You shot Monroe. Why?"

"Oh, well, fuck *him*. He's a little pissant, *way* out of line."

"What was the deal? They give you coke, you give them your dad?"

"Not my dad!" growls Nora, and Cassidy inhales sharply, takes a step back. "I told Luis at the beginning, Okay, run your money through the Gran Caribe, I'll do this little thing for you, but *it doesn't come back to my*

dad. Nobody messes with him. Then the arrogant pricks decide to blackmail him anyway."

Nora's eyes are dark, equine, the pupils huge.

"But when they *kidnap* him, and beat him up"—her voice is shaking—"I say, Forget it, assholes. Game over."

"Nothing's over. We can work this out—"

"This is the problem." She sniffs, a crooked smile. "You had your chance to work it out. We went to your house and *begged*, but you wouldn't change your Goody Two-shoes story. You could have helped my father and me. Keep walking. That way."

They reach the opposite side. A banister-less staircase takes them up to the third level.

The concourse is lit by strings of cage lights and littered with piles of steel rods. Sandbags. Small concrete mixers. Wheelbarrows and coils of wire. Nora makes them walk a quarter way around. "Down there."

"That curtain?" asks Cassidy with trepidation as they descend through a cove that leads past the seats to a black sheath of plastic like the one Joe had proudly drawn to reveal the mammoth work in progress. They had stood at the unguarded rim, looking down a couple hundred empty feet.

Nora says, "Pull it back."

Alberto rips the plastic to one side. Where there had been drop-dead open space, now there are temporary wooden barricades along the edge. Where there had been a skeleton, now they look into the almost-realized entertainment palace.

"The big picture."

"Shut up."

Cassidy stares at the empty seating, the complex crossbeams above; it is easy to imagine a silent invisible crowd filling the arena, like ghosts at the playing field in that Mayan city, come to witness a blood sport of arcane origin and mystic rules; to worship what lay at the inner core of their pyramid: a golden lion whose jaws were set in a rictus snarl of revenge.

"Three steps back. To the edge."

They do it, buying time.

"This is crazy, Nora. The police already know. They're on their way."

"I don't care. When they get here there won't be any witnesses who are alive. That should fuck their case against my dad."

Cassidy can feel the airiness behind them. She steals a look below, to an open trench at least forty feet wide. You couldn't miss it.

She recalls that parachute jump and knows exactly what it will feel like to free-fall three quick stories, and how long it will take.

"They'll arrest your dad. They'll know he set us up—"

"My dad is far away. Like I said, he doesn't have a clue about my life."

"You mean he *isn't* here?"

"She trick us," Alberto says.

Crazily, Cassidy almost cries out with joy.

A helicopter passes overhead. You can see the letters through the unfinished roof: LAPD.

"Oh, he's all remorseful, '*I can't live with what I did to that poor woman!*' and blah blah blah. He doesn't understand. It's naive to tell the truth in this world. One thing he did do. He taught me to drive a bulldozer."

She starts to back away. She is still holding the gun steadily.

"What the public doesn't know, there are accidents on construction sites all the time. Mostly they get covered up."

Alberto dives for the Beretta. It goes off at close range, the force of the discharge like a needleful of epinephrine to the heart. He twists away, Nora sprawls, gets to her knees, and comes up firing.

Cassidy finds herself on top of Alberto who is inert in the dust, cap gone, hair filled with white granules. She's trying to rouse him but her voice is just a vibration in her throat. They'd grabbed each other and rolled across the aisle like spinning river logs, protecting each other with their backs.

He gets up slowly then drops like a rock as, incredibly, another bullet explodes nearby.

She is trying to say, "*Are you hurt?*" because his face is streaked with blood. He is mouthing something in reply and struggling to his feet and there are two more helicopters which she can only see, not hear, because her hearing doesn't work.

Then she is gone, after Nora, exhaling on the effort of vaulting over a wheelbarrow. *Put it in your quads,* someone says, and she angles around the corner where she thought she saw a bobbing red hat. She runs, ducking around hoses, piles of bolts, acetylene tanks, Dumpsters and waste cans, scattering shells of sunflower seeds workers dropped on the floor, one hundred percent effort, legs laced with pain as lactic acid seizes up her calves.

Outside the open unwalled concourse, horizontal views of night-lit downtown Los Angeles speed by like film strips zipped through a projector. Cassidy keeps her eyes toward the center of the arena to avoid the feeling of being sucked right out.

She rounds a curve and there is Nora just ahead, raggedly jogging directly toward a wooden barricade set in the middle of the concourse floor.

Cassidy screams her name.

A helicopter circles the rim, spotlight searching until it finds the two of them and stabilizes.

Nora turns and faces Cassidy. Her face is dirty, tear-stained.

"I have to help my dad, because if I don't, who will?"

She gasps for breath. The gun hangs from two fingers at her side.

"Don't lean on that!" cries Cassidy, as Nora rests against the barricade.

She reaches toward her rival with a compassion that she cannot speak because the violent whipping of the blades is obliterating every tender thing; even the vacant hollow where a father's love should be. Lost, as well, in the turbulence, is the sound of the collapse of the wooden railing, so that it seems to break apart in silence.

Nora totters and slips helplessly into the open shaft.

SEPTEMBER

33

At the end of every rainbow there is an agent.

It is such an ugly fact of life that Cassidy tries to forget about it so as not to spoil the ride, but the forgetting makes it worse because inevitably, when she gets to the end of the rainbow, there *will* be a guy talking on a cellular phone, and whatever joy she was feeling, whatever wonder, will quickly turn to outrage and she will want to kick herself around the block for continuing to believe that it is possible, as a grown-up in late twentieth-century America, to live in hope.

Hope—lustful and hotheaded—is the only reason any human being would drive out to Perris in the first place, but now that hope will pay off. She has made that god-awful drive for the very last time, here to make the sign on Brad Parker and present his mother with a basket of lemon bars and miniature chocolate chip muffins. In failure, such an overtly feminine ploy would be the source of endless ragging in the scouting department. In success, however, it will be undeniable proof of female cunning and superiority. Now it is clear the mini-muffins are about to go the way of flannel knickers.

Agents.

At first glance the kitchen looks the same. Spotless counters. Refrigerator door covered with zoo animal magnets. Lingering scent of microwaved pasta in an exciting tomato sauce. A built-in wide-screen TV playing as always in an adjoining family room. The two-hundred-gallon fish tank, big as a sofa, empty. And seated at the familiar round table where they have shared nachos and carrot sticks and Brad Parker's career scrapbook in three volumes, are the young pitcher himself, Pepper and Lang, all staring at Cassidy with hands folded on the bleached oak like penitent third graders.

A can of diet soda is waiting.

Cassidy sits at her place with a smile.

"So, Brad, how're you feeling? How's the arm?"

Before he can answer the father interjects, "Warren's here. You should meet Warren."

"Great. Who's Warren?"

"Warren's in the backyard, honey," Pepper warns, as if Warren were a large and dangerous dog.

And he may well be because nobody is making a move to actually *get* Warren, in fact they are huddled together to block Cassidy's view. She has to lean way over to snake a look through the sliding glass to the yard, barren and fried in the desert heat. A pleated shade is lowered halfway down. All she can see below it are two pacing legs. Bare stocky masculine legs in shorts, no socks, gold metallic loafers. And swinging just below the knees, unmistakably, a Louis Vuitton briefcase.

Cassidy brings a clear-eyed blue stare back to the table.

"Who is Warren?" she repeats evenly.

"A friend of the family."

Cassidy: "He's an agent."

Embarrassed silence.

"Guys, I know I've been away, but I thought we were working this out together."

"We are, dear," the mom says anxiously, not the type who would ever want to upset another woman. To her face.

"You realize if Brad employs an agent we can't give him a college scholarship as a signing bonus. That's league rules."

"Warren is only an advisor," Pepper insists.

"Kind of a coach," adds Brad, obviously rehearsed.

Lang is wearing a sports shirt with leaping swordfish.

"What if I said our friend out there is a neighbor?" he suggests. "A neighbor who has an opinion? Heck, everybody on the block's got an idea of what we should do."

"And what does your 'friend' say?"

"In today's world? A hundred fifty thousand dollars."

Despite the bravado, Lang Parker cannot help sneaking an uneasy look at his wife.

Cassidy says, "We've been over the numbers. You know that's not reality for a fifth rounder. With or without an agent. We agreed on fifty-five."

"I dunno," muses the dad, trying for sly. "A kid this talented?"

He puts a thick arm around his son who slides down the chair trying to hide beneath a Lakers cap, lanky legs with no place to go.

"What is that, a new look?" Cassidy asks of a tiny blond thatch under the boy's chin.

"Yeah," he mumbles, blushing.

Cassidy throws him an affectionate glance, remembering their many talks on many soggy fields when he so earnestly expressed the desire to become a professional ballplayer. Now he can't even meet her eyes. On the mound Brad Parker is a tiger, but put him in a room with his parents and he turns into a pile of strained bananas. Well, who doesn't.

Still, she will fight before she'll lose him to some wannabe who saw the kid listed in *Baseball America* and took the first flight out of Orlando, smelling vulnerability like stale milk.

"I want to be honest with you," Cassidy says at last, resting strong tan forearms on the table. "I like Brad. I liked him two years ago and I like him today—"

"We like you, too," interrupts Lang Parker. "And we're sold on the Dodger organization. Brad wants to play ball. College can wait."

"Then let's do it."

Cassidy reaches for the $55,000 contract inside the backpack at the same time Lang goes for the handle on the sliding glass door.

"Warren's just going to sit in."

Instead of the contract, Cassidy pulls out a business card and writes down Travis Conners' name and phone extension.

"Why don't you have Warren call my supervisor?"

Groans of dismay and Pepper fluttering her hands.

"Please," she cries, "we didn't want to hurt your feelings."

"It's not about my feelings," says Cassidy pleasantly. "It's about getting the best deal for Brad. I understand."

"You can talk to Warren," the dad says, fingering the card nervously, "just as good as the front office. We have no problem with that."

"I have a problem. Because all of a sudden you're not talking to *me*."

As Cassidy stands and slips on sunglasses her eye is caught by the huge empty tank. It has been there as long as she's been coming out here— eight feet of glass still wrapped in cardboard, books on raising tropical fish piled up in the bottom. Maybe that is the clue she has missed about this family: oversized ambitions. Unfulfillable dreams. Passing them on to the boy.

"Don't go," says Brad, uncertain.

"Tell your agent to take a hike."

Silence. The guy's not going anywhere. Not even out of the backyard.

"I could easily talk to Warren," Cassidy explains gently, "but it's not the same as talking to you. I care about you. I spent two years watching you develop. You and your family mean something to me. What I love is finding a kid and having my own communication and making the sign. That's being a scout. Guys like him"—she indicates the pacing legs—"take all the fun out of it."

She shakes Brad's hand and wishes him luck and tells him that he's one terrific kid.

Then she is back on the freeway, heading west.

She gets as far as Corona before she has to pull over and cry. These crying jags have happened a lot in the weeks since Nora's death and Joe's disappearance, often several times a day. Anything can trigger them—music, a memory. The crying is helpless, deep and convulsive. She has lost interest in food and wakes up in the morning with an empty stomach and dry heaves. Yet she goes about her business, looking bright to the world. Maybe it is baseball, she has thought. Wasn't it a commissioner of the sport himself who said, "Baseball always breaks your heart"?

Or maybe it is thinking about the haphazard way it all unfolded that makes her feel sick: Monroe seeing her with the owner of the Gran Caribe at the stadium, his predator instincts aroused. Following the three of them in the Range Rover. Witnessing the accident, hiding out in the folds of the storm. Reporting to his uncle, who must have been pleased. *Transport the body. Stage the videotape. And get your ass on a plane for LA.*

Cassidy discovers she has stopped the Explorer in the parking lot of a children's furniture store near the freeway. She rolls the windows all the way down to take in the motionless fat desert air, and unfolds the letter she received from Joe several days before, postmarked Santo Domingo and worked as smooth from rereading as those original ransom notes.

Dear Cassidy,

Yesterday I went like a thief in the night to St. Sophia's to pray.

Cassidy, you have to go there. It is beautiful. The inside is inlaid with 24 carat gold. Ornate beyond your wildest imagination. You would get a kick out of the chandeliers. And a huge Jesus looking down at you from a dome . . . I can't begin to describe it.

For me there is such emotion in those vaulted archways, so many family occasions. Last night I sat there alone and saw my father as he was years ago, strutting ahead of my mother like always. It was Holy Thursday, very solemn, but you knew what he had on his mind. He wanted to look good. Be seen. Be proud. He's short in stature but cocky, king of the world when he wears his blue blazer, when he's being *Greek*, with that dignified white mustache and balding head held high. Every day of Holy Week, we had to go. I had to have perfect behavior because all the big shots were there, the doctors and bankers and every Greek actor in Hollywood.

I remember one Holy Week it rained like hell and everybody put their umbrellas outside, hundreds of wet umbrellas, different shapes and sizes and colors, leaning against the church door. All I could think about during the endless chanting and the incense and the standing up and sitting down was that our umbrella would get stolen.

Forgive this rambling. I'm on a plane but it's night and I can't see anything out the window. There is so much I want to say but this is coming out like a dog howling at the moon. When this is over I *will* be back, and *will* say those things, *and* live them, and make you believe how much I love you. I'm lonely in my soul. I want you with me now. I miss your wryness and your laughter. We should be sitting here together, on our way to someplace wonderful, drinking champagne.

Cassidy, I know you think I'm a coward. I'm a coward because I ran away from the accident. I'm a coward because I did not appear at my daughter's funeral. I'm a coward because I'm not with you now, begging your forgiveness. Everything I did, I did for a reason. The reason was you. Please let me explain.

Alberto and I traded driving all night, depending on who was least drunk or who wanted to show off. When we hit her, it was me. I saw her for a split second in the headlights, walking by the side of the road carrying a bag of *oranges*! By the time I knew they were oranges, it was too late. I got out. I made Alberto stay in the car. You were out of it, thank God. I took the flashlight and walked all the way back to where she was. Her skull was fractured open. She wasn't breathing. Cassidy, I saw her brain. What would you do? We were in the middle of nowhere in the middle of a hurricane. She was dead. I had to make a decision. The decision I made was to take appropriate action to protect everyone in the car.

Yes, it was selfish, too. I had a life and a history and a community, a family, business partners, lawyers, the biggest project in the history of Los Angeles . . . But nothing would have given that young woman her life back. Nothing good would have come of going to the Dominican police. Nothing good, for any of us.

The last six months have been a form of mental torture. The dead corpse stayed in my head. Bad dreams and sleeping pills and walking around in a daze just trying to keep it together. Then the nightmare really began, when the blackmail notes started coming. Nora never knew, but for a while I had a bodyguard watch her and the baby. What can I tell you? I was afraid. I thought I could fix it with money.

I wanted this to go away and leave us alone. I fell in love with you. My love is ruthless, it always has been. I wanted you and screw everything and everyone else. I've had the image of you and me walking a tightrope. The problem is, we're walking toward each other. Then what? Somebody falls.

Forgive me. Forgive me. Forgive me. Forgive me. Forgive me. Forgive me. Forgive me. Forgive me.

Nora. Nora. Nora. Nora. Nora. Nora.

I sat in St. Sophia's and I thought I would explode—with what, I can't even name. When you lose a child your world ends. I couldn't be there to bury her because they would have arrested me, and there is something more I have to do, so I will eat this suffering. And eat it. Swallow it down. I had no idea what she was pulling in the Gran Caribe. How could we have seen each other every day and I never knew? She shows up at the motel and assassinates Monroe and *then* she tells me. I wasn't all that surprised. It wasn't all that different from the kind of outrageous, self-destructive crap she used to get into. But when she said that she'd been dealing with this total piece of shit, the General, I thought, Jesus, she really hates me.

I'm in the fires of hell, Cassidy. I don't know how to pray. I sit on the board and give money, but last night I prayed with all my being, Let the fire bring purity, please let my suffering be acceptable to God, may He use my suffering to free Nora's soul like a dove.

I tried to cover up the accident, for you. For us. The reason I'm going down there now is for you. I tried to confess all this to Harvey, my best friend Harvey, and what does he say? "Don't tell me! I don't want to know!" So I'm hoping you will listen and forgive me. When I land in Santo Domingo I am going to turn myself over to the American Embassy. I'm going to tell them I caused the death of a Dominican citizen and take full responsibility. Then I'm going to give them the disks I copied off Nora's computer that document the General's criminal activities running drug money through the Gran Caribe. I'm going to testify against the bastard who made my daughter turn away from me, made her lie to me. I'm going mano a mano with the son of a bitch in open court. This is what I learned from my father. He suffered in order to provide for us. He was treated, basically, like the slime in the pipes that he fixed. But he taught me, Dare to be proud. Approach life with confidence and you will get what you want. Never compromise. Never walk away. Fight the bullies. Break their balls.

I've just been thinking of us on Santorini. They have such beautiful sunsets there. I saw you in a taverna on the water—your hair, your smile—and for a minute I had peace.

In that magnificent church I questioned, and God answered. Now I know that He has given me the power to bring one man to justice. I pray that this will save my soul.

> I love you.
> Forgive me.
> Joe

34

Who can say which God is in charge of these things?

Is it Ti-Jean Dantò, the Haitian trickster spirit?

Or Kalfou, vodou divinity of the crossroads?

Long ago at the beginning of eternity, somebody decided which way the earth would turn, which would determine, for the rest of time, the way a left-handed pitcher's curveball breaks on a right-handed batter.

Several days later, on the drive to the stadium, Cassidy finds herself meditating on these events: how it was ordained that Dodger left-hander Mark Guthrie would come up against the Padres' Tony Gwynn; that Guthrie would throw a curve which seemed to drop uncannily to meet the bat; that Gywnn would rip a long hard drive to deep left center where Curtis and Hollandsworth, charging for it in the outfield, would crash.

Resulting in torn ligaments and a fractured right thumb.

Which, several weeks later, would cause the phone to ring in San Antonio Municipal Stadium, informing the general manager of the Missions that Alberto Cruz was being recalled to Los Angeles.

The earth moves to the right, Pedro says, quoting Julio Bibison. *When a lefty throws, it is against the rotation of the world.*

That must be it. That must be why, maintaining a one-game margin in first place and hurtling toward the end of the season, the Dodgers called Alberto Cruz up to the forty-man roster.

It could be his speed.

Or his bat.

Or Kalfou, the Legba of Petwo, lifting her dress to show lace panties, reminding us of the mystery between visible and invisible worlds.

1:10 p.m.

Guys are dribbling into the players' lounge to get ready to work out for tonight's game against San Francisco. Cassidy is there to catch Alberto before his first major league appearance. It is early enough so the door to the locker room is still open. Doc Ramsey comes through, pulling a laundry basket on wheels.

"Throw-it-in-the-basket-and-we-will-launder-it-and-put-it-back-in-your-locker!" He swoops a T-shirt off the floor. "What've they got, soup for brains?"

There are bubbling punch and lemonade machines, deep aluminum trays filled with cold cuts and salads, a pot of chili going and one of seafood stew, and on an upper shelf above the spread, twenty round jars in a row stuffed with every beloved brand-name cookie and candy you can remember from childhood, all in the service of big leaguers' little-boy gimmes.

As Cassidy is stretching for the Oreos, teasing them off the shelf, a big arm reaches over her head and a giant hand palms the jar, taking it down and handing it to her.

"Looks like you need rescuing," Travis says.

"You got my message about Brad Parker?"

"What's up?"

"I didn't sign him."

"You promised Raymond signability was excellent."

"It was. Until they went with an agent."

"Who's the agent?"

"Warren something. I don't know. Didn't ask."

"You didn't even *ask?*"

"I was no longer being effective. I told the family to call you."

Travis flicks an Oreo into his mouth. Whole. Not pleased.

"The family got seduced," Cassidy goes on. "Now they want a hundred fifty thousand dollars."

"Horseshit."

"That's what I say."

She can see Travis pull up the Brad Parker file in his mind. It is a talent they share: to see hundreds of kids in a season and be able to recall the entire scouting report on each one with the speed of a Pentium chip.

"Parker's got a real good arm and a real good idea how to pitch," Travis says. "But no way will Raymond overpay."

"Doesn't need to."

"That's right."

"I feel bad for the kid," she says.

"I feel bad for you."

Travis gives a soulful look and immediately Cassidy becomes suspicious.

"Why me?"

"You spend two years romancing this kid, then he leaves the dance."

"The dad was romancing *us*, coming along with this line of horseshit."

"I just don't get why this keeps happening. Losing a guy on the sign."

Travis shrugs and freezes in an attitude of wonder, eyes popped, fingers splayed.

Cassidy says, "I haven't lost the one that counts," as Alberto Cruz, wearing blue warm-ups, equipment bag slung over a shoulder, enters the lounge, his long lolling stride having taken on a newly confident hip-hop attitude.

Travis eyes him darkly.

"They sure forgave a lot with that kid."

"They'll forgive a lot for talent."

Cassidy steps close and taps a silver button on the cowboy shirt.

"Which is why, Travis, you are always so understandably nervous."

She goes to Cruz.

"I came to wish you good luck."

"I got good luck."

The ballplayer smiles the good smile, a smile so grand his eyebrows fly up under the bill of his cap.

The scout grips his hand in a comradely shake but it turns into an embrace, and they hold each other as long as they can. And longer.

"Ciao," she says in a husky voice. "Watch those hips," and makes a swinging motion as he nods and heads for the locker room.

3:15 p.m.

Cassidy puts her feet up on the seat in front of her. She is in a field box over the dugout, best view in the house. In the white burned-out sky you can see the end of summer. Soon will come the division playoffs, the series, the end of daylight saving time—but now is the moment of protracted fade, before the season ends and the light turns woeful at two in the afternoon. The press box is still empty, groundskeepers rake the clay. Cassidy is simply here, in ballpark space, wondering what has happened to her in the last twenty years.

3:39 p.m.

The stadium workers prepare for the game. Although their tasks unfold like clockwork, Cassidy is suspended out of time. Although nobody else is in the stands, she can feel a presence in her heart.

The scoreboard lights up.

The escalators start running.

The food stands open. When the doors of the elevator draw apart, you can see it is crowded with hawkers wearing striped shirts and straw hats. Reporters trailing press passes hurry across the deserted deck.

On the field, TV camera people are setting up.

"It's hot. I'm getting too old for this."

"If it were cold you'd be bitching about that, too."

An usher opens a gate, allowing a group of journalists onto the red track. Even the working press is wired, this close to the game.

"Hey, whorehouse! Come over and meet this kid. Is he dumb. Even dumber than I was at his age."

It is a reporter from one of the northern papers, plaid jacket and Van Dyck beard, calling, "Watch us! We'll show you the professional way to grill somebody!"

And a gentle African-American sportswriter from Orange County, hat turned backwards and batik shirt, explaining to a visitor, "I like baseball because it's 'The Young and the Restless.' You watch it every day to see what's happening, like a soap opera."

4:30 p.m.

The Dodgers come out onto the field, the starting lineup, famous multimillion-dollar names, larger-than-life big pumped-up bodies, land of the giants.

"Okay, here we go!" shouts the trainer. "Left knee! It's the full-body stretch, dude."

Half the players are standing around joking, some dutifully rolling on their backs.

"*Whatzup?*"

And, "*Tsha!*"

And Alberto Cruz, happy as a puppy, rolling around on his butt next to Raul Mondesi, both of them laughing rapid-fire Spanish.

5:00 p.m.

The ground crew sets up the screens and the starters take BP, the coach calling, "One out. HO! Nice, double down the line. Two outs. Great play! Base hit. Man on first. Tough situation," keeping them loose, keeping them laughing like when they were kids. Everybody hits home runs. The bleachers are littered with balls.

Pedro always says, "*If it wasn't for two words in the English dictionary, everybody would be a hitter. The two words are,* Play ball!"

6:00 p.m.

They let the public in. San Francisco takes the field and the Dodgers go back into the clubhouse. The sky has claimed some pigment, warm fall blue. Cassidy is resting an arm around the back of the empty seat beside her.

She has been sitting in the empty stands, protecting this empty seat, for the past three hours.

"This taken?"

A jerk-off with long hair.

"Yes, it is."

Later,

"Excuse me?"

Two little blond boys who brought their gloves. "Someone sitting here?"

"Yes."

The boys turn at once and scramble down the aisle. Crew cuts must be in style again, at least for eight-year-olds. The afternoon sun creates twin blond coronas around the two small heads, bobbing through the crowd, undefeated and undaunted. They throw themselves into two empty seats right behind the dugout, put their feet up and hope for the best.

That's the way boys are. That's the way Gregg was, the way he taught her to be. When they took that last walk through Lithia Park she had known, although her mind and body denied it at the time, that it was very near the end: because that is when he no longer had hope.

The dogwoods had been in flower. They walked those peaceful pathways one step at a time, Gregg leaning on her for support, needing to stop and catch his breath if he spoke more than five or six words.

The goal had been chocolate-dipped soft ice cream cones at the Creek Cafe, but it might as well have been Seattle. As they inched along through the dense shade of a big-leaf maple, she was thinking of all the odd things she had seen in that park, which over the past hundred years had matured, as great parks do, into a collective dream space, where performers from the Shakespeare Festival might stroll in costume past a woman in labor being walked by two determined friends. Cassidy remembered bands of hippie children, dirty, wild. She wondered if the pair of runners that were coming at them, staring, had been shocked by the sight of her emaciated brother in such a pastoral setting.

Gregg had been in and out of the hospital all that year. He'd lost more weight. His posture had been stooped, exaggerating the barrel chest that resulted from the effort of getting air into his compromised lungs. He had been wearing thermal underwear and a thick red flannel shirt, one sleeve rolled up to accommodate an intravenous PIC line attached to an IV bag hanging from a stand which Cassidy rolled beside them with a quiet clatter, a piece of hospital equipment never meant to see the sun. The shirt was tucked into sweats but the drawstring still had so much play it hung below his knees. The bony feet were bare, long toes flexing hesitantly in a pair of rubber thongs.

It had taken scarcely more effort to guide Gregg along than the IV stand. He was nineteen years old but slight as an autumn leaf, a six-foot frame that should have supported two hundred pounds down to ninety. Cassidy was fifteen, athletically plump, hair bleached rebel platinum, chewing gum, a beaded choker, like his, around the taut, thick neck, wearing a Grizzlies sweatshirt and torn denim shorts, bare strong legs, hot-pink toenails.

The contrast between them filled her with shame.

"Can we sit down?" he had asked.

"No, bologna head, we cannot sit down."

The view from the bench had been a small meadow filled with fil-tered light. For some reason the bad kids, the street kids, liked to hang out there. They wore punk hair and Indian dresses and lay with each other in the grass.

"It's the end of the line," Gregg said, and at first Cassidy thought he was talking about the path. That he could not walk much farther on the path.

"We'll just rest," she told him.

"I told Doc Bill I don't want him to share that information with mom."

"What information?"

"I've been living with CF. Now I'm dying with CF."

Cassidy stared straight ahead.

"I don't accept that, Gregg."

"Dying? Or not telling mom?"

"This end-of-the-line crapola. It's never the end of the line. There's always hope. You can always fight."

"No," he said, kindly. "No."

He had taken her hand.

"I can feel it. This past year I've been through the transition."

Sitting, it was a little easier for him to talk.

"My energy level has been unbelievably low. The mornings are hell."

"I know—"

"I can't go through another pseudomonas—"

"Yes you can."

He had coughed. Her hand tightened around his. She prayed he wouldn't have a spell, but if he did she was prepared, a plastic bag jammed in her pocket along with the inhaler and a couple of paper tow-els. Sometimes he would cough four minutes straight. His skin would turn blue and he'd vomit.

"Mom's talking about taking that house on the coast for July—"

"Mom is wonderful. She's gold." He coughed again. "But she's in denial. And Dad's on another planet."

"You're not in denial?" Cassidy asked curiously.

She didn't really know what being "in denial" meant. She couldn't grasp the grief and the deep slow torment that had, over the past four years, arrested the vital functions of her parents; their appetites, desires, the very pattern of their heartbeats. Her mom just seemed to be there, her dad, stoical, put on a sport jacket and sold houses and coached her softball team with aggression and an expectation of excellence that went beyond the Rogue Valley to the nationals, beyond nationals to the Olympics, which was coming in ten years, when Cassidy and D.J. would be at prime age and condition to make the U.S. team. They had been marked, Cassidy and D.J., with the certainty of the hometown pecking order: their bodies were strong and gifted, they would grow into champions, it was a fact of life; she had eclipsed her brother as heir to the Smoke Sanderson legend.

This, also, was nothing but shame and guilt.

"The conflict of death," said Gregg, "it's within me."

"Then it's in me," echoed his little sister.

"That's not what I want for you."

In the clearing the street kids had formed a circle, playing that game called Hacky Sack, passing a little beanbag by kicking it with the ankles, heels and knees. One of them played a recorder. The odd hair and transparent dresses had seemed ribald, Elizabethan.

"I want you to be free."

"Gregg," she said with teenage drama. "Nobody is free."

"So there's no mystery, I want to tell you, I've thought about it." He spit into a tissue. "There's no way I'm going back to the hospital, okay? I'm going to die at home."

She elbowed him. "Don't talk that way."

He never had before. She figured it was the depressing books he had been reading. *On the Road. No Exit. The Catcher in the Rye. The Basic Writings of Sigmund Freud. The Tibetan Book of the Dead.*

"I also want to tell you"—forced to stop again—"this is tough."

"Forget it."

She stood. She moved the IV stand and the tubing played out, as if she could nudge him off the bench like a dog on a leash.

"Let's go get ice cream."

"When you went on in baseball," Gregg said haltingly, "it was really hard for me."

Slowly she sat down and put her arms around her brother. She had never known it was possible to be this close to another human being, maybe because she had never known before how close they really were: one soul in two bodies. So close, they cried into each other's eyes.

6:40 p.m.

She tries to imagine what Gregg would look like sitting in this seat, had he survived to be a man. How it would have been to have him in her life all these years; if she could, at times, just call him on the phone. If he had lived, no doubt he would have insisted that she take the genetic screening test, and maybe she would turn out not to be a carrier, and her children would be with them now. Is that what he meant when he said he wanted her to be free? Ghosts can't answer. They are gone from us. But as she waits for Alberto Cruz to make his appearance on this green field, she feels an incandescence growing in her heart, the same feeling she'd had just knowing Gregg was watching from the stands; when he was sick and she was out there playing ball. One soul, two bodies.

One forgiving soul.

6:55 p.m.

The announcer intones, "YOUR Los Angeles Dodgers!" and a full house stands up and cheers. Cassidy opens her eyes. The lights are on. The crowd, the very air, seem beautiful and polished. The team runs out and lines up, all in white. A very little girl with a very big voice from the Inglewood Children's Gospel Choir sings the national anthem. Alberto Cruz takes off his cap. He looks once at the sky. He tries to be serious. He looks down. He can't help it. He grins.

8:20 p.m.

The Giants make two errors. The Dodgers score three unearned runs in the fourth inning. Radios are buzzing with Vin Scully's soothing voice, but even he can't modulate the excitement of pennant fever: if they win this game, nine more and they clinch.

A straight-looking girl about twenty is escorted out of the stadium by two security guards for dancing on the dugout.

Cassidy will not give up the empty seat.

8:45 p.m.

Detective Nate Allen makes his way down the aisle carrying two chocolate swirl yogurt cones.

"Sorry I'm late. Knew this would happen."

"No problem."

He wades past her knees.

"Closing a case is endless."

He settles in and hands over a cone.

"Great seats."

"Better be."

"Alberto up yet?"

"Oh, he won't play. They might use him to run."

"Still, you got him to the big show."

Cassidy doesn't answer.

Nate leans around, peering closely into her face.

"You should be proud of yourself."

"I don't know what I am."

"Are you okay?"

She waits.

"I've never had very good luck with cops."

"Why not?"

"Oh, they're crazy or depressed or can't relate to women."

Allen circles a finger toward himself. "*Moi?*"

She looks at him. "You tell me."

"No, *you* tell *me*."

"Tell you what?"

"I mean, you asked me here, so, is this, now, like a date?"

Cassidy laughs uncomfortably. "I don't know—"

"I just want to make sure," says Allen, "I'm not sitting in somebody else's seat."

She looks out at the lit field. Night is almost complete, mountain ridges the last to fade. The flags move softly.

"There was someone sitting here. But he's gone, for now."

Roberto Kelly hits a homer in the seventh.

The Dodgers win it, 4–2.

Cassidy and Nate Allen trudge through the crowded parking lot. She unlocks the door of the Explorer, discouraged by the accumulated mess in the backseat, which she will, seriously, have to tackle. She has never noticed this before, but there is a wet suit tangled up in there.

Oskar Kvorcziak rolls by in the golf cart.

She takes the battered skateboard from the backseat and places it on the asphalt.

"What are you doing?"

"Just don't arrest me, okay?"

Nate Allen hangs an elbow over the top of the open door and raises his eyebrows quizzically and waits.

He gets the feeling this kind of thing, whatever it is, is going to be happening a lot.

"Hey, Oskar!" she taunts. "Look at this!"

Cassidy puts one foot on the board.

She looks ahead.

And pushes off.

Navigating downhill, slaloming between oncoming cars and shouting attendants, staying just ahead of red-faced Oskar Kvorcziak in the golf cart; weaving deftly in and out of parking cones as they come at her—one by one, then blurred together—faster than the eye can see, strobing, and then one long streak.

EPILOGUE

Dawn in Santo Domingo. *From where he stands on the roof of the apartment building in the Gazcue district, Pedro Pedrillo can see a large ship riding high on the lavender swells of the Caribbean Sea, lights still on, bejeweled and elegant. To the north, the laser beam of the lighthouse Faro a Colón, monument to dictators, continues to sweep the city, slowly losing strength as daylight grows.*

He takes a sip of thick rich coffee. It tastes sweet. Why not: three teaspoons of sugar in a small porcelain cup. He likes it that way, almost unbearable, like a high-pitched note on a guitar string that pierces the ears yet somehow seems the right pitch for this too pink, too sweet morning.

Ever since their trip to Miami, Rhonda has been hard on his case to retire. The grandchildren are growing up without them. And he has to admit, scouting Latin America has more and more become a dirty game. It is almost normal for boys to be coming now with forged documents, or expect that you will get them. Buscones are "signing" kids at the age of eleven and he has heard terrible stories how some even abuse the children. Rhonda is correct that he would have an easy coaching job in the United States.

But then he would not be driving the sugarcane roads, and find a few boys playing, and see, coming toward him in the light and shadow of a gumbo-limbo tree, the good face; the face that is open and ready to learn.

The dawn is gone. The pearly glow turns to harsh sun, the misty yacht revealed to be an oil tanker, the inspiring lighthouse beacon yet another overblown monument to political ego. Pedro can hear traffic and his nose begins to fill with dust.

Eight blocks away *a tour bus pulls out of the driveway of the Hotel V Centenario, forcing traffic on the Malecón to stop as it makes a laborious* *left-hand turn. Already the air is heavy with dust and the Caribbean Sea bright aqua with medium swells. The temperature is above eighty and climbing. The bus passes a movie theater and a row of small hotels and labors past the chirry-chingo bars along the beachfront.*

Inside, a German tour group praises the air-conditioning and stares at pastel benches set in zigzags beside the water. Despite the five-star rating, omelets made to order, packaged orange juice and American cereals, many could be observed at breakfast disinfecting their silverware with disposable alcohol wipes provided by the young tour guide. On the itinerary, besides the Parque de los Tres Ojos de Agua, is the Palacio Nacional, Old Santo Domingo, shopping at Plaza Criolla and dinner at a restaurant specializing in Spanish-style seafood. The tour guide taps his clipboard.

On the airport road the bus picks up speed and passes along a five-mile park, deep green slopes of grass dotted with flamboyant trees, wavy trunks out of an Edvard Munch painting, then rolls by a middle-class housing development painted bright yellow. There are joggers in the park and sailors strolling in white uniforms. The driver's radio plays merengue.

The bus turns into the Parque de los Tres Ojos and has barely stopped before a hustler jumps on board and bargains for protection. It is early but other tours are already there. The Germans get off, cameras swinging. Their cologne blankets the air. They walk a gauntlet of peddlers selling coconuts, peeled oranges, limes, bananas, cigarettes and candy bars from portable trays. There are tables of carvings made from stalactites, amber and onyx jewelry, and the ubiquitous Haitian paintings.

The park is shady and drippingly humid. The group descends the mossy steps and invariably somebody slips. The guide begins his speech. He has to compete with Japanese and English. He explains this is one of the city's most popular natural attractions. Its name—Park of the Three Eyes—comes from the unusual formation of three large sinkholes. Each has a different kind of water, one is bottomless. In a few minutes they will take a boat from one pool to another. As they can see, it is raining inside the cavern, and the stalactites and stalagmites are sparkling under the red and blue lamps. The natural light is dim and filtered. The heat is dense, like a hothouse, and it is hard to breathe. Those who are claustrophobic might prefer not to go on the boat, as it will have to pass through a narrow limestone tunnel.

He leads them slowly down another set of steps toward the pool. Please don't go swimming, the tour guide jokes, people have tried and never returned.

A longboat is waiting. As the group begins to climb over wet rocks, some-one spots Joe Galinis's body floating facedown. Already it has begun to swell. The arms are spread in a pointless embrace, the back of the head blown out into something indescribable. They shout for the boatman, who stumbles toward the bow and reaches for the hand, but the skin slips right off; the red streamers drifting undisturbed toward infinity stirred by the swaying of the boat into curls of watery roses.

Later the police will say the man had been symbolically shot through the eyes, a warning to others not to try to see.

Pedro leans over the wall at the edge of the roof. Below him the General and his cronies, three other retired army officers, are bringing their coffees and bowls of steamed yucca to a wooden table in a shaded part of the alley. One of them opens a box and spills out worn dominoes. Pedro watches the tops of their heads with contempt. Even now, years after Tru-jillo, that old shudder, that reflex, has never quite left him. Criminals. He would like to send a wad of spit sailing right down their necks.

He backs away. He will have to tell Rhonda his decision. There will be tears, but what can he say? "All this time I think I am holding a baseball. Now I find out, the baseball has been holding me."

Painfully, he climbs down the narrow steps to the apartment. His catcher's legs are shot to hell.

Acknowledgments

I was continually humbled during the research for this book by people who, when asked for their time and expertise, said yes.

The first person who told me, "Sure. I'll help," was Susan L. Enquist, head coach for the UCLA women's softball team. I am indebted to her and to the players and families of the Bruins for providing the background from which I fashioned Cassidy Sanderson's childhood and athletic career. Also invaluable in that regard were Kristeen Weiss, head varsity softball coach for Ashland High School, and, for Ashland lore, Michelle Galt.

Gina Satriano and Michelle McAnany, players for the Colorado Silver Bullets, gave firsthand accounts of what it was like to break the hardball barrier, thanks to Bob Hope, owner of the team and a passionate advocate of women in baseball.

A number of sportswriters unselfishly educated me about the game — Elizabeth Cosin, Mal Florence, Paige A. Leech, Maryann Hudson, Art Thompson III and the wonderful Tot and Pearlie Holmes.

For authenticity of police procedure, I am beholden to James M. Gabbard, Chief of Police, Vero Beach Police Department, as well as Sergeant David Currey and Lt. Raymond J. Barker. In Los Angeles, LAPD Detective Greg Schwein and Captain Don Mauro, Ret., of the Sheriff's Department, answered endless questions with grace and humor and became essential advisors.

There were others who gave openly of their professional knowledge: Randy Anderson, Nelson and Selma Castro, Robert F. Iverson, M.D., Greg Isaacs, Nicholas Hammond, Theodore Kyriazis, Joy Manesiotis, Nick Petnick and William F. Skinner, M.D. The sports arena described in this book (now the Staples Center) would not exist—in real life as well as on these pages—without the mastery and personal kindnesses of architect Ron Turner.

The soul of Gregg Sanderson was inspired by those engaged in the daily fight against cystic fibrosis: Joanna Fanos, Maureen Finnerty, D. J. Kaley and Bruce Nickerson, M.D., touched me enormously with their upbeat dedication. I was privileged to know William D. Biggley and Alberto Torres, two bright, articulate young people with CF who showed such courage and wit. Meeting them changed my life. May their memories, and those of all who have struggled with CF, be the inspiration for a cure.

Ultimately I owe the existence of this book to those who kept the faith during the five years it took to write. I could not have completed it without the stalwart support of my editor and publisher, Sonny Mehta; the insight and dedication of his assistant, Leyla Aker; the brilliance of my New York agent, Molly Friedrich; the patience and smarts of my West Coast agent, Robert Graham, and my attorney, Walter Teller; the laughs with my workout buddies and trainers; the comradeship of Coach Paul Henne and the Pacific Palisades Masters Swim Team; the encouragement of writer friends; and my terrific family—especially the shining spirits of my children and the abiding love and editorial skill of my husband, Douglas Brayfield. Thank you all.

Lastly, there were indiviuals who requested anonymity. In many cases they were the ones who held the key to the world of this book, and unlocked it for me. They deserve my very deepest appreciation. Well, you know who you are. And here it is.

A NOTE ON THE TYPE

The text of this book was set in Electra, a typeface designed by W. A. Dwiggins (1880–1956). This face cannot be classified as either modern or old style. It is not based on any historical model, nor does it echo any particular period or style. It avoids the extreme contrasts between thick and thin elements that mark most modern faces, and it attempts to give a feeling of fluidity, power, and speed.

Composed by Stratford Publishing Services, Inc., Brattleboro, Vermont

Printed and bound by R. R. Donnelley, Harrisonburg, Virginia

Designed by Dorothy S. Baker